KALEIDOSCOPE OF LIES

Publisher, Copyright, and Additional Information

Kaleidoscope of Lies by Keith DeClerck

ISBNs:
979-8-9921766-0-5 (Paperback)
979-8-9921766-1-2 (Hardcover)
979-8-9921766-2-9 (Ebook)

Editing by Spruce Spaulding
Cover design and interior design by Rafael Andres

KALEIDOSCOPE OF LIES

A Novel

Keith DeClerck

For Bert and Shirley McGee, my dear friends

ACKNOWLEDGEMENTS

I want to thank my lovely wife for her patience and unending support; Richard, my business agent and promoter; my parents who taught me the value of hard work; and Jesus Christ for saving me from the morass of drugs

PROLOGUE

Seattle, Washington
July 20, 1991

"Hurry up, Saber! Lay some out," Clayton said, pointing with his forehead to the web between his thumb and forefinger. He held his hand steady as Saber spooned out a pearly-white mound from a small glass vial. Clayton lifted it to his face and violently sniffed, cleaning the powder from his skin like a cheap vacuum.

Face flush with blood, Saber could see the curtain of warmth descending Clayton's body, his hands white-knuckled now, strangling the wheel of the black Porsche. He took the spoon and enticed each of his own nostrils. The chemical darkness drained down from his sinuses, anesthetizing the muscles, prowling along the back of his throat like a jackal. His nose was wet with rush, plastic and cool.

Saber licked his index finger, then plugged the mouth of the vial and coated his fingertip white with a flip of his wrist. He rubbed the narcotic into his gums. In seconds, they deadened to oak, his gritting teeth like staves of a barrel, his jaw cast in aluminum. The sensation of biting tin, saliva pooled under his tongue while his swallow constricted with the numb taste of sterility.

To cool his coke-thickening throat, he drank the last of his beer, then, using the cap of an inverted bottle, he opened a fresh brew for Clayton, and another one for himself.

The coke was exhilarating; his leg started bouncing; Saber felt the car surge as the pedal went deeper to the floor. From the corner of his eye, he saw Clayton's grin grow wider.

The road to Avondale led out of the city of Kirkland across the summer countryside, traversing the fields of wildflowers, parting the stands of evergreens.

Clayton stuck his hand out of the Targa top, funneling the air into his face, his long dishwater-blond hair flapping in the wind. The cool night air forced tears to emerge, and Saber watched the glistening moisture streak back from the corners of Clayton's eyes like the mask of a raccoon.

Clayton drummed the padded wheel with the palms of his hands. "The music is so crisp ... Saber, can you hear it? My mind is shimmering like a crystalline ball, filled with all the colors of light. I feel cracks drying on my temples, opening a chasm into my skull. I smell every honeysuckle in the meadows that rush by my window. I see every needle of every tree in the light that fans out before me. The world is mine. Mine for the taking."

Clayton cackled, then pushed his shoulders back, his arms out straight to the wheel. His lanky body was oversized for the compact seat, driving his knees to splay beneath the dash.

Breaking into a warm, tingling sweat, Saber was growing impatient. Pharmakeia's siren song was in control. "Let's see what this bitch will do, Clayton."

Clayton laughed his gutty roll and pushed the pedal to the floor. The yellow centerline blurred into a solid band while the whine of the engine vanished behind them.

As the speedometer crested one-hundred-thirty miles-per-hour, Saber felt invincible, the deception spreading through his body like the warm rush of blow. Cocaine's fingers were twisting like fresh DNA through his body. Blood pounded in his hands.

The road stretched out before them, and with it, their speed. Saber slid in a Chris Rhea CD and turned up the stereo.

Clayton smiled wider and re-gripped the wheel with both hands, his fingers curling tight. "Crank it up, Saber. This bitch is coming. I can feel it between my legs."

Saber twisted the volume knob clockwise, but the stereo was deadly silent, disturbed only by the intended light crackle of distortional rain, stroking wipers, and the muffled voice of a foreign radio announcer, as the long opening of "The Road to Hell" commenced. Saber tipped another beer, then sniffed his raw, runny nose again and again. He didn't want any of the nectar to leave his body.

At the end of the long straightaway, the road turned gently to the left and a small white gravel road peeled off from the corner. Saber's breath raised his chest higher and stronger than he had ever felt it before. He was high — really high. They were above it all — riding tall — riding high. Nothing could touch them — nothing — but the corner; the corner Clayton took too wide.

The Porsche 911 skidded out of control in the loose gravel, smacking the high-banked ditch on the right side of the road. Saber stayed safely strapped in his seatbelt, only to be crushed by the dash pushed back by the front quarter-panel of the car. Clayton was thrown free, landing two hundred feet from the car in a broken heap like a sack of garbage had dropped from the moonless sky.

As the dust settled around the 911, the motor ticking as it cooled, Saber struggled to lift his head. Torrents of blood drained the sweet nectar from his nose onto the rumpled dash. He groped for the door handle, unaware that a woman had crossed the road and was standing beside him.

She wore a negligee draped over one shoulder, her form existing in shadow, and as she bent down to peer through the hole that was once his window, the night resonated with the eerie voice of the stereo, the lyrics spoken, the music behind the words a swirling specter.

CHAPTER 1

Oil Platform *Constellation*, North Sea, Scotland
December 25, 1994

Dane sat ankle-crossed, leaning back in a plastic deck chair. He held a newspaper in one hand and a bottle of water in the other. Underneath the platform, he could hear the waves crashing against the pilings. The sky was gray and thick with remorse, and the exhaust of diesel generators lay thick on his face.

"Where'd you get that?" Quirt's voice trilled with the question, the burr thick and hoarse from pipe tobacco. He was a lonely Scotsman with a face spider-veined from alcohol and grease under his fingernails. He sat down in the chair next to Dane.

"My mother sent it from home."

"Where's that again?" Quirt rapped the bowl of his calabash pipe into his palm, dislodging the ashes, then, like setting free a butterfly from his hand, he released the spent tobacco into the breeze.

"Seattle." Dane showed him the banner for the *Seattle Post-Intelligencer* that emblazoned the top of the first page.

"Why'd she do that?" Quirt asked. He slid his calabash, bowl first, into the front pocket of his plaid flannel shirt. His teeth glistened with saliva, crisscrossed and green as blades of grass. "Seattle's on the other side of the earth. No need knowing what's going on there," he said with a point of his finger toward the west, "when you're out here."

Dane knew Quirt craved conversation; a hunger brought on by years of isolation working the oil rigs of the North Sea. "There's an article in the paper about a friend of mine. She thought I would be interested."

"What he do? Get arrested?"

Dane could see the need in Quirt's eyes, even though at this moment he wanted peace and quiet. His face possessed a sheen like wax paper, clouded as if there was a blight on his mind, the beginnings of dementia or worse. "No, he gave a million dollars to a local charity."

"Where'd he get that kind of money?" Quirt asked, folding his hands. "And then give it away? The man's a fool, I think."

Blake Hanson was no fool. Dane knew that if he'd given away a million, there were other millions held in reserve. "He's just an honorable man," he said, "giving back a piece of what he's earned. Besides, it's the man behind the money that's valuable."

Quirt got up, tugging at his crotch. "Well, I still think he's a fool. You never know when the bottom is going to drop."

Dane smiled and stroked his chin. His blue eyes held a compassionate glint.

"You know you're a nice man, Dane Avilla," Quirt said with a quizzical squint. He always pronounced the *l*'s instead of letting them remain silent. "Today is Christmas. What you be doing here, so far from home?"

Dane contemplated the answer. Not that he didn't know, but he'd never had to confess it before. Raised in relative security, he hadn't scrutinized the subtleness between good and evil, how temptation masquerades as normal and acceptable, even useful, as good.

It was no excuse, but he had simply fallen prey to a deception, allowing cocaine to slip into his life disguised as an antidote for pain. Instead, cocaine brought destruction that sprouted like a tree from his back, rooted in bitterness and grief. Until one day, in what seemed now like a distant past, he found himself heavy and stooping over with regret, seeing nothing but rotting fruit littering the ground around him.

Prostrate in a gutter in Dublin, nose raw from the sting of cocaine, stomach roiling with the thunder of alcohol, he picked himself up and relinquished his life here. "Escaping," he said at last.

"We all escapin' something," Quirt said, running his tongue over his teeth. "My father was a devil of a man. I ran as far away as possible. I'm still running, I recollect, and he's been dead nigh on ten years."

The instruments of defense against evil are tough to wield and easy to corrupt — Love, Hope, Honor, Justice, the Light of Truth — even Light will leave shadows and sometimes the darkness seems better off left alone.

"I had a dream last night I was standing outside my father's house," Dane began. "The rain was pounding down. I knew that there was comfort and warmth within, but I couldn't open the door. It was as if there was something inside of me, struggling to get inside that house, and I didn't want to infect them with whatever possessed me. I couldn't trust my own intentions."

"Truth begets Trust, Dane," Quirt said. He worked a thumbnail between his teeth. "Not the other way around. 'The truth will set you free' as it says in the Bible. You be honest, expose what's eating you, and let the chips fall where they may. Then pick them up and start over."

Strangely, there was a silver glint in Quirt's eyes and a radiance on his skin, as if all the cloudiness of his mind had cleared. Was it the calm before the storm, or the deep-seated resilience of an old soldier who had seen his courage swell on the battlefield?

Eyes searching the horizon, Dane could still feel the sting of cocaine in his nostrils. He knew her siren song well, and occasionally, could even taste her in the back of his throat. "It's hard to go home. Things change and the memories are just better off left alone."

Quirt clicked his tongue. "The North Sea is a beautiful yet treacherous place," he said. "Not sure I'd know what to do living out there in the real world. And home ... well, that's been gone a long-time past." He scratched at the stubble on his face. "Guess I'm better at giving advice than actually following it."

For the first time, Dane saw his own reflection in Quirt. The vision rendered him mute, like a fishbone was caught in his throat.

CHAPTER 2

Georgetown, South Carolina
September 11, 1995

It's impossible to predict the future when the world's foundation is made of shifting sand. Each day we stand at the constriction of the hourglass wondering what it'll be like to slip through to the other side.

The morning sun broke through the veranda doors, casting deformed shadows across the floor. Blake Hanson was staring at the ceiling, forming objects out of imperfections in the wood. On the desk lay their future caught in real estate flyers and travel brochures, thoughts of Seattle fading from his mind with each passing moment.

Tyra was lying in bed next to him. He could feel the coolness under her pillow as he slid up close to spoon her, his arm around her waist. "Good morning, Sweetie," he whispered.

Georgetown, a resolute town carved out of the tidal swamps of coastal South Carolina, was waking for the day. The doors to the veranda were open. He could hear the horse-drawn carriages clattering on the cobblestone streets.

Tyra stirred from her slumber. "Good morning."

"Did you sleep well?"

Tyra sighed. "I'm glad it'll be over soon."

Side-by-side, they laid in silent contemplation. A gust of wind flapped at the drapes, and Blake heard the clatter of leaves outside, as if unknown spirits were gossiping in the trees. The air felt smooth and dry and smelled of magnolias.

A cardinal perched on the railing momentarily, then flitted off as if a predator were approaching.

"The first place I'd like to go is Europe," Blake said, his voice caressing a conciliatory tone.

Tyra rolled onto her back. "I assume to see Dane."

Blake propped his head up on his elbow. "It's been too many years. I need to see him face-to-face."

"Seems you were closer to him than the other musketeers," she said, wiping a wisp of hair off his forehead.

"True, but after college he got an offer from BP and went to work in Houston first, then overseas."

"Was that the last time you saw him?"

"No, he came home one time for the holidays several years back. Didn't stay long." Blake was lost in thought now. "He had a girlfriend in Italy." He closed his eyes, as if a photograph or an inscription was etched on the back of his eyelids. "Can't remember her name. He hasn't mentioned her lately. I've been so busy I never asked." He scratched his eyebrow with a thumbnail. "I should've asked."

"Well, you can when we see him."

"So, on another subject, what do you want to do today?" Blake asked. "I don't have to be at work until four."

Tyra slid her leg over his and sat up on her knees. The smell of pine needles heating in the morning sun strolled in from the veranda as she unbuttoned her nightshirt. "I want to go to Pawleys Island, sit in the sand with you, and come home with a hammock," she said with a giggle. "We can put it on the veranda."

"A hammock?" Blake said, watching intently as each button was undone. "I never thought of that."

***

Hours later, when they returned from Pawleys Island, Dane began unpacking his backpack, then stopped. "It's not here," he said.

"What isn't?" Tyra asked.

"Bobby gave me a book to read, and I'm sure I put it in my backpack." He paused, placing a palm on his forehead. "But it's not here."

"Can't you just buy another one?"

"No, it was special," he said, the exasperation rushing through his teeth. "It was leather bound and had my initials, BDH, on the cover."

"Well, let's go back."

"I can't now. I'm due at the mill." His disappointment was palpable.

"Then let's go first thing tomorrow," Tyra said, attempting to console him.

Dane relinquished a smile. "I guess this means we're going to the beach again."

Tyra gave him a cheerful kiss on the cheek. "That's the ticket," she said.

Moments later, Blake left Tyra on the veranda, her feet still sandy between her toes, him musing on how the sunlight through the oaks flickered in her hair. She was sitting in her rocker, sipping iced tea and planning the exact location for the hammock he promised he'd hang in the morning.

Blake took a back-road to the mill, relishing each rock that peened off his floorboards. For out here in the rural viscera of South Carolina, he'd found his connection to life. He'd searched the streets of Seattle for meaning, pretended to take comfort and pleasure in his acquisitions, but instead anguish had followed his days.

Here in the Low Country, fate had dealt him a second chance. He reveled being part of it, and by all accounts, Blake was an intelligent man. However, naiveté had played him for a fool. He was in love with a culture he wanted to embrace, running from a culture determined not to let him go.

The steering wheel trembled in his hands, the road behind him fading into a boiling cloud of dust. Five years ago, Southeast Paper was the biggest account that Spinetti and Hanson

Engineering had ever landed, and it was Blake's job to keep the mill running at peak performance.

However, tonight an ominous purpose overshadowed that resolve, a persistent menace that he couldn't relegate to the back of his mind. Every other week, after nightfall was securely in place, he'd venture down to the Black River for the secret purpose that once had made it all seem worthwhile: trading his briefcase full of money for a new one filled with cocaine. Tonight was to be his last, and the thought made him both elated and fearful at the same time.

CHAPTER 3

Seattle, Washington
September 26, 1995

Dane joined the others gathered around and under the canvas awning that sheltered the coffin. The brightly colored trees seemed to gather in too, encircling and sheltering the grave. Some of the autumn leaves had already fallen, speckling the ground. The rest of the withering hues would fall with the temperature in the weeks ahead. Dane and his parents found a spot under the shelter a few rows behind Blake's family. Blake was being laid to rest in a grave next to his father.

Indian Summer embraced the Northwest. To the west, the Olympic Mountains were spreading their majestic heads over Puget Sound. Downtown, merchants in Pike Place Market were touting their goods to tourists in the open-air arcade. On the water, a myriad of boaters sailed Lake Washington, the Hood Canal, or the Sound itself, cruising its protected waters to the San Juan Islands or Victoria, British Columbia, the tall masts of the schooners and the sleek hulls of the power boats meshed into one in the melting pot of Seattle sailors. Yet here, in the cemetery along the road to Avondale, life had boiled down to memories, and the air was chilly with regret.

As the Pastor read from the Bible, all heads bowed in prayer. Dane tried to concentrate on the scriptures being read, but he felt compelled to lift his head. Standing next to him was a graceful lady dressed in black. Her sadness devoured his attention. Wearing a pillbox hat, her veil spilled over sunglasses, masking eyes that were swollen and red. Woven into a French braid, her blonde hair stood out against the starkness of her dress. Her presence intrigued him. He solemnly lowered his head again, but his thoughts were on her, and for what seemed like a moment, time evaded him.

Minutes had passed, the Bible was closed, and the faithful raised their heads. Dane immediately looked for her, but saw only her back as she stepped into a waiting taxi. Lost in thought, he stood there motionless, gazing at the taxi as it drove off, slowly exiting the cemetery.

"Dane? Is that you?" a voice asked behind him.

Dane's obsession abruptly ended, and he turned around. Tony Franklin was standing in front of him. He'd gained a soupçon of weight, and his face had aged, showing the anguish of his addictions, but Dane knew it was Tony. He possessed an undeniable grin that pulled the corner of his upper lip higher on one side than the other, exposing his gold-capped bicuspid. His black hair fixed in a ponytail, the well-worn Levi's and tweed sport jacket were Tony's trademark. He had on a risqué T-shirt emblazoned with a naked lady. The strip-joint moniker, Five Easy Pieces, arched across her torso. Still relaxed, still displaying his who-gives-a-damn attitude, Tony was just what Dane would've expected.

Dane stuck out his hand and Tony shook it.

"How are you Tony?"

"I'm good."

"Do you remember my parents?"

Tony looked over at Dane's parents and nodded his hello. "How's Vince?"

"Oh, you know Vince. Not much gets him down. I'm gonna go get him. He'll be happy to see you."

"That's all right, Tony. Don't bother him now. I'll be around. I can catch up with him later," Dane said, hopefully alluding to Tony that he really wanted to avoid talking to Vince today. To anyone, for that matter.

"He'd never forgive me if I didn't get him over here," Tony said, missing the hint. "Just stay here. I'll be right back." He turned, craning his neck to search over the people, and wandered off, looking for Vince.

Dane placed his arm around his mom and spoke conspiratorially to his parents. "Look, I've got to go say something to the family. I'm not sure what, but I'll be right back. Then we can get out of here."

"Sure son," his father said. "We already paid our respects at the chapel, so we'll wait over by the car."

Dane hesitantly walked over to the gravesite, where Blake's brother, Bobby, and his mom sat embracing each other. Bobby's wife, Natalie, sat next to Bobby and was staring off into the distance as their two boys fidgeted in their suit jackets and bow ties.

He quietly moved in front of them, then stood silently with one hand holding the back of the other until Bobby looked up at him. "I'm so sorry to hear about Blake," he said, looking into Bobby's grief. Bobby looked ghostly aged, his eyes sunken and shadowed with sleepless nights. "When Dad called me, I caught the next plane out. I sure wish I was here for some other reason."

"Dane? Dane Avilla?" Bobby said with a look of surprise.

Mrs. Hanson reached out and grabbed his forearm. While he was growing up, she'd been like a second mother to him. It was difficult to see her, an aging, silver-haired mother not unlike his own, in her Sunday-special print dress, burying her child. He bent down and gave her a hug. "If there's anything you need, Mrs. Hanson. Anything. Please let me know."

"I'm glad you're here, Dane."

Bobby, a balding replica of Blake, stood up and shook his hand. "It's great to see you, Dane. I'm sure Blake is pleased that you're here."

"I wish I would've been here earlier. Maybe I could've done something."

"It was an accident, Dane. No one could help him on this one."

"Well, I plan on being around for a while, so if there is anything I can do, let me know."

"Why don't you come over to Bainbridge and visit?" Bobby said. "Natalie and I have a bait shop and boat rental over there. We can have a couple of beers." He paused, then said, "If you feel like it, we can do a little fishing."

"I'd like that."

Bobby slid a business card out of his wallet and handed it to Dane.

"I get a hug too, don't I?" Natalie asked as she stood up. With or without make-up, she possessed a simple beauty. Five-foot-seven, strawberry-blonde, slender-faced with a warm smile, Dane had a crush on her all during high school; she was the older, more sophisticated, college woman. After two kids, a trifling bit overweight, but still very pleasing to the eye.

He smiled, saying "Of course" with his eyes, and gave her a big hug. "It sure feels good to be home, I wish ..." He hesitated as his voice faltered. He stepped back, holding Natalie's hands in his, and regained his composure. He looked at Bobby and cleared his throat. "I'll catch up with you in a day or two." His voice was flat and sullen. "After things settle down."

Bobby nodded in response.

He was almost to his parent's car when he heard Tony yell his name. He stopped, wiped his eyes with a whisk of his fingertips, and turned around to see Tony and Vince approaching. Vince led the way, Tony heeling by his side like a well-trained mutt. Dane held out a welcome hand. Vince grabbed it and pulled him into an egregious hug, slapping his back with both hands.

Vince was smooth, good-looking; confident to the point of arrogance; charming as a cobra just before striking. With thick black hair, a broad forehead and dark eyebrows; a muscular build in chiseled-lean proportions; and a natural golden-brown complexion; he'd turned many a woman's head, and many a man's stomach. His milky-green eyes accentuated his unblemished face, piercing deep into your soul as if locked in a stare.

Vince, Tony, Blake, himself; though baffling sometimes, Dane admired their unspoken pact. They were as different as fingerprints, yet common in bond, friends. Wherever life would take them, they all knew the implied truth: they could trust each other. They didn't always understand each other. Hell, sometimes they didn't even like each other. Yet in the end, no judgments. Strange how the glue of youthful camaraderie is stronger than the solvent of reason, leniency for a friend larger than the forgiveness of one's own conscience.

"Dane, you old son of a gun," Vince said. "How are you?"

Dane politely broke free. "I'm good, Vince. You're looking well."

"Things have been good, Dane." Vince paused morosely. "Until now." Successful people are like chameleons. They can change their speech patterns, their mannerisms, even their thought processes to fit the background they want to flourish in. "I don't know how I'm going to survive without Blake," he said finally. "I'm going to miss him."

"We all will," Dane said. "I wish I could understand it, though. Blake just didn't make mistakes."

"I know," Vince said in agreement. "I had a hard time with it at first, but it only takes one. Sometimes you just don't get that second chance. I've got a private investigator looking into it. He'll figure out what happened. I should get a report in a few days. He's in South Carolina already, checking things out."

"Hey, where are you staying?" Vince said, changing the subject.

"With my parents."

"For how long?"

"I don't know. I don't have any definite plans."

"Well, call me. We should get together."

"Hey Vince," Tony piped up. "We oughta have a party to welcome Dane back to Seattle." As much as Vince was a chameleon, Tony was a golden retriever. Honest, loyal, with a bit of Chihuahua thrown in.

Vince looked to Dane for agreement, but he'd folded up like a tent in a stiff wind. The loss was too great. He'd slipped into a void, mindlessly staring at the ground, the toe of his shoe digging under a clump of grass.

CHAPTER 4

Atlantic Highlands, New Jersey
September 27, 1995

Abandoned as a newborn on the steps of a Catholic church, Vittorio Geraci bore the name of the priest who raised him. However, his life began at the home of Antonio Maldinaro, the widowed patriarch of an east coast crime syndicate.

One evening, while the family was enjoying a pleasant barbecue, the sound of gunfire cut through the calm. Antonio and his two sons died side-by-side, their faces unrecognizable in a spreading pool of blood. Sophia, his lovely daughter and notably Vittorio's wife, suffered a gunshot to the back of her head from a .38-caliber revolver. She died facedown next to a planter of zinnias.

Miraculously, Vittorio, his six-month-old son, Michael, and the revolver escaped without a scratch. The next few years were rife with gangland wars and frequent attempts at his life, yet Vittorio's empire grew. Feared for his ruthless tenacity and ominous power, he was known as "The Son-in-Law," and to those who seek success on the dark side of the street, he was an American icon.

Vittorio was seventy years old and infectiously virile, his sexual prowess proven by his latest companion, Carmen, a twenty-eight-year-old beauty accustomed to the poolside. Encased in an armor of olive-brown skin, his body was well-toned, his face a bullet in the heart of every plastic surgeon in Beverly Hills.

A pair of sliding doors opened, and Michael entered the library. He was dressed in a blue short-sleeved shirt, white tropical-weight trousers, and tight-woven huaraches. His olive-brown skin, dark eyebrows, deep-set eyes, and broad chin gave him a formidable appearance, but behind the over-powering facade existed a gentle and confused soul. His father was sitting at his desk.

The library was a pentagonal art piece sculpted from the finest mahogany and marble. Floor-to-ceiling bookshelves lined three of its walls, floor-length windows and a fireplace shared the other two. Persian rugs covered the floors. There was a large desk, aquarium, leather armchairs, and bar at one end. At the far end, a dark-green recamier and two overstuffed chairs shared the space with a bronze eagle soaring down from a boulder that erupted through the wall.

Carmen was reclining on the recamier. She placed a book-mark in her novel, then, tossing a lap blanket aside, gracefully rose to her feet, wearing a black lace camisole and matching panties. She slipped into a blue silk robe.

Michael stepped to the side, holding one hand over the other at his waist. Carmen twisted a bun into her hair as she made her way past him, giving him a quick wink as she exited to the hallway.

"Good morning, Michael," Vito said.

"Carlo said you needed to see me. Can it wait? I was plan-ning on taking a swim and then tennis with a friend."

Vito retrieved a can of tomato juice from the bar refrig-erator, then stood in front of Michael. His iris' were yellow and brown-flecked. "We need to talk first. I'm going to take a shower. Stay put. There'll be plenty of time for pleasure."

A moment later, Michael was alone. He poured himself two fingers of scotch in a glass tumbler, tonged an ice cube from a silver bucket, then walked over to the recamier in front of his mother's portrait, which hung prominently over the fireplace. He picked up Carmen's book and smiled, closing his eyes, smelling her lingering fragrance, remembering the last time they made love. When he opened them, his mother's eyes were fixed on his; two fingers sliding down his throat.

CHAPTER 5

Seattle, Washington
September 30, 1995

The colorful sails caught Dane's eye and he could see the captain and first mate near the wheel, huddled in each other's arms, drinking something hot, coffee or chocolate, maybe a mix with Baileys or Kahlua.

Bobby idled the boat to a stop, then killed the engine. "This is a perfect spot," he said, the pulse of the outboard now quiet. "I caught some Ling Cod here last week." He moved toward the aft, the boat rocking gently as the wake of the sailboat crossed its bow, and as he sat down, he grabbed the handle of a tackle box and slid it over to his feet.

The next hour progressed in solitude, concerns gossamer as fishing lines, until Bobby piped up, "I need your help, Dane."

"Whatever you need, Bobby." Dane took a drink of his beer, then wiped his mouth with the back of his hand.

"Someone needs to get Blake's things in South Carolina."

The boat tilted suddenly, rolling on the spreading wake of the ferry to Seattle, the *Kaleetan* itself already far off in the distance.

"Sure, why don't we go together?"

"It's complicated," Bobby said, as he sat back, scratching the rim of a nostril with his index nail. "I was baffled by how much money Blake had amassed in such a short period, but he wouldn't talk about the firm or his finances. He was acting strange. I had a sense he was in trouble, and that there was something nefarious going on with Vince. I also think he had a girlfriend in South Carolina, but he was extremely tight-lipped about it."

Appraising the conversation, Dane held his chin.

"I know my little brother," Bobby said. "He had a packrat gnawing on his insides." Bobby twisted off the cap of a fresh brew. He lifted his arm, hand over shoulder, and snapped his index and middle, propelling the cap into the stern gunwale.

Dane heard the bottlecap whizz and crack, but in his mind's eye a snapshot of a woman filled his vision.

Bobby cleared his throat. "Dane? Did you hear me?"

Dane took a swig and sat forward, rolling the bottle between his palms. "Oh, I heard you, Bobby. Damn, I've seen her."

"Who?"

"Blake's girl."

"Where?" Bobby asked.

"At the funeral. She was alone. She'd been crying."

"Did you talk to her?"

"I never got a chance."

"We've got to find her," Bobby said, eyebrows furrowing. He took a sip of beer. Thoughts were coalescing behind blind eyes. "She might know something."

"I might also image things."

Dane could sense a steel bar twisting in Bobby's gut, perspiration was beading on his brow even though the air was frigid and still.

"Find her, Dane," Bobby said.

When Dane proposed again that Bobby go with him, Bobby revealed the other part of "It's complicated." In vivid terms, he recounted his return from Vietnam and the challenges he faced with a predictable list of shame, guilt and drugs. He further explained the logic he used to convince Natalie to marry him before he left, so she'd get the death benefits if he came home in a coffin.

"Thing is, I'm not sure Natalie would've married me after Nam if she hadn't already been married to me before."

"I don't believe that, Bobby. You two were inseparable. Since before I can remember."

"You weren't here when I came home," Bobby retorted.

Dane watched Bobby's eyes go dark with memory.

"I was at war with an enemy I couldn't see," he said with sudden conviction in his voice. "Spiritual warfare that is more powerful than any conventional weapons."

Dane sat back, trying to take it in, a level of disbelief eating around the edges of his intellect like weasels tearing at the carcass of a rabbit. "What do you mean?" he asked uneasily.

Bobby adjusted his hat like screwing in a light bulb to illuminate his thoughts. "Natalie figured it out first. It took me a while, but now I understand too."

"You're freaking me out, Bobby," Dane said. "Spirits?" He puckered his lips and whistled — a sound reminiscent of the Twilight Zone.

"I get it," Bobby said, a tone of reassurance in his voice. "But I didn't have physical wounds. Mine were more sinister than that: self-hatred, bitterness."

Dane was not a stranger to self-criticism. He knew how the leeches of guilt attempted to burrow holes into your heart. He took a swig of beer, hoping to swallow the whole idea of spiritual warfare.

"Bobby," he said, eager to get back on track. "I'm happy that you and Natalie pulled it together ... but what does that have to do with Blake?"

"Natalie is more forgiving than I am. But for me, if someone hurt my little brother, whoever it is, I'm going to stick a nail-gun to their head and fire off a couple rounds. Natalie knows my temperament, and she's afraid if I get involved, she may lose me again."

Dane's eyes skimmed the familiar skyline of his childhood home, trying to piece together everything he'd experienced over the last few days, while a touch of dread crept over his skin as would a wrangler watching his saddle horse finally succumb to thirst in the desert.

"So, what I'm hearing," Dane concluded, "is that you think Blake was in trouble, but you don't know how ... and Vince may be involved ... and some girl in South Carolina may know the truth, if there is such a girl ... and that there is an army of demons marching around the whole damn mess just waiting for one of us to screw up."

"When you say it that way, it sounds pretty ludicrous," Bobby admitted.

***

Tied securely in place, the *Ecstasea* nodded in the gentle swells of the lake, the yellow glow of her portholes staring like hollowed eyes into the depths. She was cloaked in a smothering darkness, a whispery rain swirling in the cool gusts of an Arctic chill.

The yacht's powerful bow jutted forward out of the black water, the profile distinctive as the bridge of a nose, the twin anchors hanging heavy like teardrops on the cheeks of her hull. Her square stern, both wide and deep, was entitled with a metallic blue-and-gold script, pronouncing name and place, a proud statement to the world.

The yacht's superstructure, climbing high out of the bow deck to the bridge, sprawled back, expansive and glorious, easily carrying a pair of fourteen-foot Zodiaks side-by-side on the sun deck, finally dropping sharply at the aft to another sun deck spanning the broad stern. Both decks were unusually barren, naked compared to months earlier, the summer furniture now folded and stowed, the long tan legs and brightly colored suits of female sun worshipers clearly absent in the cold.

Along the dock, the bow and stern lines were wound in figure eights on the dock cleats, the excess rope coiled like locks of hair on a beauty shop floor. The dock was private and secure, all quiet save for the squeaky utterings of the rubber fenders guarding the long white hull, and the murmurs of light radiating in small blooms from the service stanchions.

Fresh from the sauna and his ritualistic plunge in Lake Washington, Vince stood naked at the foot of the bed. Before him lay his most recent lady, gripping the covers in clenched fists at her neck. She flashed a devilish smile and released a hand, lifting it in his direction, then curled a slender finger. Vince tore back the covers and kneeled on the mattress, straddling her legs, towering over her like a jackal guarding over fallen prey.

She was an Amerasian enchantress, mid-twenties, her father a veteran, her mother a Vietnamese bride. A slender, fragrant flower of a woman, graced with almond-shaped eyes — obsidian chips of pure black, bright and stunningly clear as crystal. Her body was brown and full, her hair coal black and silky, her face fine and pure — she'd inherited the best of both worlds.

As the deep rhythms of Sade pulsed through the bedroom, they made love, or had sex, depending on the perspective. She was in love with him, he surmised, but Vince had no use for silly emotions.

Finished, Vince pushed himself up, Vick's hands attempting to hold him. He knew she loved the quiet time after sex, but Vince had desires too. He swung his feet off the edge of the bed and reached for the mirror, then pulled the sheet across his lap and tapped a mound on the glass. Vick slid up on the bed, sitting with her back propped against the headboard, her face twisted into a pout.

With no blade present, Vince lined out the coke with his pinkie, then licked the tip with his tongue. The powerful taste numbed his mouth, and his chest responded to the stimulus with a cool, bursting inhale.

He laid the mirror on the corner of the nightstand. With one nostril pushed closed, he held the golden straw to his nose and with a violent snort, the first line was gone. He switched hands and nostrils and inhaled again, taking up the second line. He tipped back his head, eyes closed, and breathed deep.

When he opened his eyelids, a mellifluous world awaited, his perception stilted in the present by a euphoric snowfall. Colors vivid. Thought polished to a pinpoint. The mirror appeared a hollow cylinder bored into the oak, a scattering of white left in its reflection.

"Please," Vick said, begging with a child-like inflection. "Lay with me."

Entranced by the bottomless hole, Vince pinched his nostrils and sniffed; two quick times. "Can't baby. Business." He stood, the sheet falling from his lap, and walked to the dresser. "Maybe later."

Vick pulled the sheet up over her breasts and locked it in place behind her elbows, a fresh pout protruding from her lips. Vince ignored her and got dressed.

When Vince entered the Main Salon, Chief was inching his rotund body out of an armchair, hiking up the waist of his gray slacks as he stood. Patrick Donovan was the Chief of Seattle's Metro Police. He had a potbelly, which hung over the buckle of his pants, and a melon of flesh peeking above each hip through the partially untucked tail of his white shirt. The seat cushion, relieved by his departure, sucked in air, wheezing like an asthmatic. He made his way to the bar.

Donovan's skin was greasy, his cheeks and nose florid with broken blood vessels. His hair was a thin, black comb-over. He liked food. He liked booze. But more than that, Donovan liked women. A depressing thought for him these days, since even his wife had closed that account.

The first time they'd met was at a campaign victory dinner for the mayor. Seated at the same table, Vince zeroed in on the opportunity. He gathered Donovan was proud of his service, but underlying the chest thumping was a man of despair. His career was ending, and Donovan wanted more than a wall plague and a pat on the back when he retired. Vince had hooked a bottom fish.

The reeling began a few weeks later. Slow, steady, giving him room to run. Then Donovan crested the waves, and Vince hauled the champion halibut onto the deck. He knew exactly why Chief had agreed to a second dinner: money and power; the trifecta as plain as a pinball machine lit up between his eyes: sex with one of Vince's girls. Vince just hoped Chief's carotids could handle the surge.

Behind the bar, Sean was arranging bottles of alcohol. Twenty-five years old, blond-haired and blue-eyed, with cannon-sized arms, his function was to protect and serve. Only two other commandments had been carved into Vince's stone tablets: absolutely no coke and no booze. A very strict rule that Sean followed stringently. It was easy. Impurities messed up his steroid balance.

"Where's Lance and Jimmy?" Vince asked.

"Chief was coming," Sean said. "I gave them the day off."

Lance: the name conjured visions of a Hollywood hunk; a square-jawed, body-sculpted Adonis. But, to the contrary, Lance was a farm boy from Bellingham, built like the trunk of an oak tree, cursed with the brains of an acorn. For Vince, he'd take a bullet. All because Vince had rescued him from the grill at Denny's and made him a man to be reckoned with; not some manure shoveler from up north. Jimmy, his younger brother, was freckle-faced and carrot-topped, and new to the job at Lance's insistence. Vince hadn't rendered a final judgment as to his capabilities.

"Sean, get Chief a refill, then get lost for a while ... and where's Tony?"

"I'm here," Tony said, a sluggish drawl in his words.

As Sean left, Vince quickly surmised Tony was on a multi-day binge. Heavy-lidded, his face gaunt, his lips were sticking together with a tacky-white film. The pungent aroma of body odor was suffocating.

Vince drilled him for answers, and reluctantly, Tony filled him in. Three days ago, was Jenny's birthday, and they and a guy named Dino had been partying ever since. Meth and coke and weed mostly, and booze was expected, but once Vince figured out that Tony had needled some smack, he slapped him upside the head for being so stupid.

On the street, Tony would've retaliated with a left hook. It came with the territory. But to Vince, he was submissive as a lamb. He stepped back, giving Vince room to vent.

Vince had no quarter for Jenny, and the next revelation proved his conviction. Jenny had slept with Dino to pay for the score. A ritual that was becoming more and more commonplace in their marriage. It was clear to Vince that Jenny was a train wreck, and Tony was a punk for staying with her. The episode ended like so many others, Tony wagging his head in agreement and Vince finally relinquishing his anger for his best friend.

Vince took a deep breath. There was a chalkboard in his head with fingernails scratching their way across it. He wanted to get back to the euphoria balloon that was blossoming there before Tony put a pin on it. They had business to discuss and so he poured Tony a drink and laid out some lines of coke on the bar. Not a partaker of cocaine, Chief made his way back to the armchair.

"First, Tony," Vince pleaded. "Nick is getting sloppy on the street, dishing up blow like a street vendor with a Coney Island cart. Chief's guys can only ignore so much. Straighten him out. If he gets popped again, I'm not springing his ass this time."

He glanced at the Chief. "You want to add anything?"

"Nope, you said it all."

Tony took up a line, then nodded his head.

"Second, I met with Vito and his son last night at the Palomino Room. With Blake gone, Carolina is out. For the next few months, until Vito's compound is finished on the island, deliveries will be out of New Jersey."

"That sounds dumb," Tony said. "How's that gonna work? I just figured out where South Carolina was. Is New Jersey near there?"

Vince handed Tony the tooter. "Take another line." He knew what was coming would set Tony on his ear, yet Tony never refused coke or anything else with gas, which would give himself time to explain.

"You need to work with Vito's wiseguy, Evohl," Vince said. "He'll deliver the blow on Vito's jet, then help you do the cut. If you get that right, the distribution will be the same as usual."

"Evohl? What kind of name is that?"

"What? Tony, I don't know," Vince barked with more than a slap of irritation. "He's Vito's right-hand man. He's Russian or Estonian. It doesn't matter."

"Wiseguy, huh? I'll bet he's from Wuss-tonia," Tony said with a sneer, endeavoring to sound like a tough operator.

Vince cringed and shook his head in disbelief, then ended the conversation by warning Tony not to screw up. To which Tony responded by veering onto another tangent: the possibility of throwing a party for Dane on the *Ecstasea.*

"Sounds risky," Chief said. "I understand Blake is no longer available, but couldn't you make the turns?"

"I had to make a trade. Vito doesn't want me wasting my time muling cocaine, but I want to keep Venegas as our source. I built the relationship with Venegas and even though future amounts will be substantially larger, Venegas can handle it. So I reasoned with Vito that it's better to diversify in case the Feds clip a source. In the end, he agreed, but there's a caveat."

"What's a 'caveat'?" Tony asked.

Chief piped up. "A stipulation," he said.

Tony still looked stymied, so Vince tried to put him at ease. "He wants to meet Venegas before the deal."

"Why?" Chief asked.

"I asked him the same thing," Vince said, remembering how Vito's corneas were yellow with rage, as if questioning him was beyond the pale. "Vito said, 'I won't do business with people whom I haven't looked straight in the eye.'"

Vince paused in rumination. "Then Vito locked his eyes on me and said, 'Do you understand?'"

"*That* is not a question," Chief said. "That's a kingpin marking his territory."

"I know," Vince said, re-envisioning Vito's eyes piercing him like the tip of a stiletto, and the red mist that entered at the base of his skull and bloomed out over the back of his eyeballs.

"My head was a bucket of snakes. I didn't know what to say. At that moment, I heard a piano string being drawn tight in my right ear. I wondered if I was coming down with a sinus headache, or an ear infection, or if Vito had administered twenty-two-grains of pain reliever without me even realizing he'd cocked the hammer."

"No shit," Tony said.

"Well, at least now you're on a first-name basis," Chief remarked.

CHAPTER 6

Georgetown, South Carolina
October 4, 1995

Lightning was cracking in the West, the storm steadily growing closer. Tyra moved hastily toward the back of the Inn. Flood-lights were piercing through the foliage as she zig-zagged under the oaks across the gardens. The soft glow of several warm-lit rooms illuminated its façade, the patches of serenity reminding her of a quilt sewn with images from places far away where people lived a utopian existence foreign to hers.

After climbing the trellis onto the veranda, her room, Blake's room, was dark. Tyra surveyed up and down the porch. She was alone. She gripped the long brass handle and twisted her fist. A tense breath left her lungs. Jilly at the front desk had followed her instruction.

She quickly stepped inside and closed the French doors behind her. Heavy curtains draped the entrance, dusting the hardwood floor. Her shoulders felt wrapped in a plastic film like leftovers in the microwave, her skin humid with fear.

She let her satchel and coat fall to the floor. The room felt cool, eerie, with a whiff of cigarette smoke. Her shirt damp with perspiration, her Lee's sodden with rain, she felt her way to the bed, finger-combing wisteria petals from her hair. She placed a knee on the bedspread, and slowly, like a cat, stretched out onto the bed, gently pulling a pillow to caress her head. She needed a moment to gain strength and imme-diately fell asleep.

***

Dane watched as the nightstand clock ticked off the minutes, then he saw her stir.

"You must be Tyra," he said calmly.

Tyra jumped up off the bed as if a snake had curled up beside her and backed clumsily into the desk and then the wall, rattling the desk lamp in its shade. Her breath was echoing off the ceiling.

Dane sat in a wing-back chair in the room's corner. "I'm sorry. I didn't want to scare you, but I had to make sure I didn't miss you."

"Who ... who are you? What do you want?" she said.

"I'm Dane."

"How'd you get in?" The voice came from a silhouette inching along the wall toward the veranda.

"Jilly and I became quick friends. I left the door open."

Outside, lightning pulsed through the sky. Rivulets of rain on the French door's glass cast a shadow like ink running down the walls and over her skin. Thunder followed quickly, the Inn creaking under the pressure.

"How long have you been here?" she pressed him. "You're trespassing, you know. You're going to be in big trouble."

"Slow down. I've been here ever since you crawled into bed. That was twenty minutes ago."

"What are you doing here?" she said, the silhouette inching away in the darkness.

"You're sure full of questions. I wanted to see you again. That's all. So we could talk. You left Blake's funeral so quickly. Why is that?"

"I don't have to answer any of your questions," she insisted. "Why don't you just leave?"

"Let me turn on a light, and we can get more acquainted."

"Don't do that!"

"Why not?" he asked.

At that point, the finger in Tyra's dike of emotions gave way, and tears gushed in torrents of fear and loss. Her resolute posture was crumbling like the bank of a flooding river. Dane reassured her he truly was Blake's distant friend, and that he understood her grief because he bore it too, until finally the gulps of air subsided. Punctured and weak, the slender reed of a woman slid down the wall, her legs folding like a carpenter's rule, her back slouching forward until her forehead rested on her knees.

Dane cupped her elbow and gently lifted Tyra from the floor, sitting her down in the wing-back chair. He could feel her shivering.

Dane sat on the edge of the bed. "We've got to get you out of those damp clothes," he said.

She relaxed and sat back. "No, not yet. I'm not cold. It's just nerves."

"I have to say, I am confused … about a lot of things."

"Why wouldn't you be? It's all so crazy. I don't know where to begin."

"How about the beginning? When did you meet Blake?"

"It was a year-and-a-half ago. He'd always come into the Indigo Room, and I'd wait on him. We just looked at each other for the longest time. He said he was afraid to ask me out because he thought I'd turn him down. He was always overthinking things."

"We had that in common."

Tyra took a deep breath and continued, "I was waiting, hoping he'd ask. Finally, he did, and we've been together ever since."

With a look of discomfort, Tyra retracted her chin, swallowing hard. "I'm terribly thirsty. I need something to drink."

"Here," Dane said, reaching to the foot of the chair. "It's lemonade." He twisted the cap, and Tyra guzzled it down. "I'm sorry, there's no more. I drank most of it waiting for you."

Tyra emptied the bottle, then set it on the nightstand.

She slowly passed the back of her hand across her mouth, then let her head fall back against the chair, her shoulders rounding like cookie dough in a warm oven. "Blake wanted out of the business with Vince," she said. Her voice carried a hesitation, like she was tattling on a friend. "He said he couldn't do it anymore." Tyra raised her hand to her mouth as if to chew a nail. "Only it was hard for him to quit. Vince was his friend. He didn't want to hurt him."

Vince, Tony, Blake: they were lifelong friends. Over that period, friends undoubtedly offended each other, Dane mused. It was inevitable. "I don't think I understand. Blake was worried about what Vince would think if he quit?"

"He wouldn't admit it, but I knew he feared what Vince would do," she said, her voice quivering. "Especially since Geraci was involved."

"Why would he fear Vince for quitting the firm?" Dane asked — but it really wasn't the question. The real question was subcutaneous, and it was crawling along under his skin, searching for a cut to escape through.

"It wasn't the firm that bothered him; it was the cocaine. He didn't want to smuggle any more cocaine."

"Cocaine!" Dane recoiled. "What cocaine?"

"Blake was smuggling cocaine in from South America at the mill. He never went into details, but that's what was going on. Then he'd take it to Seattle on the company jet, and Vince would distribute it. They made tons of money. Blake wanted out. We were going to be together and put all that behind him."

Dane's mind was whirring like a dust devil in Texas. He took a deep breath. "You mentioned someone else," he said.

"Geraci. Blake said his name was Geraci." There was panic in her eyes. "He's some mob guy Vince wanted to go partners with. Blake didn't like it. He didn't want to get involved with the mob. He knew he'd never get out."

Dane needed facts. He was an engineer by training and knowing how things added up came naturally. "So, what happened the day he died?"

"He went to work at the mill as usual. Next thing I know, I'm waking up in that bed," she said, pointing her trembling hand, "and he's not beside me," her voice cracking under the weight of a crushing memory. "I didn't know why at first, but deep down, I did."

She squirmed, sat forward, then back, like she was unsure of whether to stay sitting or get up and run. "I found out the next day," she said dolefully, "that he'd been in an accident. I didn't believe it. Blake was too careful. I didn't believe it then, and I don't believe it now. They killed him."

Dane smelled a dank odor suddenly invade the room, the hair rising on his forearms like a specter had slipped in under the door. "By 'they' you mean Vince and Geraci."

"Yes."

"Do you really think Vince could kill Blake?"

"I don't know. I'm sure it wasn't either of them ... I mean ... they had it done. Or maybe Geraci did it alone. All I know is, deep down, it was murder. It wasn't some stupid accident."

"So that's why we're sitting here in the dark?"

"That's right. Think about it. The police mentioned nothing about finding a briefcase of money or cocaine. It doesn't add up, and now I think they're following me. And if they are, they're probably watching the room, too."

"Are you sure?"

"This is going to sound crazy, but when I went to Seattle, there was this guy on the plane. I don't know why I noticed him. I guess it was his nose. It was huge. It was so unreal, I had to look twice."

She was staring now, directly in Dane's eyes. He could feel her alarm like a strobe light, eradicating all his reasoning and exposing all his misconceptions at the same time.

"His nose and mustache looked like one of those gag plastic faces, only he didn't have the black-rimmed glasses," she said. "Then when I'm up in Boonville visiting friends after the funeral, I see him again. Behind a rack of chips at Winn Dixie. That couldn't be a coincidence. So I rented a car and drove down here. I was scared, but I'm not an idiot. I just didn't know what else to do."

Dane could sense that whatever had happened, no matter how improbable, it was genuine enough to ward caution. He was feeling the knives of uncertainty work in his gut. He got up from his chair and walked to the veranda, peering through the curtains, skimming the landscape like a soldier intent on the enemy.

"I'm scared Dane. What am I going to do?"

Dane was not forthcoming with an answer. Thunder began pounding against the glass, visceral and unnerving, while sheet lightning was threading through the clouds as if their veins were on fire.

"I'm sure a car followed me from Boonville," she said in a whisper again. "I didn't see him, but I know he's there."

At length, he asked, "Do you know a John McTarnihan?"

"Who?" she asked, sniffling.

"McTarnihan. Vince told me he had sent a P.I. down here to investigate Blake's death. I think his name is McTarnihan. Jilly said McTarnihan showed her a P.I. license. He's been snooping around, waiting to talk with you." His eyes narrowed. "He doesn't really fit your description."

"Maybe they're working together," Tyra said, her eyes welling up again. "I'm so confused." She lifted her hand, wiping each eye with her fingertips. "I wish Blake was here."

An enormous breath of tension ballooned from Dane's lungs. In his thoughts, he could see Blake standing on a dock, and Vince and Tony racing past him, then diving into deep water. Blake looked both ways, then jumped in after them.

Dane rolled his head on a neck, stiff with regret. "I should've been here," he said.

"It wasn't your fault," Tyra said, coiling away like a leaf wilting from a hot coal. "Maybe I'm wrong about Vince. Maybe I just need someone to blame."

Dane felt her words. He saw the apprehension in her eyes. Her distress was as palatable as vinegar on a burned tongue.

Now reasoning took center stage, while emotion swooned in the back row. "I can't believe Vince is ... no" — he shook his head — "no that comes later," he said. "Right now, I must figure out what to do. Later, I'll demand answers."

Dane took in a deep breath, gathering his thoughts, circling the wagons of strength, preparing himself for action. "We need to get you out of here. Some place safe until I can check this out. Are you ready to travel?"

Tyra shook her head up and down.

"Okay, put on some dry clothes and we'll get out of here."

Tyra grabbed a clean pair of jeans and a blue sweater from the dresser.

Suddenly, they heard heavy footsteps and a knock at the door. "Miss Rivers?"

Instantly, Tyra twirled off-balance on her heel, jitter-stepping two paces towards Dane. The floor unnervingly creaked under her weight. Dane felt a chill zipper up his spine. He held an index to his lip, then pointed to the veranda. He silently lifted her coat and satchel from the floor, then cupping her forearm, led her out through the French doors and back into his room, two doors down.

"Change your clothes. I'll get rid of whoever it is," he whispered as he guided Tyra, his hand on the small of her back, into the bathroom. "Meet me in twenty minutes behind the leather shop."

Dane nonchalantly opened the hallway door, then closed it with a slam behind him. A man stood at Tyra's door, his hand poised to knock. Hearing the door bang into the jamb, he turned to face Dane.

He was short and compact, with arms too long for his body, and a thin, furry mustache grew low and straight across his lip. Light orange with a black tint, it was like a caterpillar had perched itself there, resting on the branch of a tree. He wore a green polyester sport jacket with countless snags in the fabric, fuzzy gray slacks and a lavender shirt. A charcoal homburg topped off his rummage-sale garb, gaining him a few inches in height.

"Hey buddy," the man said, the heel taps on his wing-tip shoes clicking the hardwood floor as he hip-hopped towards Dane. He pointed over his shoulder. "Do you know who's staying in that room? I thought I heard voices."

Windows lined the hallway streaked with rain, the rivulets capturing iridescent flashes of light, mimicking branches of lightning racing across the sky. From the corner of his eye, Dane noticed the profile of a figure standing by the front of the Inn. He was tall, wearing a black oil-skin Stockman's coat, plastic-covered Stetson and cowboy boots. He was standing arms-crossed under the semi-circular awning that jutted out from the lobby. A lit cigarette was in his mouth. Protruding over the cigarette, dwarfing his bushy mustache, was a fleshy awning of tremendous magnitude.

Dane turned his attention back to the oddity standing in front of him. "Sorry. No, I don't," he said.

The man pushed the homburg back on the crown of his head, exposing more of his curly hair.

"Anything wrong?" Dane asked in a concerned tone.

"No-no," the man said. "Funny, that's all. I swore I heard something."

CHAPTER 7

Seattle, Washington
October 7, 1995

FBI Agent Derek Virchow sat alone in a booth along the wall. Across a sea of pool tables, he could see the bar above which a Zenith flickered with re-runs of Gunsmoke. At the end of the bar a prostitute straddled a red vinyl stool, her skirt short, her lips bright, her bust pushed up into cantaloupes.

The Sea-Tac Strip was home to taverns, seedy hotels, ramshackle convenience stores and boarded-up windows. A gem in the community, the Alibi Room was cavernous and dark, and offered unsurpassed anonymity.

Nick Franklin had just left; the preceding hour of interrogation proving fruitless. Sure, nine months ago Nick had opened the door, but except for confirming bits and pieces that Derek already knew, he wasn't much help. Nick had lost his value. Nick would never be on the inside.

Derek already knew about Geraci and Donovan and the cops turning their heads on the street. The only revelations from Nick were about Dane Avilla, a long-time buddy who was back in town, and that soon he would need to triple his output.

When Derek asked how he would triple his output, Nick circled his head on his shoulders. Derek thought maybe he had to get all the marbles back in their holes like those cheap Cracker Jack games before he answered. When he finally did answer, it was "I don't know." When he asked him if he thought Avilla was involved, he got a weird sensation that

49

Nick didn't even remember who Avilla was. It was useless. Nick's brain was deep-fried.

The first night they met, Nick was in a Seattle DEA holding cell wearing a Dead-Head sweatshirt with cut-off sleeves, his right forearm adorned with a dull-blue tattoo of the Zig-Zag man.

That night, two facts stuck out. First, Nick got busted with five ounces of coke, which meant he wasn't a small-time dealer. Second, he was adamant about calling his lawyer, a suit Derek recognized as big-time muscle, which meant somebody with a bankroll was backing him up. So, after a little persuasion, tactics that Derek had learned in Ballbusting 101 at Quantico, Nick had an epiphany and became a snitch.

It was Jason Riker, DEA Deputy Director, who assigned Derek to the case that night. The suit, the tie, the tasseled wingtip loafers; Riker screamed bureaucrat. Derek figured Riker probably couldn't find his butt with both hands, but he also realized that Riker was a rising star at the Justice Department.

Which made Derek wonder: Why did Riker ask specifically for him? Sure, Derek's relentless determination was almost as famous as his trademark snow-white crewcut, or the purple scar that ran along his jaw where a bullet had scooped out a three-inch gutter. But Derek was FBI, and Derek didn't play scapegoat.

However, it didn't take long for the bottom line to emerge. Riker wanted to catch a train to DC, destination corner office, Pennsylvania Avenue, and Nick was his golden ticket. All he needed was an engineer who could get him through the Rocky Mountains.

Derek lit another smoke. Four previous encounters lay crushed in the ashtray next to a pack of Pall Mall straights and his stainless-steel lighter engraved with a red outline of Vietnam. The waitress brought him another beer, while some chick with green hair, short-short denims and heavy thighs was giving him the crazy-eye as she chalked her cue, the knob of her wrist protruding like a jawbreaker had lodged under her skin.

He took a sip, then sucked an inch out of his Pall Mall. The thought of Riker pursuing an investigation just to stroke his resume irritated him. But like it or not, here he sat at the base of the mountains, out of fuel.

CHAPTER 8

Seattle, Washington
October 8, 1995

Dane peeled off his coat and walked behind Vince into the Game Room, quietly head swiveling, impressed by the fruits of his trade. Tony was there, reclined on the couch with a beer in his hand.

Only four days had passed since Georgetown. Tyra was now sporting a pageboy haircut and living on a vacant schooner in Eagle Harbor, close to Bobby's houseboat. Dane knew Bobby was impatient and wouldn't wait long for answers.

The plan they had devised seemed simple. Dane was to reestablish camaraderie with Vince and Tony and discern what happened to Blake, whether accident or foul play. Whatever else he discovered was secondary. However, Vince and Tony were his friends, which made the game both dreadful and reasonable, like taking castor oil for constipation, especially with Geraci in the mix.

Vince crossed the room to hang up Dane's coat. He was prodigious, sailing over the floor in a billowy silk shirt imprinted with miniature red Ferrari's, and baggy pleated trousers the color of a faint purple bruise. Vince had an uncommon touch. Everything was effortless to him — dancing, gambling, sports, even the way he mixed his drinks. Parties got louder. Women got friendlier. Music became a visceral encounter. He had this power; an aura whereby just being allowed in his presence made you feel renowned.

"You want a drink?" Vince asked.

"Scotch would be nice," Dane said.

Vince poured two fingers over ice, then over the next few minutes, grilled Dane about his time in Europe, desperate for all the details. At the end of a long line of questioning, Dane pushed his cigarettes from the pocket of his khaki shirt, exposing the near empty pack, then held them out, showing them to Vince. "Do you mind?"

"Naw, go ahead," Vince said.

Dane stuck a filter in his mouth and pulled a cigarette from confinement.

"You been to Amsterdam?" Tony asked. "I heard good things like drugs, prostitution. All legal."

Dane exhaled as he spoke. "That's right."

"Sounds like the University District," Tony said from his half-reclining pose, the humor escaping Vince, but yielding a chuckle from Dane. The slight reminded Dane that Vince had this uncanny way of dismissing people.

"So," Vince said, putting the conversation back on track. "It's been at least three years, hasn't it?"

"Almost four." Dane eyed an ashtray on the poker table. He tapped an ash into it as he sat backwards, straddling the chair-back. "Hey, I wanted to say 'sorry' for the other day at the cemetery. I had one hellacious trip from Heathrow, twenty-two hours ..."

"Forget about it. I was edgy too."

Vince walked to the bar and replenished his drink. "So, how long are you staying?"

"I'd like to stay permanent. The parents aren't getting any younger." He hesitated, then spoke with a grin, "I hear there are some good engineering firms in town. Maybe I can find some outfit that's hard up."

Vince swirled the ice cube in his glass. "Just so happens I know of such a place."

Dane lulled a response while he raised his smoke under a cupped palm. He took a thoughtful puff, then sighed, the calming vapor exiting his nose. "What do you have in mind?"

"To be frank, I need someone to take over for Blake in Georgetown. It's a long-term contract for continuous support, so you'd need to move to South Carolina. Just come back to the office every month or two."

Dane paused, watching his cigarette roll between thumb and forefinger, measuring the proposal. "Thanks Vince, it's tempting, but I can't. I don't mind the occasional business trip, but I want to stay in Seattle."

"Well, keep it in mind."

"Gees, I can't get over this Vince," Dane said, twisting his head from side-to-side as he looked around the room. "She's a beauty. What I wouldn't give to have a boat like this."

"It's a yacht. How about two mil ... and that's used."

Dane was envious, slowly taking a sip. Teak paneled the walls and ceiling. Beveled glass light fixtures illuminated the space. Polished brass rails edged the stairs up to the sun decks and down to the staterooms. The *Ecstasea* was a graceful lady. Sitting in front of a red-felt poker table, the rest of the room was an expanse of games: foosball, pinball, darts. A baby grand adorned with a picture of a brown-skinned beauty sat in the corner. It was hard to refute; Vince had conquered his part of the world.

"Who's the lady?"

"That's Vick."

"You married?"

"Not me, Dane. That's just Vick's way of marking her territory. I could never be faithful, so why entertain heart-ache? Besides, Tony has provided me with a perfectly frightful example of 'the married man.'"

Dane looked at Tony. "How is Jenny? I haven't seen her in ages."

"You don't want to none either," Tony responded.

"She's a drunk and a whore," Vince chimed in.

"What? When you guys got married, I was jealous. Honest, I thought you were probably one of the luckiest guys in town."

Tony shrugged his shoulders, his eyes glistening with heartbreak. "Things are different now."

Vince stroked back his hair and let out a long sigh of consternation. "Different," he said. "That's an interesting way to put it."

Tony chugged his beer on the way to the fridge, while Vince mumbled an unrecognizable comment into his glass. The tension between them was profound.

After twenty heartbeats of torturous silence, Dane wanted to break the impasse. "How about we change the subject? Can we take a cruise?"

With his head down and the heels of his palms flat on the bar, Vince seemed to study his drink, until finally, he said with a pensive sigh, "Sure, why not. I haven't introduced you yet, but Sean and the boys are onboard. They can take us out." Then he looked Tony in the eye and said, "I hope you know I just want the best for you."

For Vince, it was an effort to be apologetic, his face and body contorting while he petitioned, "I'm sorry. Okay?" He waited for a nod from Tony. The signal given; his mien relaxed.

Dane raised his glass. "A toast." He waited for Vince and Tony to lift their drinks, then said, "To old friends."

***

Soon after, the *Ecstasea* was headed for Mercer Island. Tony was loading Van Morrison into the CD player. "Dane," he said, "If you is available, we was gonna throw a party. I like parties and Vince said I could have one. A welcome home sorta shindig. And since you're going to be around a while, I was thinking like Halloween, like costumes and shit would be like bitchin.'. Whatdoyathink?"

"Sure. I could use the entertainment. You'll need to help with a date, though. I don't know any women in town. Not anymore."

"Leave that to me," Vince said.

Minutes later, Vince and Dane stood side-by-side, content like long-lost brothers, drinks in-hand, gazing at the world as it slowly inched by. From the windows, Dane could see the stately houses that peppered the wooded slopes that rolled into Lake Washington. "You've been very successful, Vince. I'm jealous."

"Don't be. You know what it takes."

"Did Blake enjoy it?"

"Blake cared little about the bottom line. That was my job. But he loved engineering. His death left a black hole in this firm. One that could suck a couple of lesser men into it without effort. It's going to be hard to function without him."

"I don't want this to sound cold," Dane said, sheltering his voice under the bluesy beat of "Big Time Operators," "but Blake's death may lead to an opportunity."

"How so?"

"Earlier, you asked if I wanted a job in South Carolina. That was a nice offer and I appreciate it, but I truly want to stay in Seattle. There's just one part I left out. I've had several years of petroleum experience all around the world. Petroleum means big money and enormous opportunity."

Dane paused, recalculating his words. "Look, you can hire any talented engineer to take over Georgetown, but here, as partners, we can grow this company."

Vince's expression was unreadable. Dane wondered if his boldness was being met with amusement. mistrust, or was Vince coiling the spring on an upcoming face punch? He felt uneasy; Vince wasn't speaking, just staring with that all-knowing grin. He pursued a response. "Well, what do you think? Or do I just bleed out without so much as a snide remark?"

"I'm just ... amazed," Vince said finally. "Blake is barely cold, and here you are, asking for not just a job, but a partnership. I guess a better word for it is, I'm stunned."

"I'm sorry, Vince. Now isn't the right time. Let's change the subject."

"Oh, but I can't." He took a sip of his drink, then sucked in his checks like he was trying to extract wisdom from the aged malt. "You two always seemed to look down on me for some of my, let's say, dealings beneath the standard you'd set for the group. Tony and I were a little too hard core for the likes of you and Blake."

Vince's pupils narrowed as if focusing on an object just outside the window. It was as if a film reel was clicking slowly frame-by-frame in his head. "Blake never got use to my way of thinking. He tolerated me because we were friends and partners, but what I've seen in you today has restored my faith in human nature. Yeah, I'm stunned, Dane, but not in the way you think. I'm proud that you've finally realized that life is for the taking and every second you wait is a lifetime lost."

Dane took a gulp of scotch, relieved that he might have opened a door, just a crack, enough to get a foot in.

"Boy Dane. I believe you're sweating," Vince said, placing a hand on Dane's shoulder.

Dane pushed back his hair with a flat palm, wiping the moisture from his forehead. "I am sweating Vince, but not out of nervousness." He motioned his hand from left to right as if he was opening a curtain on a forbidden world. "When I see this kind of wealth, this kind of life. The life you have. If fate dealt me a Royal Flush because of Blake's death, well, then I'll mourn him all the way to the bank."

"You got my attention," Vince said. "Let me think about it."

***

The day progressed through the afternoon and into the evening. Sean had looped the *Ecstasea* around Mercer Island and up the west shoreline of Lake Washington. The water was smooth as silk, the weather mild, a few light rain showers pelted the windows as she slipped through the water like a salmon making its way upstream.

Dane stepped out onto the starboard deck and fired up his last cigarette. He stood arms-crossed, braced against the frigid air that skimmed over the lake and along the *Ecstasea's* length. The water was dark below. The sky above was thick with gray clouds like curds laid out on a fermentation table. He needed a contemplative smoke before venturing onto the next step of the game. The green and red running lights of the *Ecstasea* were visible at the tip of the bow. The lights of Seattle, Bellevue, and Kirkland snaked across the lake. As the *Ecstasea* slipped under the 520 Bridge, he stepped back inside.

"This might seem strange to ask, but the last time I spoke to Blake, he said you guys did some coke once in a while." It was a lie, like all lies, delivered hoping somehow the truth couldn't be known, and the seed sown would reap a harvest. Dane was looking for a reaction, but Vince remained calm, unwavering, as he eased back into his chair. Tony tipped his head and guzzled his beer, avoiding the question.

"Tell me what you're thinking," Vince said.

"Well, it's been a couple of weeks since I left Scotland, and I couldn't bring anything on the plane. Coke clears my head. Helps me unwind. Anyway, if you knew where I could get some, I'd appreciate it."

Vince turned to Tony. "Tony?" he asked, raising a quizzical eyebrow. "Do you have any cocaine?" He was trying to sound serious, like he did not know what Dane was talking about.

"Ah gee, Vince. I wouldn't know about no cocaine," Tony said softly, uneasily shifting in his seat, while wringing the beer bottle in his hands.

Vince laughed out loud. "That's why I love you, Tony. You're always good for a laugh." He looked back at Dane. "Of course. How about a line to go with your scotch?"

"Hey, I don't want to snort your stash. I can buy some."

"Don't worry about it, Dane. We can always get more. I'll be right back."

Vince left for his stateroom.

"What about you Tony? You used to hit it hard. Do you still snort?"

"Ahh–sure, Dane," Tony said, his voice low and unsure. "Sorry I wasn't like honest with you, but you been gone a lot, and well, a guy has to be careful. I've heard of dudes getting popped by old school chums who've got religion, or they're like with the law, and they turn old buddies in. I just was a bit like scared."

"That's alright Tony. I was taking a chance asking."

"By the way, I'm sorry about you and Jenny. If there's anything I can do, just ask."

"Thanks, Dane, but I can handle it."

"Well, I know I haven't been around much, but you and Vince are the only real friends I've got. I hope if I have a problem, I can come to you."

Tony sat up straight in his chair and took notice. His gold bicuspid glimmered in his smile. Obviously, it was a rarity for Tony to be asked for advice.

Vince came back carrying a couple of vials. He sat down at the bar and started lining the coke out on a small mirror.

Dane felt a cool sweat envelope his body, a cramp of nervousness tightening his gut. He hadn't snorted coke in months, the last time at the tortured end of a relentless abuse. Coke was a familiar haunt he'd sworn never to visit again. Would he be able to handle it? He poured some scotch in his glass and took a gulp, his mind whirring with sub–conscious instructions.

"There we go," Vince said as he slid off the bar stool. "The guest goes first."

Dane picked up a silver tube lying next to the mirror. He sniffed the air to clear his nostrils, then hunched over the white lines and took an inch in his left. Dane lifted his head, and his left eye watered, blurring his sight. He pushed his left nostril closed with a fingertip and leaned back over, taking another inch in his right.

"Go ahead Dane," Vince prodded. "We've got plenty. Go on. Take some more."

Dane sniffed his nose as he tilted back his head. His temples felt warm and light, like they were detaching from his skull. He hunched over again and took another inch in each side of his nose, then stepped away and handed Tony the tube.

Tony quickly edged in between the stools while Dane's mind numbed, his ears muffled to the sound of Tony's heavy snorts as he lifted a long stripe in each nostril. Tony surrendered the tube to Vince.

"Good, aye Dane," Vince gloated.

Dane nodded his head and felt the drain of his sinuses prowling his throat.

Vince stepped up to the bar and snorted a stripe half-way from one end, then switched hands and nostrils, and lifted the rest of the stripe from the other end.

Dane was unconsciously clenching his teeth, his jaw tight as a trap. He told himself: Relax — breathe deep — take it easy; have a drink. The thoughts were coming in a rush. His teeth ached; the taste in his mouth like a piece of aluminum had dissolved in his throat. He took a gulp of the scotch, the hard taste reduced to water.

Tony was lining up more coke, and Vince had walked to the stereo to place five new artists into the compact disc player.

Dane stared at the parallel lines Tony was drawing across the mirror. I'm not ready. His mind in a panic, he set down his drink and walked to the window. His heart was pumping so fiercely he thought it might explode. Calm down. Have a smoke. He pinched inside his shirt pocket, but his smokes were gone, remembering suddenly that he'd finished his last cigarette outside. He closed his eyes and took a deep breath. Every follicle on his scalp was tingling with electricity.

The music was playing loudly now, the sound of Aerosmith pounding crystal in his ears. Vince and Tony were already lifting more lines at the bar.

Vince pushed Tony aside and waved Dane over. "Here Dane, have another, before this human vacuum cleaner sucks in the furniture."

Dane knew the slippery slope had turned into a mudslide. Logic had left the building. He snatched up the silver instrument and inhaled the biggest and thickest line of all. His mind was full of doubt, pleasure, hatred and euphoria, all at the same time. Then, so that no one would take what was his, he quickly dabbed the crystals from the mirror, then lipped his finger like a hard stick of candy and spread the mendacious power through his mouth.

He stood motionless, shoulder-to-shoulder between Vince and Tony, his conscience anguishing over what he'd just done. How quickly Pharmakeia had separated mine from yours and envy from generosity and put jealousy and rage in a box with a nice red bow. There was never enough once her siren call echoed out from the rocks. Like a millionaire who needs just one more million to be fulfilled, cocaine would take your inhibitions and measure and civility as a down payment and suggest that if you could just have a little more, all would be copacetic with the world.

CHAPTER 9

Seattle, Washington
October 9, 1995

Tony sat across the table, tweed jacketed, munching on the final tidbits of breakfast. His hair banded back out of his face; he'd finished the sausage omelet in record time. Meanwhile, Dane had consumed three cups of coffee and a double order of toast.

"So Vince keeps you busy?"

Tony nodded his head. "Vince has a lot of rentals. I make sure people pay up, and fix 'em if they need fixing."

With a look of disgust, Dane sipped grounds from an empty cup, then gazed over his shoulder at the kitchen. "Did Blake have rentals?" he asked, the question an offset of his preoccupation.

"Naw, Blake didn't want the hassle. Besides, he wasn't here much."

Dane glanced again towards the kitchen, the back of their waitress disappearing through the swinging stainless-steel door. "Vince and he did well, didn't they?"

"Yeah."

The waitress gone, he attempted to concentrate on Tony. "How about you? Where do you live?"

"Wallingford. It's an older home. Vince loaned me the money to buy it, then hired some guys to fix it up."

"That was nice of him."

Dane started looking over his shoulder again, craning his neck to search over Tony, finger-tapping his cup. "Where in the hell is that waitress?"

Tony stirred in his seat. "You want me to go get her?"

"No, don't worry about it. I'm just edgy. I need some cigarettes." He began searching the restaurant again, this time for a cigarette machine.

Tony stared at Dane. "You don't snort a lot, do ya, Dane?"

Caught off-guard, Dane went flush. "Why do you say that?"

"I can tell."

Dane's face went a shade redder. "Tell what." He felt accused, the retort floating somewhere between resentment and embarrassment.

"Hey, it's okay. People who don't snort a lot get a little cranky the next morning. 'Cause like your body wants more. I get the same way if I know my stash is gone."

Tony held out a fist. "Here, take this."

"What is it?"

"Just take it."

Dane opened his hand, and Tony deposited a vial in his palm. Dane snapped his hand closed. "Gees Tony. What if someone saw you?"

"Quit worrying. It'll take the edge off."

"I can buy my own, Tony."

"Take it. It's only a half-gram."

"Well, I need to get my own."

"Okay. How much do you want?"

Dane sat speechless. He felt a dry wind grating on his patience and prickling down his neck. He had a vial of coke in his hand and was attempting to buy more. Two days ago, he didn't even snort cocaine.

***

An hour later, he parked his rental car in front of his childhood home, a two-story white farmhouse in Kirkland. The ninety-year-old house set on one acre of land, and had been his parents' home for forty years. Now high-density suburbs encroached, and it stood like a gappy tooth in a row of capped teeth.

The overcast sky was a gray nap spreading horizon-to-horizon, leveling the mountains to three-thousand feet. Dane pulled his jacket up over his head and splashed the long sidewalk past the naked rose bushes to the front porch, then up four wooden steps and out of the driving rain. He stopped to catch his breath and shake the rain from his clothes, the mere act jarring loose a memory: the fearful premonition from the North Sea so vivid in his mind's eye it scared him all over again.

He had to find a place of his own.

CHAPTER 10

Seattle, Washington
October 9, 1995

At his window, with the blinds at full rise, Vince gazed from his office to the scene of a suicide five stories below. He found himself sucked in — the sound of ambulances having drawn his curiosity. In the center of the rubbernecking horde of on-lookers, a jumper laid deformed on the damp sidewalk under a mountainous yellow tarpaulin. The police had cordoned off the area, and at the point of departure, a lone policewoman tenuously leaned over the rail, one hand clutched as an anchor, the other holding her regal-blue hat as she viewed the plummeting path.

An eight-story plunge; the choice of demise had proven to be very effective. The blood bloomed out from under the tarp and broke into a river, a crimson stain of life running into the gutter.

A voice came over the intercom, "Mister Spinetti."

"What is it, Erin?"

"John McTarnihan is here to see you."

He squinted into the distance and said, "Give me a minute, then send him in."

He pulled a small vial and a tiny coke spoon from his pocket. As with the life of the jumper, some realities needed an escape.

A quick snort later, McTarnihan entered, carrying a brown accordion file.

Vince slipped the paraphernalia back into his pocket, continuing to stare at the commotion on the street.

McTarnihan removed his coat and hat, then sat down beside them on the leather couch.

The office was splendid with pictures of the *Ecstasea*, Mount Rainier, several P.E. licenses, Rotary and Optimist awards. A bronze sculpture of a cowboy and his bucking bronco topped a low bookcase across the room.

Vince lowered the blinds past his face, the room darkening to slender ribbons of light that pervaded across the room. "Glad you could make it. You want a drink?"

"Bourbon, straight up."

Vince rounded the end of his desk and made way to a wooden globe in the corner. Then splitting away the northern hemisphere, the world revealed glasses, bottles and an ice bucket at the center of the earth. North America, Eurasia and half of Africa tilted back until a small brass chain restrained their travel to the wall.

He poured three fingers of bourbon into a tumbler. "I suppose you saw the circus outside."

McTarnihan ruefully shook his head. "Yeah. Shame. Twenty-two-year-old coed. What in hell possesses a young girl like that to take the plunge?"

Vince hesitated, thinking. "Several things come to mind," he said. He handed McTarnihan the drink. "How'd you know it was a girl?"

"I'm an ex-cop, remember?"

Vince was aware of McTarnihan's credentials: good and bad. His eyes came to rest on the folder.

"It's all right here," McTarnihan said, patting the file. "Miss Flynn in living color."

Vince slipped a paper clip off his desk and started unbending the corners. "I would've hired her anyway, you know, even without the report. She's a looker our Miss Flynn. But more importantly, she has an exploitable past." He started cleaning under his nails with an end of the straightened clip.

McTarnihan sipped the bourbon, his appearance detached.

Vince held up the back of his hand, inspecting his work. "I need to surround myself with people I can trust." He glanced sidelong at McTarnihan. "I *can* trust you, can't I, Mac?"

A fleeting grin crossed McTarnihan's face. "I'm a trustworthy sort of guy, Vince."

Vince flashed an ingratiating smile. He returned to his nails. McTarnihan took another sip in the silence.

Finally, Vince disposed of the straightened clip and swiveled to face McTarnihan. He had his elbows on the desk. His voice went flat and to the point, his palms warming as he slowly rubbed them together. "I think Miss Flynn could give me insight into Mister Avilla's motives you could not penetrate. Would you say that's an accurate assumption?"

"Very accurate. But ..." McTarnihan tweaked the end of his mustache, drifting off in speculation. "Can you trust her?"

Vince's head cocked forward; his forehead wrinkled with asperity. "With that file," he said, pointing his finger at the file in McTarnihan's lap. "She'll do whatever I ask."

McTarnihan slid guardedly behind his drink, taking a sip and politely nodding his head.

Vince laced his fingers, his forearms prone in front of him. "Okay," he said in a softer tone. "Miss Flynn will dig on the inside. You dig up everything else."

"As long as I'm paid Vince, I'll dig a hole to China."

Vince touched his wrist. "Well, it's almost five. Let's get her in here."

McTarnihan eased back into the leather while Vince walked to the door and opened it. Erin Flynn sat at her desk, typing.

"Erin. Would you come in here for a moment?"

Without hesitation, Erin grabbed a yellow pad and spun out of her chair. She touched the top button of her blouse out of habit, and with her free hand flat at a spade, she ran the waist of her skirt as if to tuck it any loose tails.

"You won't need that," Vince said.

Erin laid the pad down, and Vince held the door as she walked in, their eyes briefly catching one another; Vince, with a flirtatious gleam, Erin shyly shifting hers away.

Her countenance was demure, but the smell of her perfume instantly charged the room. McTarnihan made an ill-fated attempt at straightening his tie and nonchalantly palmed his curly brown hair.

Erin stepped away as Vince closed the door behind her, her eyes showing the perplexity of not knowing what was at hand. She turned to face him. He smiled poignantly, as if to comfort her, then walked past her to his desk, where he leaned his buttocks against its front edge and crossed his arms.

Erin stood reticently between McTarnihan and the Vince, her grace a fawn-like timidness. Long-legged and slender, a scarlet skirt and creamy silk blouse with small pearl buttons, black belt and black heels; Vince thought she looked good enough to eat. He could see McTarnihan licking his parched lips.

She's twenty-six, maybe twenty-seven, he thought. Her auburn hair was shoulder length in soft ringlets cascading past her delicate ears; her serene face jeweled with emerald eyes.

"Please sit down," Vince said, tipping his forehead to a leather armchair. There was a pleasant tone in his voice. "This won't take long."

The office had an unsettling edge, an obscurity of color melting into borderless smudges of gray-green and charcoal in the dusky light from the slitted window. Vince could see Erin struggling to remain poised. She promptly sat down, the chair and her façade starkly alone in front of the bookcase.

Hastily, McTarnihan sat up from his slouching pose, smoothing down his shirt, unmistakably noticing the slender gams that emerged mid-thigh from under her skirt. The prurient gunsight was magnetizing, and Vince couldn't escape McTarnihan's gawking stare, telegraphing his dire need of sex.

Erin crossed her legs. There was a subtle change in her calm expression. She looked at Vince for comfort. "Is there something wrong?" she asked.

"No-no. There's nothing wrong, Erin," Vince said, reassuring her. "Do you know who Mister McTarnihan is?"

"Uh-no." She paused timorously, looking to McTarnihan, then back to Vince. "I mean, he's been in the office before, but ..."

Vince broke in. "He's a private investigator."

The blood drained from Erin's cheeks. Vince could see her chest tighten like a rope had been cinched around her torso. He wondered if her heart had stopped. She slumped back into the leather, her somewhat cool demeanor melting to a puddle of fear.

"Bonnie Killough. It has a definite Irish ring to it," Vince said. "Which do you prefer? Bonnie? Or Erin?"

She stuttered, then paused as if to say more. At last, she chose to just answer the question. "Erin."

"Well, then I must say straight out *Erin*. Blowing away your pimp took a lot of courage. I admire you for that. From my understanding, Manny Ocho was a nasty man to work for."

Erin was quiet, staring at the floor, her elbows pinning the armrests, her hands together like the visor of a cap across her forehead. Her breathing was shallow.

Vince lowered his arms, placing the heel of his hands by his side on the edge of the desk. "Mac. How many times was he shot?"

McTarnihan pulled open the file and slid out three inches of paper and photographs. He fumbled down a few pages. "It was a thirty-eight; two in the gut, one in the chest, one in the groin. Two stray bullets lodged in the door of his car." Strangely, he looked at Erin with adulation, and wiped a bead of sweat from his forehead. Erin remained hidden beneath the brim of hands.

"Impressive," Vince praised her. "Six shots. The whole enchilada."

"In broad daylight," McTarnihan applauded, like it was an event to be proud of. He fumbled to another page. "Unfortunately, there were witnesses."

Erin never moved. Vince sensed the movie clicking frame after frame through her memory. "Don't keep it to yourself, Erin. I'd be interested in your recollections of the incident." He shot McTarnihan a rhetorical look. "I think we both would."

Erin uncrossed her legs, then tugged at the end of her skirt as if the exercise would lengthen the hem to her knees. Her eyes were wide, her pupils small. She licked her lips, then wiped them with the back of her wrist.

"Take your time," Vince said slowly, with a fatherly tone.

"He was a pig," she said at last, her eyes to the floor like she could see him in the weave of the carpet. Beads of sweat were forming on her upper lip. Once again, she slid her wrist across her mouth, then folded her hands in her lap.

"It had been hot and muggy all week," she started, still focused intently on the floor. "As usual, Manny was all over me in the front seat of his Caddy. I felt like furniture. A bed or sofa for him to sprawl on. He pushed his hands under my bikini top and put his lips on my neck. Then he licked me … a slow path up my neck. I hated the way he touched me. He undid his belt. Then he took my hand. He wanted me to undo his pants. Another quickie in the car, just like usual. After he'd taken all the money from my last john, by the way. I couldn't do it. Maybe it was the heat. Maybe it was his smelly arm pits or the thought of his saliva on my neck, or the thought of once again touching him down there. My mind clicked. Like a switch. Click … click … click."

"I had a gun in my purse. He didn't know I had it. I barely knew how to use it. I undid his pants like he wanted, and his eyes closed, and he eased back in the seat like he knew what was coming. With my other hand, I palmed the gun, cocked the hammer, and shot him in the crotch. The other shots I don't remember. I just kept pulling the trigger."

Erin tugged at her clothes, the fabric clinging with perspiration, then ran her hands under her legs like the leather chair was adhering to her skin.

"My, my," Vince said. "*How ever* did you get out of town?"

Erin didn't answer. She wiped the side of her neck with her palm as if Manny's saliva had reappeared. Her eyes were darting back and forth across the floor.

Feeling the silence, Vince released the question by saying, "Never mind. It doesn't really matter. What matters is that you came to Seattle, and better yet, you came to me. What has it been? Three years?"

"Three years. Four months," Erin said. She pinched the bridge of her nose, a reflexive gesture as if she was trying to quell a headache.

Vince smiled at her fondly, as if what he was about to say would be a boost to her ego. "You're a great-looking lady, Erin. Don't let the past pull you down." Vince waited, expecting a response.

Erin remained silent, motionless, then without diffidence, she sat back, and with an air of self-respect, she looked directly at Vince, and blurted out a defense. "He was subhuman. And I'm not sorry." She straightened in her seat as if the last remnants of remorse had been extinguished, a fire dowsed with pride, then began tracing a blue-ashen vein on the back of her hand with a fingertip, as if dialysis was that easy. "So, where are the police?"

Vince shifted his eyes to McTarnihan, then back. "There are no police, Erin. Just do what I ask, and all your sins will be forgiven."

Erin stared at Vince, and then switched to McTarnihan, pleading with her eyes.

Vince noticed the dread on her face and laughed. "It's a simple project. Nothing as painful as a day with Manny."

Erin focused on McTarnihan's face, her eyes drilling holes in his visage, undoubtedly searching for a hint of pity. McTarnihan blinked under pressure. His jaw was grinding. He stood up leaving the folder on the couch, and sidled to the globe for a refill, his ineptness to do anything as apparent as his wrinkled shirt, untucked, hanging out over his rear like a giant kick-me flag.

Erin's eyes followed him across the room, then dropped her head into a hand as her resolve ran out her shoulders. There was a penetrating silence, as if a coffin was being lowered into the ground. "So, what do you want me to do?"

Using the heels of his palms, Vince pushed himself up from the desk. Then, as if speaking to a child, he lifted her chin, gently tucking a lock of hair behind her ear as he spoke, "I have a friend. He's good looking, mid-thirties." Vince was speaking in a fatherly tone as gentle as the Serpent in the Garden. "He's been out of town for a long time; he needs someone of the opposite sex to befriend him."

She stared at him. His milky green eyes locked on hers — the eyes of a serpent stalking its prey. "To make this perfectly clear, Erin," he said, the words dry with cynicism. "Well, I assume you don't need me to paint you a picture."

He went to touch her again, but she grabbed his wrist and pushed it away. He had struck a nerve all right, but not one of fright.

With an unctuous grin, he backed off. He saw McTarnihan staring at him, his mouth tight with reprimand and disbelief, his hand white-knuckled around his drink.

The words slowed, and he spoke calmly, "Anyway, this friend has approached me about a job, and I need to know what makes him tick. Mere employment. Or something else."

"Like what?" she asked, a feisty edge in her voice.

Vince approached her again slowly. Erin winced and put the back of her wrist to her mouth.

"You're like a moth to a flame," Vince said, almost in a whisper. "You should really learn to keep a respectful distance."

"Well, I'm not sure what you want," Erin said with an edge of accommodation.

Vince enjoyed her spunk. "Men tell lovers secrets. I want that lover to be you." Vince bent over and braced the heel of his palms on the arms of her chair, enveloping her. Erin retreated into the cushion, her toughness waning, her face paling to stone. He scanned a lustful eye over her body. "What's the worst that could happen?" he said. "He can't get it up?"

With his face mere inches away, Erin marshaled her shoulders and looked away to the wall, avoiding his eyes, as if ignoring him would give her mind time to escape to another reality.

Vince broke into her plans. "Look at me Erin," he demanded.

When she didn't, he wedged her chin into the web of his hand, wrenching her jaw into position. He spoke slowly, delivering the ultimatum, "At no time is he to know that I put you up to this. You're to be the sweet, innocent victim of his irrepressible wit and charm and you *must* ... and I repeat ... *must* fall madly in love with him." He paused as a smile tugged at his lip. "He'll tell you everything." Vince let go of his hold.

"I won't do it," she garbled her protest, massaging her jaw. Her eyes flitted to McTarnihan standing by the globe with his amber drink in hand. To her chagrin, McTarnihan turned his back and lifted the bourbon to his lips.

"He won't help you, Erin," Vince said succinctly.

Vince was standing over her, the white noise of power like gnats in his ears. He could see the contents of her bra, and marveled at the blue veins nesting the top of her breasts, just under her skin, webbed like delicate fingers. He could feel sweat on his neck, moist and warm along the collar of his shirt, and a surge of blood in his loins.

Erin stared away; a single tear streaked down her face.

Vince could see the rage in her eyes, the rage that stiffened her body, the rage that was whistling like a freight train between her ears.

Meanwhile McTarnihan mumbled dissatisfaction into his drink as he separated the blinds, as if seeing the remnants of suicide down on the sidewalk was more comforting than what was transpiring behind him.

CHAPTER 11

Seattle, Washington
October 12, 1995

The Hawker touched down at nine-o-five p.m. and taxied directly to the hangar. A black limousine, parked beyond the yellow lines of the tarmac, waited with its motor running.

Expectantly, Tony jitter-stepped in place, cracking his knuckles and fidgeting with his ring. He'd never met a mob guy before, or a wiseguy, or any guy from Jersey for that matter. He popped a Black Beauty and swallowed it without water. Pharmaceutical speed cleared his head. He also had a long night ahead and couldn't risk coming off like a dimwit which Vince had warned him about.

Michael Geraci, looking very casual in a tan leather jacket and boat shoes, dipped his head and exited the plane first. He had a perturbed look on his face and wasted no time putting distance between himself and the plane.

Tony thought he looked like he needed a drink. He'd seen it before, that vacuous gaze that drunks got when they were hunting for a bottle. Tony stuck out his hand. "Mr. Geraci, it's nice to ... meet ... you." The greeting stretched out as Michael, without so much as a flicker of an eyelash, strode past evenly with briefcase in-hand to the waiting limousine.

Nonchalantly, Tony tried to drop the awkward appendage to his side, traipsing a small, distracted circle as the car pulled away. Then, feeling a rising pride, he lifted a birdie-finger in the air.

"Franklin," a gutty voice erupted behind him.

Tony looked over his shoulder, his middle finger still erect in front of him. "Gees!" he blurted, recoiling a stumble-step.

Approaching was an apparition, his jaw wide, his teeth large and white like piano keys. He had bleached stubble for hair, and deformed ears, as if a dog had chewed the fleshy parts. He stood six-foot-five, white like a pillar of salt, garbed in a white turtleneck and white twill pants and white patent leather shoes. The chalky fine hair on his arms ghosted his pallid, nearly translucent skin, his face unblemished, rubbery and white as a boiled egg.

He carried a silver attaché case. He pulled off his black sunglasses briefly as if to inspect them for smudges, revealing pinkish eyes, glistening like fish roe, deep-set under a block of marble forehead; then slid them back into place.

"I Evohl. We go." He was a living corpse, his tongue a whip of red projecting the only hint of life.

Tony fell back another step, then hunched and jammed his hands in his pockets. Vince had told him about Darwin. Tony had looked him up on the internet. Darwin had a white beard and a chrome dome and all these ideas about animals becoming other animals. He wondered what animal Evohl was before he was Evohl.

"We go," Evohl said again, louder than before.

Tony acknowledged Evohl's suggestion with a raise of his hand as he turned for the Prelude. He strode quickly, Evohl's shadow lurking like a gargoyle close on his heels, pulling the trunk keys from his pocket as he walked. Evohl stowed the silver case in the trunk next to two suitcases filled with Tony's tools of the trade.

Tony pulled the Prelude onto Highway 99, headed for I-405 and southeast Seattle, the trip short to their destination. The night sky was void of dimension, a luminary vacuum, pitch-black, leaving the roadway to snake before them, scalloped with artificial brightness, the streetlights strung like pearls along the neck of the highway. A mile or two passed, and Tony started squirming. The pharmaceutical speed was kicking in.

The silence was deafening. He attempted to make idle conversation with his guest, even humor. It was fruitless; Evohl remained unresponsive and distant.

Quickly, the one-sided bullshit had grown tediously dull. Tony felt he had to entertain him, but everything he said fell flat. So, he moved to a new tactic and turned up the stereo: a classic Spin Doctors CD. Could "His Blandness" be a connoisseur of music, a "Pocket Full of Kryptonite" his weakness? Sarcasm oozed from every notion that rambled through his head. He increased the volume. Evohl seemed unaffected: no tapping foot, no air guitar, not even a rhythmic nodding of his head.

Something must get a rise in his Levi's, Tony surmised. He peeled back the decibels to a Boeing 747 roar and pushed the pedal to the floor. This will get a flinch, he thought. His speed picked up weaving through the traffic, then with a Mario Andretti sureness, he passed a car on the right in the emergency lane, then floated across three lanes of traffic at ninety miles-per-hour to grab a Renton exit on the left. The car pitched to the side, tires breaking the muteness of the dry pavement with a shrill, then straightened with the centrifugal force of the banked corner, pushing the needle over one-hundred miles-per-hour. The first intersection on Sunset Boulevard rose to a crest, and as they shot the red light, the Prelude went airborne. Tony yelped with careless abandonment, then looked to the shotgun seat.

Evohl was unshakable, his hands folded contentedly in his lap.

Tony remained confused, but shrugged it off. Minutes later, he pulled into the motel parking lot, one of the many he used for the process. Dollops of light spotted the asphalt, the bulging-head and slender-necked luminaires reminiscent of Martian spacecraft from the *War of the Worlds*.

Tony drove his life as he drove his car, pushing the limits, living out on the edge. It was time to pay off the desk clerk, then spend the graveyard shift cutting, weighing and packaging the product. Which was normal, except tonight he'd have help. The white cliffs of Dover: tall, stone-faced and *boring*.

***

Vince sat bleakly at his desk, Blake's creation laying like an albatross in front of him. It was nearly midnight. The software package was worth a cool hundred-grand, and Vince knew if he could sell it to this client, others would follow.

He stared and flipped, flipped and stared. There's no way I'm going to understand this by tomorrow morning, he concluded. He retrieved a vial from his pocket and tapped out a line, then rolled up a twenty and snorted the boost quick.

He sat back, the insidious powder clearing his head. I'll make up a bogus excuse and postpone the meeting, he thought, besides Dane was on his mind. He needed his expertise. Without Blake, the firm was in trouble, and like threadbare cloth, each day it unraveled a bit more.

At length, he picked up the phone.

"Chief. It's Spinetti. Are you alone?"

The Chief was in a cheery mood. "Hang on," he said. Over the clamorous background noise, he spoke to someone else in the room, "Another rum and coke." He redirected his voice back to Vince. "Okay, what do you want? The meaning of life has temporarily slinked from my grasp."

Vince was silent, confused by the expression.

"I don't have all night," Chief said, his voice rife with impatience.

"I need your opinion."

"About what?"

"I have this friend. He's been overseas for many years, and now he's back. He wants to work for me."

"In what way?" Chief asked, his voice laced with concern.

"He's an engineer. I don't think he knows about anything else, but I have McTarnihan checking him out, just in case."

"So, what's the problem?"

"He knows me too well. Maybe better than I know my-self. If he has other motives, he could be trouble. Like I said, McTarnihan is checking him out, but I don't know how long I can keep him at bay without him getting suspicious."

"Can you use his help?"

"Sure, I'm buried here at the office."

"Then hire him. What better way to keep tabs on him than to have him around all the time?"

Vince was quiet in contemplation. He could hear Chief breathing heavy into the receiver. "Is that it?" Chief asked. "I'm busy here. I'm on second base with the barmaid, trying to cross home by closing."

"Yeah, that's it," Vince said.

CHAPTER 12

Seattle, Washington
October 31, 1995

Dane and Erin boarded the *Ecstasea*; Erin primitively alluring in a sleeveless, full-length white rabbit fur, seductively unbuttoned, exposing the scant skins of a cave girl; Dane was Dracula, maniacally entrancing, dark and flowing in his cape.

As the *Ecstasea* swayed to the chant of Enigma's "Principles of Lust," they weaved their way through the Game Room to the bar. An unknown reveler, Wolfman howled at Erin's beauty. Anklets of ivory scrimshaw, auburn hair piled high in a bone-pierced beehive, a slender neck strung with shark teeth, she'd dressed for the part, yet soared high above it, for no woman of her era could've displayed such a blend of eroticism and refined elegance in mere skins.

Vince was bartending, his face hidden behind a white hockey mask. "You kids want a drink?"

Erin discerned the muffled voice, the luster vanishing from her face. She could see Vince's milky green eyes working beneath the mask, his gaze like a scalpel on her skin.

"What's it going to be?" Dane asked, his eyes intent on hers.

She entwined her arm around his. "Make it something warm."

As Dane rattled on with Vince, the din of the crowd dimmed beneath her thoughts. He'd been the perfect gentlemen at her door, and she felt at ease with him here. He wasn't like Vince, or at least he didn't seem to be. From the start, their allure for each other seemed hypnotic. Dane was tall and lean, with a deep, muscular chest. He had gentle eyes, and he didn't talk down to her.

Dane put his palm over the back of her hand. She felt valued, not as an object to display like a gold watch or some silicone broad.

Making a noise like a garbage disposal as he sucked the last of his drink from the glass, Tony walked up behind them. He wore a three-pointed hat and the kaleidoscopic clothes of a court jester.

Dane wheeled from the bar and gave him a high-five. Tony spun backwards and stuck a hand low behind his back, slapping palms with Dane again. Off his hip, dressed as a saloon girl, was a curvy red head with snaky green eyes and a long, thin nose. Her skin was milky white, with a spattering of freckles. Dane smiled with curiosity. "Who's your friend?"

The girl tossed back her head to snap the hair out of her face. "My name's Arlene." Her voice was tinny and nasal. The sound stung Erin's ears.

Tony was painlessly drunk, absentmindedly engaged in a game of pocket pool with his hand. "But *we* all call her Lips," he haw-hawed.

Arlene raised her plucked eyebrows with a "Who-me?" gaze and sucked a fingertip as if chewing a nail. Her jumbo hoop earrings turned slowly side-to-side like directional antennas homing in on new prey. Erin watched Dane's insides melt; Arlene's expression wet, the lips gloss red and directed at him. A flash of nervousness branched over his face like lightning.

Feeling his anguish, Erin came to his rescue. "Hi Tony," she said. "I haven't seen you in a while."

Tony looked surprised. "Erin?" His eyes ran the hills and curves from top to bottom, his expression that of a starving man reading a menu. "I didn't even recognize you."

Erin's stare pinpointed Tony's crotch like a beacon. "Are you having a good time?" she jived. Then she shifted to Arlene and smiled.

Redness filled Tony's face, the blooming flower wilting in his pants. He quickly pulled his hand.

Erin held Dane by the elbow and caressed his forearm. "Nice to meet you Arr—lene." The syllables strained with mock exaggeration. The message clearly sent by female-jungle-drum: this one's mine.

Arlene stared at Erin with righteous eyes, then defiantly reached out and touched Dane's wrist. "I hope I'll see you later, honey. Don't disappoint me."

Dane shrugged with a tremor, as if a chill had run down his spine. Then, after they'd retreated into the crowd, he said to Erin, "Something about her gives me the willies."

Erin giggled. "She comes right to the point, if that's what you mean."

***

Moments later, Vince introduced Dane and Erin to Vick. She looked gorgeously edible as a luscious bunch of grapes. Purple balloons adorned her see-through dress, and a skull cap scattered with green leaves covered her head. Dane found her sweet and was absorbed by her shimmering black eyes. He told Vince he was lucky to have her. Vick blushed, a glow of belonging in her cheeks. Vince responded with a degrading remark that Dane could test-drive her anytime he wanted, then prompted Dane onto a different subject.

From the corner of his eye, Dane saw Erin cast Vick an affectionate beam. They immediately started talking with such fervor, Dane could tell their hearts had fallen on hallowed ground. After a few minutes, Neil Young rotated into position, "Unknown Legend" punched up like a request on a jukebox, and Vick and Erin strolled over and sat on the couch.

The next few introductions were a chance for Vince to pump his ego, a menagerie of Seattle's elite. However, to Dane, the best came last, Vince's body contorting as the couple approached. The mask cloaked his face, but he couldn't hide the panic in his eyes.

The cowboy spoke first. "Hi Vince. It's good to see you again." His tone was upbeat and sober.

Vince rotated the mask back on his head like a catcher staring down a runner on third base. His face was blank with surprise. Dane imagined Latin dancers doing the cha-cha in his chest. Vince unclogged his throat with a dry swallow. "You too, Michael." He stared at Michael's date. Unconsciously, his body primed, muscles pumping beneath his shirt. "Where's your father?" he said absently.

"In Jersey," Michael said. "I hope you don't mind us being here. We had nothing to do tonight."

Dane could see Vince was enamored with the brunette on Michael's arm, a French maid dressed in black and white.

"Aren't you going to introduce me?"

"Carmen, this is Vince."

Vince held her hand in a clam of his palms. "Vito speaks highly of you." He smiled at Michael. "Your father has excellent taste."

Dane could see a stab of pain crease the Cowboy's face. Either Vince's lingering touch, or the mention of his father had sliced a nerve.

Dane stuck out his hand. "Hi. I'm Dane Avilla."

Michael shook it. "Michael Geraci. Nice to meet you."

Immediately, Dane feigned nonchalance. The names, Michael and Vito, had been rolling around in his head like BB's in a boxcar, until now, when the last name, Geraci, put two successive pumps in the air gun, and the BB's morphed into 115-grain hollow points. "So, what do you do, Michael?" he said.

"This and that." Michael caught Vince's eyes. "Vince has ventured some capital into one of our projects."

"That's Vince," Dane said. "Always looking for a new way to make money." He felt weak in the knees.

"Dane is an old friend," Vince said. "He's been out of the country for a while."

Dane could sense Vince's uneasiness. He wanted to move on, direct the conversation away from business.

"Well, I'm glad Evohl told us of the party tonight," Michael said. He looked left, then right. "I should introduce you."

Vince rocked back on his heels, an invisible hand pushing against his chest. His face scrunched, his bent index finger jabbing toward the floor. "Is Evohl here?"

"I believe so," Michael said. "He told me Tony invited him." Michael craned his neck further to search the crowd. "There he is," Michael said.

"Where?" Vince jerked his head to the side to see through the mass of bodies.

"Behind the piano," Michael said.

Vince went bug-eyed.

"That's an original costume," Dane said. "What's he supposed to be?"

Michael laughed. "Himself."

Evohl proved hideous even at twenty paces. Vince raised a hand to his forehead, gripping his temples as if his skull was going to split front-to-back. His discomfort was palpable.

"What seems to be the problem, Vince?" Dane said. "Your *ax* in need of grinding?"

***

Dane sat alone at the bar. Someone was spinning old vinyl: Stones, Bowie, Bob Seger, now Aerosmith's "Walking the Dog." Erin and Vick were off powdering their noses, most likely exchanging stories like blood-sisters of the unfortunate men in their lives. Vince had moved on also, carefully mingling and cajoling the guests. Through the evening, the crowd had grown more raucous with drink and their secret retreats to the staterooms below.

Dane slipped down to the starboard bathroom to lift a few lines. The ritual was becoming more frequent and casual, the numb taste of sterility a welcome presence in his throat. Now might be the time, he thought, to do a little investigating. Vince is busy. Erin is busy. Sean and Jimmy are on the bridge. Lance is stuck behind the bar. Tony had Arlene to contend with.

He opened the door and quickly perused the hall. He could hear voices in some staterooms. Humpty Dumpty was raiding the fridge in the galley. He crept toward the bow, not knowing exactly what he was looking for. Yet he knew so little for sure. Anything would be of help. The first two rooms on the left were quiet but locked.

The end of the hall was closed off by a locked wooden door. He pushed back the skirt of his cape and pinched his wallet from his back pocket. Credit card, Driver's License, a laminated picture of a brunette in front of the Trevi Fountain.

The picture was pliable enough to make the bend, and the bolt slipped back easily. Beyond the door the hallway extended deeper into the bow, and in the dark, what seemed like a football field away, he could see a moving light, a shifting pattern on the floor, like the images cast on a wall from a TV left on in the dark. He passed some storage closets, the hum of the Engine Room growing fainter with each step. Inching closer, the light came from behind a louvered door, the dancing images sliced into long strips.

Dane crouched down, peering up through the slats. He saw a monitor with images shifting on its glass. He checked the door handle. Locked also, but it gave way quickly as he jimmied the bolt with the Trevi brunette.

Once inside, he sat on a stool and chewed a nail thoughtfully. The stool had a black leather cushion and swiveled easily from side-to-side. On the first monitor, he could see a bedroom. A baseball player had some cheerleader on his lap, his mitts filled with cheerleader squeeze. On the edge of the bed, Frankenstein was snorting a line off the nightstand.

Dane's eyes skirted the tiny cubicle. There were three monitors, each with its own recorder. One still had the static plastic advertisement slicing the corner of the screen. Headphones hung from a coat hook, its umbilical cord coiled once or twice about its ears, leaving its silver tail dangling to the console. The console was a landscape of slides, knobs, and meters. The needles on the decibel meters were bouncing, even though the volume slides were set at zero. Obviously from here, videotaping any room on the Ecstasea was possible, and multiple rooms at a time. Below the monitors were rows of videotapes, each marked with a red felt pen in block letters on white stickers.

He shifted on his buttocks and looked at the recorders once again. He hadn't noticed before, but even though only one monitor was on, all three video recorders were taping, a tiny red circle marking the display. Curiously, he pushed the rectangular buttons on the darkened monitors. Images came to his eyes in a blink, like the bright waking eyes of a giant sleeping child.

Monitor Two was the Game Room, a view high above, scanning a sea of carousers.

Monitor Three proved more interesting. Dane stared with an intensity strong enough to defrost a freezer. A stateroom set the stage occupied by a lean Stetson'd cowboy, and a French maid bent over, gripping the footrail of the bed. The gunslinger had his pistol drawn. The barrel inserted into the French maid's holster.

Dane wiped his mouth with the back of his wrist, blankly staring at the screen. He hadn't planned on invading this intimate play, and he felt as though he'd just held up a liquor store. His heart was bounding like a freight train in his ears and ashamedly he realized the tingle in his stiffened crotch.

Dane clicked off the scene, returning them to their privacy, and straightaway heard the spatter of dropped keys in the hallway. His eyes snapped straight ahead. Adrenaline shrieked into his system. He sat perfectly still, his gut turning to steel. He heard the shuffling of feet, the jangle of keys, a creaky door, then silence.

Dane reached with a wavering finger and clicked off Monitor Two. Suddenly a clack of wood-on-wood, and the heavy tread of steps. His eyes darted around the room as the footsteps approached. The handle to the monitor room rattled, the knob twisting slightly, right, then left. His lungs froze as if hit with chlorine gas, excuses rising like dead bodies to the surface of a lake.

Then the hallway visitor started singing softly: Tom Petty's "American Girl," and the lyrics faded as they padded away. Dane heard the hallway door close, and the door handle jiggle with a check at the lock. His stomach wall collapsed, his shoulders hunching as he sunk on the stool. He took a shallow breath as a cool sweat circled his skull with the odor of fear. It made him nauseous.

***

Vince lifted a mirror from the wall and laid it on the coffee table. He sat down on the couch. From vials retrieved from somewhere downstairs, he lined up two eight-balls of snow; the guests formicating like ants to a picnic. Dane slipped in behind him and perched at the bar. With all the commotion at the free coke, he had no trouble going unnoticed. Erin found him with an enduring peck and then left with Vick once more.

Vince took a quick line in each nostril, then stood, his gaze finding Evohl like North to a compass needle. Eyes cloaked in black sunglass, Evohl's body, face and soul remained stark white in the same chair he'd stayed in all night. Vince appeared steamed like a pressure cooker ready to pop a valve. Bodies circled the table, music playing, Bonnie Raitt rocking "Tangled and Dark." Vince slipped out from the crowd and exited downstairs.

Michael Geraci sat down next to Dane. They shared a drink and immediately a conversation ensued that waddled through chit-chat and weaseled around subjects they both wanted to avoid.

In the end, after thirty minutes and another drink, Dane concluded that he'd prejudged Michael. He wouldn't like him. He was the mob. Only to realize that Michael was personable, intelligent and not unlike himself, melancholy in both the worst and best sense of the word.

Carmen approached, casting beckoning eyes toward Michael. "Well, I hate to break this up," she said, "but you promised you'd get me home by midnight."

Michael touched his sleeve, looked at his watch, then at Dane. "Truth is, at midnight she turns back into a poor, meager peasant girl, and I go back to the pumpkin patch whence I came."

***

Twenty minutes later, Erin was sitting next to Dane on the couch when Vince stormed into the Game Room. Some guests were now stacked in chairs riding a wave of alcohol and coke, far out on the ocean, away from the shores of sobriety. Others were investigating rooms below decks with prurient thoughts on their minds. A few had vacated, unable to keep the pace.

"Hey, what's up?" Dane asked.

"Nothing," Vince said, preoccupied, his eyes searching the room.

Dane noticed two bloody knuckles, a bruised-colored patch the size of a half-dollar, spreading onto the back of his hand. "What happened to your hand? Do you need some ice?"

He emitted a deep sigh. "Naw, it's okay. Tony and I got into it. Too much booze. By the way, Monday. Be at the office by eight. We've got work to do."

"You won't be disappointed."

"I hope not." Vince rubbed his hand, scowled and walked off.

***

Tony was out on the bow, busy with the heaves. Kneeling, he hung over the rail, an empty bottle of Jack Daniels clutched in his right like a Nazi hand-grenade. The air was crisp with frost, the moon a fragmented ball of ice perched above Lake Washington.

"Are you okay?" Dane said, approaching from the stern.

Tony fell back from the rail onto his buttocks. His eyes hooded, he spoke with a slur, a thin strand of saliva tying the corner of his mouth to the rail. He pushed back the jester's hat on his head with both hands. "I'm good. Just fucking peachy."

Dane stood over him. "What happened to your face?"

With an index finger, Tony inspected the corner of his mouth, the bump on his head. There was a collarbone stain of blood on the jester's shirt. "Nothin'," he said reluctantly.

"Where's Arlene?"

Tony launched the J.D. into the water. "How the fuck am I supposed to know?"

"Sorry," Dane said. "It was just a question."

Tony staggered to his feet, and Dane stepped forward to hold his shoulders. Cartoon-legged, Tony swayed, but the puking was done, the taste of bile receding down his throat. A sour look pouched his face like he was sucking aspirin. He managed a belch, the smell akin to sewage wafting through a gutter grate in Cabo San Lucas.

Tony unzipped his fly and shot a fluorescent yellow stream into the water. "See that color? Them's good vitamins. That Jenny buys good vitamins."

"Where is Jenny?"

"What the fuck is this? Forty questions? I don't know. She doesn't like Vince, so she stays clear."

"Okay. Don't get excited."

"Fuck her anyway." He jostled, spreading his legs, then shook his penis to get off the last drops, flopping in around like a rubber carrot. "She was havin' friends over. Partying on the new rugs she got laid this week." He wobbled, his breath coming out in clouds. "Laid, hah! Right now, she's probably getting the big one on her deep-pile Stainmaster." He stuffed his manhood back into his pants. One hand clutched his crotch, the other jerked at the zipper.

"Why don't you sit down? Before you fall overboard."

"Oh yeah, who's gonna give a shit?"

Dane pulled Tony away from the edge. "I do."

Tony sat down with a thud, his back against the superstructure. Dane sat beside him. The deck was biting Tony's rump like dry ice, his gluteus maximus prickly as if waking from a deep slumber. He struggled to stand again, but his butt felt like lead. He envisioned the Howdy Doody punching bag he had as a kid, a base full of sand.

Dane held him down with a clothesline arm across his collarbones. "Just sit awhile, it'll do you good."

"Well." Tony hesitated, losing his train of thought. "Anyway, we din't need no new rug. Shit, for the next six weeks I'll be getting a thousand volts up my ass every time I touch a door handle, or-or turn on a faucet."

Tony coiled an open fist and hit himself on the forehead with the thumb end. "Where's Lips?"

"How should I know?" Dane said.

"Man, she's a hell of a ride. Then that fucking prick gets in my face."

"Who? Vince?"

Tony swung his head to look Dane in the face, his neck so loose, he thought his noggin might flip off his shoulders. He quickly dropped his chin to his chest, eyes closed, riding an eighty-proof head-spin.

"She's beautiful," he said dreamily. "Abso-tively beautiful."

He wiped his mouth, slobber smeared on the back of his hand. "We was in bed downstairs. Asshole yanks me off her." He stroked his jaw. "Fuck him. All I heard is Arlene screamin' four-letter words as Vince drug me off down the hall."

"What set him off?"

Tony blinked, returning to the here and now. "Ah, he was pissed about me invitin' that albino. I din't even invite that ... that other motherfucker." He began rocking his head to the coming words, shoulder to shoulder, for emphasis. "That-god-damn-my-shit-don't-stink-Geraci-asshole."

Realizing he'd just stepped in it, Tony clammed up and looked away, his mind whirring behind his eyeballs. He massaged his jaw. He could still taste the blood in his mouth. Tony dished up a blood-saliva swirl on his tongue, then spit, the sputum arcing and twisting, then finally breaking up in the wind before diving into a whitecap. His eyes opened and closed as he swallowed as if strings attached his eyelids to his Adam's apple.

"Do you want me to talk to him?"

Tony arched back in exasperation and accidentally smacked his head. "Shit Dane, lay off me!"

He shouldn't have yelled. A new throb exploded in his skull like a small atomic blast. He thought about brain hemorrhages, annihilating Vince with his fists, kicking his head all over the room like a ball on a string. He gripped his forehead, kneading his temples in a thumb-boy-scout-finger vice. Maybe Dane could mellow Vince out, he thought, but then a snapshot of Vince lit up the canvas of his eyes. "Start thinking" is what he said. "I'm sorry. Shit. Like forget it, man. It never happened."

"Look Tony. Vince shouldn't treat you like crap. Should he?"

Sounded reasonable, but Tony was buying it. "I don't know, man. I fuck up, you know. Maybe he should slap me up. Keep me straight. I'd be in a world of hurt without Vince."

Tony closed his eyes like putting a foot on the floor. His head was spinning, the acrid taste of bile creeping up his gullet. Thoughts ran in and out of his brain like streakers in church. He was confused. All these voices echoing between his ears. The Final Spin of the washing machine and he was in it. He covered his ears with palm-muffs, his fingers laced like a ducktail haircut.

"Do you trust me, Tony?"

Tony felt his scalp stretch over his ears. Pumpkinhead, he admonished himself. A stupid pumpkinhead. When the top blows off, there won't be no candle inside. He had to pick his words carefully, and that was as foreign as eating pizza with no cheese. "Ah sure ...," his voice trailed off, hoping that was enough.

"What about Vince? Does he trust me?"

Tony's hands were a bloodless knot. "Ah, we shouldn't talk about it anymore. All that stuff makes me dizzy."

Tony saw a shaft of light coming from the wheelhouse door. He wanted to follow it like walking aboard a UFO. "I wanna go Dane. Me and Arlene, we got business to take care of."

"Sit here a little longer," Dane said. "Arlene can wait. Anyway, the cold will sober you up."

Tony thought in silence. The cold felt good. Maybe he's right. A while longer wouldn't hurt — long as they didn't talk about Vince.

"You mind if I ask you something?" Dane said.

Tony had a serious hurt behind his eyes. He felt a crack forming at each temple, as if his forehead was detaching like some access panel so his brains could get out for a walk. "Naw, go ahead. Just keep it low, will ya? My head is mud."

"Why do you stay with Jenny? You're here with Arlene, and she's there with who knows who."

"I love her Dane."

"You've got a funny way of showing it."

"It's a long story," Tony said, his voice drifting off. "Jenny can't have kids."

"I'm sorry, but I don't understand."

Tony sighed, but he was gassed that Dane was interested. "When we first got married," he said, "we wanted kids. You know a couple rug-rats to keep us busy, have Christmas with. All that stuff. I didn't have much of a home-life growing up, and Jenny was an only child. Anyway, we go at it for a few years, but she don't get knocked-up."

Tony paused, licking his lips. "So, she goes and gets checked out, and like she can't have any. No tubes or something. She took it hard. Started drinking. I didn't think nothing of it. I mean, I drink like a fish right. Then she wants to do some coke. I got coke. I don't see no harm in it. But, like Jenny, she never really did drugs before. Smoke a dope that's nothin'. But the coke, it really takes hold, and she wants it all the time. Finally, I tell her no. She's like lost thirty pounds in places she din't have it to lose."

Tony's eyes narrowed with spite as he continued, "Then some worthless shit named Marty turns her on to all kinds of stuff while I'm at work. I'm not real attentive, so like I don't notice until one day I'm looking for some underwear, and I figure she might have slipped one in the wrong drawer. Only I find a syringe and a gram of heroin instead."

He looked at Dane. "I flip and she says, 'who gives a fuck,' like I don't care. Things just got worse from there."

"You try to get her help?"

"Yeah, she won't go. Remember, I'm no saint. She says I'm a kettle callin' the kitchen black, or somethin' like that."

"Doesn't that bother you?" Dane asked. "I mean, you two are just living in the same house."

Tony chewed it over for a moment. "I guess ... but I do love her, and I think she loves me, but she like hates herself because she wasn't able to give me kids, and I hate myself because I turned her on to the drugs that sent her down the shithole. I ain't gonna dump her, Dane. Hell, I ain't any better than she is anyway."

"Have you told Vince this?"

"Nope. Jenny made me promise not to tell anyone. But I guess now I fucked that up, too."

"Maybe if you tell him the truth, he'd lay off. At least he'll know you have reasons for what you do. Right now, he thinks you're just some dumbass."

"I am a dumbass, Dane. I faced that a long time ago."

CHAPTER 13

Seattle, Washington
November 1, 1995

The door to the bathroom opened and Dane floated out in a billow of steam, like David Copperfield, in some big illusion. Erin sat on the couch, letting the beehive out of her hair.

"Thanks for letting me shower before I took you home," Dane said. "Dracula's make-up was giving me a rash."

Light from a car pulling into the parking lot sent a slice of light through the curtains, elongating up a wall, then rushing at warp-speed across the ceiling toward the kitchen. There was a sound of squeaky tires muffled on the blacktop.

Dane padded to the window, a towel about his waist. Condensation had frozen in broken stars around the edge of the glass. "Look," he said. "It's snowing."

Erin eased-up beside him. Arm-in-arm, they gazed out the window. Communion wafers were falling like manna from heaven. A congruous layer covered the ground, coarse and white like the batting sewn into a quilt.

Dane smiled. "When it's white like this, the world seems so innocent."

"Unfortunately, it always melts away," Erin said. A moment later, she added, "We should probably stay here. Seattleites don't know how to drive in the snow."

"You don't mind?"

"No," she said as she gripped her elbows and shivered. "But I'm cold. Could I borrow a sweatshirt?"

"Sure, and I'll get you some sweatpants, too."

As he made his way to the bedroom, Erin studied him with a fierce intensity. If he were a candle, he would've melted on the spot, drooping over like a wilted flower. She was like a chocoholic schoolgirl at a Mrs. See's candy store. How could someone like him be friends with Vince? He must not know the truth.

Erin relaxed and closed her eyes. She could see him without looking, but like a dead fish in an aquarium, her past floated to the surface. She tried to stop the vision, but the fear sales-man wouldn't take no for an answer. *A whore, that's what you are, that's what you do, he said. He'll dump you when he finds out.*

She opened her eyes; the light breaking the trance. This was more than a one-night stand, she encouraged herself. For the first time in her life, she felt comfortable with a man, and it was so pleasant, so real. He treated her like a lady. She sucked in an air of confidence, disallowing the salesman to speak. She could tell Vince whatever she wanted to. He would have no way of knowing what went on between them.

***

A short while later, the lights were dim, and Dane had a fire crackling in the fireplace, both him and Erin reclined on a throne of blankets and pillows on the floor in front of the hearth.

They descended into an easy report, Dane's reminiscence of childhood mindful of the torment he felt for kids less gift-ed than himself and the stories about wagon trains he would conjure from a ridgeline of trees; Erin's mindful of a stepdad drunk with touchy-feely hands, and a mom who put up with it.

They talked about teenage aspirations that evolved into adult decisions, and the idiosyncrasies of their lives, both care-ful to skirt around choices that led them down the wrong path.

"Sometimes we pursue what we want, and not what we need," Dane remarked. "Those are the critical moments in life."

Erin remained silent, but her thoughts were in harmony with his.

A handful of heartbeats later, laying side-by-side, they kissed in a gentle embrace, Dane softly fingering the flute of her spine. The kiss quickly erupted into tongues, twisting in a rousing caress.

At length, Erin pulled back and let out a sigh of total satisfaction.

When their lips parted, Dane cupped her face in the pit of his hand, gently stroking her lips with his thumb, his eyes filled with a jittery energy, dancing with light from the fire.

Dane stroked back his hair. His chest, his arms, tensing seductively, a carnival of muscle to feast her eyes upon. A timorous retreat, Erin put a palm to his chest. Their time would come.

"So, tell me Dane Avilla." She hesitated, the coming question hanging loosely in the air, her eyes roaming the room. "Have you always been a bachelor?"

Dane mimicked her survey, twisting his head this way, then that. "I was in a hurry. It's a furnished apartment."

"An artful-dodger, but you didn't answer the question. Let me rephrase it. Have you always lived alone?"

Dane mulled it over, a pensive slap-tapping of his cheek. "Not always ... but I've never been married, either."

There was a sudden pain in his eyes. Erin went silent, not knowing how to proceed, wishing she hadn't pursued it.

Dane blinked. "Her name was Marcellena. Her father was British, her mother Egyptian. She died at the Rome airport ... a terrorist attack. Red Brigade, Islamic Jihad, who knows who anymore."

He paused, his palm over his mouth, swallowing a sigh. "We had a fight. She was going back to London."

Erin ran a knuckle along his jaw. "I'm sorry. I didn't realize ..."

"It's all right," Dane said. "Everyone deserves to feel love at least once." He reached out and touched her cheek in the cup of his palm, then brushed a wisp of hair from her forehead. He stared into her emerald eyes with so much conviction a lump grew in Erin's throat. "I'm the lucky one. I felt it with her. Maybe I could feel it again."

Erin swallowed hard. She'd never felt love until now. Emotions paralyzed her voice, but her thoughts whirred. She wiped a tear from her eye with an index knuckle. This was a keeper, a gentleman. A compassionate soul who cried over poor little classmates with no coordination and ugly faces and brains of dirt. He was a dreamer who turned trees into people. A man who knew that true love was precious.

***

Heartbeats slipped by, both deep in reflection. The firelight flickered across their bodies, warm on their cheeks, the soles of their feet. Tongues of flame wrapped around charred pieces of wood as wisps of smoke curled in random bursts from orange embers. Dane leaned forward, and using the poker, he adjusted the logs on the fire. A spray of sparks erupted and lifted toward the flue like a swarm of fireflies in a cyclone.

"Dane, do you think this is a critical moment?" Erin asked.

Dane reclined onto the throne. Shadows from the fire were alive on the brocade ceiling. "If it is, I don't want to screw it up."

Erin rolled on top of him, delivering a kiss so hard and flush, he felt a surge of adrenaline streak through his bones. Erin was an oral electric chair, her tongue a lightning rod, and he was strapped in tight.

Dane's nostrils flared. Rummy and unable to catch his breath, a smiley concussion bewitched him. Her breasts beneath the sweatshirt were firm against his chest. He wanted to dive in between them and hibernate for the Winter. She scared him into an eighth-grade giddiness, and he couldn't remember feeling like this with anyone except Marcellena.

She lifted her head and hooked a lock of hair behind her ear. He could feel her hips pressed to his, her long soft legs entwined with his.

Dane sensed he could make his move, but he didn't want to confuse the easiness he was feeling with the mental trappings of sex. "I want to be ..."

Erin commanded his silence, laying a finger on his lips and leaving it there. "Like my granny told me," she whispered, "sex is like making hot chocolate, warm it right, and the cup is sweet, bring the heat on too fast and you might just scald the milk."

CHAPTER 14

Seattle, Washington
November 1, 1995

Dane dropped Erin off at her apartment after she politely de-clined breakfast, then returned home and fell asleep. He woke up five hours later. The clock, a square white job with black hands and a low grinding sound in its gears, said it was 3:45 p.m. He took a shower. An hour later, after a couple of lines of coke to clear his head, he ventured out to return the rental and purchase a car.

Dane parked his new Nissan 300ZX, got out, and locked the doors with the key fob. The roads had cleared of snow, but it was dusk, and the waning light felt lonesome and cold. He strolled into Maxine's Kitchen for dinner and grabbed a seat near the front along the wall.

Save for the shotgun blast of memorabilia peppering its interior, Maxine's was a throwback to the 40s diner with the subdued drama of an Edward Hopper painting. York Pepper-mint Patties and Beechnut Gum lined the display case and coffee urns two feet tall stood guard over the kitchen.

As he slid into the booth, Dane could feel the springs in the banquette lightly jab into his rear. The Naugahyde was the color of mint Milk of Magnesia. The table itself stuck out like Mick Jaggar's tongue, thick and long and a little too wide between the seats. Several plastic covered menus stood between crystal salt and pepper shakers with dented caps and a ketchup bottle.

Above them, the wall held two eight-by-ten's. One of twelve teenybopper girls dressed in Maxine's blue-and-white softball uniforms. The second was of a bald man with narrow eyes. The caption read: Sid Bybee. 1989 Record Holder. Consumed four Maxine Burgers, four Tubs-O-Fries, four Monster shakes. Time: 15 minutes. Dane reached over and picked up a menu.

"Whatcha want, Honey?" asked the waitress. "We got chicken fried steak on special tonight. Comes with green bean casserole, mashed potatoes and a hot-cross bun."

Stitched in red script into the breast of her blue-and-white uniform was her name, Charlene. She had a 1965 vintage teased-spider-nest of hennaed hair with silver-black roots and bangs bordering her thin, brown-penciled eyebrows. Hazel eyes, lightly pocked cheeks, and nostrils rimmed burnt orange from Camels or Kents. Her mouth was permanently cocked with the silver bullets of a wisecrack. She pulled the pencil from behind her ear and flipped open the order pad she lifted from the front pocket of her apron. She was slightly bow-legged with toothpick gams, and Dane was intensely studying her knobby knees. An image of a white-bonnet'd bespectacled hen chasing the debonair Foghorn Leghorn around the barn-yard popped into his noggin.

She put a hand to her hip. "Hey Honey. You want me to come back? I'm flattered ... I think ... but my legs aren't on the menu."

"Oh, sorry." Dane squinted at the name sewn above her breast. "Charlene. Can I call you Char?"

"No. Not unless you're a big tipper. If you are, you can call me anything you want."

"You know I've never seen you in here before," Dane said. "Are you new?"

"I came out of retirement to help while Janet ... you know, Janet? ... she got her gallbladder removed this morning. I used to work the breakfast crowd."

"You did? Then you probably know my dad. Tiago Avilla."

"Big T! He's your Pop? We go way back."

What till Mom finds out, he thought. "Oh yeah, Big T is where I got my good looks."

"Maybe ... but I think I see more of Brita in you. Especially the hair."

Dane was feeling weird. Thoughts of Mom and Dad and Charlene in some kind of sick geriatric love triangle tickled his brain. He almost blurted with laughter. "Oh, so you know Mom too."

"You betcha, Honey. I worked here for fifteen years ... until I retired and landed a high-paying executive job. Actually, my husband died and left me a bundle. So now I watch the grandkids and sell Avon. Needless to say, you get to know a lot of people in fifteen years. So, what'll ya have? Sid's waiting for his burgers."

"Sid Bybee?"

"Yeah. You know him?"

Dane looked down at the menu and thought of taking a tour of the place to catch all the local yokels in action. "Oh, never mind."

"So, what is it, Honey? See anything you like?"

"Well, if I can't have you, Charlene, I guess I'll settle for the special."

Charlene smiled, then leaned over with both hands on the table, her order pad in one, a pencil in the other. Her uniform was zipped down from the neck to a pea-sized freckle nestled in her wrinkled cleavage. A gold cross dangled in front of his nose as she whispered into his forehead. "If I didn't think you were so full of kimchee, I'd take you up on it, Honey. I ain't had nothing of your caliber in twenty years."

Dane never looked up. The torchy smell of an Avon original, Birdbath or Firestorm, filled his nostrils.

"Not to say that I ain't up for it," Charlene said. "I could use a stud like you to put the curl back in my hair."

Dane spoke to her freckle. "Well, in that case, I'll also have a cup of coffee and a bucket of oysters."

Charlene straightened up with a pleasing smirk wrenched on her lips, one cheek coiled high and pink over the corner of her mouth. He could tell she liked his spunk. She slipped the order pad back in her apron pocket; the pencil wedged in behind her ear. The tip disappeared into the teased nest. "What's your name, Honey?"

"Dane."

She turned and took a step toward the kitchen, then stopped and stepped back. "Oh, by the way, one bucket wouldn't be near enough." Then she slipped into that wisecrack grin. "Ask your pa. He can tell ya."

Dane felt his chin bounce off the table as Charlene yelled out, "Chicken Fry. Order up!"

***

For a Sunday night, Maxine's was bustling, and Dane was working his way through an excellent dinner when suddenly somebody sounded off, "Harrumph ... harrumph."

Dane looked up to pinpoint the sound. The guy was seated at the dining counter.

"Harrumph ... harrumph." The guy kept at it, hawking a deep phlegmy cough into his fist, like he had the jawbone of a donkey stuck in his throat.

Dane finished the steak and was taking the last bite of his mashed potatoes when, "Harrumph ... harrumph." The guy started at it again. "Harrumph ... harrumph." With it came the sound of a fist slamming down on the bar.

Dane thought the guy was choking on a piece of meat or a dry bun. His hands were coiled in a double fist in front of his mouth. "Harrumph." That one came deep and raspy from somewhere near his kneecaps. He had on a short sleeve cotton shirt and the muscles in his Popeye forearms jumped like Chinese dragons on parade. The guy next to him pushed a napkin in his direction.

"Harrumph!"

That did it. Dane slid to the end of the seat, a Heimlich maneuver on his mind, but before he stood up, the napkin guy turned his head. Dane stopped like a crash test dummy hitting a steering wheel with no air bag. Nose. Dane felt bloodied by the sight. It was Nose alright. Even at twenty paces, that tree stump was unmistakably buried in the center of his face.

He eased back into the seat, deaf and dumb, sliding closer to the wall, feeling dismembered like Ren without Stimpy, or George without Gracie, then caught his mouth hanging open, cold and drafty like where Indians used to hang their meat.

He shut it, a palm over his face. Hold on, he thought. A coincidence? Hardly. Just chill out. Relax. Finish your dinner. Notions strafed his thoughts like a P-38 Spitfire homing in on a platoon of ground troops. No. I'm done. Get the bill and get out.

Dane began drumming a panicky paradiddle on the table with spider-like fingers. If they were here for him, he surmised, he'd never make the door. He took a deep breath, then he saw her: Sweet Charlene. He raised a flickering finger and got her attention.

Charlene glided up to the table. "What is it, Hon? Want more coffee?"

"No thanks. I wonder if you can squeeze out a look at the two guys at the counter. One of them just had a fur-ball caught in his throat."

"I don't need to look, Honey. I ain't never seen them before."

"Are you sure?"

Charlene put her hands on her hips. "Look Honey, I thought we went through this before."

"Okay-okay."

"Say, Hon, you're about as white as the sheets on my bed. What's the matter? You in trouble?"

"Why do you say that?"

"I may have lived a sheltered life, but I know what fear looks like. And those boys are either thugs or cops. So, if you need help, say so, and I'll get you out of here."

"I don't want you involved, Char." Dane pulled two twenties from his wallet. "That should cover my tab."

A tear welled up on the dike of Charlene's eye. "My late husband called me Char." She wiped it away with a fingertip. "Listen, you Big Lug. Right now, I want to embarrass you with one of my patented butt-grabbing hugs. Instead, you walk toward the door, and I'll stall your friends with some of my mindless chatter."

"Thanks Char. For the record, I'm still on the up-side of the law."

That wisecrack grin came back. "Boy, you wear me out with your constant BS."

Dane stood up and Charlene walked him halfway to the door, talking in a low babble, like they were ancient friends.

When Dane hit the sidewalk, he noticed a man leaning against a gray sedan across the street. The glow from his cigarette lit up the eaves of his fedora. He rounded the corner toward the parking lot, thinking: How many are there? — a brainwave before erupting into a full sprint towards the ZX.

CHAPTER 15

The radio clicked on, and somewhere in the middle of Stevie Ray Vaughn's "Tin Pan Alley" Dane woke to the blues congested, his head plugged with a nasal funk. He slapped the alarm clock. A fuzzy silence returned to the room. It was Monday morning, soon to be his first day at Spinetti and Hanson Engineering, or S.H.E., as the company logo proudly displayed.

When he arrived, Erin was waiting. She greeted him professionally, then showed him to his office, Blake's old office, with a view of the park. Once there, she greeted him again with a long good-morning kiss. It was eight o'clock. Vince would be in later this afternoon.

***

Vince returned about four o'clock and called Erin into his office. Dane was still busy in his, deciding if the wastebasket should sit in the corner or next to his desk.

Vince closed the door. "Sit down Erin. You want a drink?"

"No, thank you." Erin sat down in the leather armchair across from the desk.

Vince poured himself a scotch. "How are you and Dane getting along?"

Erin rested back and crossed her legs. "I think we're doing fine."

"So, did you fuck him yet?" Vince asked.

The question bit hard. "Why don't you ask him," Erin said.

"Oh, that's no good. Of course, he'll say yes. He has his reputation to uphold."

Erin couldn't stand how arrogant he was. "How about we get to the point, okay Mister Spinetti? I have work to do."

"The only work you have, Erin, is what I tell you to do." His tone was forceful and systematically degrading. "So, have you fucked him or not? I don't need a three-page report."

Erin uncrossed her legs and hunched forward, palms on her knees. "Yes, damn it," she said, her voice teeming with disgust. "We did it in front of the fire, over the back of the couch, on the table. You name it, we've done it. I'll probably do him in his office before we leave work."

Vince started a slow walk of intimidation towards her, a chord of sardonic disbelief in his voice. "Oh, really." He sat with a leg-up on the edge of his desk.

Erin was breathing hard. She felt stupid and toyed with. Every muscle from her waist up wrung tight like a dishrag.

Vince brushed back his hair with a finger rake, then spoke. His voice was relaxed, his words to the point. "So, has he told you anything of importance?"

Erin's shoulders stiffened, and she lifted her face to stare at him. Her rebellious spirit was about to riot, the normal mode of defense she'd learned on the street, and she felt an overwhelming surge of smart-ass on her lips. "No, we've been too busy fucking. Remember?"

Vince watched his lower leg swing, pivoting at the knee, simply amused by the action, simply amused at the situation. "Gees. Feisty aren't we."

When he didn't attack, Erin exhaled a ball of tension from her chest. "It's a bad habit. I need to learn how to control my temper." Her torso unknotted, her shoulders going limp. But that god-awful question was still hanging in the air like a heavy scent of betrayal. She swallowed a dry urge to get up, then she answered, to just get past it. "And no, he hasn't told me anything of importance."

Vince stopped swinging his leg and looked at her. "Get me what I want Erin. The last time you were in that chair, I restrained myself. You don't want to see me unrestrained."

CHAPTER 16

Seattle, Washington
November 11, 1995

The week passed in a blur with Dane trying to get up to speed at S.H.E., and except for a couple of lunches out, Erin and he had hardly seen each other.

"The moon was a ghostly galleon tossed upon cloudy seas," Dane said. "While Bess the black-eyed daughter plaited a love-knot in her hair. Watch for me by moonlight, I'll come to thee by moonlight, be sure my lady fair."

"How poetic," Erin cooed.

"It's from the *Highwayman*. A poem I learned as a kid. I reworded it a little. It's about unbounded love and sacrifice."

Erin adoringly stared at him. His eyes were beaming.

"Usually, the brightest star in the sky is a planet: Venus or Jupiter or Saturn," he said. Then he pointed a finger toward the southern sky. "See those four stars? That's Orion. Two are his shoulders and two are his feet. In the middle, the three stars lined up in a row. That's his belt. And hanging down from the belt is his sword."

"A sword?"

Dane raised his hand and pointed again. "Yeah, see that cloudy area below the three stars?"

Erin's chin slid forward as she squinted. "Like a fuzzy spot?"

"Yeah, that's Orion's sword, actually the Orion Nebula."

Erin turned with a puzzled face.

"A nebula is where stars form. Right now, we're looking at baby stars that were born light years ago."

The sky was a purple bruise, the moon an eyelash near the horizon. Erin searched the universe, the gleam in her eyes like that of a child's. "What's that star called?" she asked.

"That's the Dog Star."

Erin nuzzled into his shoulder. "How do you remember poetry ...and stars?"

"I told you. I was a weird kid."

The night was on a dip toward freezing, a handful of clouds like giant puzzle-pieces were sailing east to join at the mountains and leave a picture of snow-covered slopes. Dane lifted his arm and adjusted the blanket around Erin's shoulders.

Erin continued searching. "I used to look at the stars. We'd camp out in the backyard and every so often we'd see a Shooter. They were meteors, you know, shooting stars, but we called them Shooters. I never knew what any of the actual stars were called, but they sure were beautiful."

"It doesn't matter what they're called," Dane said. "None are as beautiful as you."

Erin kissed him. He returned the favor.

After dinner, they'd made their way through Queen Anne to Magnolia Bluff, where they spread a blanket on the ground, and from their perch, the iron ground spilled off into the ocean. Across the Sound from Seattle, the lights of Winslow were in the distance.

Erin stayed quiet, simply soaking it in. A ferry to Victoria B.C. cruised north toward Whidbey Island, leaving a low hum, a guttural hush of the diesel engines in its wake. From its portholes, small circles of light reflected in the water.

Dane spoke now with caution. "Erin. I haven't been completely honest with you."

Erin's head turned slightly, looking away toward the ferry that slowly melted on the dim horizon. She stared out across the Sound for a long-long moment, and then she peered into his eyes. She couldn't speak. Her heart froze. Hurt before, she wanted no part of it now.

"It's not ..."

Erin went on the defensive. "What is it, Dane? I've heard them all."

"It's not that I didn't want to ... I truly didn't know how."

Erin was partially deaf, partially blind. She sat quietly in a fog, waiting for the bomb to hit; he had a wife, a girlfriend, he wasn't ready for a relationship. Erin trembled with non sequitur thoughts as a sudden chill circled her shoulders.

"I should've told you the truth about Marcellena," Dane said.

"Marcellena?" she probed. "Is she alive?"

Dane shook his head.

The answer wasn't what she'd expected. Erin pulled herself together. She looked deeper into his eyes and saw a man drowning in need of help. "What is true, Dane?"

"The truth is ... when she died, I went off the deep end, and ... I got drunk. A lot. Like for weeks, more like months. I started doing drugs, anything that passed my way. Especially coke. I got belligerent and mean. I went looking for fights and found plenty. She was gone. I couldn't handle it, Erin. I couldn't function."

Beneath the blanket, Erin gently stroked the back of his hand, listening, caught up in the rush of his words.

"I was so strung out on cocaine, one morning I woke up literally lying in a gutter," Dane continued. "Until then, 'lying in a gutter' was only an expression. A term used for someone who was worthless, a derelict. But there I was ... in all my glory ... I was the derelict; beaten, robbed and left for dead in a Dublin alley. That was the turning point, I guess. I knew I was going to die if I kept it up, and it wasn't what Marcellena would've wanted. She would've wanted me to remember her but to carry on. I had to get my life back on track."

There came an uneasy silence while Dane rocked with visions of the past. His eyes watered with grief and shame.

"So, what did you do?" she said.

"I knew of some that went to rehab … most failed."

Erin sat pensively. She could feel Dane's hand trembling and she knew it wasn't from the cold.

"So, I used some of my connections in the oil industry and stranded myself on a rig in the North Sea," he said. "I figured being isolated, I'd have no choice but to quit. I stayed out there for thirteen months. Then Blake died. That's what brought me home."

"Why are you telling me this now? You sound so urgent. Like you won't be here tomorrow," Erin said. "I'm glad you told me, but whether you told me today, or told me next month, it wouldn't change anything. Wouldn't change how I feel about you."

"I want you to know the truth. I don't want there to be anything held back between us, and well, I think I love you."

Erin squeezed his hand. "I love you" — the words she thought she'd never hear. Then she thought of her connection to Vince, and it pulled her gaze off across the Sound, the crash of waves on the shore below filling her ears. Truth. I can't tell him now, she thought. If he knew what I was supposed to do, spy on him, that I was a whore — she corrected herself — am a whore. He'd leave me for sure. Her eyes welled with tears, her shoulders trembling with fear.

Dane pulled her close. "Erin? Why the tears?"

"I'm scared Dane. Scared that I'll lose you."

"You won't lose me."

Locked on his side, Erin hugged Dane with all her might, wishing this night would never end, and immediately began thinking of what she'd tell Vince. It had to be believable, but not the truth. If anyone deserved to be lied to, it was Vince Spinetti.

Suddenly, Dane pointed to the sky. "There! Did you see it?"

"I did! A Shooter."

"Make a wish," Dane said.

"I already did."

***

Vince was sitting in a leather armchair, staring out over Lake Washington. Through the window, the city lights wiggled on the water. A single spotlight over the fireplace stained the chamber with gauzy shadows of melancholy, while the haunting sounds of Enya held the mood in its grasp. A capless bottle of scotch and a coke mill lay on the side table by his arm.

He hit auto-dial and Tony picked up. "Hello."

10,000 Maniacs were screaming in the background. "Tony? This is Vince."

"Hello-hello."

Vince raised his voice. "Tony. It's Vince. Turn down the music."

Vince heard the receiver drop with a crack, then the muffled sound of a sweaty handgrip before the music deadened to a low rumble. Tony's voice came back to the phone. "Yeah, Vince. What's up?"

"What're you doing?" Vince asked.

"Uh-h-h …"

"Dumb question," Vince said. "Let me try again. How long have you been partying?"

"Uh-h-h …"

"Who's there?"

"Umm, just Marty and Jenny and me. Marty brought over the new 10,000 Maniacs CD. You oughta hear it."

"I just did," Vince said.

"You got 10,000 Maniacs *Unplugged?*" Tony asked.

"No stupid," Vince said. "Over the phone." He sighed. "Why do you let that son of a bitch in your house?"

"I don't know."

"Are you ready for this week?" Vince's voice was low and mollified. He lifted his drink, the ice rattling against the glass.

"Yeah but, do I have to let that Evohl guy go with me again? He makes me uncomfortable."

"Yeah, you do," Vince commanded softly. His throat was husky, the tone gloomy. "You don't have to entertain him. Just do your job."

Tony spoke tentatively, "Okay Vince, but I don't like him."

Vince slurped his drink, a small chunk of ice wedged in his cheek. "Look, I have to go back east for a few days." He spit the cube back in the glass. "I'll be back late Thursday. Please don't mess it up, Tony. I'm counting on you."

"Don't worry Vince, I won't mess up."

The consequences of a screw-up with Geraci now in the fold were deadly, and Tony was like playing tag with a loaded gun. "Why doesn't that make me feel better?"

Vince sat up straighter against the back of the chair, trying to bolster his resolve. "Just pay attention and stay clear of Dane while I'm gone."

"Why?"

"Never mind."

Vince leaned over and grabbed the bottle by the neck, pouring a smooth amber river into his glass. "When I get back, we'll all go out for a drink or something. Just you, me and Dane."

"Are you okay, Vince? You're kinda quiet. You're making me nervous."

"I'm fine." Vince took another drink.

"Why are you going east? You gonna see Geraci?"

Vince wedged the bottle in his crotch. "Yeah. Pleasure trip. Vito wants to show me a good time. Now that we're partners and all."

"Can I go with ya? I'd sure like to meet him."

"Believe me Tony, he's not God. He may think he is, but he's no different from you or I."

"I'd still like to meet him."

"Well, not this week. I need you to handle the shipment. It's important."

"I wish I could make some decisions."

"Tony, now that Blake is gone, I'm counting on you for a lot more than I used to."

"You let Blake make decisions."

Considering that compassion wasn't normally one of Vince's virtues, he was uncharacteristically a picture of se-renity. "What's this about?" he asked.

"I miss Blake too," Tony said. "And I know you've been thinkin' about him. But I ain't stupid. If I were dead, bet you wouldn't be sitting around moping. You'd have a party."

"That's not true, Tony," Vince said in a protective tone. "You're my best friend." He hesitated, his mind lulling with distant thoughts. "But you're right, Tony," he said at length. "I have been thinking. Thinking about all the good times you, me, and Blake had before we started the coke business. I was thinking about all of us, and where we'd been, and where we've come, and where do you and I go from here?"

"Gees Vince, I know you is my best friend, but like I don't have any idea where to go from here. I don't even know what I'll be doing later tonight. I never was much good at figuring things out."

CHAPTER 17

Seattle, Washington
November 13, 1995

Derek Virchow sat alone in the tree-lined park, the points of his rear numbing on the cold wooden bench. About twenty pigeons were cooing and marching in disarray at his feet, waiting for the crumbs of his lunch. In twenty minutes, he had to meet Riker in the Federal Building across the street. He could hear its flagpole lanyard clanking in a light breeze. Director Cartwright was stepping down, probably by next April. The article was on page three of the Wall Street Journal this morning.

Derek was in damage control, and he could feel his blood pressure rising. The veins on the back of his hands were swelling. He fired up a calming smoke, took a medicinal drag, then quickly exhaled, laying out a fan of carcinogens like a crop duster.

Early on, they'd both agreed that nailing the twenty-mule team without nailing the wagon master would be unacceptable. Now Riker was in a tizzy. Derek had feared this moment, when Riker would get over his skis trying to boost his credentials to land Cartwright's position.

Nearby, a couple of teenage girls dressed in Dr. Martens, nose rings, and plaid skirts leaned against a tree sharing a joint. Their rebellion was blatant. Derek wished Curt Cobain had never left grungy Aberdeen, allowing Nirvana to infect the Northwest, even though the last thing he felt at the moment was bliss.

***

Tony's house was a one-and-a-half-story Craftsman, white with black shutters, built in the 50s, with a small square wooden porch. Dane rang the bell. An older neighborhood, he surveyed out the homes that ran the other side of the street. Tony's house wasn't the best kept. It needed paint. The flower beds were full of weeds, and grass had grown tall between the pickets of the fence.

The door swung open, and Jenny greeted him with a tentative smile. "Hey, Dane."

Dane stepped into the entry. "Hi Jenny." He bent down and gave her a hug. She felt frail in his embrace. Her hollow breasts melted against his chest.

"Where's Tony?"

Jenny moved across the living room, throwing a hand down a hall toward the back of the house. "He's asleep in the spare bedroom." She flopped down on the couch, propping her bare feet up on the edge of the coffee table.

Double-hung windows streamed dusty light into the room. Jenny's unkempt hair formed a frazzled halo in the sunbeams. There was an awkward silence. Dane cast with a woman he no longer knew; Jenny bound, self-conscious of the difference.

Jenny lowered her feet and grasped a purple bong from the coffee table. She loaded the silver bowl with marijuana and lit up. The water bubbles burst, each round chamber releasing THC to her lungs. The ball glowed, then diminished, finally sucked with a whoosh into the bottom of the watery tube.

Jenny held her breath in gagged snorts, a warm flush peeling down the skin of her neck. She arched her back as if goose bumps were inching down her spine, exploding like detonated land mines. She spoke as she exhaled. "You want me to wake him?"

"I'm awake," Tony mumbled, shuffling into the room, socks scuffing the carpet. He had on boxer shorts and a Black Sabbath T-shirt. Absently scratching his scrotum, his eyes half-closed in sleep, he made tracks for the fridge. "What's up Dane? What are you doin' here?" He grabbed a beer from the Kenmore.

Dane surveyed here: empty beer bottles and food takeout boxes strewn on the coffee table; built-in cabinets with beveled glass doors stuffed with an assortment of dishes, pictures with or without frames, and liquor bottles. The odor of moldy beer, patchouli incense and cigarette smoke raided his nostrils. The new rug needed vacuuming. From where he stood, he could see dishes piled high on the counter by the sink, a litter box in the fireplace. Heaps of clothes, like visiting relatives, hogged the two living room chairs.

At length, he answered, "Thought I'd stop by. I've been trying to reach you." It wasn't the truth. The truth was: Vince was out of town, and he figured he could work Tony into telling him more about the coke operation. Another truth hit him like a warm rush. He also wanted coke, making his way here like a bloodhound follows blood.

Tony rounded the kitchen table and sat down on the hearth. "Well, sit your butt down."

The chairs were full. Jenny patted the cushion next to her.

Dane pulled off his coat, threw it over the back of a clothes-filled chair, and sat down beside her. Her blouse was paper-thin linen and baggie on her bony frame, gaping open, missing the top two buttons. From here he could see the brown areolas of her small breasts, her tiny nipples no bigger than pimples bumping the surface. Sharp bones protruded from her shoulders. She wore an old pair of hip-hugger jeans with nickel-size buttons in front and a drawstring to cinch-up the back. Up close, her pale skin was anemic-yellow-gray and there was a dull ache that lived in her chestnut eyes. Lines made nets about them, and fainter lines crossed the corners of her mouth, her expression dry like Death Valley.

Jenny lifted her pack of cigarettes from the table. "You want one Dane?" Tony didn't smoke, but Jenny did: low-tar menthols.

"No thanks, I'm trying to cut back." It was true, sort of, but he couldn't stand menthol and would've lit up one of his own, except they were in the car.

Jenny fired up, then laid the cigarette in an already heaping ashtray. Out of habit, she slid a stringy lock of hair behind an ear.

Dane recognized the motion, the habit that remained as the only sign of her youthful innocence. She felt his gaze and turned to him, eye-to-eye, to only see Dane quickly shift his eyes away as if he'd found something heartbreaking in hers.

He felt as though he'd deserted her and as he stared at the floor, tiny fishhooks snagged at his guts. He searched for something to say, any idle bit of conversation to relieve his mind. At last, he said, "I like your new rug, Jenny." It wasn't as bad as talking about the weather, yet Dane felt stupid that he had nothing else to say.

"We needed it. The old one was shit."

"If you'd've cleaned it once in a while, it woulda lasted longer," Tony remarked.

"Oh, fuck you, Tony," Jenny said calmly, reaching for her cigarette. She took a puff, her face emotionless, her demeanor like an apathetic cat. "I don't see you running around here like Paula Dean cooking or cleaning anything."

Dane felt uncomfortable for bringing it up and hurried on to something else. "Where have you been, Tony? I've been trying to get hold of you since Saturday."

Tony looked like he'd been on a sleep-in-your-own-puke drunk. His complexion was white with a green tinge, his eyes sunken. "I've been here. Sick. I must've gotten into some bad food or somethin'. I've been shootin' acid out my ass all week."

Jenny piped up after a slow exhale, "The only thing you been getting into lately is that Arlene chick. No wonder you got the runs."

The words cut deep; blood and tears welled in Tony's eyes. He lifted his beer to hide his emotions.

Jenny packed another bowl and handed the bong to Dane. He knew not what else to do but take it. The cool smoke filled his lungs. He gagged down a few coughs. For a moment, his eyes were walking around in the back of his head, then they came back to the scene at hand.

A tall lanky man with glassy eyes, three-day stubble, and skin yellow like rotten teeth came down the hallway from the back of the house. He had on a pair of floor-dragging jeans that rode low on his hips and no shirt, socks or shoes.

"It was nice seeing you again, Dane," Jenny said. Then she got up and padded to the back of the house, pulling her blouse up over her head as she disappeared down the hallway. The butt-less lank walked back through with a beer. He never said a word. A tattoo of a dragon was sprawled across his back.

Tony was sitting quietly, swilling his beer. A chirping sound came from the mantel. He stood and retrieved his beeper, silencing the noise. He read the message to himself.

Dane heard Jenny giggle and then a door close. He dropped his voice to a whisper. "Tony?" Dane jutted his chin to the hallway. "Who's the guy?"

Tony took a drink. He stared down the hallway, wiping the beer from his lips with the back of his fist. "I don't want to talk about it. What's up? Why are you here? No one comes by this shithole just for a visit."

Dane looked sheepish and rueful, caught with his pants down, another knife to add to Tony's back. "I need some coke." Some truth was better than none.

"What makes you think I got any?"

"I was hoping you could get me some."

The beeper went off again. Again, Tony read the message to himself. He looked at the wall clock. The time was five-fifteen. His eyes darted to the back of the house and his leg started jiggling like he was late for an appointment. As he stared at the carpet, a pensive look invaded his face like he was calculating amounts in his head.

Tony licked his lips as if his mouth were dry with a lie. "I'm supposed to go over to mom's tonight for dinner, so I don't have time to pick up none."

Tony's mind stuttered. "Yeah ... well, I bought an eight-ball last night for myself. I can sell you that."

"I don't want to take your stash."

Tony was impatient now, his movements sporadic and disjointed. "It's not a problem." He got up and went toward the kitchen, then stopped, turn one-eighty and walked down the hallway. "It'll be about five-ten minutes," he said over his shoulder. "I've got to change my clothes." He went into the spare bedroom.

"That's all right. Take your time," Dane called after him.

Tony stepped back into the hallway. His shirt was already off. "Get yourself a beer," he said. "They're in the fridge."

Besides a few condiments, a chunk of orange cheese carpeted with green fuzz, a half-gallon of sour milk, a Ziploc with a tiny brick of what looked like hash, and a dry half-eaten cinnamon roll on a red plastic plate, Dane found out that beer was about all that was in the fridge. Unless, of course, you include the cordless phone, which was on the middle shelf.

Dane laid the phone on the counter and shut the fridge door. He took a guzzle of the beer and left the kitchen. The beer stung the inside of his throat. He couldn't believe that Tony was in the spare bedroom, probably weighing out his coke while his wife was in their bedroom with the skinny Dragon.

When Tony came back from the spare bedroom, he'd split an eight-ball into two vials. Dane paid up, then laid out a line for Tony and one for himself.

"Hey, let's get together after you go to your mom's," he said, trying to raise Tony's spirits. "We can shoot some pool, grab some beers."

"Naw, sorry Dane," Tony said, his voice downtrodden and bleak. "I got some stuff to do tonight."

Dane knew why Tony was being elusive. He had deliveries or pickups to make.

"But call me tomorrow," Tony said. "I picked up a hundred hits of Dilaudid. I was gonna just hang here for the day and do some up."

***

Sitting in a cozy spot at a table next to the pizza parlor's round fire pit, Dane's knee was running like a rocker arm. The coke he'd snorted on the ferry to Bainbridge Island on top of what he'd snorted with Tony had lasted longer than he expected, and the buzz was making him anxious.

The waitress delivered another pint of beer. She was about forty, with brown eyes and blue hair. "Your pizza is almost ready. I can keep it warm if you like until your friends get here."

Dane had guzzled the first beer, hoping it would bring him down a notch. "No worries," he said. "I see them coming through the door."

Tyra walked up first. She was wearing a blue jumpsuit and a white angora sweater. The floppy turtleneck reflected a peach hue about her jawline. Bobby peeled off his coat and hung it on the spindle of a straight-back chair. Dane's coat occupied the other spindle.

Dane gave them both a hug, then they all sat down. Tyra and Bobby sat side-by-side across from Dane. Bobby tossed his cap on the brick hearth by the fire.

The waitress showed at the end of the table. "The pizza will be out in a minute. What would you like to drink?"

"Beer," Bobby said.

"Root beer for me," Tyra followed.

"What kind of beer, sweetie?" the waitress said, smiling at Bobby.

"IPA," Bobby replied. "Whatever's on draught."

She purposely smiled again at Bobby, then walked off.

Tyra elbowed Bobby. "She likes you," she said.

Bobby's bald head turned bright carmine, as if being smiled at was an act of adultery. He straightened the collar of his red plaid shirt. "How long have you been here?"

Tyra grinned at Dane playfully.

"Not long. Twenty minutes."

A sharp excitement rose in Bobby's voice. "So, tell me what's up. Have you found out anything?"

"Some things, but nothing about Blake. I don't know Bobby. This might take longer than I thought."

"What do you mean?"

Dane was feeling complacent. The new job, Erin, cocaine. He wasn't sure he wanted anything to change. "Well, I can't expect Vince to just roll over and tell me everything, can I? We haven't been that close over the past few years."

"No, I guess not, but how long Dane? Vince knows how this went down." Bobby smacked his fist into an open palm. "It's going to be a genuine pleasure knocking ..."

"Hold on Bobby. What if it was an accident, like the police said? Can you handle that?"

Bobby was huffing through his teeth. Tyra laid a hand on his forearm. "Calm down Bobby. Let Dane tell us what he thinks."

Dane took a drink of his beer. "Well, if something nefarious happened to Blake, I know Tony wasn't involved. He's a sidekick, not a decision maker. Vince might know what happened, but I can't picture him doing the deed. Blake was his friend. He might be scared the same will happen to him. If Geraci did something, we've got to let the police handle it."

"Hey, you're talking to an ex-SEAL. I take care of my own."

Dane chuckled sarcastically. "Have you seen the kangaroo pouch you're carrying?"

Bobby steamed. Obviously, the sense of being hog-tied, inadequate, unable to contribute, galled him. "Look Dane ..."

"No, you look, Bobby."

"Excuse me," Tyra said, interrupting. "Bobby, I know you're impatient and Dane, you're like Blake, reluctant to budge until every duck is in position. But I don't relish the thought of sitting here eating pizza, listening to the both of you going round-and-round about it. If we can't be constructive, let's just enjoy some time together. Okay?"

Dane and Bobby were paralyzed by her frankness, their mouths hanging open like they'd been shot dead by her simple truth right as the waitress approached. She was smiling again, but Bobby kept his head down and averted his eyes. She set the pizza and drinks on the table with a pile of napkins.

For the next half-hour, while they worked through the pizza, Dane filled Bobby and Tyra in on what he'd accomplished without mentioning his recent delving into the coke bin, ending with an account of the monitor room and how he almost got caught.

Tyra was appalled. "He makes videos of people without them knowing it."

Dane held down a grin, remembering the passion play on Monitor 3.

"I never did like that SOB," Bobby said. "Excuse my French, but it's true. Do you think there's enough information on those videotapes to nail Vince and the rest?"

"Could be."

Bobby's back went ramrod straight. "Why don't we take them and hand them over to the police?"

"Look," Dane warned. "The mission was to find out about Blake. Not send Vince and Tony to jail. I'll figure out what's on the videotapes."

Someone cranked up a Neil Diamond tune on the jukebox, and suddenly, the chair holding their coats tipped over backwards. Two boys were struggling over possession of a handheld video game. When they careened into the chair, the coats and the chair went over.

The kids said nothing, not even "sorry," the jostling ending as the older boy ran off with the prize in his hand, the younger in pursuit. Bobby set the chair back on its feet and looked around to see if anyone was claiming the kids as their own. No one even shifted an eye in his direction.

Bobby's head tipped to the shoulder as if he was looking at a foreign object under the chair. He reached down and when he stood back up, he was holding a cylinder of white lengthwise between his thumb and forefinger.

Dane lunged forward and snatched the vial from his hand.

"What is that, Dane? Is that coke?"

Across the room, a waitress dropped a tray of glasses. Tyra nearly jerked out of her skin.

"Sit down and shut up, will you, Bobby?"

Dane had kept his voice low and under control, but the words, the insolent look, they hit Bobby like a slap in the face. "What in hell are you doing, Dane?" He raised his finger accusingly, pointing at the white-knuckled fist that coiled the vial. "That's coke isn't it?"

Tyra grabbed Bobby's forearm and eased it down. "Calm down Bobby."

Bobby shot a condemning look at Tyra. "Did you know about this?"

"No, I didn't," she said defensively.

A red tide of anger rolled up Bobby's neck over his face. "What is it, Dane?"

"Sit down, Bobby, and let him explain," Tyra urged him, tugging on his forearm.

Bobby sat down, holding Dane in an icepick stare.

"It's simple. If you want to get in deep with a drug dealer, you've got to look like you do drugs." The grilling he was getting from Bobby perturbed Dane. "Is that so tough to understand?" His voice was indignant.

Bobby was quiet, holding his forehead in his hand.

Tyra looked conspicuously around the pizza parlor.

Dane patted the back of her hand. "Don't advertise it. No one saw."

Bobby had a queer expression drawing out his face. "Are you on coke?"

"No, why?" Dane sniffed without knowing.

"Because that looked like coke and you just sniffed."

Dane self-consciously wiped his nose with his index knuckle. "You're exaggerating Bobby."

"You've been high this whole time, haven't you?" Bobby said.

Dane looked away.

"You snorted some of that crap on the way here, didn't you?"

Dane continued to look away.

Tyra grabbed his wrist across the table. "Dane. Did you?"

Dane went on the defensive. "So, what if I did? What difference does it make?"

Bobby was peeved, but could control the volume, his words coming out in a boiling hush. "Damn it, Dane! That stuff will mess you up."

"I can handle it, Bobby."

"Dane," Tyra stopped him. "Bobby is only trying to help."

"I get it, but I have to play the part, or Vince and Tony will never trust me."

"Is Vince here?" Bobby asked sardonically. "Is Tony here? Last time I looked, we are alone having pizza, not a line between friends." Bobby stood up and leaned over, his palms flat on the table. "Evil walks about seeking whom she may devour. Don't be a fool. She'll kill you."

"She who?" Dane asked, bewildered.

Bobby grabbed his coat from the chair, then stepped around behind Tyra to get his hat from the hearth.

"Where are you going?"

"Home."

Bobby walked off, slipping his arms into his coat sleeves.

"Bobby ... c'mon, sit down," Dane called after him.

"Let him go Dane," Tyra said.

Things got deathly quiet even though the pizza parlor brimmed with people. Dane thinking about what kind of fool he was, retracing all that'd happened. Tyra was silent, poking at her pizza with a fork. At length she asked, "Why?"

"Why what?"

"Why tonight?"

Dane was quiet, deciding whether to answer.

"Please Dane, tell me the truth. Blake had a problem, but he kicked it. Do you have a problem?"

Dane sighed as all the thoughts from his past streamed through his head. "It's a long story, Tyra. I'd love to tell you about it sometime."

A log collapsed in the fire pit, sending up a shower of sparks, and out of nowhere, McTarnihan was standing at the end of the table. "Mind if I sit down?"

The sight of him was surreal. There he was with that on-the-road-staying-in-flea-bag-hotels look to him — a Hawaiian print shirt under his green polyester sport jacket and a rainbow trout tie. The knot loosened at the collar. He had on a topcoat unbuttoned down the front, his homburg cocked back on the crown of his head, his fly half-unzipped so you could almost see Argentina.

McTarnihan looked down at Tyra with a warm grin.

Tyra stared back with the pitiful eyes of a woeful child, begging for mercy.

"And who might this be?" McTarnihan asked.

Tyra returned a tentative smile like she had crooked teeth.

Dane's tongue was tied in knots, his mind rushing from corner to corner of his skull, trying to come up with a phony name.

Tyra held out a trembling hand. "And you are?" she asked, with as much cool as she could muster.

McTarnihan shook her hand, stepping closer. "John McTarnihan." He didn't let go. "You know, you look familiar. Tyra Rivers. Is that correct?"

Tyra let out the weak cry of a yearling caught in a snare, jerked her hand free and with the heel of her palms pressed to the edge of the table was teetering between whether to bolt or stay. She looked dazed, like everything inside of her was shouting and rushing in different directions, fear giving her a dozen eyes searching every which way for an escape.

"Easy Tyra ... easy," Dane said low, but in a reassuring tone.

McTarnihan wiggled out of his topcoat and draped it over Dane's, then three-finger pinched his hat at the crest and hung it on the other spindle. He sat down in Bobby's vacated seat next to Tyra. "I won't try to stop you, Miss Rivers, if you decide you must leave ... but I'd rather you stay."

Tyra looked to Dane for the answer, and Dane nodded the okay.

"Good," McTarnihan said. "Let's talk."

Dane focused sharply on his face. "What do you want, McTarnihan?" His voice was raised in accusation.

McTarnihan was as calm as a case on Thorazine. "Was that Blake's brother that just left? He's stockier than the little brother, isn't he?"

Dane had no choice but to talk to him. He knew about Tyra and could blow everything wide open with Vince. "What do you want?"

McTarnihan held a grin like a jailer who holds the keys to the cage.

Tyra chewed her lower lip.

McTarnihan snapped his fingers over his head, the sharp clicks calling the waitress. "I need a beer."

"What kind?" she asked.

"Anything, as long as it's draught."

The waitress hustled off, McTarnihan casually eyeing her as she walked away.

"I suppose you've told Vince about Tyra and me."

"Frankly, no I haven't."

"Why?"

"I figured there was no use getting her involved unless I had to."

Tyra piped up, "And now you have to?"

"That's up to you. I don't owe Spinetti anything."

The waitress came back with the beer, and McTarnihan paid with cash. He took a giant gulp. "Ahh, that's better."

Dane was fidgety for a smoke. McTarnihan caught on and pulled out a baggy from his vest pocket with two generic cigarettes inside. He untwisted the twist-tie that held the plastic bag shut and offered Dane a smoke. McTarnihan fired Dane up, then himself.

Holding the smoke between his index and middle, McTarnihan worked the twist-tie, smoke rising like a jet trail to gather in the overhead, imitation, stained glass lampshade. "You see, I'm a curious animal. Always have been. That's why I was a police officer, and now a private dick. I just want to know what kind of scam you're running."

McTarnihan waited a dozen heartbeats, letting the implication sink in. "Vince is paying me to check you out, Avilla, but you seem to be just a working joe with one thing in common with Spinetti: Blake Hanson. So, when you hide Miss Rivers here, yet try to get in close to Spinetti, it makes me wonder."

"We don't need to tell you anything."

"That's true...but come this weekend, I meet with Spinetti to give him what I know, and depending on what you tell me here will decide what I tell him then."

"If you work for him, what difference does it make what we tell you?"

McTarnihan eased back in his chair, took a languorous drag, then exhaled. "Maybe if I tell you where I'm coming from, you'll feel a little easier about letting me in."

Dane nodded with the go ahead.

"When I was on the force, I had a partner, Patrick Donovan. Ever heard of him?"

"No."

McTarnihan had wound the twist-tie into a pretzel. He tossed it on the table. "Well, Donovan is Police Chief and Spinetti has him in his pocket. Chief looks the other way. Spinetti increases his pension. Get it? Only thing is that when we were partners, I got into a little trouble. I shot this kid in an alley. Problem was, I was drunk, and the kid didn't have a gun. Anyway, Donovan always had a lot of pull with the upper echelon, so I don't do jail time. Only now, I'm his favorite whipping boy."

McTarnihan paused with a narcotic drag, then exhaled as he spoke, "I think he was waiting for that night. Waiting for the guillotine to drop."

He grabbed a rectangular napkin from a pile on the table and placed it in front of himself. He tapped an ash into his palm, waited a second, then dropped it on the napkin. "Well, he got what he wanted. I lost my badge, my wife, my respect, everything."

He stared down at the table. "I used to drink to get loaded. Now I drink to forget. Booze is a multi-tasking skinflint."

He looked at Tyra, who was stiff as a board beside him. "Sorry miss, you don't want to hear philosophy." He refocused on Dane. "Then comes Spinetti and because he's Chief's friend, I get to dig up dirt on all kinds of people." He paused, reminiscing on a thought. "Frankly, I don't like the way he uses the information."

"That's why you never mentioned Tyra to Vince."

"Exactly. I figure why drag her into it? But," he said, pausing again, "I'm curious. I want to know what she knows. Only you come along, and poof, she's gone."

He looked at Tyra. "I would've never hurt you, Miss Rivers. I just wanted to talk."

Tyra had been as rigid as a corpse, but with the last settling disclosure, the muscles in her shoulders and neck relaxed.

McTarnihan continued, "You know, I'm not stupid. I guess I may dress a little on the loud side, like some half-wit used-car salesman, and I could take off a few pounds, but what the hell, I have no one to impress. I was a good cop. A damn good one."

He tapped another ash on his palm and then on the napkin. "I've known for some time these guys were felonious, but I guess until now I didn't think anybody cared."

Dane had listened unblinkingly, his freshly lit cigarette burning down to a fragile and perfect cylinder of ash before crumbling across his knuckles. He snuffed the rag in his ashtray.

"What changed?"

McTarnihan moved some scotch from a flask in his vest pocket to his beer and tipped back a big blast. Beer tainted with scotch ran from the corners of his mouth like a Fu Manchu. "It's a personal thing." He wiped his face with a meaty palm. "But in a nutshell, I don't like the way these assholes do business, and in particular, I don't want to see them messing up any more innocent girls."

Tyra appeared emotionally drained. "What makes you think you can help us, or that we can help you, or even want to?" Tyra asked, her cheek resting on the flat of her hand.

"Well, it obvious to me you're running some sort of scam. You tell me what it is, and if I like it, I tell Spinetti only what I want to. That leaves you free to do your thing, and if it works, I'll love watching Spinetti get his balls whacked. Either way, Spinetti pays me. I have nothing to lose."

Dane looked at Tyra and there was agreement in their eyes.

"Okay McTarnihan. To use your term, in a nutshell, we want to know the truth about Blake. That's all. We don't know for sure it was an accident, and if it wasn't, we want to know who's responsible."

McTarnihan laughed.

"What's so funny?"

"I figured you guys were trying to dupe Spinetti out of some money. But you want nothing but the truth. I'm pleasantly surprised, that's all. These days, it's rare to find people interested in something less tangible than dollars."

McTarnihan's cigarette was burned to a nub. He was alternating looking at the napkin and the palm of his hand. Dane slid the ashtray over in an act of covenant.

"So, is it a deal?" Dane asked.

"Why not."

Over the next few minutes, McTarnihan told Dane and Tyra all he knew about Blake and that horrible night at the mill. His voice was dreary and monotone. The air became thick with despair. The tale ripped a hole in Dane's guts; and in her eyes, Tyra's heart was being sliced to the quick.

"I am suspicious, though," McTarnihan said. "It's too coincidental. Even though the facts point toward accident, my nose smells a hit: a big fat Geraci move."

"Do you think Vince was involved?" Dane asked.

"I can't say. I don't like Vince, but that doesn't make him a killer."

With that disclosure McTarnihan was finished. It was now time for Dane and Tyra to spill what they knew. It didn't take long and most of it McTarnihan knew already.

"Well, I have to go," McTarnihan said touching his watch.

At this point in the conversation, only one detail haunted Dane's mind, the word "coincidental" resurrecting a memory from Maxine's. "Are there more of you?"

"More of me. God, I hope not," McTarnihan answered. He slid his arms into the sleeves of his topcoat, then using both hands adjusted it across his wide shoulders.

"I mean, do you work alone?"

McTarnihan wiped his mouth with a fingertip brush, then picked up his hat. He worked the brim in the palm of his hand. "If I know what you're asking." He paused, looking to Tyra, then back to Dane. "You should be more careful. If I can track you down, so can someone else."

CHAPTER 18

Atlantic Highlands, New Jersey
November 15, 1995

The Hawker descended out of a slate-gray sky, touched down and taxied into the hanger, the nose of the jet dipping as it came to a stop. Watching from inside the limo, silver rain beaded and ran on the windshield. Vittorio tipped back the last of his drink and gazed with delight. Carmen had been gone for almost two weeks, and he was expecting a splendid evening.

The stairs folded out from the plane. The co-pilot came first, then Michael and Evohl close behind. They stood on the concrete of the hangar floor, face to face, a final discussion. As they talked, the co-pilot dragged a thick black power cord to the plane and plugged it into the fuselage. Evohl turned and walked off, disappearing into the hangar office. Michael flipped up the collar on his jacket, then clutched the throat of the bomber like a shawl and ran to the car.

"Father," Michael greeted him. Rain trickled from his hair onto his brow, and he wiped his face with a palm.

"Where's Evohl going?" Vittorio asked, the ice cubes clacking in his glass as he set it on the bar. "I need to speak with him."

"He's going to stop at Krinkov's and pick up some borscht on the way to the house."

Vittorio looked back into the hangar. Carmen still hadn't deplaned.

Michael pressed the intercom. "Let's go home, Gino," he said to the chauffeur.

Alcohol soured in Vittorio's mouth. "Where's Carmen?"

The question bore a serpentine hush; nerves coiled, ready to strike. The limo pulled toward the gate, the street, en route to the mansion. Michael hesitated. Another private jet touched down, a spray of mist swirling from its tires on the damp runway. "I had her stay behind," he finally admitted. "She has more to do at the compound."

The answer irked Vittorio. "I thought she was done?"

Michael poured some scotch in a tumbler. "It's a thirty-million-dollar compound. It's going to take her a while."

"Are you sure you didn't have her stay for other reasons?"

"Like what, Father?" Michael grimaced in his drink.

"You know 'what'," Vittorio said adamantly.

Michael sniggered and sipped his drink.

Vittorio ran an index finger under the collar of his turtleneck. "You know, Michael, treat me with more respect. You're not irreplaceable."

"That sword cuts both ways, Father. I've had a good example of how to eliminate meddling family members."

Vittorio squeezed his thighs, feeling a discomfort in his muscles, the same feeling he'd get after running five miles. He wondered if the feeling would be similar if he injected someone with diluted bleach. He could see the back of Gino's head, and Gino's eyes, in the review mirror. A dim fog pervaded the interior of the coach, muddled by the cabin lights. He thought about elbowing Michael in the temple. The blow would surely daze him, at least. He had a garrote in the console. Michael was strong, but the element of surprise was in his favor. Then a quick ride to the pier ...

"Face it, Father," Michael said.

The words jarred Vittorio from his dark thoughts.

"You need me more than I need you."

Vittorio hesitated, stepping back from the edge of a familiar haunt. "How so?" he said at length.

"You're an old man," Michael said in a whisper, his head turning from the window. "All your protection has figured that out as well. They're already calculating who'll take your place, where their allegiance should lie, and the logical choice is me."

Michael tilted the tumbler side-to-side that rested on his knee. Vittorio watched him warily. It was as if Michael was weighing consequences on a set of balance scales. "You butchered my mother, then hung her portrait in the library. Why? So she could watch you give the family business to someone else? I don't think so."

Vittorio was morosely quiet. He heard a gunshot in his mind's ear, and saw blood pooling on the terrazzo, Sophia's raven hair strewn about her face.

Michael slammed down the rest of the scotch, then calmly set the glass tumbler on the tiny bar. "One day soon you'll be riding in a limo for the last time, Pops. The kind they take to the graveyard." Michael punched the intercom button. "Drop me off at the corner. I've got to get some fresh air."

***

Vito entered like a dry wind, grating teeth, setting the room on edge.

Vince stood immediately. "I hope it's all right. Manfred let me in, and I found myself a drink," he said, holding up a tumbler of single malt and ice.

Vito had his hands stuffed in the pockets of his ivory slacks. He wasn't smiling. His fingers were working overtime with vehemence. Coins were jangling out an eerie dirge. He walked to the windows and stared out over the bay. It was nearly dusk.

Vince felt ill-at-ease, slipping a free hand in the front pocket of his chinos. "Where's Michael?" he asked.

Vito spun from the window. Like being tugged by an invisible puppet string, the corner of his eye started dancing. A tic of rage. "He's got other things on his mind besides business."

Animosity flooded Vito's mind. Vince felt the heat of his antagonistic thoughts and sat down. A light sweat circled under his button-down shirt, clinging the khaki fabric to his shoulders.

There came a knock, and the mahogany doors to the library slid open. Carlo, Vito's bodyguard, stood in the doorway. His stony expression, his aura of death, he was exactly as Vince remembered from the Palomino Club.

Vito squared his shoulders and pulled an upturned palm from his pocket. "Where in the hell have you been?" he barked.

Instantly, Vito's stare melted Carlo's menace to a puddle on the floor. "I got held up in traffic, Mister Geraci."

"Is it done?"

"Yes, Mr. Geraci."

"When Evohl gets here, send him to me."

Carlo nodded his head, and the twin mahogany doors rapped together in front of his twisted face.

Vince set down his drink. "Do you want me to leave, Vito? If you need to be alone for a while, I understand."

Vito headed for the bar. "No, Vince, that's all right. Michael and I had a minor disagreement, that's all, and well, if you had a son, you'd see what kind of upheaval that can cause."

Vito poured a scotch and shot it down like it was water. He poured another. "That's better. Are you ready for this evening? I took the liberty and arranged a companion for you. Carmen was going to join us, but she stayed in Seattle."

Amused by the mention of her name, Vince said, "That's too bad." His words giving no meaning to his thoughts. "I suppose we can do something else this evening."

"Are you kidding? I've got a table for four at Spagos, box seats at the hottest show on Broadway, and then we'll hit the clubs." A roaring laugh erupted deep in his chest. "By morning, you'll be crawling on your hands and knees. New Jersey women are merciless. You will be delightfully exhausted. Like that suit selling moron on TV, 'I guarantee it.'"

Like a sudden earthquake, Evohl's voice rumbled from the intercom on Vito's desk. "Mister Geraci. I am Evohl. I need to see you."

Vito reached over the desk, pressing a small rectangular button. "Come in Evohl."

"We must speak alone."

Vito shrugged his shoulders. He set down his drink and left the library.

Vince browsed around the room, admiring the metal sculpture of an eagle perched on a protuberant boulder, the portrait of Vito's long-past wife, the vastness of his personal collection of books. He stood before the windows, sipping his drink, overlooking the bay when Vito returned.

Vince turned from the window and Vito gave him a look, transmitting both judgment and curiosity with equal shares.

Uncertainty circled Vince like a tornado. "Is everything okay?"

Vito was doing his best to remain calm. "They could be better. I have received some disturbing news. Who is Tony Franklin to you?"

"Why? Did something happen to Tony?"

"He is all right ... physically."

Vince got the gist of it. "What did he do?"

"There was a problem concerning the shipment Evohl delivered yesterday."

"What happened?"

"Is Franklin more than an associate?"

"He's an old friend. We've known each other for years."

"I see," Vito said, his voice trailing off as if his mind had walked into another room.

Vito needed Vince like a vampire needs a dim-witted blonde. He'd coax and harbor him until he'd sucked out every ounce of life, then discard him as an empty shell. Vince knew that from the beginning. Yet the payoff was too alluring, and although a formidable opponent, Vince counted on his youth: a silver cross, and his intellect: a wooden stake, to save him in the end.

"What happened Vito?" Vince asked. "Did they get busted?"

"Could have," Vito said. "When Franklin picked up Evohl, he was drunk. Evohl offered to drive, but Franklin refused. Franklin was driving erratically, being childishly reckless. Then he beat someone up at a convenience store. A cop arrested him."

Vito was losing his temper. His voice had slowly ramped from negligible aversion to an angry plateau, now exploded, "Dammit Vince, they had four kilos of coke in the trunk of that car."

Vince was in knots. Tiny aftershocks from the explosion shook his knees. A twitch invaded his left temple.

Vito stroked back his hair, the gesture seemingly an effort to calm himself. His eyes were piss-yellow with rage, his neck sinewy, his face a leathered omen slashed with deep-rooted malice. He took a deep breath.

"Evohl convinced the officer that he had nothing to do with it, and that he'd drive the car home," Vito said. "Evohl is quite disturbed about it. This is the second time Franklin was driving recklessly with a load of coke in the car. The first time I let it slide. Now he gets arrested to boot."

"I'm sorry, Vito."

"Sorry! What if the police impounded the car and had them both hauled off to jail? Sorry doesn't cut it."

There was a disquieting silence. Vince leaned against a bookcase. His thoughts were foggy, unsure how to proceed. Vito was pacing, his ire apparent.

Finally, calmly, Vito stated the facts, "I want Franklin out."

"Out?"

"That's right ... out."

"Exactly what do you mean by 'out,' Vito?"

Vito's voice was smooth like molasses, but pure cider vinegar. "I had a man working for me once. Money ran through his fingers like shit through a goose. Women hung off each arm like grapes from a vine. He partied at the best clubs, got drunk on the best liquor, drove the best cars. Flash the money, flash the clothes; he had to be a big-wheel."

Vito stared at the ocean for a moment, a scowl curling in his face. "You see that buoy a few hundred yards out in the surf?"

Vince came closer to the window. He pointed with a crooked finger. In the gray-green light of dusk he could see a battered orange buoy with a red-light blinking slowing atop. You couldn't see it on the outside, but on the inside, his arm was pure Jell-O. "That one?"

"Yeah. Mister Big-Wheel lies five-hundred-feet out and three-hundred-feet down from there. Mister Big-Wheel was big trouble waiting to happen. I stuck a .45 to his lips and shut him down."

Vince opened his mouth to speak, then hesitated, and merely shook his head.

Vito laid a hand on Vince's shoulder, started massaging it like he was his dad, getting his son's throwing arm ready for the big game. "Cops can let many things slide, but when you keep shoving it in their faces, they can't ignore it."

Vito dropped the massage, lightly slapped Vince on the back of the head. "Get rid of him, Vince, or I'll have to."

"What if I have him do something else? Something less noticeable."

"If you can make it work fine ... but if it doesn't, friend or not, we will have to handle the situation."

Vince chewed it over. Dammit Tony. This was a possibility he'd never calculated.

"You'll learn Vince. In this business, you either die old, rich and wise; or you go out young, poor, and stupid." He looked to the ocean and jutted his chin toward the buoy. "The stupid ones end up out there."

CHAPTER 19

Seattle, Washington
November 19, 1995

"It's a chance I'll have to take," Vince said with some finality, buttoning the last button on his khaki shirt. "I'm surrounded by morons."

A heavy sigh echoed over the phone.

"Present company excluded, of course."

The apology came late and stunk of phoniness. With it came a short languishing silence. Vince checked the crease in his Dockers, tucking in his shirt, and pushed on. "Let's face it, Chief. Lance and Jimmy are fine at doing what they're told, and Sean is smart, but they're not street smart. Not like Tony."

He zipped up and buckled his belt, phone wedged ear to shoulder. "With Blake gone and Tony out. I've got no one else to turn to."

"Okay, hang on," Chief said.

Vince heard a chair creak, a lewd mix of tacky music and suggestive utterances dying in the background. Vince imagined Chief kicked back in his easy chair, feeling imposed upon, the strings of hair on his bald scalp matted with a sex-craved sweat, the rendezvous with his collection of pornos interrupted.

"Of course, you know, I'm out of the question," Chief said.

"I know. That's a given." Vince started pacing. "I just wanted to inform you and ..." Vince hesitated, a disquieting stab. His uncertainty was like oil on water, marring the cool surface.

"And ..."

"And get your opinion," Vince continued. "You're all I've got now."

"I see. Considering I'm your last bastion of intelligence."

"C'mon Chief, you know what I meant."

"Indeed, I do. Well, let's see, from what you've told me ... hmmmm ... I'd say it's a good move, but ..."

"But what?"

Chief paused, his breath heavy, a phlegmy rattle in his throat. "I'll only say this once. You've got to be prepared to eliminate any problems if they arise."

"I understand."

"Have you told Geraci?"

"No. Absolutely not. Geraci wants results, not problems. I need to handle this on my own."

"Well, I hope my advice has been of value?"

The message was obvious, not in the words he'd said, in what words he avoided. Chief's chair creaked again, and Vince knew more was coming. The price was being determined, one second languishing on to ten.

Chief spoke up again. "Look Vince, I'm sitting here staring up at the dappled white orange-peel ceiling of my study, thinking how it looks like my wife's cellulite butt, and the videos aren't cutting it anymore. I need more than money this time, Vince. I need a woman. A young woman. Understand?"

CHAPTER 20

Seattle, Washington
November 26, 1995

Dane entered the Main Salon, ruffling rain from his hair with a towel. "Is it ever going to stop?"

There was a heavy chop on Lake Washington. Rain sheeted the windows, a relentless downpour blurring the sight.

"Probably not until July," Vince said as he handed Dane a beer.

Dane sat down on the couch, towel in his lap. "So, what's up?" he asked. "You said you needed to talk."

"Let's wait for Tony. He should be here any minute."

Vince tore open a blister pack of AA batteries, loaded them into the CD player remote. A moment later, Annie Lennox's *Medusa* spun, the volume low, her singular voice galvanically poignant.

Dane pulled out a vial and lined up a snort on the coffee table.

Vince touched his wrist, grimaced at his watch. "Why is it Tony can never be on time? It's like a game with him."

"When was he supposed to be here?"

"At four, just like you. But you're here, and he's not."

Dane handed Vince a tooter. "Here, take this. It'll settle your nerves."

Vince leaned over and snorted the line, quick and easy, then fell back into a chair.

"Howdy pardners," Tony said. "Looks like it's party time."

"Give me another," Vince said, gritting his teeth. "I'm going to need it."

Dane quietly laid out another line for Vince, wondering how these two could be the best of friends, yet continually at each other's throats.

Tony piled onto the couch next to Dane. Without asking, Dane began sculpting out another set of lines.

A rank odor infiltrated the close quarters. Vince sniffed the air. "What is that?"

Tony ignored him and concentrated on Dane's progress.

"You smell it, don't you Dane?" Vince ran a finger under his nose, eyes squinting.

Dane sniffed the air like a bluetick hound, nose up, all senses cued on to the scent.

"What is it, Tony?" Vince asked. "Tell me what you put on to cover up the booze."

Tony picked up the tooter on the tabletop. "I'm not drunk Vince," he said.

Vince's nostrils flared. "I asked you what it's called."

"*Riot Poor Homey.*"

"'Poor homey' ... like a sorry black dude?" Dane asked facetiously.

"Where's it made?" Vince jumped in. "South Central? The Crips got their own cologne now."

"Really, I tell ya." Tony pulled a small towelette packet from the pocket of his Levi's.

Vince's hand darted out like a snake, clutching the packet from Tony's hand. He looked at the label. "Franklin," he said with a chuckle. "You're priceless. 'Poor Homey', shit. It's *Pour Homme,* you idiot. *Pour Homme,* that's French. It means: For Men. It's *Riot for Men.* Not *Riot Poor Homey.* "

"Let me see," Dane said. He tore the corner of the packet, took a whiff. "That's the stuff all right."

Tony flipped them both off, then began hoovering a line. After a second line, he got up, went to the fridge, and opened a beer.

Vince got up and followed. He poured himself a shot, slipped it down, and poured another. As Tony returned to the couch, Vince stared vaporously out the windows of the salon.

Dane caught his distance. "Hey what's up?"

"Nothing. I simply don't know where to start."

Dane looked at Tony.

Tony slid back in his seat, a quick non-committal flash of his eyes before he tipped back a long, deliberate guzzle of beer.

Dane looked back at Vince, thought of a cigarette, then dismissed it. "Start with what?"

"We've been friends a long time, haven't we, Dane?"

"Sure … long time."

"And even though we've been miles apart sometimes … physically … philosophically, deep down we've known that we could always trust each other, right?"

"Sure, sure," Dane said. "What's this about?"

"What I've got to tell you Dane...you cannot repeat to anyone," Vince said. "Do you understand?"

Vince had a look on his face as if the president had just clued him in that a first strike was eminent. "Do you understand?" he repeated.

Dane looked at Tony. Tony turned away to the windows, safe behind another guzzle of beer. "Okay, I understand," Dane said at last. "But what is it?"

Vince downed a second load of whiskey, stood with palms flat on the bar before him, the crystal shot glass glittering like a diamond at his fingertips. "An opportunity … but where to start?"

"How about the beginning?"

"The beginning … whoa, I don't have that much time. Tony, why don't you start by telling Dane what happened."

"You mean about Marty?"

"Yeah, Marty."

"He had it coming," Tony said.

"Maybe so, but the guy looked like someone had taken a mallet to his face."

"He had it coming, Vince."

"Just tell Dane how it happened," Vince said.

Tony paused, gathering thoughts, then said, "Well, it was about nine o'clock Wednesday night and me and Evohl ..."

"Geraci's albino?" Dane asked.

"You guessed it," Vince said.

Tony was stifled. His face contorted into words: How could he talk, tell the story, if they kept butting in?

Dane saw the frustration in his eyes. "Go ahead, Tony," he said apologetically. "I'm sorry I interrupted."

"Well, okay. Him and me, Evohl. We stop at the 7-11 over on Lexington Avenue, you know, by the old Burger Bar. I needed a Pepsi, one of those big thirty-two-ounces. So I go in the place, and as I'm going in, I notice Marty. He's outside the front doors leaning on the hood of his car, that piece of shit Oldsmobile he drives. Anyway, I go inside, and I can see him and a couple of guys really yukking it up out there. And the guys are looking at me through those glass doors and smiling and laughing, pointing and mouthing words to me. I can't tell what they're saying, but they're looking at me, you know, like I'm some kind of jerk. So, I pay up and step out the door ... but I'm going to ignore 'em and just get back in the car with the albino, when I hear Marty say Jenny's name. It was like ... a shot. That's all I heard."

Tony took a guzzle of beer, one eye squinting, remembering Marty's words like a corkscrew in his temple. "So, I set my drink on the trashcan, and like stripped down my straw, you know, so I can listen. That's when I overhear Marty say that Jenny was the boniest fuck he'd ever had. I had my back to him, but I heard it plain as day. I know he was saying it loud on purpose, you know, so'd I'd hear, but he really pissed me man. So, I told him to shut up, and he laughed, kept talking trash to those guys ... said she looked anorexic, but she couldn't be, 'cause she was hungry for his stuff all the time. I was crazed, sorta outta my mind. I was gonna kill the motherfucker."

Proud as if his sudden virility put him in the ranks with other action-heroes, Tony elaborated. "I pinned him down easy on the hood of that Oldsmobile, like he was aching for it, and wailed on him good till his face was mush."

Tony glanced at Dane, his eyes twinkling with amusement. "Like some gooney bird with hemorrhoids had dropped a load there."

"Some gooney bird did," Vince smirked.

Tony looked at Vince for a long, long moment, waiting for more. He'd missed the joke, went right over his head like eighth-grade math.

Vince laughed, knowing Tony didn't get it. "Jenny's been sharpening old Marty's pencil all right," Vince said to Dane. "Next, she'll be taking on the whole Ticonderoga factory."

Tony frowned.

"What did his buddies do?" Dane wanted to know. "Just stand there and watch you beat him up?"

"Sure. What do they care? They thought it was funny."

"So, continue," Vince prodded. "The store manager calls the cops."

"First time, I have ever seen anybody call the cops," Tony said, "and they were there in like seconds. Must have been a Winchell's around the corner or something," he haw-hawed.

No one else laughed.

"So, what happened?" Dane asked.

"I've got assault charges pending," Tony said, smiling like he'd just won the Lotto.

"Gees Tony. This is serious."

"Don't worry Dane," Vince said. "Marty will drop the charges."

"How do you know?"

"I know. Leave it at that," Vince said. "But that's' not the end of the story."

Tony began stuttering, "No-no-no. There's more."

Vince held an open palm to Tony — a stop sign without lettering. "I'll finish it, Tony."

"You see Dane, the rough part is Evohl was in the car," Vince said. "The police, of course, had to question him."

"He did nothing," Dane said. "So, what's the problem?"

"There was coke in the car. Four kilos."

Here we go, Dane thought. An Oscar performance was about to take place. "You're kidding. You mean grams, right?"

"No kilos. In the trunk."

"Ah-ah, so what happened?"

"Evohl talked them out of searching the car. Said he would take the car home."

"And they bought it?"

"They didn't really have any reason to search the car. It was a fight. Besides, Tony wasn't in the car, and no reason to suspect there was any coke to be found."

Dane turned to Tony. "Are you nuts? Four kilos of coke. Where'd you get it?"

"It was mine Dane," Vince spoke up. "It was my coke."

"What!" Dane exclaimed. Shock, disbelief — it was all there in his eyes, his expression, his voice. He was a shoo-in for the hefty gold statue.

"Which now brings us to the business I wanted to see you about. I need to distribute the coke, and Tony can't do it," Vince continued. "One more screw up ..."

"Hold it," Dane said. He had a finger pointed at his own chest. "You want me to do it?" Then he drank a theatric sobering of beer before he set the foaming bottle on the table. "I don't think so. Anyway, I don't get it. Why do you have four kilos of coke and why is Tony distributing it?" It was uncanny how well he fit the part.

"Blake and I started this business a long time ago," Vince said. "Blake would bring the coke in from South Carolina, Tony would distribute it, and I kept everything running smooth. When Blake died, I had to get it somewhere else, so enter Geraci and his boy the albino."

"Michael Geraci is a dealer?" The lines just kept coming, naturally, ad lib.

"It's a family business. Problem is Tony has been screwing up royal lately. On the first delivery, the very first mind you, all he was supposed to do is pick up Evohl and the coke and go somewhere safe and cut it up. But no, he had to show off, be Mario Andretti, his Prelude a friggin' Indy car. His driving upset the albino, and so he tells old man Geraci that Tony is reckless. Which he is."

Vince shot a baleful stare at Tony. "Of course, Geraci is pissed, but he let it slide. Then on the next delivery Tony shows up drunk and gets arrested for assault. When Geraci told me, I couldn't believe it. Of course, I had to hear it from old man Geraci, because bonehead here didn't call me."

Casually, he turned back to Dane, like that business was behind him, but he couldn't hide the seed of rage that was planted in the green fields of his eyes. Vince poured another shot and took the blast fast, throwing back his head. "But now Geraci wants Tony out."

Vince looked at the ceiling in disbelief. "Amazing. Brain-child punches out Marty and voila' the cops appear. Who'd a figured."

"He had it coming Vince," Tony said.

Coke, the sedative, became coke the incendiary. "You idiot! Of course, he deserved it. But use your head."

"I did what you told me. I wasn't drunk."

Vince glared at him.

"Well, that drunk anyway," Tony followed.

"You don't get it, do you?" Vince said.

Tony was defiant. "I suppose you could've done better?"

That did it. Anger was a river, and it was about to crest its banks. Vince came at Tony from behind the bar. Tony jumped up and started backpedaling for the door. "Nah-nah-nah," he bleated.

"Nah-nah-what? You got something to say, say it."

"Nah-nah-nah, I didn't mean ..."

Vince grabbed a fistful of black-and-blue Van Halen T-shirt, holding Tony at the chest. SLAP! A palm moist with anger welting skin; the sound was sharp, shattering like breaking glass.

"Didn't mean what? You didn't mean to," — SLAP! — "be a fool?"

"Didn't mean to," — SLAP! — "mouth off?"

"Didn't mean to ..."

Vince went to slap Tony again, only Tony raised his forearm and blocked the blow. A definite no-no.

Vince looked to the side like Michael Jordan faking a pass, then SMACK! Vince hit him, roundhouse, the concussion ripping Tony's head back and to the side, his body a staggering pirouette, his eyeballs rolling up in his skull like cherries on a slot machine. He fell to the floor, his head smacking the coffee table with a crack of either wood or bone, then deflated like an air mattress, flat.

The violence was so quick, Dane saw the furniture run in all directions, then the next thing he knew, Vince was standing over Tony like a maul at the state prison.

A slash of Tony's blood scarred Vince's cheek. He wiped it clear with the bridge of his index.

Tony struggled up on his elbows.

"Get up," Vince snarled the taunt. Jugglers twitched the length of his neck.

Stunned, Tony rolled over, cloudy-eyed, his lip pulped by the shot, blood glistened on his teeth. His tongue clucked the roof of his mouth.

Vince's body tensed. "Come on asshole. You want more?" His words were slaps of anger, but his expression was detached, a slick of cool sheltering indifference.

Tony's hair drew black gashes across his face, his left cheek red with slaps. He was probing his ear with a fingertip as if an ice pick of pain was ringing in its depths. He had a walnut surgically implanted in his temple.

Tony blinked, his eyes trying to focus. Blood flooded his mouth, ran out on his chin. Self-consciously, he palmed his crotch like his fly was open and his privates were showing. "What I do?" he asked.

Dane was stunned, paralyzed by the abruptness, drawn by the savageness, in awe of the violence.

Caught between Vince's legs, Tony began squirming like a claustrophobic buried alive.

The resistance spurred him. Vince grabbed a fistful of Tony's shirt and lifted his chest off the floor, his arm cocked with a knuckle sandwich, cold and dry with no pickle.

Dane lurched forward and pulled Vince off, wrestling him back away.

Arms held from behind by Dane's restraint, Vince's hands were claws splayed in front of his chest. "Let me at him Dane. I'll shell him like a peanut."

"Calm down Vince. Calm down."

"Let go Dane!"

"Not until you calm down."

Tony scrambled like a crab across the floor, bumping into the wall, his eyes panicky.

"Okay." Vince wrenched his shoulder free. "Okay."

He walked off to the windows, then pivoted. He jabbed the air at eye level, pointing two fingers, index and middle, like one wouldn't be enough to get the point across. "It's no use. He pushes me to it. Dammit! Somebody's got to beat some sense into that son of a bitch."

Back to the wall, Tony clambered onto cartoon legs, his self-esteem slurred behind clenched teeth, his lips silently mouthing words of indignation.

Dane got in front of Vince, holding him at bay with palms flat to his chest, theirs a fandango of action-reaction.

Like he was a pesty fly, Vince kept trying to swat Dane's arms away. "Leave me alone, dammit!"

"I will when you calm down. Just walk away, Vince. Walk away."

At length Vince gave up, and paced back to the windows, a panther caged.

Dane sucked in a cold load of air, and the transformation was complete. Somewhere in the middle of all that violence, he'd arrive at his destination. However, conceit had raped his innocence, reducing Blake to shadow.

Dane abandoned his beer, made his way to the bar, grabbed Vince a tumbler and one for himself, filled them with whiskey. He delivered the sedative. "Here. Take this."

Tempered breath waning, Vince's eyes skimmed the turbulent water. He was taking measured shots of whiskey, rocking slightly, lifting the left leg, then the right — a pent-up motion, like he was barefoot in cold muck.

Suddenly, the music died, and the absence left a deadening vacuum as if ear drums had snapped.

Dane looked over his shoulder at Tony, then took a swallow of the whiskey himself, the warm liquid spreading quickly, inducing a brief, spatial calm.

"So, what now? What happens to Tony?"

Vince stared out the window. "Geraci wants him out."

"You mean ..."

"That's right. Dead."

Tony rubbed his neck, cringing, his gray horrified gaze one of a dead man with a shiv in his guts.

"Can't we get Tony out of town?" Dane asked. "At least until Geraci calms down."

"I'll handle Geraci. But I can't have Tony anywhere near Evohl. The problem is, I've got four kilos to distribute, and another shipment coming Thursday. I need you to distribute the coke and meet Evohl for the next shipment."

"And if I don't?"

"It's your loss, Dane. I'll find someone else."

"What about Tony?"

"Tony will get you started. Then he's out."

Dane looked at Tony, suddenly feeling extremely bold, eminently superior.

"So, what's in for me?"

"You'll be compensated nicely."

"Nicely," Dane snickered. "Is that like I get to wash your car and shit like that?"

"Hey! Don't screw with me, Dane. I'm not in the mood."

***

For the next hour, no one said a word, and in the quiet, Dane found truth and fabrication walking around in the back of his mind. He wondered what it would be like to be finally behind the veil. In the past, he'd despised cocaine for the destruction it had caused, but now it was an enchantment that nullified all rational thought. His throat was thick with euphoria and Pharmakeia was the puppet-master swirling above his head.

Finally, mustering enough courage to speak, Tony said weakly, "Vince?"

Over the last hour, mellowed by the narcotic effects of time, Vince had been relieved of his hostility. "Yeah Tony, what is it?"

"Vince, I wish you would let me explain. I got problems. I know that. But I can change, 'cause like I don't want to be cut out. You gotta give me another chance."

"I wish I could Tony. Maybe if we get some time under our belts."

Tony went to the windows. "I can't talk to you," he said to no one in particular, but there was a fear in his voice, his reflection a premonition of one already on the outside looking in.

Vince stood behind him, put his hand on his shoulder. What came next was an odd voice, half whisper, half command, an echo of the inner man buried in the avalanche of power. "Just do as I tell you, Tony, and you'll be fine," Vince said. "It's not like we can go cruising anymore, cranking up Blue Oyster Cult and smoking reefer out of a gas mask. We used to bend the world to fit our way. Things are different now, some things don't bend, and you need to realize that."

Tony took a deep breath, then blew it out as if he knew the party was over. Dane figured he was already daydreaming about Arlene or being a rock star. Neil Young, no-no-wait — Billy Idol.

Confident and willing, Dane gave Vince an obsequious smile. He was in deeper than the Pacific.

CHAPTER 21

Seattle, Washington
November 27, 1995

Tony and Dane sat at the curb in Tony's Prelude under a row of sycamores dripping in a dark and whispery rain. Out of the mist, a gelatinous man approached, lumbering down the sidewalk. He had the gait of a walrus and breath rose from his mouth like the belch of a furnace.

Dane rolled down the passenger window and the big man leaned in on his elbows, the car dipping under his weight. He exhaled, hot and sticky in Dane's face. He had glacial cracks in his tongue. Instinctively, Dane inched away.

The deal was quick — two ounces of blow — but Barry was short two-hundred dollars, had been for four weeks, and Tony was PO'd.

"So, what's it going to be, Barry?" Tony asked.

Barry stuck out his arm, wrist curled, fingers down. A gold bracelet lay over the back of his smooth pigskin hand. "How about this? It's brand new. Fourteen carats. Cost me three-fifty."

"Barry, I told you 'bout that fuckin' bracelet last time. I suggest you strap a catcher's mitt over your butt, 'cause next time I see that bracelet, I'm going to shove it up your ass."

In the end, Barry coughed up the money.

***

Next stop was to the 21st Century, a tattoo parlor, where Randolph Scott, a tattoo artist, lived in a backroom apartment with his mom. He wore a black dew rag and a skull earring and had black images curling up his neck onto his cheeks.

The place was a sty reeking of cat urine, marijuana roaches, and stale beer. There was a kitchen and dining room all-in-one, the living room set off to the side. Two doors led from the living room, probably bedrooms. The kitchen sported worn linoleum tile, grease-dripped cabinets and a water-torture faucet. Next to the kitchen was a bathroom. It had a washer, dryer and a heap of clothes in it. The living room was green shag — matted carpet that hadn't seen a vacuum since the Jurassic Period — and cluttered with furniture Goodwill wouldn't accept. A small brick fireplace with more ash in it than Pompeii blessed one corner, a nineteen-inch Zenith on an empty beer keg blessed another.

The walls were rife with odd crayon stick-figures and swatches of wallpaper. The only framed picture was that of a wolf overlooking a snow-covered valley of fireplace-smoking cabins hanging cockeyed next to the bathroom door.

Dane's first impression: Randolph was psychotic; precisely as Tony had warned: a bi-polar-manic-depressive-schizophrene with a skin disorder. One minute he's smiling at Tony, to himself, then he's staring at Dane, talking about people with rabbit eyes. His x-ray vision focused five feet behind Dane's head.

Randolph stood quickly and walked toward the cupboards. He opened a drawer by the stove, then took off his shirt and started rubbing oil onto his arms, his chest. He was covered with tattoos, a real-life *Illustrated Man.*

"Ma!" Randolph blurted.

A woman, taken with a look of bewilderment, sat on the floor of the living room. She was short and dumpy, with overworked, burnt orange hair. Her skin was as yellow as stone-ground mustard. She had on a faded dress and was sitting with her back to the wall, knees pulled up to her chest, watching reruns of Bonanza. Dane thought she was a pile of laundry until her head jerked.

Randolph called her to her feet, "Ma, get up. Rub this on my back."

The old woman got up off the floor, not gracefully mind you, hitching her dress to her waist and rolling onto her knees, then using furniture for support clambered to her feet. She loaded herself into a pair of furry slippers.

Up close, she was frumpy and fetid. A bona fide county fair champion. Dane imagined five blue ribbons tattooed on her chest. Randolph stuck the bottle of oil in her hand.

"This stinks!" she proclaimed.

"Shuts your nose."

Dane could see the frustration in Tony's eyes. Tony's backpack was on the floor, the flap unbuckled. Sixteen ounces were on the table.

"Hey, I don't want to be rude," Tony said, "but I got other business tonight. And besides, the twenty-mule-team out front looks real fucking eager to snag some blow."

Randolph told his mom to beat it. Then, from the same kitchen drawer that held the oil, he grabbed a stack of bills. Tony thumbed the stack, easily counting the bills like a machine at the bank, then shoved them in his backpack.

It took another twenty minutes for Tony to convince Randolph that Dane wasn't a fed.

***

When they piled into the Prelude, Tony pulled a pistol from under his armpit, concealed inside the familiar tweed jacket. It was the first time Dane had seen him with a gun.

Dane stared at it through a smoke trail; the blued steel gave no hint of reflection.

"Go ahead," Tony said. "Take it."

Dane flicked his cigarette out the window.

Tony laid the pistol in Dane's palm. It felt cogent in his hand. He took a sight down its barrel and mimicked a few shots at a passing vagrant.

"Pretty cool, huh? You gotta get one," Tony said. "Randolph is psycho, and some punks just need to know who's in charge."

"It's a fine piece, Tony," Dane said as he handed it back. The molded grip left his palm clammy, evidence of its insidious charm.

***

Next stop was a grocery store in Bellevue on Bel-Red Road. Bellevue was high end, a respite for the wealthy.

Upon arrival, Tony popped a stick of gum in his mouth and went into the store, carrying a travel mug. The connection's name was Abby, the wife of a surgeon. According to Tony, the drop was genius. Wait for the right moment, then swap travel mugs in her cart. He was now back in the car with a mug full of money.

Dane made a face, both amused and surprised. "She's a housewife?"

"Yep. She told me once she was an ex-chanteuse turned wife and mother." Tony screwed up his face. "Whatever-the-fuck a chanteuse is."

Dane grinned. Having seen the street-side of Tony all evening, it was nice to know that Tony was still simply Tony. "Chanteuse is a French word. It means: A female nightclub singer."

"Well, we both know how good my French is."

"So, what do we do now?"

"Usually I split, but tonight I left her a note taped to the mug. You need to see each other since I'm out. Just like I told Barry and Randolph."

While they waited, he explained how Abby scored for all her housewife friends and that she took all the risk and they benefitted from her generosity, and that she was never short on a payment, and how she had four kids, a dog, three nice rides and a house on the lake, and how she convinced the hubby it was better to shop late at the 24-hour grocery after the kids had crashed.

"I know her brother," Tony said. "He works for the Kirkland Fire Department."

"Sounds like you might have a crush on this chick."

Sticking an accusing finger at his own chest, Tony made a poor attempt at acting shocked. "Me? Shit. I don't crush on no chick."

Tony gazed back at the storefront. His words were in denial, but the look on his face was pure, smitten puppy-dog. "She's good people, Dane," he said.

A few seconds passed, then Tony turned from the window. "Anyway, you got to watch yourself with these assholes. Especially sniffers — glue, paint, their brains are shit ... but not Abby."

Dane nodded without saying a word.

"It's not what ya think, either. I don't want to like do her or nothin'. Not that she isn't nice and all that, but she's gentle. Like a bird. One of those white jobs that do that *drdrdrdrdrrrrr* thing." Tony made a cooing sound, vibrating his tongue.

The action reminded Dane of Tony in the sixth grade. Bird calls and blow-darts were Franklin specialties.

"So why do you do it, Tony? I mean, if you don't like it, why do you keep selling?"

"Ahh, I don't know. I used to get an ounce and sell off enough so I could snort for free. It was the same with all of it: acid, weed, whatever. Remember Pecker Billson? One good eye, bald at sixteen. He used to snag these monkey tranqs at the zoo. At least till he got fired."

Tony hesitated, lost in space. "So, like, what was your question?"

"Why do you do it?"

"I like drugs Dane. Makes the days go by."

"I mean selling. Vince has you pushing a lot of snow. If you don't like it, why don't you quit?"

"I am quit, Dane ... Remember? You's doin' it now."

Dane was taken aback, the revelation hitting him square in the face.

Suddenly, Tony snapped back in his seat. "Hold it. Here she comes." His tone became protective. "Let her look at ya, but don't be gawkin'. It'll scare her."

"Okay Tony. I'll give her my best ephemeral smile."

"I din't say you was trying to pick her up."

Dane grinned. There was no use explaining.

CHAPTER 22

Seattle, Washington
November 28, 1995

Tony and Dane emerged from an alley onto King Street. To the west was the International Church of Elvis, complete with T-shirts and photo ops with the King, and Biosphere 6000, a coin-operated art gallery and dietary breast enlargement center. To the east, prostitutes: women, men, teenagers. Only blocks from I-5, the train station, the Kingdome, and the waterfront docks, it was a carnival of sexual persuasions.

The streets were quiet now as the bottom of the ocean, abandoned except for the hardy, deep-water few. After Abby, they made an eight-ounce delivery to a 7-11 clerk on Alaskan Way. Sweeney was his name. A billiard ball. No hair, no ears, barely coherent. Then they stopped at the downtown bus terminal and left twelve ounces in locker 411. Dane had slipped the small orange key onto his ring. It was now one-twenty-five a.m.

The smell of fermenting garbage was everywhere. Dark puddles splashed beneath their feet. Here old building facades of ornate cast iron had been left to rust, painting a river of orange on the sidewalks.

Across the street was a ten-story tenement, two windows lit, staring out into space like the yellow eyes of a disfigured giant. On the ground floor, next to the Rebellious Shroud (purveyors of goth clothing), was Mary's All Nude Revue.

The marquee was pulsating, advertising the Christmas extravaganza starring Suzie Beaver: *Look What Santa Found Under*

The Mistletoe. Dane followed Tony close on his heels, stalking the shadows with eyes, ears and nose.

Parked thirty-feet from the entrance was a pearlescent black 1934 Panel Delivery, hopped-up for the street, with Cragar mags and wide, low-profile, white-letter T/A radial tires. Windowless except for the required three up front, the rear doors were welded shut and body-shopped smooth. An air-brushed mural covered the expanse, picturing a dark-haired enchantress wearing a sheer lace wedding gown, standing on a molten lake, her breasts and the velvet hinge at the apex of her generously parted legs exposed. Around her, succubi were ascending to a zeppelin with male victims in tow.

In a slow, watchful arc, a black-and-white rounded the corner and parked on the other side of the street, exhaust billowing, a narrow two-lane blacktop of separation.

The policemen stared, cloaked in blue.

Tony nodded his recognition of their power.

The policemen returned the gesture in spades.

"You know those two?" Dane asked, surprised.

"Not by name," Tony remarked.

The policeman riding shotgun fired up a cigarette. He had deceptive eyes under bushy dark brows, and a cheap smile filled with nicotine teeth. The driver had a pencil-thin mustache, the lines of his face gathering at the corners of his mouth in a ganglion of spite.

"Belltown to Central. You'll learn their faces. You'll learn what they want — drugs, money, women — each has their own price."

A Lincoln Mark V sailed by, stereo blasting. The driver was a grainy relic with a mohawk, shaved sideboards, and a steel-brush mustache, the boat riding on a high tide. Slight weave. Excessive speed. The patrol car stormed out in pursuit.

The music faded as the Lincoln floated away, turning the corner two signals down, but out of the beat that lingered, Dane put together the lyrics: Moody Blues, "The Other Side of Life."

With a startle, the door to Mary's flew open and a man in a wheelchair emerged, the dented Sheetmetal-skinned door straining on its hinges.

"Hey-hey Tone," the man said. He was hunched over slightly, propelling the chair with his grip on the handrim at his side. They were angled in for speed and comfort, while two small hard-rubber wheels supported the front of the chair and gave it balance. The chair had a low back, lightweight magnesium frame, and no handles for pushing — a sport model.

"Hey Clayton. How's it hangin'?"

A bag of atrophy from the waist down, Clayton grimaced at the question and flipped Tony off. Then he laughed. A gutty roll that lacked one vital element: a smile.

With physical artistry, he pulled a wheelie as he spun one-eighty, ending up parallel to a sliding door, which had been custom-fitted into the side of the Delivery. He threw Dane a curious eye, said nothing, then unlocked the door.

Clayton had long dishwater-blond hair, and a black beard and mustache meticulously groomed. He wore fingerless leather gloves, one hand supported by a wrist brace, and a tan leather vest over a western shirt. His legs were vacant in his like-new denim pants; his withered thighs strapped to the chair. Rattlesnake cowboy boots set cockeyed on the feet supports. Ingrained on his face was a perpetual frown, his forehead intense and worried, his jaw muscles tight, as if he expected trouble during the second-half of every minute.

Dane tried to ignore the handicap, but it was of no use, and he ended up staring inanely, feeling inadequate and superior at the same time.

Clayton slid open the door, and whatever rue Dane felt because of Clayton's lower body stature was vanquished by an incredible upper body display. Clayton undid his thigh straps, and with one swift motion, his tremendous upper body strength prevailed. He grabbed a brushed aluminum pole, spun from the chair and immediately was sitting on the floor of the

Delivery looking out at Dane and Tony. He picked up his chair, folded it, then stowed it into a slot in the back along the edge.

Clockwise from the slot was a bed that had several pillows on it. Up the far side was a split bench seat upholstered in black button-tucked leather. The driver seat was button-tucked, facing the rear, the passenger seat the same, facing forward.

Using only his hands, Clayton moved with ease across the floor and into the driver's seat. He swiveled the passenger seat around and nodded to it. Dane got in and sat down. Then Tony got in and closed the door. Clayton turned on the dimmed overhead lights.

"You want a beer or something?" Clayton asked as he lifted the section of bench closest to him. Inside was an ice chest, two bottles of hard liquor and a small carved wooden box.

"Yeah," Tony said.

Clayton handed Tony a beer, then looked at Dane, unsmiling, unblinking. "How about you? You want a beer?"

"Sure," Dane said, holding his ground. On the surface, he was disenchanted with Clayton's stare, but under it he felt something familiar, which kept the meddling voices of uncertainty away. "By the way, don't I know you from somewhere?"

"Could be."

Tony choked off his guzzle of beer. "Shit man," he said, looking at Clayton. "This is Dane Avilla. Hell, I din't think of introducing you guys. I thought you knew each other."

Eyes locked on each other, there was a nervous quiet between Clayton and Dane, the odor of a pine tree freshener lingering like a bad dream in the shadows. Dane remembered Clayton being long and lanky, always with a mischievous grin. He looked older now, his face a fist. Existing in the stare was mutual recognition: life had ravaged them both.

"Sorry to hear about Saber," Dane said at last.

It was obvious Clayton had been snorting heavily prior to their arrival. The flaps of his nose were red and swollen. His demeanor was a calculated rage. Clayton tried to hide his anguish under the pretense of an amused grin, but his violent and self-pitying temper was only skin deep and burned red in his eyes like a polluted sun on the horizon.

He looked out the side window. A street punk walked by on the sidewalk, his face angry with zits. He wore a tie-dye sweatshirt with a hood under a leather jacket that has more studs in it than a Michelin snow tire, and more zippers than a dress shop. The hood was off his head, a mound behind his neck as big as Quasimodo's hump.

"Not much to say," Clayton said. "That was one fucked up night. You got my blow, Franklin?"

"Twelve OZ's."

Clayton opened the carved wood box and pulled out an envelope. "Count it. It's all there."

"Naw, I trust you, man."

"By the way, next time I need sixteen. Yakima and Pasco are expanding."

"Ho-ho. Things are dialin' up all over."

"Oh yeah, and that college chickee you sent my way... the one with the tight ass. She's working out fine, too. UW is experiencing a snowstorm."

"All good news. I think we ought to smoke to that," Tony said. "I scored some Thai stick we can Bogart."

Moments later, Tony fired up the joint, and after he took two indulgent puffs, passed it to Clayton.

Just then a dancer came out of Mary's, stood with her back to the wall, shifting from foot-to-foot in her six-inch heels and knee-length coat. She fired up a smoke.

She was gazing into the middle distance. Dane sensed a brushfire was burning behind the façade.

"She must be pissed about something," Clayton remarked. "The way she's smoking, tobacco stocks have bumped four points in the last twenty seconds."

Clayton took a pull, then gagged down a toke as he handed Dane the joint. "Did you see my girl?" he said in a voice that sounded like it had been squeezed from a balloon.

"Girl?" Dane responded before he took a drag.

Clayton let out his breath. "Circe. She's a goddess of sorcery, or Pharmakeia."

Dane shook his head while holding in his toke.

"She's painted on the back of the van."

"Oh yeah, we saw her," Tony piped up. "Nice looking patch."

"I met her the night Saber died," he said, his mouth holding a raw, honest look. "On the road to Avondale."

Dane let out his smoke and Tony and he exchanged puzzled glances.

"She was there?" Dane asked with an air of incredulity.

"Damn straight. I was laying out in the field. Couldn't move, but my eyes and ears were working fine. She was talking to Saber in the car."

"No fuck?" Tony said.

"Yeah fuck," Clayton said. "She looked just like the mural. Fucking nice. And she had a voice that was as smooth as that college babe's ass."

"Where is she now?" Dane asked, feeling power like a brooding wind blow through the Delivery.

"All around, man. She is skilled in the magic of transmutation, illusion, and necromancy. I went to a psychic, and she filled me in. Then I looked her up myself on the Internet."

"What's all that shit mean: Trans-Mutant-Negro-Nancy?" Tony asked.

"It means she can alter her appearance and conjure spirits of the dead to perform magic," Dane said.

"No shit." Tony took a hit, then passed the Thai stick to Clayton.

Clayton rolled the joint between his fingers. "She told Saber he'd ventured onto the highway to hell. He thought it was his mom."

"What'd he do?" Tony asked.

"Shit man, he died," Clayton said before taking a drag.

"Well, that don't sound cool. Sounds like this bitch is weird."

"Enough," Clayton bellowed. Anger brought a blue vein to Clayton's forehead. "I've said enough. I can feel Saber creeping in on me. Pulling me close to the ground."

"Gees Clayton!" Tony spouted off. "You on some kind of windowpane? Whatever it is, I want some. You's talkin' like Walter Shakespeare or somethin'."

"Hey, blow me Franklin."

"So why'd you paint her on your van?" Dane asked calmly, trying to get Clayton back on the subject.

He handed Dane the smoke. Took a deep breath, then said without compunction, "Simple. Sorcery is Pharmakeia. Pharmakeia is drugs. I love drugs. I love Circe. Long as she's around, she'll keep me coming back to the altar."

"You mean as long as her spirit is present, you can never kick the addiction?"

"That's right. She won't let me. But who wants to? Addiction is the only hobby I got."

"So, you want her around," Dane said. It wasn't a question, more a fact.

"Fuck yeah. She's seductive, erotic, irresistible. I don't even have words, but when I'm high, she comes and straddles me with those hips...it's like an avalanche breaks free."

"For real?" Tony said.

"Real enough. Look at me. I can't get my rocks off."

"Don't be embarrassed," Tony said, like an apology.

Clayton chuckled as he massaged his thigh. "Embarrassed?" He stared at Tony, then Dane, then said, "You try pissing in a bag, uncorking your ass each morning so you can take a shit. I'd say I'm past embarrassed."

Poignant words from a pusher sitting in a demonic van next to a strip joint in a dark part of town. Dane took a pull of his beer and felt nothing. His life was blurring into one big hodgepodge of nonsense. "Does she talk to you?" he asked. Nonsense or not, he wanted to know.

"Damn straight. And she talks to you too. Otherwise, you wouldn't be in my van smoking dope and selling coke. You just don't know it. But man, I'm telling you. If you dial into what she's offering, she'll take you into the Orgasmatron, a universe of sex and ecstasy where all those chicks like Aphrodite hang out. You can't get that in the physical."

Dane said nothing, petrified like a man with his head in a noose, waiting for the floor to drop out.

CHAPTER 23

Seattle, Washington
December 15, 1995

Dane woke face down in bed, swimming in a pool of sweat, struggling to break free from the sanguine visions of a malicious coke dream.

He rolled to his feet and started making connections in the enigmatic region at the edge of sleep. The nightmare exploded. He was alone. In his apartment.

He took off his T-shirt and wiped his underarms with it. The clock showed six p.m., straight up and down. It'd been weeks since Dane's first night with Tony learning the ropes, even longer since he'd seen Erin, except those few times in passing at the office, those days when he made it to work.

***

A shower later, Dane made his way to Nick's Coney Island (a run-down hole-in-the-wall beer-joint-restaurant that had to be the original in-your-face sports-bar with a twenty-seven-inch Magnavox tuned permanently to ESPN), covering the ten blocks at a clandestine pace, keeping to the darker side of the darkest streets, a careful eye peeled over his shoulder. He sat in the back along the wall in a vinyl booth.

The waitress, named Deanna, a comely brunette with a confident smile, approached, took his order, administered a cup of coffee, then retreated to the kitchen.

Nick's had an obnoxious bell that rang anytime someone entered the establishment. The sound would almost make you bite your tongue. The bell went off and Dane jerked a look at the door. His brain went tilt. Nose and Popeye. He instantly huddled over his coffee like a fugitive on the run.

Popeye wasted no time. He walked right up to Dane's table and sat down, sliding in across from him, wearing gray Dockers and a light-blue ski jacket. Nose wore a trench coat over gray slacks and pulled up a chair at the end.

"Do you mind?" Dane said. "I'm eating alone."

Popeye forked a smoke and shrugged, waving his cigarette hand. "Don't mind us. We thought you could use the company."

Nose followed suit like a trained monkey and lit up. Only he smoked Marlboro instead of Pall Mall.

"Who are you guys? You don't think I know that you've been following me?"

"Oh, we know plenty about you, Avilla. Everything, including your dress size." Popeye pulled his identification. "I'm Derek Virchow and this is Special Agent Paul Bradley."

Bradley flashed his badge, then slipped it away, quickly checking down his shoulder at the rest of Nick's to see if anyone had paid particular attention.

Dane was relieved and angry at the same time. He felt no imminent danger — supposedly they were the good guys — but they'd scared Tyra, scared him. They merited a little consternation. So, he got cocky because they deserved to talk to a cocky malcontent.

Holding his coffee cup in a clasp of hands, Dane's forearms laid flat on the table. He threw a hitchhiker's thumb at Bradley. "So, if he's *special*, what are you?" he quipped.

Virchow had taken a mammoth suck off his cigarette. "Super special," he said, stretching his neck, exhaling an immense cloud that formed a low-pressure frontal system along the ceiling.

"Well, I know I'm not as special as you FBI types, but can I make a teensy-weensy suggestion?"

"Go ahead."

"You need to budget some funds to get this guy a nose job. It's probably the only man-made object besides the Great Wall of China that is visible from outer space. He couldn't sneak up on Al Capone, and rumor has it he's been dead since 1947."

Deanna waltzed back to the table. "You two want coffee?"

"Yes, please, with cream," Derek said, flipping over his cup. "Bradley?"

"Thank you. I'll have a cup of decaf, with cream, and five lumps of sugar."

Deanna was pouring Derek's cup. "Sugar and cream are on the table. I'll have to get the decaf."

"Why don't you just order a Seven-up and get it over with," Dane cracked.

Deanna sped to the counter, grabbed the decaf and Dane's order. She slid a coney and macaroni salad in front of Dane and filled Bradley's cup.

"So, what can I do for you?" Dane said.

Derek had abandoned his cigarette to the ashtray. He was holding his coffee cup up to his lips with both hands, elbows on the table. "A little birdy told me you were a friend of Vince Spinetti."

"So, what of it?"

Derek slurped loudly, eyes wincing. The coffee was molten lava. "I've checked you out, Avilla. You're not his type. So, what gives?"

"He's an old friend."

"Naw-aw-aw," Derek drawled, setting his cup down on the table. "This goes deeper than that." He reached under his jacket to his shirt pocket and threw a three-by-five glossy of Tyra on the table — new haircut and all.

Dane peered down at the photo. He ate a fork load of macaroni attempting to conceal his nervousness.

"I can tell you're frustrated. I know you're on a mission and it's not going as planned. It's like that girl in high school. The one with a steel trap for a bra. You can't get your hand under it and the clasp is equipped with a four-tumbler combination."

"This is a joke, right?" Dane circled his index, pointing at his temple like he was winding up a string, setting a clock, or dialing a rotary phone with no finger-hook.

"You're crazy. I don't know what you're talking about."

Virchow looked at Dane with no friendliness in his eyes. "We know all about you, Tony Franklin, Spinetti, Geraci, long-gone-buddy Hanson."

"You guys know nothing," Dane remarked. "Otherwise, you wouldn't be here talking to me." Dane made a move, done talking, headed for the street.

Virchow's hand darted out like a snake snaring Dane's wrist. "I don't think you know what you've stepped in, Avilla."

Dane stopped, one leg in the aisle.

"Calm down," Virchow said. "You smoke, right? Have a cigarette. By the time the smoke is over, if you're not comfortable, I'll leave."

Dane looked at Virchow, then at Bradley.

Bradley winked at the suggestion and tapped his hard pack against his index knuckle, smooth white cylinders of tobacco emerging.

Dane hesitated, then pulled a smoke from the pack.

"That's better." Virchow flicked his lighter. An orange-tipped blue flame wavered.

Dane leaned into Virchow's cupped hands for a light, then collapsed back against the seat.

There was silence while Virchow lit up another cigarette from the butt in his mouth and stabbed out what curiously looked like a roach in the ashtray. All the while, Bradley kept moving his hands and adjusting his tie.

Virchow let out a sighing lungful of carcinogens. "Let's talk."

Dane looked at Bradley, then back to Virchow. "I feel out-numbered."

Virchow and Dane locked eyes in silent concentration, until finally Virchow said quietly, "Bradley, take a seat by the door."

Bradley's head started bobbing like a seismograph needle during the Big One. A good little soldier that Bradley. Snuffing out his butt in the ashtray, he looked thoughtful for a moment, like he wanted to say something, then went away without saying a word.

Dane took a calming pull on the Marlboro. "It's your show," he said on the exhale. He held the cigarette up, the filter buried in a tripod of thumb and fingers like a tiny white flagpole burning. "There's only three-quarters left. You'd better start."

"Okay ... Spinetti's a drug dealer. Franklin's his main mule and Geraci's the goose that laid the golden egg."

"So, if you know so much, why don't you arrest them?"

"Spinetti's not dumb and Geraci's slipperier than snot on the end of your finger. We've got plenty on Franklin, but we want the big boys."

"What do you need me for?"

"I don't need you, Avilla. This is a courtesy call. I'd hate to see someone as squeaky clean as you get hit by flying debris."

"Oh, I get it. This visit is out of the kindness of your heart. I'm touched. Deeply touched." Dane crept low in his seat, trying not to crack a smile at his own wit.

Virchow's face coiled into a fist. "Okay smarty-pants. Bottom line. You either tell me what you know or go down with the rest."

"I can't help you," Dane said.

Virchow flicked an ash. "Friends. This is about friends, isn't it? It's like holding a tit for the first time. You don't want to let go."

Dane remained quiet. A smirk rising on his lips.

Heat rose in Virchow's neck. He began pacing, sitting down. "Listen, forget what you think you know, Avilla. I want you to back away from this."

Dane took a complacent drag, letting Virchow cool his heels. "You ever back away Virchow? You don't seem the type."

The question made Virchow think. He rolled his cigarette between his thumb and forefinger, staring at the rising stream.

"But you want me to."

Virchow laughed, buried his cigarette with its comrade, then brushed his hands together over the ashtray as if pieces of tobacco had stuck to them. Or was he a modern-day Pontius Pilate? "You're in over your head, Avilla."

"Maybe."

Virchow possessed a certain calmness in his voice. "What is it? You got a wild hair about Hanson. This isn't a game of pin the tail on the donkey."

Suddenly, the thought of the FBI on his case dampened his attitude. Dane administered a puff of courage. "Sorry Virchow. Vince recently hired me into a cushy position. Besides, I need the job. I have several bartenders around town depending on me for support. By the way, what makes you think I won't tell Spinetti about our little meeting?"

"Simple ... you want something, Avilla. Why else hide the girl?"

Dane chewed it over but gave no answer.

"You know, there's one other option here we haven't discussed."

"And what might that be?"

"I need someone under the sheets."

For a moment Dane thought about what he'd gotten himself into. It wasn't exactly where he thought he'd be at this point in his life. He never dreamed of being a drug dealer. Major League Baseball pitcher was a dream, engineering was a reality, but the here-and-now had slipped in so easily. Vince and Tony were not squeaky clean, he knew that, but the thought of driving nails in their coffins made him seasick. It was like trying to decide whether to cut off your arm because it was caught in a trap, or to take your chances to see if someone would show up before you starved to death.

"I'll take it under consideration."

"Don't wait too long. The offer has an expiration date."

Dane felt a vial in his pocket, hard like a forty-five-caliber cartridge. He'd been cast as the hare, Virchow the tortoise, and he knew all too well the moral of the story. "When's that?"

"When I get tired of waiting."

CHAPTER 24

Seattle, Washington
December 16, 1995

Dane dressed quickly, gave his teeth the once over, then ran a brush through his hair. While he was at Nick's the night before, Bobby had left him a phone message — two, in fact. They agreed to meet at Maxine's at eight in the morning.

Bobby and Tyra were waiting at a table inside, Tyra warming her hands around a mug of hot coffee.

Dane sat down across from them. He looked at Bobby, then Tyra. "Have you ordered?"

"Just coffee," Bobby answered. He waved his hand at the waitress.

Maxine's was packed, a mix of blue, white and no collar workers.

Charlene bopped up to the table, her usual mien of spunk and spice. "What's-your-order? Hey, look what the cat drug in. Still one step ahead of the opposition?"

Dane chuckled.

Bobby and Tyra stared. First at them, then at each other.

Dane caught their dilemma. "Char and I go way back." He looked at Charlene. "Did we decide I could call you Char?"

"You call me anything you want, Honey. Just call me tonight," she said, then shrieked with a laugh.

From the kitchen, the cook yelled, "Charlene! Number nine. Pigs in a blanket."

"Okay Stan," she called back. Then, under her breath, she said, "Idiot must've got his Jockey's shrunk in the dryer. He's been after my butt all morning. You kids want to order? Or should I come back?"

The three of them looked at each other, then Dane ordered first, Bobby second, and Tyra finished with a strawberry waffle.

Dane put a hand on Charlene's forearm. "Lots of coffee. I need lots of coffee."

"Okay Honey," she said, pushing the pad into her apron pocket. "I'll be back with the mud in a minute."

With Charlene gone, an anxious hush befell the table. Dane felt Tyra was receptive, but big-brother–Bobby reeked argumentative.

Finally, Tyra broke the silence. "How've you been?" she said in a voice that carried a hint of criminality, emerging from the same place where spite and malice also fester.

"Not too bad," he replied. "How've you been?"

"Good," Tyra said. "Bobby and Natalie have been ..."

"The only ones around," Bobby jumped in.

"Don't get on me, Bobby. I've been busy."

"Too busy to call?"

"Stop it," Tyra protested. "We came here to have a nice breakfast."

Bobby's face was turning red. He took off his cap, and his scalp was already carmine with frustration. "Maybe you came here to have a *'nice breakfast'*, but I came here to get some answers."

The conversation went quiet again, each sipping their coffee in contemplation until Charlene delivered the food and a comment. "It never surprises me," she said to Bobby's red face. "Nobody can piss me off more than a good friend."

Having said her "peace," she ripped the ticket from her pad and slipped it face down on the table. "Looks like we need more coffee," she observed, and left.

Once again, quiet hung over the table like an ominous cloud, and in the black silence, they ate until every morsel was finished. In the aftermath, coffee was administered in sips. Charlene kept it coming, just as she'd promised.

"What 'opposition' was Charlene talking about?" Bobby asked at last.

"Some cops wanted to talk to me about Vince."

"What'd you tell them?"

"Nothing."

"About the same as you've told us."

"C'mon Bobby. Lay off. I've told you all I know."

"That's BS, Dane."

Dane shrugged his shoulders and chuckled like Bobby was ignorant.

"Tell him Tyra," Bobby demanded. "Maybe he'll listen to you."

Dane looked at Tyra with accusing eyes.

Tyra stared back without saying a word.

"See," Dane smirked at Bobby.

Then Tyra spoke up, breaking her reticence in Bobby's defense. Deep down, maybe in Dane's defense too, "You *have* changed Dane. That first day we all were together, you were so happy to see Bobby, you were happy to be with me, and together we were going to find out what happened to Blake. But something has changed. I know you didn't start out to do it this way, but all we want to do is help you."

"I've told you before," Dane came back. "Vince had nothing to do with Blake's death. And as far as the business ..."

"Business," Bobby snapped. "So that's what you call it."

"Vince isn't doing anything that a thousand other guys aren't doing every day."

"Oh, so that makes it right. Sorry, Dane. Wrong is wrong and right is right."

"Dammit Bobby. You're so righteous."

"Screw this. I don't need this," Bobby said. Until now, his voice had only tapped the ceiling. Now the roof was in jeopardy. "I thought you were Blake's friend. I thought you were going to take this to the end. Isn't that what you said? You said we were partners too, but I guess you were just shining us on."

"I am not," Dane said in defensive, his voice decibels higher. "I told you ..."

Suddenly Charlene interrupted, speaking in a forceful whisper as she gave Dane and Bobby a twisted eye of reproach. "You boys want to keep it down to a dull roar over here. Not everybody wants to hear about all your damn problems."

So astutely pointed out by Charlene, their lack of civility became an embarrassment. "Okay-okay," Dane and Bobby said in reluctant unison.

Charlene refilled their cups with coffee, and without a further mention left.

After her departure, Dane went on in a lowered voice, "I told you, Bobby. Vince had nothing to do with it. He's a friend."

Even whispering, Bobby's words came across as a shout. "Oh, so that's it. Vince is a friend. Well, I'll tell you what Dane Avilla: friends like Vince Spinetti you don't need. He's not the Vince Spinetti you knew years ago, and you know it."

"That's who I am, Bobby. You don't give up on friends unless they give up on you. Besides," Dane said caustically, "Virchow can't make a move until he gets someone on the inside."

"Virchow? Who's Virchow?"

"I told you about him, Bobby ... him and Nose, or Bradley, or whatever his name is."

"Nose?" Tyra said.

"You've said nothing about a 'Virchow,'" Bobby said. "And the last I heard, you didn't know who 'Nose' was."

"You've seen Nose?" Tyra asked, dismayed.

Dane started fumbling back through the pages of his coke-distorted memory. He was sure he'd mentioned them before.

"So, Virchow and Bradley is it? They're the cops?" Bobby asked.

"FBI," Dane responded.

"FBI!" Bobby shrieked, then he looked around Maxine's, seeing if anyone had heard him. He lowered his voice again to a whisper. "Let's start over. You've met *'The Nose'*," — Bobby over-emphasized the nickname with a sardonic twist — "and he's FBI."

"Why didn't you tell me?" Tyra asked.

"I just found out," Dane said, trying to regroup.

Tyra blinked her eyes in astonishment. "I've been sneaking around all this time and he's FBI?"

Dane spoke to her. "I didn't know Tyra. Until yesterday."

"When were you going to tell us?" Bobby asked with a chuckle under his breath. "Or do you need a snort first?"

"Shut up, Bobby. For once, just shut up and I'll tell you. These guys are not a problem."

"Not a problem," Tyra and Bobby came back in unison.

"No. They're not," Dane said forcefully. "They want information on Vince, and I wouldn't give it to them."

"Are you stupid?" Bobby kept hammering away. "They'll arrest you."

"Bobby, they want Vince. More likely Geraci. Not me. They're Feds. They want kingpins and mobsters. Guys that will put the Feds on the front page, headlines; red, white and blue talking points. They don't want to deal with street punks. They leave those for the local yocals to shove around."

"Street punks," Bobby said. "You mean like you?"

A tinderbox ignited in Dane's chest and raged up his neck.

"You're a fool, Dane," Bobby added. "Dumber than Blake ... if that's possible."

Tyra sat dumbfounded, shaking her head in blue disbelief.

In the back of his mind, Dane knew Bobby was right, but his reasoning was clouded. He'd ventured into a world he thought he could handle, but somewhere along the way he'd gotten sucked in, and though he'd deny it, he was running in waist-deep water, growing tired and getting nowhere towards his initial goal.

"Look Dane," Bobby tried to reason with him. "I'm only trying to save you from yourself." He looked sidelong at Tyra. "Blake couldn't see through Vince either." Then he paused, refocusing his attention on Dane. He scratched his cheek. "Why don't you let us help you?"

Dane was thinking privately that Bobby was a jerk. Resorting back to the con, Dane thought he could smooth Bobby's feathers with more smoke and mirrors. "I'll handle it, Bobby," he said with all the shrewd politeness of a slick politician.

"What about Blake?" Tyra asked. "I thought we started all this to find out about Blake."

Dane looked at Tyra with conciliation in his eyes. "I'm sorry, Tyra. We may never know the truth about what happened to Blake."

"So you're giving up," Bobby alleged.

Dane was getting bored with the accusations. He had just tried to be nice. In Bobby's immortal words: "Screw this." He wanted a line.

"And what about all the coke you're doing?" Bobby said.

You want the truth. Close-but-no-cigar. Dane grinned with impudence. "Bobby, you don't know nothing. I don't even really like it. I just use it for a boost sometimes. Look, I've been working super hard. Engineering isn't like running a tackle shop."

The ridicule cut deep. Bobby looked at Tyra with wounded astonishment, then focused back on Dane. "I feel like I'm talking to a wall," he said. "We can see it in your eyes, Dane. You say you despise the drug, but your pomposity has erected a monument to its power. You're not fooling anyone."

Dane shook his head in disbelief, his eyes closing as if to erase what he'd just heard.

Bobby gazed at Tyra, regret welling in his eyes. "He's bored with us, Tyra. The whole time we've been here, he's had that look. Like how I feel when I go clothes shopping with Natalie. Now I know what she goes through as I hang on the clothes racks in sheer boredom, and I don't like it one bit."

First Erin, then Virchow, now Bobby and Tyra, Dane was burning all his bridges. Bobby got up and left, and not knowing what else to do, Tyra followed, looking back.

CHAPTER 25

Seattle, Washington
December 17, 1995

The sunrise streamed in through the office windows, casting long shadows across the face of its walls, leaving dark images on the floor like Nagasaki or Hiroshima.

Erin picked up the stack of paper from the corner of the desk, bound them with a thick rubber band, and loaded them into her knapsack. Weeks had passed; this was the last run. She took one more look around, pointing with her hand, as she mentally checked off the list: file cabinets, desk, computer.

Erin slung the knapsack over her shoulder. There was nothing else, and so, with her mind clear that she'd done her best, she headed for the door. As a reward, she laid on a track of raspberry lip gloss. The air became sweet with its touch.

With only a few steps toward freedom, Vince's computer called her back. It made a ding. A diminutive sound with a ponderous effect. E-mail. She stopped, her head cocking to the side in spurred thought. Faintly she could hear the hard drive paging. She stepped closer, back to the desk. The computer screen was blank except for Vince's screen saver — Johnny Castaway searching for a rescue ship — but the LEDs were flashing erratically, red on the hard drive, yellow and green on the modem.

Overwhelmed with a sense of foreboding, she suddenly felt ticked at the world. She was done. She had put on her lip gloss. Yet vines of chicanery pulled her into Vince's chair, her knapsack dropping to the floor in purblind motion.

Each week she backed up Vince's hard drive onto one Derek had supplied, but Vince, the consummate gamesman, had meticulously kept his E-mail clean, reading, then deleting, most likely with the aid of a digital destroyer.

The PC set at an angle on the desk. She moved the mouse and Johnny disappeared, revealing a wallpaper of Budweiser Girls lying on a beach towel, three across, the words: Bud — wei — ser, spelled out across their waists. Located across the bottom of the screen were many icons. The Email icon had a letter in it.

To access the email, she'd need to enter the computer password into a box that hovered in the center of the screen. Below the box, a message read: "Please enter your eight-digit password."

Erin looked to the ceiling, searching her mind for words Vince would use. "Asshole," she said out loud. An amusing thought, but that was only seven letters.

She put an elbow to the desk and tapped her lips with her forefinger, thinking. She found the word "engineer". "E-n-g-i-n-e-e-r," she whispered, counting each letter as she typed them in. She hit "Enter." The computer spit back another message: "Access denied."

She knew the software would probably only give her one or two more chances, then the computer would lock her out. If that happened, Jenna Rowaite, S.H.E.'s system analyst, would get involved. Only she had the access and know-how to bypass passwords and unlock the whole mess if Erin jammed it up.

'Spinetti', that has eight. Sweat was running down her ribs. She heard a click and fired a look at the doorway. She felt a foreboding, like the prickle on your back when eyes are upon you, or the fleeting reflection of a shadow in the corner of your eye. But nothing came.

After a dozen raucous heartbeats, she concluded she had imagined the sound, or was some piece of office equipment turning on or off.

Still on the tip of her tongue, she typed in the letters, s-p-i-n-e-t-t-i, then punched "Enter" with a resounding stiff finger. Again, the computer spit back the message: "Access denied." Only this time, a second line appeared: "You have one grace login left."

Was it worth it? Taking a chance at a password for a message that could be as mundane as Joe Blow from Such-and-Such Company requesting So-and-So to do this-or-that. Or might it be important? She kicked back in the chair and started playing "Chopsticks" with her forefingers in a slow recital along the edge of the desk.

Finally, she rose to a conclusion. If she screwed up, she'd contact Jenna, make up some phony excuse — she was, after all, Vince's secretary — and have Jenna fix the problem before Vince came back to the office. He was scheduled out until Thursday. Plenty of time for Jenna to work her magic.

She looked to the door again in case she'd been wrong and now Freddy Kruger was standing there — the strong silent type with razor blade hands. Still nothing.

She put her head down. "Predator," that has eight. She chuckled to herself, shoulders jiggling. Vince was a predator, but he wouldn't use that for a password. He'd use "sexyhunk," or "machoman," or "immastud." She giggled to herself. He thinks he's so cool. "Bigprick" was her overall favorite.

Elbows to the desk, she tented her hands while her eyes floated from side to side. What could it be? Then, right in front of her, hanging on the wall in a black frame, was her answer. Sure. His pride and joy. His showy piece of materialism for all the world to see: the *Ecstasea.*

Why not? She decided and typed: e-c-s-t-a-s-e-a. Then she hesitated for a second on keying in the "Enter," considering her choice one last time, but when she did, the box disappeared.

Erin's eyes sparkled with elation. She marshaled her shoulders forward, her body angled over the desk, her face glued to the screen. She clicked the Email icon.

The message was from NJG Associates. A company she wasn't familiar with, nor had seen in any of the files. She clicked on the name, and the message came into view. It was a short cryptic message, two sentences with no sign-off. It read: "Contractor to be terminated. Project timelines will not be affected."

Thoughts of what the words could mean were racing through her suspicion like a commuter train. Her heart quivered. Her hands were sweating. She pulled down a menu, and with a click of the mouse, she sent the E-mail to the printer. Either way, substantial or not, she'd give it to Derek to decide.

Behind her on a walnut table, a laser printer fired up like a miniature turbo-prop jet preparing for take-off. Her freedom was seconds away. She closed the message; the words shrinking instantly to the mailbox. Then, with another click of the mouse, she shrank the mailbox back to a small icon at the bottom of the Budweiser screen. The little envelope was gone from the slot, but it was minor. No one would ever know of her access. She'd step out to her desk and, in seconds, send Vince a message, something bogus, enough to put a letter back in the slot. And then everything — everything would be as before.

Then keys rattled, the sound a sudden threat to her ears. Someone was coming in. She checked the desk clock: 7:45. Her mind screamed: Who in hell is coming here at 7:45 on Sunday morning?

Erin shot for the office door, closed it to a crack, and with a furtive glance through the side glass of the entrance, she could see Vince bending over to pick up his keys; hot coffee in one hand, a newspaper wedged under his arm, a briefcase set on the concrete beside him.

As Erin raced back to the desk, she heard the lock rattle again. This time with success. She stood in horror looking at the Budweiser Girls, knowing that it would be seconds before Johnny would reappear.

Erin stepped back, looked down muddled, and upon seeing it, lifted her knapsack to her shoulder. She had to escape. But how? She opened the office door.

Vince saw her at a distance, eyes widening at first recognition, then narrowing to focus. "Erin? What are you doing here?" he said.

Erin wanted to ball up like a potato bug, but it would be of no use. He'd squash her as simply as snuffing out a cigarette. "Work," she said, as it was the only thing that came to mind.

"Work? What work?"

In the corner of her eye, Johnny had not yet reappeared. "I had some typing to do." She stepped forward slowly from the doorway, keeping her body as a shield between Vince and the computer screen. "The report to Union Camp you wanted sent on Monday. I ... I didn't finish it on Friday."

Vince moved from the entrance, watchful and predatory as he moved closer, slow like he knew what was up.

Erin panicked, fluttering like a dove with a wing full of birdshot, and struggled for more words as she moved toward him, trying to keep his view of the screen at a distance. Suddenly she found the words. Words that left the taste of vinegar in her mouth even before she'd said them.

"Vince, you know," she said, sliding up in front of him. "I'm glad you're here, and we're alone. I've been trying to deny it, but I'm attracted to you. More than I thought possible." She administered a teasing smile. "Dane is a boy when it comes to sex."

She put a palm flat on his chest. It felt despicable to touch him, but time was crucial. "I want a real man to make love to me. Someone who can teach me something. I hate always having to lead the way."

Vince's eyes gleamed with conceit. He took a cool drink of his hot coffee, then brushed by her, downing the last of his coffee on the way to the desk. He chucked the cup in the trash.

Erin turned in shock at what she expected him to see.

Vince set the briefcase down behind his chair and tossed the newspaper onto the desk. He curled a finger at her, summoning her to his office.

Erin inched toward him. Next to Vince, Johnny was back, searching the distant waters with his giant eyeglass. She breathed a sigh of relief, letting the knapsack slide from her shoulder.

Immediately, he grabbed her by the back of the neck and kissed her violently. She wanted to heave, but held back. She could surrender her body, but it wouldn't be love. Like a pro, she responded to his lips, pulling at his sleeves.

He slid a hand to her breast and squeezed, her nipple found by his thumb under the thin shield of her athletic bra.

Erin knew the moves. She'd learned her previous trade well and fell back into its clutches with purpose. She undid his belt, then the zipper of his slacks, finding his manhood with her probing fingers.

Vince maneuvered her toward the desk. He pushed her down onto the hard surface, shoving the newspaper and other desk paraphernalia to the computer end.

Once on the desk, Erin resigned herself to the fact he would have her — physically, but not mentally. A stunning actress, she tore the kerchief from her hair and threw it to the floor as if her hair burned with passion. She shook her head brazenly, fanning the flames.

Vince hooked his thumbs over the waist of his slacks and pushed them down with his underwear. His dagger emerged. She tried, but couldn't look at him. She rolled her head to the side, and trembled at the sight, her eyes finding the email, waiting face-down in the printer tray. Russian roulette: that email put a bullet in her cylinder.

Vince was groping and grunting. She had to maneuver. He had her jogging pants pulled off one ankle, his body wedged between her knees, kissing her neck, pulling her panties to the side.

She tried to sit up, but he was too strong and held her down. His fingers were everywhere, places she didn't want him to be. His invasion sent a shock straight up her spine, and she cried out. Vince responded with a primal grunt and heavy breathing.

She forced herself up on one elbow. "Oh baby," she said. "Let me take over."

Vince groaned, but never let up.

She had only seconds before the grotesque invasion would escalate, her mind suddenly decisive of what she had to do. She pried his arms loose with more gentle urgings.

Vince pulled back and let her up. Erin turned him around by the shoulders, then began unbuttoning his shirt, kissing his neck, his chest, his abdomen as she worked her way down.

Vince eased with what he thought was coming. He set his buttocks firm on the edge of the desk, leaning back on his palms. His eyes closed; his head rolled backwards.

That's when she hit him.

Looking from beneath the awning of an eyebrow, she spied the desk clock, the pen and pencil set, the telephone, the green-shaded desk lamp. She grabbed the paperweight inscribed with Vince's name, and as he writhed, lost in animal beginnings, she slammed it into his temple.

Vince rolled off the desk, stunned, bouncing off his chair, landing flat on his chest.

Erin scrambled, pulling on her pants, snatching her knapsack from the floor, and as she exited the front door of S.H.E., she saw Vince on his hands and knees, crawling to the door of his office, screaming her name.

CHAPTER 26

Seattle, Washington
December 17, 1995

It was three in the afternoon, and as soon as Dane came through the door to the Main Salon he knew someone was wallowing in drink, for the smell of scotch lay thick in the wind.

Vick was there, casually stunning, wearing black stretch stirrup pants and a bulky Donna Karan sweatshirt. She had a delightful smile on her face.

Vince, however, was in an untied bath robe, bare-chested, wearing a pair of black silk boxers underneath. He had a snarl on his face that either came from pain or anger, or both.

Dane went straight to the refrigerator and grabbed a beer.

Vick kissed Vince on the cheek, then exited for the dock. Vince had given her a wad of money and was letting her use the Porsche to go shopping.

"Where've you been?" Vince asked, a slur in his voice.

"I went out for breakfast and took a drive. I got back an hour ago and caught your message. What's up? You sounded urgent."

Vince held his mussed hair out of the way, angled his head, and showed Dane the yellowish-brown egg on his temple. "This is what's up. I frigging got mugged."

Dane came closer. "Wow. Where'd it happen?"

There was a mirror of coke on the table. Vince leaned over and dished out two lines. He took one himself and slid the mirror toward Dane. "Have some," he suggested.

Dane set his beer on the coffee table. He took the tooter from Vince and then waited for a reply, a quizzical look in his eyes.

"This morning at the office," Vince said, then hesitated, as if the coke was neutralizing the scotch, clearing the smog away like a stiff breeze. "I caught Erin in the safe. She got away with almost twenty grand."

"Erin," Dane yipped. "You're joking."

"No, unfortunately I'm not."

"Well, go on," Dane requested. He took a toke, then slid the mirror back to Vince.

Vince followed suit. Then, as he was rubbing the leftover onto his gums, he began recounting the events at the office, "I saw the safe was open. Then out of nowhere WHAM! she hit me with a paperweight. When I woke, she'd split with the cash."

Something didn't add up, and Dane wondered what web of deception was being spun in his regard. Erin was not a thief.

Vince fingered his cheek, his nose. "I think my face caught the chair on the way down."

A seagull dipped down to the level of the windows, soaring on an invisible cushion of air. Dane downed a swig of beer, rubbed his knuckles along his jaw. Vince was quick. Even as a child. Used to tick off Dane's father the way Vince could make up alibis so fast. Traversing his stories was like walking through a minefield. You had to be judicious with each step. "So, what are you going to do?"

"I thought you might know where she is."

"Why don't you call the police?"

"I don't want Erin in trouble. I just want my money back."

"Well, I guess I could drive by her apartment."

"Please do. If I get the police involved, who knows where it could lead?" Vince said. He got up off the couch and stumbled over the corner of the coffee table.

Dane jumped up and caught him, grabbing his upper arm and opposite shoulder. "You okay?"

"Yeah-yeah," Vince said, trying to steady his near empty drink. "Frigging knot on my head won't let up." He found his way to the bar, relying on the furniture, and poured another. Once he had his glass full, he staggered back to the couch.

Vince pulled a Playboy to his lap and started leafing through the pages. "I probably should have McTarnihan find Erin," he said at last.

From his chair, Dane could see Lake Washington's skin quivering. He let out a ruminating exhale. "Let me find her."

"Might be better if Mac takes over. I know you have strong feelings for Erin."

Dane's mind was working double time. He wanted Erin's side of the story first-hand. He stole a drink from his beer. "I do. But what she did is wrong, for whatever reason."

Vince started mindlessly flipping through the pages of the magazine. He had a grin on his face like a Cheshire cat.

"What's so funny?"

"Oh nothing. It's just every time I think of McTarnihan, I have to laugh. He's such a cornball."

"If he's such a cornball, why do you use him?"

Vince tossed the magazine on the coffee table and re-counted the story of how McTarnihan and Chief used to be partners and how a drunk McTarnihan shot an innocent kid in an alley and Chief saved him from jail. Dane had heard the story before from McTarnihan, but he listened intently as Vince put his spin on it.

"Besides being weird, he does a thorough job," Vince said in conclusion. "He was a good cop."

"A good cop? He shot a kid while he was drunk," Dane replied. "I don't think that ranks him high on the list for merit badges."

"Life isn't all black and white, Dane," Vince said as he slid the mirror in front of himself.

Vince lined up some cocaine. He chuckled, leaning over his work, elbows to knees, razor blade clicking the glass, then smoothing out the manufactured mounds into long thin curved lines. "Can you keep a secret?"

"Sure," Dane replied. What else was he to say? He stole another drink from his beer.

The sharp edge of the razor was wiped clean with a moist fingertip, both sides, the taste of white put to his gums. "McTarnihan didn't kill that boy," Vince said, looking up at Dane.

The revelation spurred a momentary lapse in the conversation, Dane calculating if he wanted to know. "Well, if he didn't. Who did?"

"Chief did," Vince said. A smile rose on his face that was twisted with admiration. "I've got to hand it to Chief. Simple, yet brilliant. You see, the Chief is ... well, he likes it both ways. He'd die for a splendid piece of ass, but occasionally, he's bent on a more muscular envelope. You catch what I'm saying?"

Dane felt a knot tighten in his stomach.

"Chief was paying the kid," Vince said, "but then I guess the kid figured blackmail would up the ante. So, one night while on patrol, knowing that McTarnihan can't turn down a drink, Chief gets McTarnihan loaded, or at least points him in the right direction, then pumps a .44-mag in the kid's chest using McTarnihan's gun. The rest is history. Chief becomes Chief. McTarnihan ends up McTarnihan."

The words "Protect And Serve" bounced from wall-to-wall in Dane's cranium, hollow like Ping-pong balls.

***

Derek Virchow sat alone at the back of the sanctuary. It had been years since he'd been to mass. Yet he'd come here several times in the last nine months at Erin's request. She felt safe here. Saint Paul's Catholic Church was on the outskirts of Redmond. Built in the early fifties, the church was constructed of red brick with a large, round stained-glass window over the main doors.

The sanctuary held an eerie silence. An empty whoosh from the heating system. The subterranean hum of a sound system left on. The ticking of a mechanical clock. Even the tongues of the vigil lights held silent prayers. As he shifted his weight, the long pew of yellow oak creaked beneath his weight, the sound deafening in the heavy silence.

He touched the band of his wristwatch. Erin is not coming, he decided.

He walked outside to the edge of a concrete planter, one of two large rectangular raised beds that flanked the passage-way to the main doors. All the rose bushes had been cut back, blanketed with sawdust for protection from frost. He sat down on the planter's edge.

In the distance, through a rectory window, he could see a priest sitting in a straight-backed chair with a glass of wine in his hand. The amber glow of the room put features to the face of a rough-hewn man.

He fired off a smoke, noticing the yellowing between his index and middle finger, then followed the bell tower spire to the black sky. The moon was thin as a nail-clipping overhead. He pulled a hard drag, and a bad feeling overtook him like a fever chill.

CHAPTER 27

Atlantic Highlands, New Jersey
December 17, 1995

Michael squatted at the edge of the hot tub, balancing on the balls of his feet, and brushed back his hair with a finger-fork, taking an opportune glance at Carmen who sat across from Vito in the bubbling torrent of chlorinated water.

Vito registered the glance. He was enraged by Michael's youthfulness, saw the lust in his eyes, and felt his grip on Carmen slipping. He thought of shooting Michael in the face.

"Carmen. This is private," Vito said.

Carmen got up, water running from her lime-green bikini, and padded to the house.

Vito crushed an empty water bottle between his hands and tossed it onto the pool deck, then stretched his arms out along the rim of the tub.

"It seems Spinetti has a secretary with inquisitive eyes."

"What does she know?"

"Not sure."

"Lose her," Vito said. "Things are about ready on the island, and we don't need some nosey broad gumming up the works."

Michael snorted, his eyes gleaming with utter delight. "He did. Lose her I mean."

Vito slapped the water and "Shit" fell out of his mouth.

"She got away from him. He doesn't know where she is."

"What time is it?"

Michael looked at his watch. "Eight-fifty."

Overhead, through the glass roof of the pool house, the moon was set in a blood ring. "With time zone changes, Evohl should be able to get there by midnight. Tell Evohl to rouse Spinetti on the way. Get him out of whatever sack he's in and find this broad with the sharp eyes."

CHAPTER 28

Seattle, Washington
December 19, 1995

Lying awake in the seedy darkness, Erin listened to the arrhythmic clanking of the worn-out Heatilator, blowing out its stale warmth. In the currents, the curtains swirled as a dervish, dancing on the light of yellow lamps that lit the alley behind the Union Hotel.

The clock read six-eleven a.m. Erin propped another pillow behind her head and gazed about the tiny room. The sheets reeked of mothballs; the pungent odor of tobacco was inescapable; she could hear the toilet running in the bathroom.

She had to leave Seattle. Virchow would probably lock her up if she stayed. Vince would probably kill her if he could find her. She already had the number for a taxi written on the hotel pad. By eight she'd be at the Flying J Truck Stop in Issaquah melting into the breakfast crowd, watching and waiting, at some point catching a ride with an eighteen-wheeler headed east toward Spokane.

Then there was Dane. Like the confusion that exists where the ocean meets a rocky shore, she churned the impulse over and over in her mind until she concluded: if she didn't make the call now, she never would.

She picked up the phone and five seconds later, Dane was on the line. Groggy but awake.

"Where are you, Erin? Vince is looking for you."

Erin gripped the phone tighter, every muscle constricting. "I know. Did he tell you why?"

"He said you stole some money from him," Dane said. "Twenty thousand, to be exact. I saw the knot you put on his skull."

"It was in self-defense. And I stole nothing from him." Erin started sobbing. "He's lying," she cried.

Dane remained cool and distant, but after a basket of heart-beats, Erin regained her composure and asked that he reserve judgement until she'd finished all she had to say.

Dane agreed and remained silent while she began.

She started in Oklahoma, recounting the abuse of her step-father, the move to California, how she couldn't find a job, was cold and hungry, and how Manny took her in, gave her a place to stay, eventually put her to work as a prostitute, and how in the end she left him dead in his car.

She heard Dane catch his breath a few times, but most of all, he was quiet. While she related her story, sorrowful emotions racked her, but she held the tears at bay.

"I ran Dane. Hard and fast. Until I ended up here in Seattle. Please don't hate me."

"Erin," Dane said. "I don't hate you."

His words gave her the courage to go on, so next she described how she'd landed the job at S.H.E., and how she fell in love with Seattle, eventually volunteering in the children's ward at Swedish Hospital; and how FBI Agent Derek Virchow was waiting for her one day outside the hospital.

"Virchow?" Dane asked, his words inquisitive and awe-struck in unison.

"You know him?"

"Unfortunately."

"Well, he knew all about me ... and he said he needed my help. He said he'd free me from my past if I helped him gather information."

Erin smoothed down the fabric of her pants. The next part of the story would be the most difficult of all. The sorted tale of how Vince approached her at his office, how he knew of her past too, and how he used that knowledge to force her into spying on Dane.

She changed hands and moved the receiver to the other ear. "To make a long story short, he set you up with me on Halloween for one reason and one reason only. He figured if we were having sex, you'd let your guard down and spill your guts about your actual intentions."

"I don't know what to say. It's a lot to process. I fell in love with you Erin. I thought ..."

Erin sighed. "It doesn't matter now. I was copying the last of the files for Derek when Vince walked in on me. I thought he was going to kill me, so I hit him with a paperweight. Believe me or not, that's what happened."

"Where are you, Erin? We need to sort this out."

"Dane, I'm scared. I don't know how much of what I've told you stack up against your friendship with Vince. I can't take the chance. Face it, it's hopeless for me now. Hopeless for us. I just needed to tell you the truth before I left."

CHAPTER 29

Seattle, Washington
December 19, 1995

Dane couldn't sleep. Like a six-foot stick of dynamite, he rolled around in his bed, kept flipping his pillow to the cool side, until finally the nagging question banished him to the living room. Erin had blown him out of the water. Would Vince really have killed her?

Still in his boxer shorts, he started pacing around the room. Their conversation had died in a blur. After hours of thought, he had some things he wanted to say. Some things he needed her to know.

He thought of Virchow. Call in the cavalry and let Virchow know what had happened. But would Virchow listen to him? Would Virchow consider him an accessory?

Dane felt like the floor was falling out from beneath him. His stomach was in his throat. If Vince was lying to him, who knew what demands Geraci had leveled in his regard?

Then a picture of John McTarnihan streaked through his brain like a falling star. Sure, McTarnihan was a little weird, but he had offered help at the pizza parlor. And now, thanks to Vince, Dane knew the truth about the kid in the alley. Knowing the truth, any loyalty McTarnihan had towards Chief or Vince would surely die.

After all the years of mental torture, he'd hate them. For what they'd put him through, he might want to kill them. And bottom line, Vince had said it himself, "He was a good cop." McTarnihan could find her.

Dane went to his desk. He shuffled through the top drawer, latching onto McTarnihan's business card.

He punched up the digits on his cordless phone and sat down on the couch. McTarnihan answered, clear-headed on the first ring. The sound was cavernous, like McTarnihan was in a room without furniture.

"It's your dime," McTarnihan said.

"Erin Flynn."

There was a calculating moment of silence. "Erin Flynn," he said, then left the rest of his thoughts dangle.

"Sounds like you know her," Dane said.

"Yeah, I know her."

"Has Vince talked with you about her?"

"No."

"Vince caught her going through his files. He didn't appreciate it. I need you to find her. She might be in danger."

"Might be? Of course, she's in danger. Has been for some time. But why are you calling me?"

"That's a fair question. Are you sitting down?"

Dane heard a chair screech across the floor, and over the next few minutes, he conveyed the story Vince had told him about what had actually transpired in the alley. The night McTarnihan's life took a downward turn.

When he completed relaying the story, McTarnihan sighed. "All these years, I thought I'd killed an innocent kid, and both those jackasses held it over my head."

"Now you know why I called you."

CHAPTER 30

Seattle, Washington
December 20, 1995

Dane pulled into the lot of a run-down convenience store, slithering the ZX into a corner slot near the payphones in the dark. Stevie Ray Vaughn was bleeding eardrums with "Scratch and Sniff", the legendary guitarist pounding the ZX with a blues-rock hammer.

He whiffed a crude line off the back of his hand, then took a pull from his tequila. Alcohol was wet on his lips. He hadn't eaten and was looking for a quick meal: a microwave burrito and a paper boat of chips and cheese, maybe a candy bar of the chocolate variety. He canned the music, then swung a foot out of the car.

Dane could've chosen to take beer on this trip, whiskey, even vodka. The refrigerator carried a six-pack, cold and drizzling with an icy sweat; the cabinet over the stove held a wide selection of fifths and pints, but he chose tequila. Warm, gut knotting, worm preserving tequila.

If you want to get to Angryville, tequila is the ticket. Care to brutalize your body? Then tequila is the fist. Do you want to get down so low you can't get up? Tequila is the shovel to dig your grave. And if you want to kill or be killed, tequila is the bullet with your name on it.

It's Mexican piss in a bottle. All the anguish of an entire civilization liquefied, then sealed in a glass grenade, waiting to take over a victim with its hatred and fight. The more you drink the angrier you get, the angrier you get the more you drink, until finally you either puke up what boils in the pit of your stomach, or you punch out a window, a mailbox, a signpost, or a face.

Dane was looking for trouble. He was looking for a fight. The coke was keeping his brain alert; the tequila was taking the pain in his head and jamming it into his fists.

Dane burst into the tiny store, jaw grinding, eye burning, like he'd been ripped off, beat up, and now it was time to get even. He pushed his way to the nacho bar, loaded up a pile of chips, pumped on a slick of chili and cheese, and then tossed a bean burrito into the Radarange. He twisted the timer like it was somebody's nose, one-minute, nuclear power, then stood there impatiently, tapping the side of the microwave with a stiff, punishing index finger as though he was trying to coerce a confession out of it.

The oven finally gave it up — dinged five times, then its light went out. He took his food to the cashier. Raj was behind the counter. Dane eyed his name badge, then stared at the towel wrapped into a pile on his head.

"Iz that all?" Raj said with a thick ginger accent indicative of Calcutta or Bombay.

"Yeah, I'm finished."

While Raj worked the cash register, Dane felt the chill of cold flesh brush against his arm. A pint-sized Grandma with copper-frosted electrocution hair had squeezed in next to him, setting her buttermilk and Depends on the counter.

She was ancient, curled over like a walking comma, her skin so dry and flaky, one stiff breeze and she'd blow away like dust from a tabletop. She was a quivering old bag like the udder of a cow, wrinkled and sagging to the ground, incontinent, perfumed with Mary Kay or Avon products to an odor just shy of a rose-scented diaper pail.

"You know," she quavered, "you look like my son-in-law, Jerry Neufeldt. He's in draperies and linens over at Sears. Do you know him?" Her cheek-flesh hung like rouged handbags under her eyes, the pink make-up thick and powdery.

Like I know everybody in the world, Dane thought. Oh, of course, I know Jerry. What's the matter with me? We go way back. "No," Dane said.

"He's a very nice boy," she said, making a sincere attempt at an already ill-fated conversation. "They got in a whole new shipment of lace shams the other day and he called me first thing. He's so good to me. Does your wife need any shams?"

Just what I wanted to do tonight, Dane contemplated. Snort a few lines, polish off a bottle of Cuervo and stand in a Third World 7-11 and make idle conversation with Grandma Jones going over the nuances of shams and drapery rods. Maybe Mister Raghead could transform one of her shams into a new lace bonnet.

"I'm not married," he said. He felt like screaming, but his voice was like butter. His mother always told him to be polite, especially to priests and the elderly.

"Oh, that's a shame," she said. Her mind whirred vacantly. "I have a great-great-niece about your age. She's a little plump, and a bit of a wallflower, but she's got a big heart ..."

'Plump wallflower with a big heart' — Sounded like an advertisement for an abandoned dog, personal column Morse code for a failure with men. "Sorry, I'm gay," he said. The interruption a Hail Mary to throw her off the trail.

"Oh, that's okay. She likes to have fun, too."

"No, I meant: I like men ... sexually ... you understand?"

She just stood there staring with her droopy, bloodhound eyes. Dane could see that what he was saying was not registering. It was as though the flag was still at half-mast. Okay, he mused, let's be blunt. Perfect. He was in a blunt mood. "Okay, listen close, Granny. I like to date men, wear women's clothes, paint my toenails. Haven't you seen a talk-show on guys like me, like on Donahue or Sally Jessy Whatever-her-name-is?"

Raj's face was changing colors, about ready to erupt into a full-blown snit. Flabbergasted into silence, Granny's eyes were white saucers of disbelief, but at least she wasn't talking. No more yakkity-yakkity-yak.

***

The stale burrito and greasy nachos went down hard with the tequila, but Dane struggled through until the last chip was devoured, his taste buds more magnanimous than his hunger, his stomach more sociable than his attitude.

He'd been drinking since high noon Pacific Sulking Time. Now it was 8:00 p.m., nearly thirty-six hours since he'd spoken with McTarnihan, thirty-six hours since the flashbacks began: It was Marcellena; they had a fight; she ran in a huff, back to London, dying in a rampage of blood. Likewise, Erin had vanished. The logical conclusion was: it was his fault. At least that's what the tequila was telling him.

The ZX pulsated, rocking to the Cowboy Junkies' "A Common Disaster" and "You Must Be Evil" by Chris Rhea. He was on a collision course with self-pity and rage, neck deep in a kaleidoscope of lies.

His journey led him to the Central District, Rainier Avenue, the Forbidden City, an exceptionally rough part of town. A place where poverty and segregation kept the residents at their worst. Prides of men gathered around their Cadillac cars, lounging on the hoods, reclining in the lush seats, radios blasting with a gang-banger beat.

Dane wanted to beat and be beaten. Eventually he dropped anchor at the Dancing Bare, a bunkeresque strip joint with low concrete walls and a flat roof just off Yesler Avenue. Iron bars crisscrossed its windows.

He pulled the ZX into a quiet spot in the back behind a couple of junk cars and a mound of scrap lumber and sheet-rock leftover from a remodel job. Razor-sharp concertina wire rimmed the roofs of all the broken-down buildings in sight. He imagined Minsk, or Chernobyl, looked like this, something eastern bloc, the structures stained with polluted-brown rain.

Fifteen minutes later, after refusing to keep his hands off the merchandise, Dane found relief for his angst at the hands of Johnny Drago, bouncer and ex-longshoreman. Fifty minutes after that, he was in the Harborview Hospital Emergency Room, being stitched up for his stupidity.

CHAPTER 31

Seattle, Washington
December 21, 1995

Dane could feel his face and hands swollen like an acromegalic as he picked up the phone.

Bobby answered on the second ring. "Hello."

"Bobby?" Dane's voice was harsh, his throat raw.

"Yeah, who's this?"

Dane felt paste in the corners of his mouth, remembering the pariah he'd seen in Pioneer Square, their lips glued together with a spermy-white cream, high on Haldol and Thorazine martinis. To top it off, ever since he'd gotten up, napalm had been shooting out his rectum, compliments of Raj and his chili and cheese.

"Bobby, it's Dane."

"What's the matter, you sick?"

Dane stood at the kitchen counter, holding his body weight erect with the heel of his palm. The force had creased his skin, cutting the blood flow to his hand. His fingers felt numb, like dowels of wood. His mouth watered with nausea. He spit in the sink.

"Self-inflicted," he said.

Over the past few weeks, words had passed between them. Words you can't take back; words that cut deep and heal thin. After a few zingers meant to offend and humble Dane in the same breath, Bobby cooled to his usual concerned self.

Dane understood. Bloodletting the wounds was Bobby's way of letting go. A few apologies later, the reason for the call exposed itself: Dane wanted to talk, but deep down, what he was seeking was forgiveness.

***

At five-forty-five p.m., Dane met Bobby at the ferry dock in Winslow.

"When you said 'self-inflicted,' I didn't realize ..." Bobby adjusted his cap. "What happened?"

For the next few minutes, while Bobby groaned and sighed, Dane summarized the events leading up to and including the night of the Dancing Bare.

"Cops involved?"

"No. Two hours at Harborview Hospital, but please keep the Dancing Bare to yourself. I feel stupid enough the way it is."

"This is certainly a giant mess you've gotten yourself into."

"I'm sorry. What do you want me to do, Bobby? Don sackcloth and repent while you bury me in a pile of ashes."

Bobby grinned an acquiescent smile. "Okay then, but before we go to the house. I've got to ask."

"No. I'm not high," Dane said.

***

Natalie met them at the door, the youngest son swinging from her arm, attempting to draw her back into the kitchen for a taste of dessert before dinner. She wore a tan, square-neck housedress with a red-and-white checked apron. She stuttered a welcome as she shook free of her younger son, then dried her moist hands on the apron. The strange look on her face was one of concern, the stitches in Dane's face the primary object of her attention.

As the boy crawled toward the kitchen on all fours, Dane touched the stiff black caterpillar the doctor had sewn onto the bridge of his nose. Besides the stitches, cuts and broken blood vessels remained, running disjointedly from cheek to jaw like the ganglion of veins in a bloodshot eyeball.

Natalie gently touched his wrist. "Can I get you anything? Bobby has a couple pain killers leftover from when he broke his leg."

"No thanks Natalie," Dane said. "Luckily, it looks worse than it feels, and whatever pain there is, I deserve."

Natalie heard the oven door open, and without further ado, she rushed for the kitchen, a mother's voice booming.

Bobby led the way to the living room. The older son was sitting on the couch reading a comic book. He asked him to go help his mom in the kitchen.

The boy left the room while Bobby sat down in his green easy chair under a gooseneck reading lamp, took off his cap and laid it on the end table by his side. He stroked back remnants of his hair. "Can I get you something to drink?" His baldness glinted under the light.

Dane sat down on the couch. "I could use a cup of coffee."

Bobby went to the kitchen and came back with two cups.

"So? Do you want to talk about it?" Bobby asked.

"Last night?" Dane shifted in his seat, pulled an ankle up on his knee.

"No. Where we go from here?" Bobby said.

Dane was silent, uneasy.

"Have you thought about what I mentioned before?"

"You mean about the videotapes?"

"Yeah. I could slip in and get them. Easy. I'm sure of it."

Dane hesitated, unsure if Bobby might erupt if he once again nixed his plans for a raid of the *Ecstasea*. "Bobby. I appreciate the offer. And I don't doubt your skill to pull it off. But I have a crazy idea about what to do."

"Is that supposed to surprise me?" Bobby said.

"No ... not really."

Bobby whistled softly through his teeth. "Well, let's have it."

"The plan involves Tyra. Do you think she'd go along?"

Just then, the door opened with a waft of cold air, and Tyra stepped in from the darkness outside.

CHAPTER 32

Seattle, Washington
December 26, 1995

Crossing the 520 Bridge, Lake Washington spread to the shoreline like a sheet of black iron pitted by raindrops. Tyra was pensive, staring out her window, the moonlight like oil on the water's surface.

Dane was dressed in slacks, a quarter-zip sweater, and a light brown leather jacket. "Vince likes women," he said bluntly. He let his eyes roam from Tyra's toes to her hair. "He'll certainly like you. Just flirt with him. He'll never leave your side. I shouldn't be gone over five-ten minutes."

When she said nothing, he tried to reassure her. "Don't worry. You got this."

She nodded her head.

***

When they entered the Main Salon, Vince was standing at the windows. Casual, wearing chinos and a button-down shirt, his skin was dark-tanned and smelled of expensive cologne. He hadn't seen Dane since before the Dancing Bare and was quick to comment on his appearance, although his eyes were glued on Tyra.

Tyra wore a leather miniskirt, black and snug, matching waist-length jacket, high heels, and silk stockings. Underneath the jacket, she wore a yellow corset crop top, stretched tight — accentuating her cleavage — and short enough to leave a delectable slice of midriff for tasting. Over her shoulder, a satchel hung from its leather straps.

"I got blindsided by some guy in a bar," Dane said.

"Who's your friend?" Vince asked. His eyes were the color of cool mint, brimming with arrogance.

Tyra blushed under the force of his captivating stare.

"Well, thanks for your concern, *bro*," Dane said sarcastically. He put his hand on the small of Tyra's back and edged her forward. "Taylor, this is Vince Spinetti. Watch yourself. He could charm Joann Woodward into thinking Paul Newman's a bum."

Tyra stuck out her hand for a shake, and Vince took it. However, instead of a shake, he kissed the back of her hand.

"See what I mean."

"Don't listen to him," Vince said, still clutching her hand. "Taylor," he said as though he were caressing her name, "I'm very pleased to meet you."

Tyra retrieved her hand. "It's nice to meet you too."

Vince helped Tyra out of her jacket and Dane slipped out of his. Vince took the coats and hung them in the closet. "So, can I get you both a drink? Wine? Liquor?"

"I'd take a scotch on the rocks," Dane said.

"Do you have any champagne?" Tyra said. "I normally drink wine, but I'm feeling elegant tonight."

Vince sidled in behind the bar. He poured some Glenlivet with ice in a tumbler and slid it across to Dane, then uncorked a bottle of champagne and poured a sparkling glass. He delivered it in person, guiding Tyra to a leather armchair with his arm about her waist. Dane moved to the couch, throwing a glance at the lake, the glow from the *Ecstasea's* running lights like quicksilver on the surface.

"So, you two are going out on the town?" he asked. The question was rhetorical, served up to amuse. "Dane usually never gets past Burger King and a can of beer. Although, I guess *it is* coupon night at the Renton tri-cinemas."

Tyra looked expressionless at Dane, then gave Vince a charmed smile.

Dane ignored him. "You asked me to stop by. I thought tonight was as good as any. You look like you have a date."

"Met her at a gas station. Can you believe it? I was filling the Porsche; she was filling her Jag. Her legs are an art form. Can't wait to unpack her other treasures."

"Good to hear. What's Sean up to tonight?" Dane asked.

"He's got Chanel in the Game Salon. I'm assuming down to her panties by now. As long as they clean up after themselves, they can screw until they're blue in the face."

"Where's Lance and Jimmy?"

"Why?"

"Oh nothing. Just curious."

"It's Tuesday, Dane. You know it's their night off."

"Oh yeah," Dane said, trying to sound enlightened.

Vince poured himself another drink, then turning serious, he looked at Dane with questioning eyes. "We have to talk, Dane. Do you think Taylor would be comfortable in the Dining Salon? Or better yet, why don't we go up to the bridge, and she can stay here?"

Dane stood up. "First, I have to visit the little boys' room," he said. "I'm sure you won't mind having Taylor all to yourself, although I don't know if she's got enough in her arsenal to protect herself."

"Oh, Dane," Tyra said with a laugh and a wave of her hand, "what can he do in only minutes? I'm sure anything Vince would have in mind would take all evening." She gave Vince a volatile, impish grin before a sip of champagne, and Vince was quick to respond.

***

Dane headed for the stairs to below decks, leaving them with a parting comment, feigning concern under his breath. A flutter of black anxiety rose through his chest as he descended the stairs as though a flock of starlings had broken the grips of gravity and exploded skyward.

Jimmying the lock as before, moments later, he was in the Monitor Room. He could see Tyra and Vince on Monitor 1. Tyra was sipping her drink. Vince was sitting on the arm of the couch next to her chair. Sean and Chanel filled Monitor 2, naked, engaged, their entangled limbs writhing as though in pain. Monitor 3 was off. Only Monitor 2 was recording. Obviously, a slow night.

A stack of unused videotapes set on the console. Dane had to work fast. Everything he needed was in the room: blank videotapes, white labels, even the red marking pen.

The recorded videotapes had labels with names, some had dates, a few had odd nicknames. From the titles with female names, many were sex videos, he deduced. That left ten others. In the end, he chose four, a couple with names he recognized, a couple on instinct.

For each one, he smoothed out a fresh label with his thumb, and forged a duplicate, each letter one-by-one as the original. Once done, he slipped the forgery into the original slot and set the original to the side.

Then something mystic broke his concentration. Vince and Tyra were still on the Monitor 1. Chanel was on her back on Monitor 2, blowing smoke rings in the air, and Sean, well, Sean was gone.

Dane's mind imploded. He went to grab his original tapes, but knocked two to the floor, then picked them up, laid the pen back where he thought he'd gotten it, then changed his mind and put it somewhere else. He straightened the blanks again, the fake originals again, then backed out of the room, pulling the door shut, locked behind him. Right or wrong, the light was left on.

The hallway was alive with shadows. Thoughts blew in and out of his head as though his mind were a tunnel, visions like dried leaves on the wind. He rounded the corner by the galley, groping in the semi-darkness. He felt for the bathroom door and heard the toilet flush.

The sound pinball'd in his head. He felt the stack of video-tapes grow heavy, sweaty in his palms. He backpedaled. The door opened and Sean came into the hallway. Dane stopped dead in his tracks, his mind going over the options like a Rolodex of choices.

Sean walked off down the hall toward the Game Salon, naked, toweling his crotch, not noticing the man who was standing in the semi-darkness of the hallway that ran from starboard to port.

With quiet deliberation, he entered the bathroom, placed the videotapes in a stack under the sink, and climbed the stairs back up to the Main Salon.

***

"Everything okay up here?" Dane asked, as if it were a joke.

"Fine," Tyra said.

"Super fine," Vince added.

Tyra took a gulp of champagne, then wrinkled her nose as if tickled by the bubbles.

Dane picked up his drink.

"What took you so long?" Vince asked.

"My stomach is a mess. Too much holiday food."

"I forgot to ask. How was the family?"

"Good."

Vince looked at his fingernails, a fleeting remembrance in his eyes. "I skipped the trailer-court Christmas with Ma, Pa and Jack Daniel's again this year." He looked at Tyra with an acute frankness. "The Spinetti's are into slaps, black eyes and verbal abuse," he said, "instead of the traditional silk tie, fancy perfume and Red Ryder BB gun."

Dane shot his booze. He didn't want to get sidetracked. "You ready to talk business?" He touched his watch. "I don't want to miss our reservation."

"Sure. Make yourself at home, Taylor. Dane and I will be on the bridge for a few minutes."

Like they'd gone over it in the car, Tyra chimed in. "Vince, I need to check my make-up, do a few girlie things. Do you mind?" Her voice quavered. "Where's the bathroom?"

"Downstairs." There was a modicum of suspicion in Vince's voice. He pointed a vertical palm at the stairs, then flexed his wrist right while saying, "At the bottom of the stairs, take a right. First hallway, another right. The head is right there on the left."

Dane fiddled with the cuticle of his thumb as Tyra snatched up her satchel and disappeared below deck. He then moved Vince onto a new subject. "Have you seen Tony?"

"Not lately," Vince said. "Talked to him on the phone. He's handling a remodel job at the Rachel Street Apartments. What about you?"

"Nothing. He's being elusive. I think he's mad."

"About what?" Vince said, a hint of agitation in the question. He left his perch on the end of the couch and edged back to the bar.

"Being replaced."

"He'll get over it," Vince said.

"Yeah, but on the street, you should've seen him. He was king."

"A guy messes up; you pay the consequences."

Consequences. Dane thought about that for a second. Vince-the-pot calling the kettle black.

Vince took a washcloth and ran it under the faucet, twisted it damp and wiped down the bar. "I know I haven't told you this before," he said, "but I'm grateful. Things have been running very smooth since you took over."

"What about this deal with Erin?" Dane asked to get a reaction. "I thought you'd be more interested in whether I've heard from her. Twenty thousand is no small chunk of change."

"Do I need to ask? I figured if you knew anything, you'd be telling me." Vince stopped wiping and gazed at Dane. "So, what about it? Have you talked to her?"

"She called me a week ago. Told me you were full of it. She wouldn't tell me where she was, though. I didn't press it. Haven't seen or heard from her since."

"Me neither," Vince said as he resumed wiping. "My guess is she's on some beach in California sipping a Piña Colada."

"Yeah maybe."

"Do you have any doubts?" Vince folded the washcloth and laid it on the edge of the sink.

"About what?"

"She said 'I was full of it.'"

"I can't trust her. She was lying to me about several things," Dane said. "She admitted it when we were on the phone."

Dane looked toward the stairs. "Besides, there are plenty of ladies out there."

Vince leaned onto his elbows over the bar and nodded his head.

"Let's get business over with," Dane said, looking at his watch. "I'm running out of time."

"It's not much really," Vince said. "I'm going out early to spend the day with the old man. Sean, Lance and Jimmy will be with me. Unless you want to go out early, you'll have to find your own way."

"No problem. I know where it is. Is it alright if I bring a friend?"

"Taylor?" Vince asked.

"It's a possibility," Dane said. "Depending on how well things go tonight."

"No problem," Vince said. "Just remember, this is business first, pleasure second. I know Geraci will want to meet you. He's an intimidation freak. He likes to show his power, so that everyone knows he's the boss. Venegas will be in late. So, while I'm with him and the old man, I'll need you to keep an eye out. I know Michael will be there, Evohl, plus several more of Geraci's men, but I'd feel better if I knew you were watching things."

Dane nodded in consent.

"A lot of guests will be coming in from the East Coast," Vince went on. "I want you to bring plenty of coke. Also, when Venegas gets there, keep a sharp eye on his men. I don't want them snooping around and making the old man crazy."

"What about Tony?"

"What about him?" Vince said, his voice full of indignation. "He isn't coming. Geraci is hard enough to handle without intentionally cocking the gun."

"Just wanted to know in case he asked."

Vince was quiet. Several heartbeats passed between them.

"Is that it?" Dane asked.

"One more thing. Johnny Smart is going to be shuttling a bunch of broads over from Friday Harbor. I want you to pay him when he gets there. Ten grand. He'll say it's more, like we made some other deal, but ten is what we agreed upon."

Vince rolled the sleeves down on his shirt and started buttoning the cuffs. "That's about it."

Seconds later, Tyra reappeared from below deck, her purse slung over her shoulder, heavy with four video cassettes.

CHAPTER 33

Seattle, Washington
December 30, 1995

Dane folded the newspaper and tossed it on the table. He'd been checking the personal columns every day for a week, waiting for a response to his ad. The ad he'd placed to draw Erin out. Today did not differ from the rest. Nothing. The thought thickened in his throat like phlegm from an allergic reaction, sickening him with her absence.

He called McTarnihan. The story was the same as him. He'd keep looking. His voice sounded small and beleaguered.

***

Later in the day, Dane drove to an Urgent Care, got his stitches out, then to an electronics store and bought a palm-sized recorder, voice activated, sixty-minute tape. Then he called Tyra and set the schedule for the following day, New Year's Eve.

He knew Bobby was working his way through the videotapes. They were incriminating, but nothing yet about Blake.

Early evening, he made a few coke deliveries, then returned to the dark of his apartment, spending the rest of the night spacing out in front of the TV with a six-pack of beer and an endless supply of the white powder. *Treasure of the Sierra Madres* was on channel 39, Bogart at his paranoid best.

CHAPTER 34

San Juan Islands, Washington
December 31, 1995

Henry Island was acres of rock and fir trees. On it, Geraci's compound was born from stucco and stone, overlooking the ocean from Kellett Bluff. Within its walls were the mansion, two quaint guest houses, even smaller servants' quarters, sweeping verandas, marble statuary, extensive flower gardens with fountains, waterfalls, and glimmering pools. There was a pavilion of glass connected to the mansion chambering a pool, sauna and whirlpool spa.

The perimeter of the compound was twelve-foot-high stone except for the edge that bordered Kellett Bluff, a sheer rock cliff that was more formidable than any man-made wall. A guard kiosk set at the front gate and two more at extreme ends of the bluff, equipped with an arsenal of MAK-90s, AK-47s, Glock pistols, and Weatherby shotguns sawed back to the magazine with their plugs removed.

The rooms at the rear of the mansion faced southwest over the bluff, looking toward Vancouver Island, British Columbia. Most notable of these was the library with three of its five walls jutting out for a full panoramic view of Haro Strait, and the eighty-foot-tall flagpole that carried the Geraci Crest flapping in an onshore breeze. Between the bluff and Vancouver Island lay the Canadian border, a line in the water 1.4 miles away.

It was eight p.m., and most guests had gathered in the Great Room. They'd arrived by float plane, helicopter and yacht, chartered or private craft.

It was a caste system of partygoers. At the top, suits bent on criminal intent, sharing the lofty realm with the idle rich. A step below trawled the sycophants, their smiles welded in place. Lower still, the personal assistants and bodyguards, not considered part of "The Life," but essential to its existence. Then the basement, not deemed a level at all, mere servants, cooks and cleaners.

Dane grabbed a pair of champagne glasses from a passing waiter and handed one to Tyra. From where they stood, he could see into the pool house, the swimming pool lights emitting a pallid smoke into the clear blue depths. Overhead, a catenary of Japanese lanterns bordered the poolside, their reflection quivering on the surface of the water, floating on the glass windows like bright balloons escaping skyward.

Tyra wore a décolleté dress, red and snug with a climbing hemline, high heels with severe spikes. Dane was in departure from his normal attire and wore pleated black trousers and a button-down shirt tucked in at the waist.

Moments later, Vince arrived like a gust of wind. He was incredulous, wearing a white silk shirt, the front left unbuttoned down to the xiphoid. His hair combed back, glistened slick and black; the milky green color of his eyes twisting like protean smoke, threatening all who ventured there to be sucked into the vortex.

Vince's eyes were immediately all over Tyra like a diamond cutter, looking for imperfections. By the intensity of his gaze, he wasn't finding any. "Taylor. You look ravishing." He took her hand, leaned in, and stole a kiss from her cheek.

"This is quite a layout," Dane said. "Geraci spent a wad on this one."

"If you only knew." Vince angled his head over his shoulder as if expecting an oncoming train, then spoke low below the crowd. "Thirty mill. Easy money. Like most people save nickels and dimes in a quart jar."

Absently, Tyra looked off across the strait.

"Beautiful, isn't it?" Vince said following her gaze.

"Yes, it is." She stepped ahead, through a glass door, out into the shadows of the terrace. Dane and Vince followed. It was cold, but not unbearable.

Earlier on the journey to the island, they'd watched the sun dip below the Olympics, turning the horizon pink by its flare for excitement, then fade, leaving a skiff of high-altitude clouds turning brass in the dusk. Now the sun had escaped the curvature of the earth, leaving the atmosphere scorched with the blackness of night.

Tyra gripped the rail, scouring the skies. "It's so dark," she said. "Look at the stars. Like glitter on a black velvet dress." Her eyes were wet, her cheeks full of color.

Illuminated by the lights of the compound, the waves were breaking against the bluff; the foam leaping high into the air. A gaggle of seagulls huddled on an outcropping. Dane pointed his chin to the dock below them in the distance, down three flights of metal stairs that switchback their decent of the rocky bluff to the water. "Is that Vito's boat?" he asked.

"The *Insatiable*," Vince said with some fanfare. "A one-hundred-and-seventy-three-foot motor yacht with a thirty-two-foot beam and twin Caterpillar screws. She's a Benetti of Viareggio, Italy. A heliport on the bow, six palatial staterooms of imported marble and gold leaf, sweeping staircases and a skylight lounge adjoining the spa deck. What more could a mobster ask for?"

"Isn't that an Excalibur 45 docked opposite Vito's?" Dane asked.

"That one is Michael's," Vince said. "The *Screemin Mee-Mee*. An ocean runner with twin 502s."

At the far end of the dock, a sea plane approached, water spray cyclonic off its prop. The engine chun-chun-chunked to a stop. The pilot stepped onto the pontoon, then the dock, tied up and began letting off more guests from the mainland.

Sean appeared and summoned Vince to his side, speaking like a conspirator in his ear.

Tyra was now peering into the raven water. Her skin was as smooth as alabaster. Dane stepped close and held her hand.

Without warning, a private smile invaded her cheeks. "What is it?" Dane asked. "What do you see?"

"Oh nothing."

"C'mon, you're not smiling for nothing."

Tyra leaned closer so she could whisper in his ear. "I was wondering what creatures lie out there beneath the waves." She hesitated and shot a look over Dane's shoulder to where Vince was standing. "But then," she continued, "I had this thought of Vince as a puffer fish, his ego so puffed up he exploded into a million pieces."

Dane whispered back in her ear. "If only we could be so lucky."

***

Minutes later, they were back inside. A sextet was playing high-brow tunes, and Vince was pointing out the more notorious guests, when from out of the crowd a man came sidling through the people.

"Howdy, Vince." His voice was clear and brisk with a Texas twang. He looked fiftyish, tall and lean, with a white scar under his left eye that had puckered, resembling an asterisk. He wore black cherry cowboy boots and a black curl-brimmed hat that set down low over his eyebrows. In his shirt pocket he carried makings for hand-rolled cigarettes.

"Luc-k-k-y, my man-n-n," — Vince seemed glad to see him — "I see you made it."

"Yessir, Vince. It took some doing. But *I am here.*" He rested his hand on his rodeo buckle. As big as a gladiator shield, it winked in the light.

He looked at Tyra, Dane, then back at Vince. Dane thought his gaze was vacuous, focused on a place somewhere in a mired distance. He noticed Tyra turn her head, as if she'd found something repulsive in his eyes.

Vince followed with introductions all around, then from the other side of the room, a large man was waving Vince over. "You get acquainted here and I'll join you later," Vince said. With that, he left.

"So how do you know Vince?" Dane asked.

"Vince is expanding, and I got most of Idaho and Montana corralled."

"Oh, I see," Dane said.

***

"These cops," Vince said precariously. "Can they be trusted?"

Chief was sweating. His shirt had a yellow smile in the armpit of each sleeve. "Sure," he said. He loosened his tie. "Vito asked me for a little support. He said he felt shorthanded tonight." He ran a knuckle under his eye, wiping away a crescent of perspiration. "Don't worry so much. These guys are in it for the money. Hell, Martini runs a chop shop out of his backyard, and Kelly grows his own dope."

Vince dumped off his glass on a passing waiter. He was uncomfortable that Geraci had bypassed him and went straight to the Chief. He was brooding over the situation when his eye picked up on one of Johnny Smart's girls heading toward the pool. She was barefoot in a flowered sarong, bronzed by a tanning bed, wearing a fluorescent orange bikini top. She had a twenty-two-inch waist, smooth as water over stone.

"Check her out," he said, nodding his head to point out the girl. "Wouldn't that be a roll?"

"No doubt, Vince," Chief said. "There's enough flesh in this room to give a statue a stiff, but I don't see any of them running over here to meet me."

"Maybe ... maybe not." Vince put a hand to his chin thoughtfully, his eyes transfixed as if he was dividing by zero.

"What?" Chief rocked on his heels as if his loins were boiling, his tongue quivered as he spoke, "What-what are you thinking?"

Like a Grand Master of chess, Vince was thinking several moves ahead. He knew money was soon forgotten, amounts fading from memory as easy as childhood dreams, the one-dollar-bill the same color and size as the fifty. But sex was indelibly etched in a man's brain, the experience returning at the mere flick of a mental switch, whether lying in bed at the end of a long day or driving down the freeway. Chief would be forever in his pocket, deeper than ever before.

"As I remember, I still owe you for some advice. I was thinking you and Vick ..." He let the rest of the thought dangle.

"Vick? Don't be jerking me around Vince. It's not funny. You mean *your* Vick?"

"One and the same."

Chief tottered from foot-to-foot, his patent leather wing-tips languishing under his shifting weight. He pointed across the room, the hair on his forearms glistening like animal fat. "That Vick?"

"Now take it easy, big fella. I'll arrange it. However, the next time Vito comes to you for a favor, remember who your real friend is."

Vince raised his hand in the air and caught Dane's attention. Vick was conversing with Tyra. He motioned all three of them over.

Arriving first, Dane asked, "What's up?"

"Dane, this is Chief Donovan."

"Glad to meet you," Dane said. "Vince has spoken highly of you."

They shook hands as Vick and Tyra approached, setting the mood ablaze with their piquant fragrances.

Vick was wearing a black silk dress, cut to mid-thigh, her shoulders bare. Her hair was wound tight like a camellia bud upon her head, her neck exposed long and sensuous. Her lips were cinnamon candy, sizzling red, yet icy sweet, wet like a lollipop lick. She carried a snifter warmed with dense green absinthe. She gave Vince a kiss on the cheek and immediately latched on to his arm, evidently where she felt safe.

Holding his drink in both hands, Chief nudged Vince with an elbow, a look of impatience tightening his lips. Vince turned and whispered in Vick's ear. Abruptly, a cast of horror sucked the skin taut over her cheekbones. She stepped away.

"Excuse us for a second," Vince said, pulling her by the arm out of earshot.

Chief ran a finger around the inside of his collar, loosening it from the folds of flesh that engulfed it, his shirt sticking to his chest in an adulterated sweat, his dark nipples wet like gravy stains on the fabric.

***

Dane stood on the landing at the top of the stairs. Behind him, a series of suites lined corridors tunneling back from the landing like the fingers of a hand. Below him, the party was in full swing.

At the bottom of the stairs, one of Vito's men, Danny "The Mutt," was monitoring access. A guy with a heavy chest and short legs, "The Mutt," had a pockmarked face and cauliflower ears, and Dane thought he resembled a cross between a bulldog and a shotgun blast.

Dane could feel his heart beating anxiously, the rhythm now a blur. He'd paid off Johnny Smart in a suite at the end of the ring-finger corridor, then as soon as Johnny left, Phar-makeia convinced him with a rational adeptness that a few lines of white would help him stay in focus. He was now riding a wave of energy like a surfer slipping a North Shore curl, his throat thickening, numbing with the sterile taste he'd grown so accustomed to.

Tyra was waiting for him below, and while he stood grip-ping the banister trying to compose himself, Vito entered the Great Room like a dry wind parching lips with the whisper of his name and now stood at the far end like Tiberius or some other roman ancestor of his, chin up, arms hanging loose at his side, setting the room on edge. He wore a white banded-collar shirt buttoned to the top under a black sport coat and white pleated trousers with cuffs.

Suddenly, Vick streaked by Dane, her heels clicking in a panic down the stairs. She'd emerged from the middle-finger. Her hair was down about her shoulders, her lipstick smeared, her mascara running in black tears down her cheeks. They made eye contact, hers electric with shock, his staring blankly confused.

Tyra too had seen her decent, and after a quick look of concern at Dane, she followed Vick down the hallway.

From his perch, Dane turned his attention back to the forum. Vince lifted his eyes, and with a tip of his head, flagged Dane down from the stairs.

Dane felt heat rise through his neck and stretch like a net across his face as he made his way through the people, some of whom were puffing casually on Trinidad's or Cohiba's.

Sidling into the cocoon of parasites that surrounded Geraci, Dane didn't know how Geraci would accept him: a welcome addition to his collection of flunkies, or as if a cancerous cell had now entered the bloodstream.

Geraci looked at his face. The skin around his eyes puckered with thought.

Dane stared back like he'd nothing to fear, wondering if Geraci could see through the facade.

"Vito, this is Dane Avilla," Vince said above the clamoring voices. "The man I told you about."

Geraci had a grip like a prizefighter, seizing Dane's hand as if to wring water from it. His yellow eyes were flatly suspicious, and he had a face so brutally strong it looked as though it'd been cut from a single piece of steel.

No words passed between them. Dane remained quiet in fearful reverence as Vito's reticence thundered with calculation. Dane assumed Geraci measured every man he met, some for profit, some for aptitude — some for a coffin.

Vince squirmed at the tenuous stillness. His Adam's apple appeared stuck in his throat like a giant hairball, but at last was relieved when Vito turned and nodded his head, a slight gesture acknowledging his first impression.

Next to Geraci was Constantine Berragucchi. He had a face so sharp you could slice bread with it. On his arm was a woman several inches taller than himself, half black, half Cherokee Indian, her skin dull like a copper penny. She had a honking laugh. He didn't introduce her.

Next to Berragucchi: Benny Malto. A dark complected man with close-set eyes wearing a sport coat the color of a potato sack. He smelled of gunpowder. His wife wore a Mennonite cape dress, her hair coifed into a tight chignon. She kept pulling her compact from her purse, checking her make-up, and replacing it. Their daughter, early twenties, had pale green eyes, which kept opening and closing with her mouth agape as if she were in the throes of a barbiturate meltdown.

It was hard for Dane to imagine that these two men were connected. If you saw them on the street, you'd probably feel sorry for them because they were meager and ugly, and their wives were odd and quirky, and by the minute Malto's kid was losing grip.

Vito asked Dane to join Vince and him, then walked toward the library, slowly like a diplomat at a fundraiser, peeling off fawners like skin from a snake, at different intervals stopping to deliver a wise quip, kiss a woman's cheek or the back of her hand.

Dane followed as requested, and so did a pair of Geraci bodyguards, one with dull eyes and a flat nose; the other had a body as hard-ribbed as a pumpkin, a scar slick and brown like an earthworm across his cheek.

As they entered the library, Geraci's men peeled off to stand watch outside. The library was mahogany and lined wall-to-ceiling with books, with several large windows that overlooked the ocean.

The wood was rich, the fabrics luxurious, the leather masculine and smooth to the touch. It was as Vince had described: all that money could buy.

From behind the bar, Vince poured a round of scotch. He proposed a toast to the future, and all three men shot down the malt.

Vince reloaded their drinks as Dane wandered the library, admiring the fine collection of books. There were jackets imprinted with names like Hemingway and Kafka. Some looked like first editions. He noticed a copy of *The Adventures of Tom Sawyer*, his favorite, but refrained from touching it.

The fireplace was ablaze, flames licking the throat of the firebox. Geraci kept pushing a ring around on his pinkie finger while his eyes studied Dane with an intensity that could boil water.

Unable to ignore his gaze — like one could not ignore pliers tearing away strips of cheek-flesh — Dane became electrified with thought. Could Vito hear the voice-activated recorder whirring under the lip of the bar? It was only inches from where Vito was standing. If so, how long would it take for Vito to put two-and-two together and come up with his sorry butt?

From previous conversations with Vince, Dane knew that if a meeting between Venegas and Geraci materialized, it would happen in the library.

So, after they arrived, while Tyra engaged Vince in conversation, he slipped into the library and concealed the recorder beneath the bar.

It wasn't a fool-proof plan, as if any deception ever was, but it was the best he could devise, considering there were no stores that sold guaranteed plans for situations like this.

"Vince tells me you've been friends for a long time," Vito said. "Friends are hard to come by. How is it you two are still so close?"

Dane's eyes narrowed, his pupils constricting, remembering the chapter where Tom Sawyer decided: "Yes, they had forced him to it at last: he would lead a life of crime." He licked the dryness from his lips. "Well, I suppose we're more like brothers than friends."

Vito moved behind his desk, a grin in the corner of his mouth like a conniving hyena. He sat down in his high-back leather chair. He put a foot up on a drawer and buffed away a smudge from his shoe with a tissue. "So, tell me, what is it you expect to see from *our* relationship?"

The back of Dane's fingers rubbed along his jaw in contemplation, the fine grit of a twelve-hour beard grabbing at his skin, but what Dane said showed no signs of hesitation. "Money. I expect to be a rich man."

"And power?"

Dane slipped a hand in his front pocket and ambled toward the desk, staring down as though a thought were crawling on the floor in front of him. "No," he said with a pause. "Money. I'll leave the power to you."

Leaning back into the leather, Vito formed a cathedral of fingers in front of his chest, tip-to-tip, elbows to armrests. Colorful fish swam behind his silver hair. His face was stony as polished agate. "It's good to have you onboard, Dane. Don't make me eat my words."

Then his eyes dismissed him like one hangs up a phone. "Now leave us."

Their meeting was over. Vito, the man of few words, each syllable designed for maximum effect. A taste of brass flooded Dane's mouth like he'd just swallowed a .38-round-nose, yet he wanted to leave the same way he came in — with some semblance of control.

He stepped to the bar, topped off his scotch to show he wasn't prone to panic under pressure, then tipped his glass in thanks, and left, sliding close the doors behind him.

CHAPTER 35

San Juan Islands, Washington
December 31, 1995

Restrained like a storm in a bottle, Vito moved around to the front of the desk, his hands were flexing at his side. Moments earlier, Vince had informed him that Venegas wasn't coming.

"You said you could handle this."

Sometimes it's hard to know whether to speak up or shut up. Excuses don't always defend, sometimes they escalate. "I thought he'd change his mind," Vince said. "And I didn't want to concern —"

"I'll decide what concerns me!"

Patches of red were blooming on Vito's neck, the smell of his cologne souring on his skin. The odor ignited Vince's saliva glands, flooding his mouth with spit.

"I'm the lightning Vince, and you're the thunder. Destruction is in my touch ... the best you can do is make a lot of noise."

The skin on Vito's face was knuckle-tight and ridged with bone, like a leather-gloved fist. He was coming unglued like a wet newspaper tearing apart in the wind.

Vince blinked as if a twig had snapped behind his eyes, and suddenly Vito was at the bar filling a glass three-fingers-full of scotch. He shot it down like water, and with it the iron in his shoulders melted, the muscles in his neck relaxed. His jaw slackened. His eyes cooled.

He supported his buttocks on the front edge of the desk, crossed his arms. "Have I made myself clear?" His voice was chameleon — seconds earlier spitting fire, now cool as ice.

"Crystal." Vince pushed his scotch away with his thumb.

Vito's legs were out straight before him. He clasped his hands together over his crotch and looked reverently at the ceiling. "My father-in-law, rest his soul, would never tell me the whole of anything."

Vito's eyes came back to Vince. He pulled an earlobe. "Obviously, Venegas is out."

Vito's temper had calmed, but for some vain reason, Vince felt that keeping Venegas *in* was worth the risk of re-igniting the gasoline in Vito's bowels. "No disrespect intended, Vito, but why?"

Vince had a palm out, face up, pleading his case. "Venegas has the product, the quality and the price. He can deliver. I promise."

"Call it a character flaw, but I want to put a face on my accomplices."

"Look, Venegas wants to keep his exposure to a minimum. I get it," Vince said. "There are outstanding warrants for his arrest in the U.S."

"So, he didn't come to your party." Vince flipped his wrist, waving a dismissive hand through the air. "So, what of it? This is a night of celebration. We don't need a bunch of his *pendejos* smelling up the place."

There was uncertainty wrestling with confidence behind Vito's eyes.

"I'll arrange for him to be here the day of delivery," Vince said.

"At this point I'm unsure of your ability to persuade him," Vito said with a pause, "but changing horses now will take months to correct."

"He'll come," Vince contended. "He has too much to lose."

Vito paused in contemplation, gripping the edge of the desk. A chipped block of ice was sweating itself to death in the sink. Vince watched it melt in silence — ten — twenty; thirty seconds.

"Tell Venegas if he wants the sale, he'll receive half the money upfront by wire," Vito said at last. "The cash balance will be here when he arrives. He'll have to come get it."

Vito started pacing the floor, one hand in his pocket, the other on his chin. "Assuming Venegas accepts, he'll transport the product to the open sea to a predetermined drop. We will relay the coordinates to him by encrypted Internet message. Captain Bodega, whom I'll introduce to you later tonight, will pick up the shipment via his vessel, the *Nez Pierce*, a converted trawler, then bring it into the straits."

"From there," Vito continued, "divers will bring the shipment to a secret entrance in the bluff: a five-foot diameter hole bored into the basalt fifteen feet below low tide. The entrance is camouflaged, but easily found if you know where to look."

Vito walked to the window, motioning Vince to follow. Outside, the Geraci Crest flapped on a flagpole at the edge of the bluff, its serpentine form engulfed in a whitewash of spotlight.

"The flagpole marks the entrance and will direct the divers to the tunnel. Once past the netting, the divers will bring the cocaine another sixty feet under the compound where the tunnel takes a ninety-degree turn, rising straight up out of the stone into a cavernous lab below where we now stand. Below this very library." Vito jabbed a finger at the floor. "Hidden from view."

"In the lab," he continued, "the cocaine will be cut, weighed, repackaged and sealed in watertight bags. Then once again, using the tunnel, it'll emerge back into the Sound where the *Nez Pierce* awaits. She will transport the final product to Seattle."

Vito walked to the bookcase that spanned the wall to the right of the aquarium. One at a time, he tipped four books out at an angle from the shelves. "First there is *Tom Swift*. May the journey be so. Next Poe, *House of Usher*, for we'll usher in a new regime. Then O. Henry, *Strictly Business*. And finally, *Huck Finn*, let the adventure begin."

The bookcase eased away from the wall, a motor whirring somewhere in the depths below, and revolved to the right, revealing a stairway that wound down into the lab. The air rose out of it like a chimney, cool as a cavern, yet void of any smell, like breathing midnight sky or inhaling a dream. Vince followed Vito down the stairs, their shoes resounding off the metal treads and basalt walls, the slender stainless-steel rail slipping through his hand. The lights came on, triggered by electronic sensors.

Below, a capacious sculpture in gray basalt and glinting stainless steel emerged. Two long stainless-steel tables with sideboards set in the middle. Along one wall was a stainless-steel sink and two stainless-steel, industrial-size bread mixers. In the corner, a bathroom, all stainless-steel.

It was hospital clean. Operating room bright. Sterile and white and devoid of life, like the product that would be unbundled, cut and repackaged here.

Vince saw the metal hatch to the tunnel, closed, with a heavy handwheel on top, resembling a hat with a pompom. Above it was an electric winch with cable and hook, the yellow cord of the control pendant festooned off to one side.

"Can I open it?" Vince asked.

"Absolutely," Vito said. "But be prepared. It's heavy."

Vince spun the wheel counterclockwise until he saw the latches recede, then lifted the handle.

The walls of the shaft were mottled with shadow from the work of air-chisels. Vince could smell the basalt, musty with dampness, but the overpowering pungency was one of brine. There was a metal ladder attached to the wall of the shaft that showed signs of rust, and it descended into the water at a level ten feet below the top. At six feet, Vince could see a ring of algae marking high tide.

He saw his reflection on the flat surface of the water, the light of the room above him a halo about his head, then from the underside of the hatch, which was saturated with condensation, a drip plummeted to the water, rippling the surface, allowing him to see into the depths for an instant where he found crustaceans already accumulating — squatters on Geraci soil.

Once back in the library, Vito tipped the books back into place, a boast of cunning on his lips, as the bookcase swung back into position.

***

Elbows on the terrace railing, hands laced, Dane's eyes scudded across the black expanse of ocean. "Venegas isn't coming."

Tyra brushed a strand of hair from his forehead. "So what now?"

"Well, I can't leave it. Even if there's nothing on it, eventually someone will find it."

"Midnight might be a good time," Tyra said, "with all the commotion."

In the distance, freighters and fishing trawlers crossed paths in the Straits, reduced to pinpoints of light. "So how's Vick?"

"A mess," Tyra said.

"I'm sorry Tyra. I know you just met her."

"She needed help," she said, her face flushing with anger. "Vince told her it was business. His way or the highway back to being a stripper ... oh, I could kill him."

"So where is she now?"

"She left about ten minutes ago for Friday Harbor with the caterer's set-up crew."

Dane sighed.

"I tried to change her mind," Tyra said, "but she was determined to leave."

Perpetual waves moved like marching armies toward the shore, the sound of muffled cannon fire manifest as they broke across the rocks in battle. Contemplation had a saddle cinch tightened around Dane's ribs. He fired up a smoke. "Thanks for being here," he said.

Tyra placed her hand over his. Dane saw the moonlight flick in her hair, saw the lunar radiance shoot diamonds from her eyes.

Tyra kissed him on the cheek. "I'm going back inside," she said. "I like fresh air, but I'm getting cold."

Michael Geraci held the door as she reentered the mansion. He joined Dane at the rail. "Who's that?" he asked.

"My date," Dane said.

"Nice looking woman."

"Speaking of beauty. Where's Carmen tonight?"

Michael took a drink of his bourbon. His eyes were wet with alcohol. "She's lying low upstairs in her suite. The old man is on a rampage."

Dane rolled the filter of his cigarette between his thumb and forefinger. "It's none of my business, but I see the way you both look at each other."

"I saw you in the library with the old man and Vince."

Dane looked away toward the ocean. "Changing the subject?"

"Maybe," Michael admitted, "but having you around makes me think of a man walking into a china shop carrying a ten-foot piece of angle iron. No matter how you turn, shit's going to get broke."

"What makes you think I want to break things?"

"Just a feeling. I don't like many people. But for you, I'll make an exception."

"I must say you aren't what I expected, either."

"How so?"

"You're not like your father."

"True. My father doesn't like anyone except maybe Popes and Presidents, and that's simply because he figures they're the only guys carrying bigger sticks."

"Why don't you get away from him?"

Michael cocked his head and put his palms in the air, acknowledging the absurdity of the situation, yet conceding his inability to escape its reality. "Same reason you can't walk away from Vince. Too much water under the bridge."

***

With midnight approaching, the soiree was kicking into high gear. A DJ was spinning dance music to a crowd steeped in alcohol. Dane made his way upstairs for a quick snort before rejoining Tyra.

One of Johnny Smart's girls was standing at the banister. She wore a pink organdy dress, the hemline swaying high on her thighs in rhythm to the music. Her eyes were glazed, the whites tinged red from reefer hits.

As he climbed the stairs, he thought about the recorder. He knew a shipment was coming soon, but when and how and where?

He assumed the 'where' was the compound. It was secluded, on its own power source with no access roads, and one dock controlled by Geraci. Half the island was a bird sanctuary. It's a fortress in the classical Bondian style, he thought. Goldfinger would've been proud. He'd have to retrieve the recorder, but he assumed the 'when', and 'how', were not on it.

Dane opened the door to the suite. He was at the end of the pinky-finger. But he wasn't alone.

Lucky was lying on the edge of a canopied, king-size bed, one foot on the floor. He had a needle stuck in his arm, riding a thick blue vein like a giant plastic mosquito, his vacant eyes rolling up in his head like lemons on a slot machine.

His left arm was tied off with his bolo tie slightly above the elbow. He worked his jaw, but no words came. A handful of candy wrappers laid like crumpled flowers on the bed — a junkie four-course meal. The burning nub of a candle flickered on the nightstand.

Lucky's chest slackened as his breath left his body in a prolonged sigh. He'd entered a fourth dimension where cement sidewalks turn to sponge, where shapes fold and words take on different meanings from mouths that spew watery sounds from hollow faces.

Dane locked the door and closed it behind him, leaving Lucky — Roy Rogers with his horse, Silver — to melt into the surroundings.

CHAPTER 36

San Juan Islands, Washington
December 31, 1995

"You're sweating," Tyra said. "Are you okay?"

"Yeah," Dane said, the answer trailing off. He knew she was studying his face, trying to find some criminality there, her eyes-tinged electric-blue and liquid with adrenaline.

After seeing Lucky, he'd dipped into the upstairs bathroom and snorted a mass quantity. That was only ten minutes ago. His eyes were sinking into his head. Across the room by the buffet table, Dane saw Vince and Vito standing face-to-face, palavering, probably trying to decide who'd replace him after he was dead.

It was easy to sense Tyra wanted to say something. Her breathing was shallow and her eyes penetrating his skin. She laced her fingers around his and squeezed his hand tightly, like a rope on a cleat tied to an anchor. "Someday," she said, drawing out the word. "I'm going to help you kick this face-less enemy."

Dane was cognizant enough to see her concern. She was typical of someone who held the welfare of others above their own.

"We'll get to that," Dane said. He swallowed hard, his throat plastic and cool.

"In a matter of minutes, it'll be midnight." He pointed his chin toward Vince and Vito. "The Bobbsey Twins are over there, busy instructing Fate. I saw the albino exit the terrace door a minute ago, and Michael is nurturing another drink at the bar. It's now or never."

He slipped his hand free from hers. Tyra held a look of terror in her eyes. He felt a chord strum in his breast and put his hands on her shoulders. His eyes came to life. "Don't worry, mon chéri. I put the damn thing in there. I'll get it back."

***

Dane made his way to the library. The guests were milling about, speaking empty words filled with lust and the pride of life, their eyes aglitter with the moment as though they lived easily in swarms of merriment all their lives. Inconspicuous as a flu virus, he slipped unnoticed into the library.

His heart was pumping so hard his palms felt stiff with blood. He wiped a knuckle across his lip, his nose running with apprehension, his mouth watering as if he was chewing aspirin. It was so quiet he could hear a clock ticking — or was it his own clock counting down the seconds till expiration?

Dane fumbled for a light switch along the wall, found it, and clicked the first in a row of four. A pair of wall sconces lit up across the room. He shot to the bar, to the recorder hid beneath its lip.

He slipped down onto one knee and pried it loose, the two-sided adhesive giving way, then pressed the adhesive in between a folded dollar bill and slipped it into his trouser pocket.

Dane could hear the buzz of the aquarium pump, feel a dull ache congealing in the fluid of his knee, and as he stood, like a welder's arc, the light within the room burst with intensity.

"I bother you," Evohl said. He was standing like a monolith in the doorway, the din of the party behind him.

Dane glanced at the door in cool shock and lowered his voice. "Bother me. You're joking." He felt like he'd just swallowed a thumbtack.

"So, what you do here?" Evohl asked.

Even though he couldn't see them behind the dark sunglasses, Dane felt the albino frisking him with his eyes. He sidled to the back of the bar, his skull tingling like a beehive, hiding the recorder at his side behind the spade of his palm. It felt like a tarantula in his hand, alive with consequences.

"Uh-well ... you've got me by the short-and-curlies here," Dane said, trying to inject some humor into the moment. Once behind the bar, he slipped the recorder in with the dollar bill.

The albino didn't laugh. He was so impassive; a match could've been struck off his jaw and he wouldn't've even flinched.

"I don't want to lie to you. I was raiding Vito's scotch."

Then, as the fabrication unfolded in his mind, Dane felt a knot of anxiousness unravel in his chest. "I had some earlier with Vince and Vito and heck, what can I say? I wanted more."

"Interesting," Evohl said, grinning his toothy grin, the way a major league pitcher would after delivering a curve ball that left you corkscrewing in the dirt. His pearly-whites were like a row of grave markers in Arlington Cemetery. Dane could smell cigar smoke on his clothes, garlic and basil fecund on his breath.

Dane put an unlit cigarette in his mouth. "If you think I shouldn't, please turn the other way, or else pull up a stool and I'll pour you a drink so we can toast the New Year." Was there a tremor in his voice? he mused. He wanted desperately to sound secure.

Evohl kept one palm flat on the bar and slid a tumbler into position in front of his massive body. Dane took the gesture as a "yes" and positioned a tumbler for himself, then laid out two fingers in each glass.

"A toast," Dane held up his tumbler. "To you, to me ..." Dane lost his train of thought, realizing he had an unlit cigarette waggling from his lips.

"To scotch," Evohl raised his glass, his upper arm bulging, a balloon full of lug nuts and ball bearings.

Dane pulled the cigarette from his mouth. "To scotch," he said, mimicking Evohl's deep accented voice. Then they clicked glasses and downed the scotch.

Evohl wiped his mouth with the back of his hand. His neck was like a tree stump, the thick trapezius muscles at the base like massive roots gnarling into his shoulders.

Dane poured two more fingers into each glass. He felt the blood throbbing in his neck, felt sure Evohl could see the panic in his eyes. Once again, he inserted the unlit cigarette between his lips. "Do you know much about books?" As soon as it left his mouth, he knew it was an inane question.

Evohl scratched his grainy neck, his fingernails thick as tortoiseshell. The corners of his mouth curled down, and conjecture drew lines on his forehead. Dane felt a stiletto pierce his façade.

Suddenly, the door opened, and Lance strolled into the room. A breeze of party sound floated in with him. "Oh hey, Mister Avilla," he said. A nanosecond later, he noticed the albino, and his upbeat mien disintegrated.

Dane welcomed the addition, even though now he had four eyeballs to keep track of. "What's up, Lance? I thought you'd be outside, keeping us safe from all those things that go bump in the night."

Evohl swiveled his head, shadowing Lance's movement.

"Mister Spinetti sent me to get his bottle of champagne." Lance pointed with his finger. Behind the bar, a bottle of Dom Perignon was shoulder deep in a sweating ice bucket.

Dane wanted to pace, like a cat finds panic in a rowboat on water.

"You trying to quit smoking, Mister Avilla?" Lance asked.

"Huh?"

Lance looked at his watch. "My pop used to run around with a dead cigarette hanging out of his mouth. He said it was his way of quitting smoking."

"No, I ..." Dane hesitated, his voice fading black, realizing the unlit cigarette was still dangling from the corner of his mouth. He could feel the albino looking at the side of his face, stripping away the layers of deception like a meat slicer.

He began slapping his pockets, looking for his lighter, until a flame wavered in front of his face. Evohl held the source in his hand. Dane leaned in, lit up, and took a nervous puff.

Lance went behind the bar, lifted the bottle from the ice, and wrapped it in a towel. "Anyway, Mister Avilla," Lance said, looking at his watch again. "In like two minutes it's twelve-up midnight, and I don't want to miss out on the broads giving out lip-locks when the ball drops. You get what I'm saying?"

The words were like a "Get-Out-of-Jail-Free" card. "Oh yeah, I hear you loud and clear," Dane said. He squashed his cigarette in the ashtray, then gave Evohl a make-shift salute. "See you on the other side of midnight."

CHAPTER 37

Seattle, Washington
January 2, 1996

The lamps were down, the only light coming to the walls from a video muted on the TV. A single burner hot plate glowed searing-orange in the flickering darkness like a coil sun, the heat flushing his cheeks as he leaned over to intake the stream of brown smoke that at first burst with a mushroom cloud, then writhed into the air with the tail of a snake, a hash ball the size of a BB melting like butter on the sizzling surface.

Tony choked down the hit — eyes bulging under pressure, the sensation of veins rupturing in his temples — and as the music waned between songs, Tony heard Jenny at the far end of the hall, the bedroom dim, the walls undulating with sadness from the tongue of a candle licking the cooking spoons of smack.

Ziggy had arrived just after midnight. A guy with a goatish face, he had a long protruding nose rising to a plank forehead, eyes as lifeless as pennies, and a straggle of hair hanging from his chin.

Jenny loved smack like most people love ice cream. Tony heard the bed creak under the weight of their bodies. He erased the sound from his mind, then dropped another ball to the red-hot burner, the next song winding up on the stereo, The Cure stinging his ears with "Fascination Street."

***

She got up from the bed, and up on one elbow, Vince studied her derriere while she walked for the bathroom, his eyes glued to the tight twitch of her butt with an intensity that could impregnate. The light of the bathroom behind her emphasized her curves, and he had an overwhelming desire to swallow her whole in one gulp, like a cartoon Taz would swallow a ham.

He'd woken at midnight from an early slumber with a sexual craving so intense he couldn't waste it. He called Tracy, and she came right over. She was always ready to party and loved her cocaine and chocolate and whiskey sours. Beyond perfection, she kept her body manicured like the greens at Augusta, and her ample cleavage would bring tears to a priest. He couldn't help but notice the way her legs moved in a skirt, like scissors flashing in the midday sun, her butt like two cats in a bag, each trying to fight their way out.

Tracy came back to the bed, those scissors flashing, the cats out of the bag, her lips glistening like fresh morning dew. She slid beneath him, and he felt the warmth of her thigh against his, and his desire pulsed deep inside.

He kissed her neck, one side, then the next, while she squirmed and moaned, her body writhing like a trout on a hook. He was coiled with sexual energy, and for the next hour, he'd have his way with her, slow and smooth, exactly like he planned, like they were soaring for another planet, a thousand miles from the Earth, weightless and free.

***

The bourbon went down hard, straight with a twist of regret. Dane wanted to apologize for his failings, yet the indescribably sad feeling he carried inside couldn't be translated into words and instead, he felt his heart being dug out with a dull spoon.

He knew what he must do, but his mind kept see-sawing, Pharmakeia's thumb on one end, sobriety on the other. His lungs felt white-capped with anxiety, like someone else knew the score and how far he was in debt.

After midnight, it was windy in the trees and the sky was full of rain, the windows rattling occasionally with an angry fist. He closed his eyes and let the alcohol take him like spice travelers on Dune to another space and time: Summer; a twirling sprinkler casting rainbows on the wind; the soft click of the oscillating fan as it changed directions; kids running and playing, splashing their feet.

And he realized no matter how close you get to the mirror, all you see is yourself. You look for a crack in the vision, something to prove it isn't real, a ripple in the silver, but it's you and only you and there is no getting away from it.

***

Jason Riker eased back in the leather chair, his thin briefcase in his lap, then rested his elbows on the chair's arms, holding the morning edition of the *Post-Intelligencer.* The headline read: "CARTWRIGHT TO STEP DOWN."

He blew a torrent of frustration through his teeth as he laid the paper to rest in his briefcase, then snapped the lid shut. Riker knew in his conceited heart that if this investigation was a success, he'd be a definite candidate for the Director position. He had Cartwright's ear. Now all he needed was a couple of sweeping strokes on his golden resume, the caliber of a Geraci, the originality of a Spinetti, and all his dreams would come true.

Yet he could still hear his words like a broken record — Virchow and his old school mentality. Words like: "Hang tight" and "Have patience," but Riker's day was coming now, not later, and without a little grease on the wheels of justice, his ace would show too late.

Riker erased Virchow's countenance from his head — his burr haircut, his skunky cigarettes, his continual demands — and replaced it with Geraci's head mounted over his mantle and "Director" lengthening his name.

He straightened his tie, picked a stray thread from the arm of his dark gray suit, and peered down at the crease of his pant leg that lay precisely over his kneecap, admiring the shine on his week-old Ballys.

In the office where he sat, there were trophies galore, short ones, tall ones; a prestigious bronze running back stiff-arming his way toward the goal set prominently on a fluted pedestal. On the wall, plagues and diplomas hung next to autographed pictures of local celebrities, and a snapshot of Ronnie, Nance and Tip O'Neill at a political event.

The opposite wall was a bookcase filled with law books, their spines deformed in the long morning shadows by a sun rising in the windows behind a walnut desk, a perfect yellow plate cracked by the limbs of a towering maple tree in the courtyard. On the front lip of the desk was a triangle of wood, which read: *Hollis J. Green, District Attorney King County,* in bold script.

Riker set his briefcase upright by the leg of his chair, then lifted an eight-by-ten of the wife and kids that sat on the corner of the sprawling desk. The wide silver frame felt heavy in his hand. His wife: beautiful and chic; he was envious.

"You approve?" a booming voice questioned from behind him.

Riker jerked, throwing a look over his shoulder, his heart climbing in his throat. "Oh-wow, you caught me by surprise." He took a breath, replacing the photograph, then stood to shake hands with the imposing figure of Hollis Green. He had an enormous grip that nearly swallowed Riker's hand.

Green set a brown accordion file on a worktable in front of the windows. Rays of sun broke off his square shoulders.

Regaining his composure, Riker said, "You have a fine-looking family. You can see the boys take after their dad."

Green moved papers from one section of the file to another.

"Actually, I was admiring your nameplate, too," Riker said. "Mine is polished aluminum. I guess the county makes out a little better than us Feds," he said with a feigned laugh.

"It was a gift from my father," Green remarked, turning now from the accordion file, pulling off his suit jacket, hanging it in a corner closet before sitting down behind the desk. He was a trim, fit black man, with large sinewy hands, and eyes so black they shined with reflective light. He had a chin as wide as his temples, shoulders an ax handle across, and a neck ridged like the slopes of Mount Rainier. His white shirt was impeccably pressed, the letters HJG monogrammed into the pocket. He wore black suspenders, jade cufflinks, a crimson tie and dark wool trousers. He leaned back in his chair and laced his hands behind his head, his biceps threatening to tear at the fabric of his shirt.

"So, what can I do for you, Mr. Riker," Green said.

Green was well known in political circles, was a member of all the right golf courses, and had lunch with the most influential of judges. Educated at Stanford, he had a razor-sharp mind with a shrewd, maniacal edge that could terrify the worst offenders. In addition, there were rumors that Hollis Green also aspired for the Senate.

"Thank you for seeing me on such short notice," Riker said.

"My pleasure." Green put his hands in his lap, rocking slowly with both feet on the ground. "So, want brings the DEA to the hallowed halls of the county courthouse?"

"Not to waste your time, so I'll get right to it."

"I appreciate that," Green said. "I'm expected in court at nine-thirty, and Judge Fartwell is an intolerant SOB."

"Fartwell?" Riker said.

"Insider joke," Green said. "Let's have it." He leaned forward, putting his thick forearms flat on the desk, his Lincoln-log fingers toying with the edge of the blotter.

Riker readjusted his position in the chair, shifting his weight first left, then right in the seat. "We have a man in our possession that has knowledge of cocaine trafficking in the Seattle area."

"A snitch," Green said, coming to the point.

"Precisely. This man, Nick Franklin, has steered us toward some big players, and as a result, we have several mules that we could convict today."

"Good-good," Green said, nodding his head. "How can I help?" His eyes never left Riker's face.

"I'm hoping you can, but as you well know, these mules are mere spokes in a wheel, and frankly sir, we're tired of only derailing these organizations for a short period, allowing them to fix their operations quickly and pick up again where they left off faster than we can regroup. No sir, this time we want the hub. Take out the entire apparatus, some would say."

"I see." Green sat back in his chair, appearing to read memories from a secret tablet suspended over Riker's head. "I seem to remember the name Nick Franklin," he said. "He's got a sheet?"

"Oh yes sir," Riker said. "Reads like a comic book."

"Perhaps, does he have an older brother?"

"Yes sir, Tony Franklin. He and Nick are both a part of this organization, but they're not the focus of our investigation."

"Now I remember." Green's eyes dropped back onto Riker's face. "But you say they're not the focus. Then who is?"

"This must be kept in the strictest of confidence," Riker said with a hint of superiority.

Green stroked his large rawboned jaw with a hand that sparkled with a diamond Rose Bowl ring that was big as a Mercedes. "I don't write a gossip column, Mr. Riker, and I'm not in the habit of spilling the beans."

"I'm sorry, I didn't mean to offend ..."

"You haven't. Merely setting the ground rules, I understand. But let's get to it."

"Thank you, and I will," Riker said. "We have evidence of an association between a businessman here in Seattle, Vincent Spinetti, and one of the most notorious men in organized crime, Vittorio Geraci."

Green appeared shocked by the revelation. "Geraci?" he said. "I thought he was strictly East Coast?"

"Not anymore."

"This gets better by the minute," Green said ardently. "Please, go on."

"For months we've worked every angle on these two, trying to get any piece of evidence that will tie them to the trade, but so far, we've got nothing concrete to go on. Franklin has provided us with the best information he can, but it's not enough."

"Seems Geraci is more agile than a cat. No matter how you flip him, he always ends up on his feet."

"He is cunning, but so was Gotti," Riker said.

"But it sounds as though you've reached an impasse," Green said. "These apes never connect themselves with the workers on the street."

"There's a third man, Mr. Green, and this is where you come in. He appears to be close friends with Spinetti, and we're almost certain he's a part of the operation."

"Well, who is it, man? I'm all ears."

"Patrick Donovan ... Metro Chief."

Green averted his eyes and swiveled his chair to the right in mild shock. His eyes became lost under the maple tree in the courtyard, focused on a small wooden bench that was still cold and blue with shadow.

"I understand Donovan is a friend," Riker said.

Green rubbed the back of his neck. "Not socially. But on a public service level, yes, we're friends. We've worked together on many cases."

"It may be hard to believe, but he wouldn't be the first cop to stray, supplementing their income from nefarious sources," Riker said.

A nervous tic, Riker played with his ring, slipping it on and off his finger. "What I need from you is information, Mister Green, but I take it by your reaction, you knew nothing of his involvement?"

Green shook his head, kept looking oddly out into space, a calm perplexity in his mien, like he was trying to decide which offer to take — the money or what's behind door number three.

"I hoped you were already running an internal investigation on Donovan," Riker said. "A long shot, but worth a chance. I know this must seem out of the blue, but can we get to him? You know, make him talk."

"With what?" Green bellowed, his shoulders shooting up to his ears. He turned to face Riker and stared with an amused glare. "You said yourself you've nothing to go on except his acquaintance with this Spinetti fellow."

"Possibly ..."

"I know nothing of his personal affairs, Mister Riker," Green said cutting Riker off, "and do not know of any crime. What do you think ... that I have some special power over Chief Donovan? I'm afraid not. I know this much; you'd better have something more than a casual acquaintance to go on if you want to confront Chief Donovan and bring him down."

Green stood up behind his desk and touched his wrist, checking the time. He paused with a thought, then concluded, "Look, I don't know if he's dirty or not, but he's a smart man, and if you confront him with this, he'll laugh in your face and call you ludicrous. You'll never break him unless you've got some hard evidence, eyewitnesses, videotape, something that ties him to the crime. Otherwise, you're simply showing your hand."

Riker felt a twinge in his neck and heard the voice of Derek Virchow in Hollis Green's words.

CHAPTER 38

Avery Beck was a detective in the South Precinct. McTarnihan and he had graduated from the Police Academy together, and Avery was there the day McTarnihan turned in his badge. He had shoe brush eyebrows, and a toupee that looked like a handful of horsehair sprayed with shellac.

McTarnihan was apprising the area, his eyes slick with grief. Yellow cordon tape was strung through the trees, other officers were milling about, a black body bag lie in wait at the side of the gravel road.

"Ahhh," Avery said, his nose angled upward as if the air were blooming with lavender. "I love the smell of creosote and slaughterhouses in the morning."

McTarnihan stroked his orange caterpillar mustache.

They were standing on a gravel access road a quarter mile in from the primary thoroughfare, forty feet from the edge of the Duwamish River. Empire Meat Packing was behind them. Two-hundred-feet further, the road ended behind Stinson Ltd., a company that produced utility poles by impregnating skinned fir trees with creosote.

"A vagrant found the body," Avery said. "He runs a trapline along the river. Over by his shack, he's got a crawdad pot in the river."

Avery was looking downstream. McTarnihan saw a wood frame storage shed with white paint that had blistered and curled into strips like plucked chicken feathers.

"Does he know the Duwamish is the most polluted river in the state?"

Avery spit on the ground. "Can't say. Although dining here is probably fresher than the dumpsters downtown."

McTarnihan adjusted his homburg.

"Do you want to talk to him?" Avery asked, pointing his chin toward the vagrant, who was sitting on an upended bucket twenty-feet away, smoking the tarred stub of a hand-rolled cigarette. He was a purple-faced derelict with more wrinkles than a shar-pei. His clothes were layered in places as thin as cheesecloth. On his head, he wore a nubby brown stocking cap low over his ears.

McTarnihan shook his head.

Avery gestured to an officer to dismiss the vagrant.

"The victim had her hands zip-tied behind her back, then suffocated with a plastic bag. It's a produce bag used in most grocery stores. She had bruising consistent with being held down. Evidence is secure, photos complete, and the M.E. has come and gone," Avery said. "You want a look before we bag the body?"

McTarnihan wiped sweat from the band inside his hat, then looked back down the slope to where the body lay, his throat as dry and scratchy as burnt toast. He was hoping he was wrong, but he had only one way to find out.

Avery blew a nostril to the ground. "By the way. How'd you know South Precinct would get the call?"

McTarnihan shrugged. "Everybody knows the Duwamish is Seattle's favorite dumping ground."

McTarnihan heard a beep-beep, then saw a forklift enter the back of Empire's white cinder-block building from a raised cement dock. Several cattle cars set on a rail spur at the far end of the building, the cows inside bellowing in frantic desperation, awaiting a sure bullet in the head.

Between the plant and the road were huddles of old processing equipment inside a perimeter of chain-link fence topped with razor wire. Overgrown with grass and bull thistle, the fence was wallpapered with windblown sheets of paper and plastic. The air smelled of blood and guts and fat boiled in a vat, with a hint of creosote thrown in for good measure. The sound of motors whirring, conveyors clanking, and steam vents hissing, was incessant.

After McTarnihan sidled his way down the steep embankment of thick grass, hanging onto the branches of bushes for support and digging his heels in the soft earth, he stood at a place leveled out about the size of a billiard table, alongside which several fifty-five-gallon barrels were buried waist deep oozing a black muck through rust holes. He could feel his heartbeat in his face. The sun had come up bright that morning and even though it was still January-cold, the insects were boiling in the tall grass.

Ten feet from the water's edge, Erin lay on her back, her body half-buried in wind-blown leaves as if a thousand hands were there to hold her. McTarnihan brushed a few away from her face. They felt heavy with deterioration — full of death.

Her clothes were torn. Her skin had blackened to the powdery color of charcoal, leaving those areas in contact with the earth a pale gray. Extensive areas of muscle were gone — ravaged by animals. The stench was overwhelming. He peeled a stick of spearmint gum and stuck it in his mouth.

The rising sun was touching the river now with its heat and steam rose like wood smoke from the surface, faintly haloing the river with a ghostly humidity, while long-legged water bugs scooted along on the stagnant surface.

McTarnihan stared at the body and somewhere deep inside an animal broke loose from its chains. He wanted to shout, wail with ball-fire anger and eternal damnation at the world, but his throat felt as dry and thick as a razor strop, and the rage just roiled within him.

A flock of starlings were circling over the river, venturing closer to see what was up. An ugly bird, raven-black with yellow eyes. Some were perched in the surrounding trees, gawking, squawking, eavesdropping, compiling a report for the netherworld.

He sank with disappointment, his heart plummeting fast and devastating like a ship with its underbelly gored, while in the background all he heard was the birds squawking and the cows bellowing and the drag chain at the creosote plant pulling logs going clankity-clankity-clank.

CHAPTER 39

Seattle, Washington
January 3, 1996

Tony Franklin sat at the curb in his Honda Prelude, a Stones CD spinning in the dash, the afternoon sun bright through his windshield, warming the interior of the car. He could imagine Jaggar doing his antics on stage. Never saw him in person, but he got an electrical short in his jaw thinking about the purple barrel acid he'd dropped at an Aerosmith concert at the Kingdome once.

From the corner of his eye, his head bobbing slightly to "Some Girls", Tony glimpsed his brother Nick coming off the steps of the apartment house where him and his ole-lady Arial lived on the second floor in a run-down three-room dive. Dressed for success, Nick wore his patented acid-wash Levi's, which he always wore slung low so everyone could see what boxers he had on. A Hamm's T-shirt with that dopey bear on the chest, rounded out his attire.

The Rasmussen was a two-story brick building in the low-rent part of Edmonds that had two wings that met at a slight angle at the entrance. Over the door, "Rasmussen" was spelled out in neon like it was some great place to be, which always made Tony laugh, because it was a dump; but Tony did like the way when it rained and it was dark at night that the purple-and-gold neon looked whispery, like cool smoke against the brick.

He had little use for Arial. She was okay to look at in a Cyndi Lauper sort of way, but from the first day they met, they were like opposite poles of a magnet. You could only get so close before some unseen force stuck a palm in your chest and said, "Stay back asshole, I feel your vibes and they make my teeth ache."

Of course, it could've been "bitch" instead of "asshole" depending upon which pole was doing the talking, but for instance, she'd told him once she felt "impinged." Tony looked it up and told her the next time he saw her she should take some Ex-lax 'cause it always seemed to help him. Arial flipped him off, then told him he was an "ignoramus."

Tony looked that up too — hell, he was just trying to be nice — but it was like that between them all the time. They didn't like the same food, the same movies, the same music. Nothing. And another thing was Arial liked these kitschy oil landscapes you can get at the Greenwood Inn up in Marysville on every other Saturday from some starving artists that sold the pieces of shit for like ten bucks or eight-fifty if you pressed them hard, and she'd hang the damn things all over the place.

Boats in a harbor, sunsets on the ocean, green meadows in the mountains. Tony hated those paintings and Arial knew Tony hated them by the way he'd told her he hated them, so with that and because of the other things, Tony would never go in, and he'd simply pull up to the curb and wait for Nick to come out.

Why she threw away the bare-chested Mexican broad on black velvet, the one with the big bazookas he'd given them for Christmas a few years back he'd never know, but when Tony heard Arial had chucked the painting, it was like "the final straw in the camel's mouth." He decided then and there he was never gonna set foot in her landscapy apartment again.

The door locked; Nick rapped on the passenger-side window with his red knuckles. Tony opened the door from the inside. Tony had on a pair of black denims and a white AC/DC T-shirt under his tweed jacket.

"Hey Bro," Tony said, as Nick slid into the seat. "How's it hangin'?"

"Can't complain. Arial made me a berry pie. Well, really, she made herself a berry pie, and I got to eat some hot out of the oven with ice cream. Shit, being eight months pregnant can be a drag, but she sure is cooking a lot more desserts these days."

Nick stuck one of his high-top sneakers up on the dash, pulled a joint out of his T-shirt pocket and fired it up with a butane lighter that had a whistling three-inch flame. "So, why's Vince want to see me?" he asked, holding his toke and sounding like a balloon with the air leaking out.

Tony pulled out onto the street, edging past Nick's green '67 Impala with the tore vinyl top and the rusty quarter panels. It was parked at the curb with one flat tire.

"I don't know, man," Tony remarked. "If I knew all what was in his head, hell ... he just said meet him at Shilshole Bay."

Nick started digging through the roaches in the ashtray. "Well, shit, he's never wanted to see me before." He found a spent paper match, split it with a thumbnail, the crotch of the forked stem perfect as a makeshift roach clip.

"Be cool Nick. Things are changing. If Vince wants to see you, he must have a good reason. Maybe it's time for you to move up."

They made the I-5 on-ramp in minutes and merged into the hoard of traffic moving toward Seattle. Nick held the clip to Tony's lips so he could toke.

When Tony exhaled, he hesitated with a rush, blacking out for an instant as he passed a rock truck in the fast lane. When he came to, he said, "Holy shit," then slipped a vintage Aerosmith CD in the dash, cranking the sound just shy of bleeding eardrums.

***

Derek Virchow was stuck in construction traffic, blood pressure high enough to blow the gaskets out of a big-block Chevy. He hadn't moved in fifteen minutes, but the topper was he'd just gotten off the phone with Bradley.

Kulich, Bradley's stakeout partner, had left for urgent care with a festering hangnail. Soon after, Spinetti left in his Porsche. Bradley followed, but stopped to pee, so he lost him. When he got back to the stakeout location, Spinetti's yacht had sailed. Now both Spinetti and his yacht were missing.

"That's perfect," Virchow said with enough sarcasm to flay skin. "Bradley, the next time I see you, that's if I don't stroke-out first, you'd better be wearing a diaper."

He snuffed out his cigarette. "Now find that boat! Or you'll be behind a desk so long you'll root into the carpet."

CHAPTER 40

San Juan Islands, Washington
January 3, 1996

The *Ecstasea* was floating in two-foot swells sixty miles north-west of Shilshole Bay Marina. Earlier in the day she'd traversed the Ballard Locks, then cruised south of Whidbey Island until now five hours later, she sat poised at the east end of the Straits of Juan de Fuca, centered over the imaginary line between Canada and the United States.

They trolled for fish, watched the sunset like a welder's arc, cutting the Olympic Mountain Range from a black piece of steel, then as a full moon rose over the Cascades flat as a communion wafer, they retired to the Main Salon, indulging in copious amounts of coke and alcohol, until now it was nearly midnight.

Nick was sitting at the bar and Vince was behind the bar, busy twisting the lid off a bottle of bourbon.

"Gees, eight months," Vince said in a concerned voice. "What do you do with a broad who's eight months pregnant?"

Nick shrugged his shoulders, lost as to an answer.

"So, Nick, do you want to know why I brought you on this glorious fishing trip?"

Dane had been wondering the same thing for hours. Vince's magnanimity always came at a price.

"Sure-sure," Nick stuttered. "Tony said like maybe I'd be moving up."

"Moving up, huh?"

Vince stared at his drink for a torturous span of time until Nick asked, "So why *am* I here?"

Ted Nugent's "Stranglehold" was on the stereo. Looking Nick in the eyes, Vince replied, "Simple, Nick. You've been talking to the Feds."

Dane had heard Nick's fateful question but couldn't believe the stinging answer. Tony's face turned a pale blue, his hands like blocks of ice. It was like someone had kicked open the door to Antarctica, and in the chilled silence, Vince's answer floated like a nerve gas cloud. No one wanted to breathe. Dane dropped his forehead to his hand, his mind heavy with consequence, realizing why Nick was aboard.

Tony uttered a simple word of disbelief. "What?"

Nick rubbed his palms together, his shoulders limp and lifeless. Dane could see it in his eyes. They'd grown dull, shaded with uncertainty.

"Is that right, Nick?" Tony asked, moving to within a foot of Nick's face.

Nick stared at Tony with pleading eyes, then nodded his head.

"Yeah but, you didn't name any names did ya?"

Nick was silent, but the answer was clear.

Tony glanced at Vince, then back. "Yeah but, you were in big trouble. Right, Nick?"

Nick stared at his feet. A bubble of saliva formed at the corner of his mouth.

"Yeah but ..."

"Enough with the 'yeah buts' Tony," Vince said. "Nick sold us out. Didn't you Nick?"

Vince waited for an answer. They all waited for an answer. Something concrete to confirm or deny. Tony turned away and fell into a chair.

Vince paused snickering in the wretched stillness, then put on a face so smooth you would've thought it was an angel's wing. "Just tell me what you did and maybe we can fix it." He said it so calmly, it was almost like he meant it.

Dane knew better. He'd been around long enough to know that Vince was straining like a tree heavy with snow, serene at the moment, but at some point, he was going to snap. His mind started racing, thinking of a defense.

Tony threw his head back on the chair and stared blindly at the ceiling.

Vince walked to the intercom and called Sean down from the bridge. Then walked an aimless circle, a hand cupped on the nape of his neck. "So, Nick," he said at last. "Remember earlier we were talking about character? You know, owning up to problems?"

Nick wagged his head, his face a burlesque of apprehension.

"So why don't we do some character building? Start, let's say, by you telling me what happened. From the beginning."

Dane pulled a cigarette and watched Nick's throat muscles try to swallow the truth.

Nick shifted his weight on the barstool. "Maybe if I had another drink. I think my mouth is dry."

Vince slid a finger along the bar with a dreamy expression. "Sure Nick. Have a drink. Have a line. Take your time." He slid the bottle of bourbon in Nick's direction, then laid the tooter by its side. "Just don't let the clock run out, Nick. I have the patience of a heart attack. One minute purring like a kitten, next minute ... well, you get the idea."

Sean came in. He had Jimmy with him. He told Vince that Lance was at the helm.

Vince nodded his approval, then turned his attention back to Nick. "Oops," he said with a jerk, grimacing as he laid a palm to his chest, twitching in mock cardiac arrest. "I feel pain, Nick. Do something."

Nick's bourbon eyes grew large and bright. His face was drawn and hard. Then, as the show Vince was providing subsided, he placed a well-chewed pinkie in his mouth. "It's not as bad as you think," he said in a patronizing voice that sounded feeble at best.

Dane stared at the yellow-gray lines of sweat half-mooning Nick's armpits, then watched Sean shake his head as he took out a towel, held it under a cold spigot, then twisted it damp and laid it around his own neck.

Vince picked up his glass and made wet rings on the bar. "Let me jog your memory. You remember Mr. Hollis Green, don't you Nick? That big black D.A." — he held up his hands, palm facing palm like he was holding an ax handle by the ends in front of his face — "The one with the shoulders about yea wide. You know, the one that let you off on a technicality the last time you got popped for possession. How do you think that happened, Nick? Think God was looking down that day and just for the hell of it, he slapped old Saint Peter on the back and said, 'Hey Pete, let's give this poor asshole a break'." Vince shook his head. "I don't think so Nick."

Vince finished his bourbon with a quick flip of the wrist, then set the glass down and slid it away with the back of his fingers. "I'll tell you what happened. Hollis is as crooked as a bolt of lightning, and not surprisingly, he's in my pocket. All two-hundred-and-seventy pounds of dark meat so deep he ain't ever gonna see the light of day. All these political types need donors, Nick, and when he heard the bad things you've been saying, he felt compelled to tell me. So how about it, Nick? Are you gonna tell me what's what? I've plumb run out of patience on this."

"Maybe Hollis is playing you for a fool," Tony said with enthusiasm, like maybe he'd found a loophole for Nick to crawl through.

"Tony, shut up will ya?" Vince said with derision. "Nobody plays me for a fool. I may know fools, but no one plays me for a fool." He looked at Nick, his eyes hard as granite. "At least not more than once."

Again, Nick didn't answer. He sat on the barstool, picking his cuticles, one leg bouncing like it was made of flubber.

Vince looked at Sean with resolve in his eyes.

Sean took the towel from his neck and tossed it in the sink, then walked around the end of the bar. Before Nick could back away, he grabbed Nick's arm at the wrist, and with a quick twist, wrenched it up between his shoulder blades. Nick popped up off the barstool like a Jack-in-the-box and started dancing on the balls of his feet. Tears of pain welled in his eyes. Sean could have ripped his arm off at the shoulder, as easily as a drumstick detaches from an over-cooked chicken.

Nick was squealing like a stuck pig. Tony jumped out of the chair, bumping into Dane in the confusion.

"Nick," Vince said. "I'll have Sean stick your arm down your throat before this is over. Make it easy on yourself and tell me what I want to know."

"Okay-okay." Nick was choking out the words. "Let me go. I'll talk."

Sean let go, and Nick touched the pain in his shoulder with his hand. He started treading back and forth, massaging his shoulder, adamantly trying to explain the situation to his benefit.

Vince sat back on a barstool to listen. Dane and Tony stood stone-faced at the revelations. Sean moved behind the bar and got himself a bottled water to drink.

Animated by fear, Nick's face was full of blood. It was a toady supplication, prancing around in front of his master, like a dog slavering for a bone.

It took ten minutes to spew it out. How he got caught at the border. How the Feds put the screws to him. It was exhausting. For everyone.

"So, what do they have?" Tony said out of left field, as though he'd caught the act, but missed the plot.

"Cops get info, Tony. They don't give it," Nick said sarcastically. "But I never said nothing about Geraci."

That admission was the nail in the coffin, and things got as quiet as a casket six feet under.

Tony spun toward the windows. Dane knew Vince had told Tony explicitly to never mention Geraci's name to anyone, and he knew the proverbial *shit* had just hit the fan.

"Geraci! Geraci!" Vince started barking. "You told them about Geraci."

"Calm down Vince," Dane said, raising a palm. "Calm down." In between his fingers was the cigarette he'd pulled minutes before, unlit, now nearly torn in half by the crush of his hand like tension had torn the belly out of the room.

"Calm down! Calm down!" Vince howled. "Do you know what he's done? If Vito ... Dane if Vito ever finds out. There isn't a hole deep enough to crawl into. We're dead. We're all dead."

"I understand," Dane said, "but flipping out now will not produce any answers. It was bound to happen. The FBI has been after Geraci for years."

"How do you suddenly know so much?"

There was a hint of suspicion in Vince's question. Dane had to be quick on his feet. "It's been in the papers. I do read, you know."

"Don't get smart!" Vince's neck was flaring. Then he wiped his mouth with the back of his hand, his eyes holding a manic gaze. "I just can't let people shoot their mouths off to the police. Understand? It's unhealthy."

"Okay-okay, but let's talk about it. There's got to be a way out." Dane knew in the back of his mind that desperate men do desperate things, and that knowledge was like a turnbuckle between his ears.

"There's what?" Vince said. "A way out?" Then, like he'd answered his own question, it hit him. Vince's expression became set, his eyes rigidly curious.

***

Minutes later, Vince pushed Nick to the aft. Pearl-sized drops of rain pocked the swells and exploded on the gunwales like

Fourth of July fireworks. The water around the *Ecstasea* was aglow, yellow with submersible light; the aft deck was dimly ethereal in the shadows cast by the shifting bodies.

Dane was nervous. "What are you going to do, Vince?"

"Yeah, Vince, don't go crazy here," Tony said.

"You shut up," he said, pointing a finger in Tony's face. "I told you to straighten him out. What do I have to do? Ram some backbone up your ass."

A cold northerly sliced through the deck, a pelting downpour in its wake. How quickly hair and clothes became dark with rain. At that moment, even though it seemed strange, Dane could smell the dank and musty odor of wet dogs.

"Tell Lance to keep her steady," Vince began giving commands, "and pipe some music out here. I hate the sound of rain."

Jimmy ran inside. His Glock slapping at his ribs.

"There's a way out of this," Dane said.

"Only the hard way," Vince replied.

"I don't believe that. There must be ..."

"Cut the bullshit, Dane. You know as well as I do, something must be done. Like taking out the garbage, either do it or die in the stench."

"Okay-okay, but what you have in mind, think about it." The stiff wind had turned Dane's ears to pinpricks of ice. His hands were stinging as if black thorns were blossoming between his knuckles.

"Think about *what* Dane? There's a leak in the hull," — Vince tilted his head toward Nick — "tell me how I keep run-at-the-mouth-Nick quiet."

After a three second intro of crackling electronic static, a set of bongos came over the speakers, and then Bryan Ferry singing "Limbo." Nick looked at Dane, then at Tony. Tony was pacing the stern, his head heavy, chin-to-chest, as though there was an anchor about his neck.

Vince seemed relieved at the sound of the music, as though the voodoo rhythm was taking the sting out of his thoughts like Novocain for his brain. "I want you to know, Nick," he said, the apology coming in his acknowledgment, not his voice. "I didn't plan it this way."

"Listen, I-I-I-I can fix this," Nick said in a fearful stutter. His ears were turning white along the edges. His T-shirt was clinging wet, his ribs like strangling fingers.

"Fix it?" Vince winced as though a dentist's drill had severed a nerve. "It should've never been broken." Then he slapped him so hard, Nick's eyes went off like popcorn, and a gush of blood fanned out below his nose. Nick licked at the mustache of blood as it crept into his mouth.

Vince was breathing heavily, balling and unballing his fists. There was a tremolo in his throat as he spoke, "You ever get so angry, Nick, that you just want to beat something...smash it into tiny pieces?"

Nick nodded his head slowly. His eyes were stippled red with fear.

"Let's say you have a cat." Vince went on, as though he was trying to connect a valid reason to his actions. "And no matter how much you pet it and feed it and give it a warm place to stay, it keeps crapping on the carpet, and after a while, you tire of cleaning up after him."

Vince paused, head bobbing like he knew he was right, his hands held out, palms angled up, as if he was the Pope receiving the multitudes. He smiled, a slight crook in the corner of his mouth.

It felt as if there was a question hanging in the air like a noose. Nick wanted to answer, but to what, and with no credible reply, his mouth fell open in a stupor, his brain the consistency of wet cement.

In the next instant, Jimmy came back from inside. Nick's eyes averted for a second, maybe two, but to Vince, the casual distraction was like a slap in the face. It was as though Nick didn't care, was giving him the "bird" without lifting a finger. And this lack of respect came like the nail that finds a tire on the freeway at seventy miles per hour — sudden and explosive — Vince couldn't keep it on the road, and suddenly his knee exploded into Nick's groin with the force of a Louisville slugger.

The pain was ear shattering, screeching from the back of Nick's throat, and he fell forward, heaving from deep inside.

Tony lunged for his brother, only to have Sean throw an arm across his chest.

"Easy, Tony." Vince pointed at his friend. "I wouldn't want Sean to show you what steroids can do."

Nick was on his knees, face to the deck.

By this time, Bryan Ferry was into "Day for Night," and Dane would've happily made the trade.

Vince motioned Jimmy for the deck hose. "I trusted you Nick," he said. "It was implied the first time you snorted a line of my coke."

Huddled at Vince's feet, Nick was whimpering like a dog being reprimanded for chewing on the couch.

Pushing his way erect, Nick sat back on his heels just as Jimmy began washing down the deck, scouring Nick's lunch toward the sea. In the wash, Nick's legs were being drenched in cold water. He was drooling profusely as if he had a mouth chocked-full of marbles. He struggled to his feet, hanging on the gunwale, steadying himself against the roll of the *Ecstasea*. His eyes were wet from retching, his breath was that of a mule's. "I'm sorry, man," he uttered, his voice thick with lament. "Please, don't kill me ... Arial ... the baby."

Dane came up behind Vince's shoulder and, hoping to inject some calm into the decaying situation, said low to his ear, "Vince. C'mon man. There's no need to get rough. We can ..."

With that, Vince turned to speak, looking Dane straight in the face. He raised his voice so that Tony could hear him, too. "Dane, I'm only going to tell you this once. Either you are with me or against me. But if you keep undermining what I'm trying to do here, I'm going to suspect that you're against me."

"I'm not against you Vince. I just ..."

"Dane, this isn't a discussion," Vince said. His mien was mulish. The rain was running out of his hair. "I don't want this to turn ugly for you, Dane. Nothing would piss me off more than for that to happen. So, are you with me or not?"

Still blocking Tony from any approach, Sean had twisted enough toward Dane to show his hand on the grip of his Glock. Dane could feel Tony's eyes wandering on the side of his face as though his pleading gaze had morphed into boots with calk soles.

"Well?" Vince waited a heartbeat for a reply. "Because this is the absolute last fucking time I'm going to talk about it."

Staring at Sean's hand, Dane backed away, the answer in his retreat, and any thought of resistance ran for the back of his skull. The body will do strange things when faced with adversity, the chemistry beyond magic, and like a morphine junky he fell into a dream, disconnected, everything slowing and subtly changing shape.

Suddenly, Nick tried to run. Where to was anyone's guess, but when an animal is cornered reason becomes a luxury.

Jimmy quickly pinned him to the wall, Nick's eyes frantic with the knowledge he was too far from home. Immediately, Sean was there to grab an arm. Like two men wrestling a sail in the wind, they slowly moved him back to the gunwale. Back into the rain. Back into the direct path of Vince's wrath.

"You know, Nick, for what it's worth," Vince said with almost a sense of cajolery. "I always liked you ... but what you've done ... I ought to put your head on a pole and split it like a peach; let everyone see what happens when trust is broken, or maybe ..." He let the word "maybe" drag as he pulled Jimmy's gun from its holster. He held it up between their faces, looking at it as though he was marveling at the facets in the Hope Diamond.

Dane could see the gun reflecting in the saline shine of Nick's eyes. The blued steel showed no glint in the light itself, but it didn't have to flash to show its power. The knowledge was inherent. Tony stood agape, impotent.

A tiny voice whispered in Dane's ear. "No religion can save you now." Then Dane felt his mouth turn to sand, felt his muscles solidify as lead, and in his mind's eye he saw the heels of his shoes click to the deck as though they'd suddenly been magnetized.

Without a hint of indecision, Vince pointed the gun in Nick's face, point blank.

Nick's face was a cartoon character: skin wind-tunnel-taut, teeth clenched, lips twitching, eyes rigid, white saucers of shock.

And then it happened, as simple as a twig snapping under your feet, or a body joint cracking when you roll out of bed. Vince pulled the trigger. The Glock jerked upward in his hand; the breech sliding back, then forward, first with the pressure of escaping gas, then with the slam of the breech spring. Instantly, the back of Nick's head exploded, and the sound of the muzzle slammed into the air.

As if an afterthought, Nick's head rocked backward, the force nearly pulling his body free from the clutches that held him, then fell forward as if there was a rubber band tied between his forehead and the deck. In the blink of an eye, the bullet had chewed a hole through the back of his skull — seven lands, four grooves, two full twists — spitting teeth and cartilage, blood, flesh and bone out into the ocean. The strange human mixture floated on the dark water in chunks of red, like chum spread for passing sharks.

The gun had gone off so abruptly, Dane yipped like a dog. He saw a red corridor of light contort and screw into his brain and, as quick as the click of a trigger, the night was transformed into a scene straight out of purgatory. He saw all the players standing on the aft deck, bodies steaming with an angry heat in the soaking rain, three hits deep in some pyric hallucination. Pulling a palm down over his eyes, he wiped a warm pink mist from his face and knew Nick was upon him. He tasted copper. He tasted death.

Thick cords of blood were pumping from the back of Nick's head, running over his shoulders, down his arms en route for his Zig-Zag man tattoo. The music was blaring, though the volume had never changed.

At first, Tony looked like he was drowning, fighting for the breath of a different place and time. Heat smolders without oxygen, but when the fuel is plentiful — with a gulp of air Tony burst into flames. He rushed at Vince, revenge twisting in his mind like a piece of barbed wire ripping caution from ear to ear.

Immediately, Sean dropped Nick's arm and clotheslined Tony across the throat with an elbow. He went down, a crush to the windpipe, yet in an instant with the fury of hatred cyclonic in his loins, he scrambled back to his feet, fighting for any inch of the asshole who'd just shot his brother.

But it wouldn't be. Vince whipped the pistol through the air like one would strike down a mad dog, tearing a jagged line down Tony's jaw. Tony went down as though he'd simply blown a fuse, losing shape like a hot-air balloon crashing into the ground.

Jimmy started keening, a siren from the back of his throat, Nick's body hanging heavy like a sack of mud from his arm, the blood advancing over his fingers.

Sean pushed Jimmy aside, and Nick's legs folded. His torso slumped immediately down in front of the gunwale. As he collapsed, a rush of air left his body up through the tunnel in his skull like a giant sigh of relief. His head was tipped back now, laying on top of the gunwale as if in a pillow of deep sleep, his mouth open jagged in a hideous scream, blood running down the side of the *Ecstasea* to the Sound, dying the water like Kool-Aid dumped into a glass of cold water.

Dane watched the light die in Nick's eyes, all the fanfare of a match in the wind. Now deadness stared blankly at the stars, yet some circuit in Nick's brain hadn't got the news — his left leg was twitching like an out-of-control paint shaker.

Jimmy kept wailing, his incoherent agony deafening.

Vince started yelling for Jimmy to shut up, pointing the gun in his face, driving Jimmy back toward the bow. Like a roast left in the oven too long, Vince's muscle tone had changed, sinewy and hard; his face had taken on angular proportions, dark and razor-edged; and there was this horrible smell. Murder had an odor, and Vince was basting in it.

Tony's jaw must've been broken, for it was ballooning blue and black, swelling with blood in a painful erection. His right ankle was twisted, his foot pointing inward.

Dane could see the grip of hands left on Nick, the outline of unwanted restraint, purple fingers as ghosts on the skin. Panic gave way to remorse.

A powerful concoction: the smell of gunpowder, the singed flesh of a muzzle blast, the burgeoning reek of blood coagulating, then turning brown in the cotton fibers of clothing; the unnatural sight of a man left with his eyes bulging, skin white as chalk, his brains dangling from the back of his skull like spittle hanging from the lips of a drunkard; the cry of a fellow human lost in the wails of that simian creature that lives in all of us, the sound sharp like a barb through the heart — Dane stared out at the ocean and gagged down a retch.

"Sean, dammit!" Vince yelled. "Shut him up."

Reacting on sheer impulse, Sean pushed Jimmy toward the bow, ineptly speaking words of consolation. They were still in sight when Vince called behind them, "And get me the anchor from the skiff."

Tony was lying on his side against the gunwale where he'd fallen, an advancing pool of Nick's blood edging along the deck, gathering at his head, soiling his hair, brother-to-brother.

Dane couldn't help but stare, not knowing whether to shake him awake or let him sleep through the misery. Finally, at some point, he turned to Vince and yelled, "Do you have any idea what you've done?" He wanted the question to be forceful, to invoke some feeling of remorse, but through the emotional swelling in his throat, his voice came out pitifully thin.

"All too well," Vince replied, the apology in his words, not his meaning. "I just saved our necks."

Suddenly, the music died. Someone had cut it short. Vince stared at the bow, wondering. The rain was blowing off the eaves into the light, and in the relative quiet, the drops denting the ocean sounded like lead shot falling on the deck. Dane saw the last coals of heat rise in steam from Nick's body in a whisper, like silver swirls of breath. He could smell the diesel and hear the purl of the engines beneath his feet. Rivulets of water traversed down his thighs, cool inside his pant legs, the feeling curiously reverse in direction as though an army of snakes had come, bent on devouring him for inaction.

Then, as if on the edge of a dream, Dane saw Tony stir. He wanted to say something, reassure Tony that what *had* happened was an illusion. A result of the coke and booze. But there were no words he could say to make this pain go away and his tongue turned to water and soured in his mouth.

Tony crawled along the gunwale, helpless, like a dog on two legs, calling up every ounce of courage he could from that hollow that lives in the pit of one's stomach. Words formed on his lips — condemnation, reprisal — but no voice would join with his thoughts, and as he lay there in the struggle, Dane knew his life had thickened, the future lost, the present heavy and muted. Life had become blurred, but if Tony knew it, he pretended he didn't, for in his eyes burned the flame, Dane could see it, and with one simple look he told Vince of his erring ways.

Vince saw it too, but would have none of it. "I told you Tony," he said. "God dammit, I told you." He couldn't look at him anymore. It was over. He turned away.

Sean came back with the anchor, a three-gallon bucket filled with cement that had a chain buried in the center of the cylindrical rock, and a short section of nylon rope left from where he'd cut it free.

"Take off your belt," Vince ordered Sean.

Hypnotized with disbelief, Dane heard the cold slap of leather as Sean zipped the belt free of his pant loops.

Lying on his side, Tony squinted into the glare of the spotlight with watery gray eyes. His lips were purple with cold. He ticked a finger on his chest, then looked at Dane and out of a wet typhoon of visions came a mysterious thought on the wind. "I wonder," Tony said softly, "if Stevie Ray Vaughn felt this way when he knew the plane was going down."

Following Vince's orders, Sean positioned Tony back-to-back with Nick, his belt fashioned around their necks. He tied the skiff anchor to Tony's leg. Then, using another length of rope cut from a fender line, he cinched them together at the waist.

"Tie them up good," Vince said. "I want nothing bobbing up and washing ashore." His words were absent of emotion. It was as though Tony and Nick were merely a bundle of newspapers to be set out for recycling.

Sean nodded as he set the bucket of cement up on the gunwale.

"So, this is how it goes," Dane remarked snidely. "Well, ain't you the man ... more like a cheap ..." Then he paused, for Tony was staring at him, the look in his eyes, the slight shake of his head pleading for him to stop before Vince gave him a similar ticket to hell.

Vince never said a word, motioned with his arm, waving the gun as if it were a handkerchief.

Strong as an ox, Sean could raise Nick and Tony to their feet with no help. Nick's dead weight pulled the neck-belt tight, forcing a choking cough from Tony's throat. Then, with a grunt from Sean and a sharp intake of air from Tony, the human bundle went over the side.

Somehow, in a last attempt at life, Tony grabbed the gunwale, hands slick with blood. He stared long and hard at Vince, an infinite sadness in his eyes. Nick's weight was pulling at his neck; the belt had torn into the skin; blood came thick as pitch seeps from a tree. Yet, with uncommon strength, he held on.

In a last-ditch effort, Dane pleaded for Tony's life. "Vince, think of what you're doing. This is Tony. Tony Franklin. Think about the countless hours we've spent together, out on the lake, riding in his car. Hell, that old Studebaker of his was like our first apartment. And–and what about the laughs? We had good laughs, Vince, great times. What about those?"

Vince was unwavering, staring out over the ocean, kneading the gun in his palm. Sean had his hand perched once again on the firm rubber grips of his pistol. Dane surveyed the possibilities: Was there some way to win against the Steroid Boy, the maniacal Vince, and the two guns they had cocked and ready? He realized the only hope was in his words.

"Listen Vince. I'm not trying to undermine you. I'm not trying to do anything at all except make you think about tomorrow. You do this and you'll never be able to go to sleep at night knowing that you killed your best friend. And he is, you know. Tony has taken many a punch for you, Vince. Hell, most of them from you. And he's always been there, always. If anybody was to say a bad word about Vince Spinetti, watch out because Tony Franklin's gonna kick your ass. He's loyal, Vince. Right now, he's upset, but once he sees what Nick has done, he'll get over it."

Vince turned and looked Dane in the eyes. His face was slick with rain, his clothes clinging to his skin. He raised a hand and snapped his fingers. "Sorry Dane. No can do. Business is business. Everything else is secondary."

"Secondary? Life is secondary. Tony is secondary?"

"Afraid so," Vince said.

"Okay then, asshole, but don't cheat Tony by letting Sean do the dirty work. You do it."

A smile ripped across Vince's face, first flashing it at Dane, then to Tony. "Bon voyage asshole," he said, then that quick — switch on, switch off — he pushed the anchor from the rail.

The sound came like hellfire, the splash of the water sharp, more like a shattering of glass. Tony jerked with the weight, his white fingers straining, his lips moving, his voice mute, then his grip gave way and, like a ghost, he slipped into the black depths of the ocean.

It was so quiet now; it was as if they were standing in a meadow after a midnight snow. Dane didn't think he would do it. He didn't think Vince could kill his lifelong friend. Dane thought once he had thrown down the gauntlet, and Vince faced the criminality of cold-blooded murder, then it would end. He was wrong.

Words ran through Dane's mind: coward, pussy, asshole, jerk — but coward stuck. Sweat burst from the pores in his forehead, a frigid sweat, like water dripping from a melting snowball, and growing from the stillness a dark peal rose in Dane's ear — the whoosh of a cement anchor streaking toward the six-hundred-foot bottom, pulling Tony and Nick in its path.

Funny how life will turn on you. On the way to his death, Nick had been upbeat, cocky, expecting a promotion. What he got was 9mm, 115 grain.

And then there was Tony. A man of limited vision. A man with a heart of gold. He had done life the hard way, colliding with everything, even the air he breathed. But he didn't deserve this.

***

Time passed by. Dane didn't know how long. He had no watch. There's no way to measure that kind of time, anyway. They had moved in out of the rain. Jimmy had washed down the evidence from the aft deck. The *Ecstasea* was three miles off Possession Point, cruising back for the safe arms of Lake Washington.

Already flipping back through it in reverse, Dane was searching the evening like a videotape on rewind. Could he have changed things? Could he have done something different? Instead of impotently standing aside, should he have gone down with Tony and Nick? With memory as an unwelcome vision, he would battle this forever, one side of darkness remonstrative, the other side pleading it was useless from the beginning, as though standing in quicksand, for the more he'd struggled against Vince the worse things had gotten.

"You must feel pretty large at this moment," Dane said. "Killing two people and all."

Vince shrugged the smallest shrug that could be shrugged. "I'm having a hard time putting a finger on it. The adrenaline-fed sense of omnipotence was charged for sure, but I had no way of knowing until that moment whether I had the balls to pull the trigger."

Vince dumped a small pile of coke on the web of his thumb and forefinger, then smiled the faintest smile. "You must feel some guilt for the outcome."

"Why? I didn't kill them."

"You didn't stop me either," he said. Then he lifted the line easily into his mind.

Dane felt the heat of anger rise in his chest, heard the collective hum of Tony and Nick's blood coursing through his ears. At that moment, he wanted to tear Vince's tongue out. But what purpose would it serve? Vince would only try to rule the world as the first mute dictator.

From the windows of the Main Salon, he saw the skeletal fingers of a tree branch float by on the back of a fallen log, and it resurrected the sight of Tony's fingers losing grip of the gunwale. Now his fingers ached, and he wanted to dip his face in the cold water.

Dane walked to the aft deck, out of the snickering view of Vince. The night air felt weary on his skin. Murder had come like a rodent, scurrying along the walls, hidden from view, carrying the wet kiss of pestilence, and once bitten, spawning a worm that feeds on your soul. That worm was in Vince now, and Dane wondered when his day would come. The day when Vince would decide that murdering another friend was beneficial for business.

It was there, standing under cover from the rain, when he saw a glint of light in the shadow. A flash at the base of the stern no larger than a marble, but bright as a flare. As he walked closer, and saw it clearer through the gathering light, he choked hard, but the tears still came. For laying in the dark, in the slender line where the gunwale met the deck, Dane found Tony's gold tooth. Knocked clear of his mouth when Vince pistol-whipped him. Jimmy had washed it down but failed to notice its shine.

He picked it up, clutching it in his palm, and instantly a knot of regret swelled inside him. He felt naked and ashamed, his throat scorched by murder, and as though a boulder had broken free from the mountainside, a ball of acid rose out of his stomach and flowed over the stern.

The cold rain of Winter will warm in the Spring, and darkness will shrink in the light of day, but guilt, you can't puke up like too much tequila, and forever and a day, just to the left of his sternum would be a hollow ache in his chest where his heart used to be.

CHAPTER 41

Seattle, Washington
January 7, 1996

The funeral home was an angular building of gray brick, black iron and minimal glass. A pair of plaster lions bordered the entrance, which was covered with a blue canvas awning. The lawn was elevated behind a parapet of brick, which also served as a flower planter along the sidewalk. Dane sat smoking a cigarette on the parapet, legs crossed, jacket open; a single thought on his mind: the night they danced to "Delta Rain," and how the lyrics spoke to their loneliness.

It was five p.m. Behind him, a few persistent flowers hung on in the dead of winter like barflies at the last call for drinks. The trees guarding the lawn were wet, the conifers particularly green. He'd been there for nearly two hours, smoking, observing, afraid to go in. He'd come early to ask for forgiveness, but he couldn't work up the nerve. Much of the time he'd spent talking to himself, trying to convince himself that sitting outside in the cold wasn't an effort to keep a safe distance from the palpability of Erin's death, but more because he enjoyed being frostbit and uncomfortable and it gave him the opportunity to smoke an inordinate number of cigarettes, which was a vice he'd been neglecting of late.

Earlier in the day, Jenny called. She had Arial on the line. Dane lied to keep them calm. Arial was especially wound with the baby on the way, Jenny calmly curious, for it was not like Tony to be days from home. Lying came easier these days, but

Dane knew Jenny wasn't convinced, and he could still feel the strained shiver in Arial's voice.

Now, as day turned to night, the sun had a jagged piece cut out of it by the Olympic Range and darkness was prowling the streets. Dane heard a squeal of tires as McTarnihan's Lincoln swayed around the corner, approaching from the East. One headlight was burned out, but the big American car almost drove itself. For appearance's sake, McTarnihan held the wheel in a ten-and-two grasp. He roared past, then swerved into a parking spot.

In a few minutes, he was standing in front of Dane.

"You okay?" McTarnihan asked.

"Yeah," Dane said, glancing down the sidewalk. "I'm fine."

"Why don't you go inside?"

"It's a long story."

McTarnihan was wearing a black sport coat, white shirt, black pants, black shoes. His hat was conspicuously missing, his curly hair wet and freshly combed, parted as neatly as a surveyor's rule on the left side of his head. He even had on a black tie.

Eyeing the suit, Dane was quick to ask, "What gives John? I've never seen you in a suit that wasn't a statement in clash."

"I rented it," McTarnihan spouted. "Any other questions?"

"No," Dane said with a smirk, putting his cigarette out on the brick.

The inside of the funeral home smelled of disinfectant and vanilla candles. It was deathly quiet, save for the tattling of red streamers blowing from the vents. Dane and McTarnihan stood side-by-side, uneasy as Catholics in a Foursquare Church.

"I wonder if they have a can?" McTarnihan said.

"I'm sure they do."

McTarnihan wandered off.

"In the meantime," Dane said, "I'll figure out where they have Erin."

"Can I help you?" asked a chic-looking lady wearing a black skirt stretched tight as mermaid skin, a V-neck blouse, and a black onyx necklace. She had perfectly coifed cara-mel-ombre hair. At first glance, she seemed like one of those snoopy broads you see on the train or meet in a line at the bank: their eyes like scalpels, their attention zeroed in on your business.

She was mid-forties, but well-kept and recently altered, the curve of her breasts up firm and high, protuberant against her blouse as she breathed. Her butt was smooth and hard, her thighs marble-tight inside her skirt.

"I hope so," Dane said. "We're here for Erin Flynn."

"Let's sit down." She swished off toward an office, her mermaid tail swaying, stirring up the current.

Once inside, Dane sat down in a chair with wooden arms. She sat on the edge of the desk, the vee of her legs like a gun-sight aimed between his eyes.

"My name is Monique," she said with a smile of conse-quence. Her eyes shimmered in shadow like a lake in moon-light; her contacts tinted chemical green. "May I ask a ques-tion?" She bit her lower lip and held it there a moment, as if deciding whether to bite it off and spit it out or leave it on a while longer.

"Depends on the question," Dane replied.

She crossed her legs, showing a more generous sweep of her thigh. Dane tried to keep his eyes where they belonged.

"Well, I was curious about this situation from the start. Most of our clients die of old age. Are you her husband?"

She had a nice way of talking, smooth, half-cynical, yet not hard-boiled. She rounded her words well. "No," Dane replied. He absently studied the lovely lines of her neck. She was deeply tanned. "Why? Does it matter?"

She looked at the door for a moment, then put a smile back on her face. "Not really. I was just curious."

"Oh. For a second I thought maybe I'd get a discount off the price if I answered the question correctly."

Her eyes flashed at that. They were very seductive. "I wish I could give you a discount, your loss and all, but ...," she spoke in a whisper, an ocean of sincerity deep as a birdbath. "Anyway, you answered the question correctly. I mean, I don't care if it was honest, you see, only so long as you know it was the answer I wanted to hear." Her words, her breath, they were like an obscene tongue in his ear.

"So, there was more to it than a simple verification. Like there was a deeper meaning for you."

She got up and closed the door gently, as if she didn't want to wake a sleeper. "Would you like a drink?" she asked.

"I don't know."

Her tongue darted between her teeth, glistened her upper lip. It wasn't forked, but it had the same effect. She poured two bourbons, her nails a jarring cherry-blossom coiled around the glass.

"I've never thought of drinking in a funeral parlor before." He remembered Clayton, and how Saber thought he was talking to his mom, yet Clayton was convinced it was Circe. "Are you trying to seduce me?"

Her eyes flashed again.

"So, what happens next?" His tone became hard and degrading. "Is there a play book? Or do I simply fall headlong into the abyss?"

"Well, I don't know if I like your attitude," she carped. She did her best to be incensed, coming on like it was her first taste of crudity.

"Where's Erin?"

She looked away. "Parlor B."

Bobby, Natalie, and Tyra were standing in the foyer when Dane returned. McTarnihan was with them. Bobby was wearing a brown suit too small for his shoulders with trousers too tight at the waist. Natalie had on a dark blue dress with a white lace collar. Tyra was dressed in dark slacks and a black chenille sweater.

"What's wrong Dane?" Tyra asked first, seeing the disgust on his face.

"Nothing. This place gives me the creeps. Where are the boys?"

"At home," Natalie answered.

"We got a sitter," Bobby said. "You okay buddy? You look like you've just been mugged."

"Yeah, well, I feel like it too."

The five of them filed into the parlor. It was empty of people, unless you considered Erin, who had been cremated. Her urn set on a marble pedestal at the front of the room. Everyone knew there would be no formal memorial, no coffee and cake with the family, no well-chosen words by an unfamiliar pastor. Even Erin's mother had no interest in burying her child. After their brief meditation, she would be interred at the same cemetery as Blake on the road to Avondale.

Dane guided them up to the urn. Natalie reached out and took Dane's hand, and Tyra took the other. Bobby stood next to Natalie and held her hand. McTarnihan closed the ranks and stood next to Bobby, the last link in a concave chain around Erin. Over the next several minutes, each in their own way, they dealt with Erin and her demise.

Once finished, Dane gave Natalie a hug, then Tyra, and then Bobby, and with a pair of fingertips, he wiped a tear from his eye. When they turned to leave, Virchow and his side-kick Bradley were seated in the back. Dane led the way to the exit. Virchow and Bradley stood and stepped into the aisle.

"What are you doing here?" Dane said. Their coats smelled of rain.

"Paying my respects," Virchow said.

"That's a laugh." Dane looked around the room. "Seems like a person as good as Erin would've gotten more respect than this."

"I'm sorry, Avilla."

Dane went for the door. When he stepped outside, he could smell the ocean, though the wind carried only rain falling in grubby curtains across the street. Virchow was on his tail.

Bobby and the rest filed out behind them. They all stood under the awning over the entrance.

Virchow instantly fired off a cigarette. Dane stared at him with a wagonload of contempt.

"You want a smoke?" Virchow said, holding out his pack. He had on a white-collared shirt and a V-neck sweater under his trench.

"Thanks, but no thanks. You know you've got a lot of nerve showing up here."

"I wasn't sure of the situation. The least I could do is pay for her ..."

"Death?" Dane said with a raised voice. "The Feds coming through with a little bonus money for a job well-done."

Dane trembled with anger and even in the cold he was overheating, for along with his grisly thoughts of Erin, still vivid in his memory were flashbacks of Nick and Tony going over the side, their demise of which he also attributed to Virchow's incompetence.

Virchow pulled off a long strip of foil from the pack of cigarettes and folded it neatly. "I *am* sorry, you know. I didn't want it to end this way."

Dane stood silent, the tendons in his neck popping, twanging like banjo strings.

"Lot of good that does her now," Bobby threw in a comment from behind.

Bradley had taken up a position on the edge, rolling a toothpick on his tongue. He was dressed in cowboy boots, pearl button shirt, and bolo tie. His oil-skin coat was stiff against the breeze, his substantial nose casting a shadow on his face.

"Look," Virchow said, giving Dane a sidelong glance. "Maybe we should go talk. There's a pizza joint on Monroe. Do you know the one I mean?"

"I'm not socializing with the likes of you, Virchow. There's too much sand in your K-Y." Dane tossed a thumb over his shoulder. "Why don't you and Jimmy Durante take a hike? I've had enough BS for one day."

Virchow ignored him. He looked down at his foot and stirred a pattern on the damp cement, like a big-league pitcher considering his next pitch. "So how does it feel to be driving the mule team these days, Avilla? I hear Franklin's been put out to pasture."

Dane remained quiet.

"Avilla, I could bust you for wearing Levi's on Fridays, or smoking cigarettes with filters," Virchow said. "I could put you away so fast, your shoes would have to be notified you'd left town."

"So why haven't you?"

"Avilla ..." Virchow took a drag off his cigarette and exhaled as he spoke, "Let me lay this out to you in a way that I hope you can understand. I know this is a traumatic time for you, but I've been very patient. I could've hauled your ass in weeks ago. Put you away for ten easy."

Suddenly, things got quiet. Except for the raindrops popping on the canvas like gunshots overhead, it was as if someone had yanked the plug on the audio. Bobby pulled the knot of his tie loose. Tyra and Natalie each took a step closer to each other. Bradley started breathing stertorously, like the toothpick was now caught in his throat.

Dane looked across the grass. Crooked shadows from the naked tree limbs swept back and forth across the banked lawn. "Is nailing Vince worth that much?" Dane said. "Or is it Geraci that really fuels this fire?"

Virchow hesitated with an answer, taking a languorous drag of his smoke. Once he exhaled, he spoke. "I'd be lying if I said I didn't want to see those two piranhas off the streets," he said. "I'd like to see both of their polished asses rotting in a cell. But I'm running out of time on this Avilla. Soon I'll be going with what I've got. And I promise, you and Franklin will be the first to go."

"Maybe you should listen to him, Dane," Tyra said, the dread in her eyes intense.

"Well, I'm glad somebody's thinking," Virchow added. "By the way, speaking of Franklin. Have you seen him lately?"

Dane stared out at a tenement across the street. The windows were filled with a hard and yellow light. No one else said a word. The pause was like walking on broken glass, but Dane ignored the question.

Finally, Virchow tossed his cigarette to the ground, grinned, and took up a prizefighter's stance. "Okay, Avilla, let me have it. If that's what you need ..."

Dane spun on the invitation and shoved the heel of his palm into Virchow's nose. In the same instant, a gush of blood exited south. Bradley jumped forward, but Bobby stopped him.

"Wow!" Virchow said, backpedaling from the blow. He pulled a kerchief from his pocket while motioning Bradley to back down. "Gees Avilla, I was kidding. You nearly broke my nose." He wiped the blood, looked at it, folded the kerchief, and wiped at it again.

Bobby and Bradley eased their grip on each other. McTarnihan waved off a couple under an umbrella, passers-by who'd seen the commotion, their expressions suddenly frozen by the events.

However, Dane was still bouncing on the balls of his feet, adrenaline surging, eyes wide and bright, his nostrils flaring white like he was inhaling ammonia.

"I guess I deserved that," Virchow said, wiping the last of the blood from his upper lip.

Bobby grabbed Dane's forearm, reeled him in. "Cool it, Dane. What are you doing?"

"I feel like a pressure cooker, Bobby. I don't need this crap. Not today."

"But you can't go off smacking cops in the face."

"Can't we do this another time?" Tyra asked.

A subversive rain was falling now, the water sluicing off the gutters, down the sidewalk, the banked lawn puddling like Minnesota.

Virchow stuck another cigarette in his mouth, his fingers yellow from years of scissoring the Pall Malls between his index and middle.

"You had her in an impossible position, you know," Dane said. "She had no way out."

"And if you would've helped me out in the first place, this whole mess would've been over by now," Virchow retorted.

In a show of support, Tyra moved over and stood off Dane's shoulder, where she gently held on to his arm.

Bobby looked at Virchow with a raised eyebrow, then welcomed Natalie to his side. A solitary drop of water had bled through the canvas and with uncanny precision fell, spotting Virchow's cigarette and putting out the fire with one quick blow.

"Looks like it's time to go," Bobby said as Virchow studied his suddenly extinguished smoke. Then the four of them — Bobby, Natalie, Dane and Tyra — turned and, disregarding the rain, walked off, conveying the show was over.

Holding out a fresh smoke, McTarnihan gave it to Virchow with a slight smirk. "Here, have one of mine," he said. "I promise this one won't blow up in your face." Then he left too, catching up to them on the sidewalk with a heavy stride.

CHAPTER 42

Seattle, Washington
January 8, 1996

Dane hung up the phone. Vince had called. The shipment was coming in on Saturday, and they spent the first fifteen minutes going over the details. The rest of the conversation was like talking to a stranger. To Vince, killing Tony and Nick solved a cancerous problem. It had to be done. To Dane, their demise left him lost in a quagmire of malevolent emotions.

It was spiritual quicksand. He couldn't think. Nothing was adding up, and that's when the coercion began, obsession speaking reason as all vices do. Cocaine will bring equilibrium to a sea of indecision. Cocaine will open your eyes and help you understand. The lying was incessant.

But you can't hide rotten wood for long under a layer of latex enamel, and the demons were creeping, so he took the rest of his coke to the bathroom and flushed it down the toilet, only to stand at the rim a nanosecond later, wishing he had more.

Once that tornado hits, your next best move is to stick your tongue in a light socket or run. He had to get out of the apartment. Get some fresh air. Get some space between him and the minefield of addiction.

A mile down the road, his cell phone rang.

"Don't you ever turn on your phone?" Bobby said. "I tried the landline, but —"

"I leave the cell in the car," Dane said with a snap. "Sometimes you've just got to be left alone."

"What's wrong, Dane? Don't let those razor blades of guilt start again.

Dane shifted down, took a sharp corner, then sped up the long ramp onto Highway 520. "So why'd you call?"

"Remember the videotapes ..."

Dane interrupted. "Bobby. We've been over this."

"Let me finish," Bobby said.

Beep-beep.

"What was that?" Bobby asked.

"My battery is going dead."

"Can you plug it in?"

"I don't have an adapter. Just hurry."

"Okay-okay. It's a long story, but the bottom line is one videotape was defective and wouldn't rewind completely. I didn't want to break it by forcing it back to the beginning, so today I took it to a friend who owns a camera shop in Winslow. He rewound the entire videotape onto another cassette."

Beep-beep.

"What's the point, Bobby?"

"There's a section of videotape we hadn't seen."

"Go on."

"The first part of the videotape is Vince sitting in a chair for a few minutes," Bobby said. "Then a young guy comes in... bodybuilder type. Vince gets up and they talk."

Dane heard Bobby shuffling around.

"I'm holding the phone by the TV so you can hear what's on the videotape," Bobby said.

Ten seconds went by, then Dane heard Vince's voice, followed by Sean.

Vince: "Did you replace the recorder?"

Sean: "Yes. I'm recording us now as a test."

Vince: "Good. Verify it's working. Then rewind, and have it ready to rerecord."

The phone rings.

Vince: "I've got to get this. Come back after you check the equipment."

A second ring.

Vince: "Hello."

A five second pause.

Vince: "I understand."

Another pause.

Vince: "No, I agree. Keep the two kilos as payment. Blake is my problem. I should pay for it."

Another pause.

Vince: "Sure, tell him I appreciate it."

"Then Vince hangs up and just stands there with this blank look on his face," Bobby said. "A minute or two later, the video jumps to a different time of day, and there are three people in the room. I know one is Patrick Donovan. I've seen his picture in the newspaper. The other is Tony. The switch must be where the videotape got bound up. So, unbeknownst to Vince, the earlier part never got erased."

Beep-beep.

"Dane. Listen. This is proof. Vince had Blake killed."

Beep-beep.

"Dane, are you listening?"

Beep-beep.

Dane was listening, but the words made no connection. His mind was whirling like a dime-store top. He was driving on instinct, a third eye connected to his brain. Blake lie buried in a casket while the rest of the world had blurred into submission.

"Dane? Answer me."

"Look, Bobby, do me a favor. Keep the videotape to yourself."

"But ..."

"Just until tomorrow, Bobby. I've got to think."

Beep-beep.

"We'll talk tomorrow. I promise."

Beep-beep.

The line went dead.

There's a line you cross when you know there is no way back. For Dane, it wasn't as simple as a chalk mark on the sidewalk scratched there by a child, nor the yellow blur that crosses in front of your car as you go head-on into reckless-ness. This line was drawn across his chest — a fence of pro-tection for his heart. The wire was made of trust; the posts buried deep in the soil of fraternity. Within its border was truth; outside was a world crafted of lies and illusion.

He threw the phone in the seat, then slipped a pint of tequila out from the glove box and laid back a slug of liquid eraser that would've made the Space Needle disappear. The heat spread like a brush fire down his body. But there was no elixir that could erase the blemish he carried like a cancer to his soul. The burden of Erin and Tony and Nick, not least of all Blake, couldn't be cut out with a knife, let alone scrubbed away with alcohol.

His foot pressed to the floor. A sour knot tied in his throat and his heart felt like it was drowning in heavy water. He drove and drove and drove and drove, aimlessly, until he knew not where he'd been or where he was going, streaking along empty crowded straight-aways, running lights and ignoring signs, twisting down winding roads with a screech in his wheels, making no more head way with his life than a worm in a bait can, until he found himself at the Bluff — the Bluff where magnolias explode from the earth in passions of color — the Bluff where Erin and him had shared their love under a bright ceramic moon.

From the pavement, he slid the car sideways into the tall grass, and swung open the door of ZX, stepping out in one effortless motion as the car came to rest in a hush of blades. He rushed for the cliff, the rocks to catapult him into obliv-ion, the trees speaking in echoes and murmuring his name. He stood at the precipice of death and stared down at the remnant of his life.

And then, as if a quarter had been stuck in a jukebox, a song played — a Dylan dream — issuing forth from the in-terior of the car like a molten hymn. It resembled a funeral march, a haunting tempo of organ, drums, and dreamlike guitars. Two bars in, off in the distance, caught in a world of electronic ones and zeroes, a dog cried out in lament, and in his soul the words reverberated like they were his very own.

His chest heaved with a collective stir. Even his willful persistence couldn't change the past, and the contemplation of suicide was not the way forward. Shadows had engulfed his life, and there would be no rest until he could set this burden aside. It was on his shoulders, for, fair or not, an old siren song, Pharmakeia had slipped back into his life innocuous as a twist of smoke and set his world on fire.

He dropped his head, his chin spiking his chest. The lies and darkness were everywhere, and time was running out. He wanted to go back to the North Sea and forget he'd ever left its fierce solitude. In the distance, he could hear church bells ringing, and coyotes, standing on the left side of darkness, guffawing at his expense; while a stone grew cold in his chest, for he knew what they were telling him: the law as God designed it is not for the faint of heart.

CHAPTER 43

San Juan Islands, Washington
January 12, 1996

The moonlight was pewter on the flatness of the ocean, a welcome change from the night before when drizzle fell like static on TV. The *Nez Pierce* sat poised on the water, the wind southwest, a slight nod in the trawler's bow. In the distance, a black freighter steamed away to the east.

Her crew worked feverishly on deck, wrestling a cargo of three nets abandoned by the freighter minutes before. They had hooked them with a grapnel and with swift determination dragged them aboard. Each net held two watertight parcels. The total catch: six parcels of high-grade cocaine.

As with most conventional fishing vessels, the *Nez Pierce* attracted little attention. However, the *Nez Pierce* was far from "conventional". Airtight compartments below deck, and a hull equipped with an egress hatch near the keel, worked in principle like an overturned glass in a sink of water. The incompressible air allowed divers transporting contraband to pass back and forth without detection, below the waterline, even in the light of day.

Out on the deck, the five-man crew broke out cigarettes and shots of Wild Turkey. Even Captain Bodega joined in the celebration. In an ocean of uncertainty, the whispering curl of sedative smoke, and sweet bourbon spreading like warm rain through their chests, brought a brief island of calm.

Then once again the *Nez Pierce* rumbled deep in her belly as if she'd swallowed a thunderhead, her bones creaking against the roll of the water as she got under way, while far-off in a king-size bed of satin, Vito Geraci rolled over in an ocean of his dreams.

CHAPTER 44

San Juan Islands, Washington
January 13, 1996

Bobby leaned back into the cushion and adjusted the trim as the Black Thunder XT roared across the sound. Equipped with twin four-hundred-fifteen horsepower inboards, the trip from Eagle Harbor to Open Bay would take slightly over an hour, the forty-three-foot LOA of the Black Thunder able to maintain an average seventy miles-per-hour even with a three-foot chop on top of six-foot swells.

The customized helm seats allowed for standing or sitting and molded to one's body like a grip. At this speed, standing was preferred. Opposite him, Tyra was glued to her brace by the power, her eyes watering at the speed. They were both wearing wet suits. Bobby's black with red flaming bands across his calves. Tyra's was navy blue, wrapped in a thin yellow spiderweb.

The night before, Dane, Tyra and McTarnihan met Bobby at his houseboat. Natalie served pizza and beer and kept the boys out of earshot of the discussion.

They'd considered the what-ifs. There were too many to count. Too many to safeguard. But by the end of the evening, they'd decided on a plan and agreed that once they started, they'd carry through until the end.

Straight ahead lie Henry Island. A rocky protuberance with about as much character as a toothache. Their base of operations, Open Bay was due west of the compound on the opposite side of the island. Tyra glanced at Bobby, his intense face read like a manual on procedure and calculation. Down in the hold were the scuba tanks, the spearguns, the flippers and masks. Behind her on the deck lay the propulsion gear that would speed them underwater. Tyra fretted over her inexperience, the concern gnawing in the pit of her stomach.

Her first dive was two days ago. Bobby had been an excellent instructor, disciplined, calm, decisive. His experience was immense, albeit dusty, and came back to him with ease and confidence. She'd learned quickly, but wisdom comes from experience, and she hoped her lack of it didn't prove fatal for her or someone else.

The sun had crested the Cascades and was climbing higher over Seattle in the distance, a red ball of fire unable to remove the chill in her bones. She eyed the black resin handle of Bobby's knife, its sheath strapped to his arm, and wondered what revenge raged behind his gaze. Then Bobby smiled at her. A quick parting of the lips. Not a flirtatious smile. Not a cordial, meaningless smile, either. A genuine smile that deadened the pounding hull against the surf, a smile that quelled the riot in her chest, a smile that muffled the growl of the strung-out engines as if a rag had been stuffed down their throats, and best of all, even for an instant, a smile that voided any thoughts of impending doom.

***

The sun riding high in the sky gave the clouds a landscape all their own, their shadows casting murky stains upon the water. Vince anchored the *Ecstasea* a hundred yards offshore while Lance and Sean readied the skiff. As usual, they were packing their sidearms. Dane was wearing denims and a Ruger .380 under his jacket. Ironically, Nick and Tony were anchored only a mile away.

Vince loaded the money onto the skiff. Two large silver cases carrying a million apiece in large denominations. He had on a pair of ivory chinos, deck shoes, a silk shirt of saffron and blue, and a brown leather jacket. Dane got in behind him, coiling the rope in his hand, and with a shove of a foot, Jimmy sent them on their way.

The motor kicked over easily, a puff of blue smoke and the water churned from the prop, a cloud of chopped seaweed in the storm. Soon the *Nez Pierce* would deliver fifty kilos of coke to Henry Island, and Venegas would leave with four million in cash, four million in electronic funds, a bargain at any price.

Earlier, Vince had insisted on a snort to clear their heads. Dane was reluctant, but Vince wouldn't take no for an answer. In the end, Dane took a vial for himself, unable to resist her charm. Thirty minutes later, Dane felt like his pump was about to cavitate, as though Circe was working his heart with an angry thumb. But it wasn't only Circe who had grown angry.

It started the night of the Dancing Bare, first angry at himself; then guilt, unable to rectify the wrong, mutated into revenge, reaching a crescendo the night of the funeral home, when he remembered something Erin had told him the morning before her disappearance. "The day I killed Manny," she said, "we both died."

Then, when Blake's demise was revealed, "the straw that humped the camel" as Tony would say, he remembered Erin's words. He didn't understand then, but now he knew what she'd meant: if he acted out of revenge, he'd never recover. He'd be left guiltier than before, no better than those he wanted to avenge. Guilt would track him down until he sought refuge in the grave.

That's when he ended the blame game. However, forgiveness doesn't satisfy consequences, and they were closing in like a one-eyed freight train. They'd crossed the Rubicon. Dane knew Geraci would never let him quit, and Vince could never set it all straight, even if he wanted to. The best Dane could do now is set up the chess pieces and let fate run the board, hopefully without Bobby and Tyra discarded as sacrificial pawns.

Dane watched the eddies swirling off the stern. For weeks he'd assumed this moment would bring him happiness, but now happiness had been erased from his senses just as bleach takes the color out of your jeans. He felt like he'd swallowed a napalm burrito, burning deep inside. Consequences had turned all that he surveyed a shade of hell, and the antidote was to be as malignant as the disease.

They tied the skiff up at the end of the dock, the cargo of silver cases unloaded. Vince led the way, Dane pulling up the rear with one case, Sean behind him with another. Vince ordered Lance to position himself on the dock and wait for Venegas to show.

The stairs from the dock were steep, zigzagging their way up the rock bluff sixty-feet vertical to the base of the compound. Set in concrete cylinders bored into solid basalt, the heavy aluminum structure was stiff beneath their feet.

Dane felt a shiver course down his spine, his denim jacket providing little protection from the cold. He hadn't selected it for its warmth. It was easy to maneuver in, and he figured it would be easier to recover from a cold in the head than a bullet in the brain.

At the top of the stairs, one of Geraci's men was standing expressionless in sunglasses, holding an Uzi machine gun across his chest. He had a dimple chin and straight chestnut hair. His sweater was the color of robin's breast.

Vince proceeded to the library. The mansion was cold, blue with shadow. Outside the library door was another man in olive slacks, Mexican huaraches, and an island-print shirt. He was wearing a brown shoulder holster, but sitting down, his gun was in his lap. There was a white rag over one knee and a squeeze-can of oil by his left foot. The man looked up. His eyes were lifeless as tar. He told them to go in, his voice revealing a Caribbean accent. Mister Geraci was expecting them. He had an Elvis ducktail, which gave the Negroid look a whole new feel. He went back to cleaning his pistol. That gave his laid-back island look a whole new feel, too.

The winter sun was shining through the massive windows of the library, the room bright with its energy. Vito and Michael were sharing drinks at the bar. Evohl was like a snow-covered mountain seated in a chair by the desk, wearing a sport coat, slacks and crewneck sweater — all white, of course.

"Where do you want these?" Vince asked, referring to the cases.

Vito pointed with a look. "Put them over there by the others." The aging criminal had on dark slacks and a banded collar shirt of a tawny hue.

Sean and Dane placed Vince's two million by the desk next to the two million that Geraci had prepared. Four enormous silver dominoes. Dane wondered what would happen if one was kicked over.

"So, are we all set?" Vince asked.

"Our end seems ready," Vito said. "We'll soon see if Venegas can keep a schedule."

Vince instructed Sean to leave, then moved closer to the bar. Dane melted into the wall, noticing Michael's bloodshot eyes alluding to a sizable buzz in progress.

"I have five men besides Evohl," Vito said. "I assume you brought Lance."

"That's right. I left him down at the dock to wait for Venegas."

"Good. So that about does it. Eight men, Evohl and the three of us, make twelve. I don't think Venegas will cause us any trouble."

Michael poured himself another drink.

Vito put his hand on Michael's wrist. "Slow down. We need all our wits about us today."

Michael shook loose of his grip, then knocked back the vodka in one pass. A dribble escaped the corner of his mouth. He wiped down his chin with a palm. "I hope you weren't counting on me using a weapon, Father. I can't seem to hit my mouth with a glass, let alone a man with a gun."

Vito chuckled at some private joke, then let it known for all to hear. "I'll just use you for a human shield if the need arises."

Michael found no humor in the statement. He poured more vodka into his glass.

"So, no one else is here," Vince said. "No service staff?"

"Correct."

"What about Carmen?"

"I sent her to Jersey."

"How convenient," Michael said, his lips shiny with delightful inebriation.

"Michael, let me warn you once more," Vito said. "I don't need any trouble from you today. If you wish, I will have Evohl relieve you of your wit."

Vito glared, while Michael cracked a knuckle against his jaw. Their rift over Carmen was as obvious as snow in a snowstorm, tempers flaring like static off a doorknob.

"In a matter of minutes, Venegas will be here," Vito said. "Do I need to remind you what's at stake? Fifty kilos of uncut coke. Once processed, three-hundred-thousand grams. At eighty a pop to the street players, that is a cool twenty-four million." Vito was twisting his ring — clockwise, counter-clockwise — as if the motion was calculating the numbers.

"So, if you wish to play the court jester, you'll be doing it alone, locked in a room of Evohl's choosing. Have you caught my drift? Or do I have to make myself *perfectly* clear?"

Michael had a snarl on his face. "No, I got the idea," he said. "No need to ramble on."

"Good. So now I suggest, Evohl, that you and Michael and Dane all wait in the Great Room where you can see Venegas' seaplane approach. As well, the *Nez Pierce* should appear soon."

Vito glanced at Dane with an incredulous eye, then said, "Vince, I wish to speak with you in private."

***

In the Great Room, two more of Geraci's men were standing by the windows. One tall, sinewy, with a blade face. The other shorter, fatter, his head the shape of a darning sock, his skin greasy like bacon rind. Michael directed them outside. Dane saw Darning Sock head down the stairs to the dock. Blade Face went toward the front of the compound. Both were packing MAK 90s from a sling over their shoulder. After a few minutes of idle conversation, Michael left in search of a sandwich. Dane presumed, more likely, there was a bottle in the kitchen.

Dane stared out over the Straits, a sliver of light piercing his eyes as the sun skipped across the water. From here, in between the flashing swells, he could make out Vancouver Island. At the Empress in Victoria, they're probably just finishing afternoon tea, he mused, while I'm here ... he let the thought die. He felt as if he was neck deep in three hits of speed. His breathing was shallow and cold down his throat, his skin crawling with apprehension.

Slipping in quietly behind him, Vince pointed his Walther behind Dane's ear. The muzzle bit into his scalp as if a tick had settled in for lunch. Dane spun in one swift motion, his hand diving under his jacket for the Ruger.

"Hey-hey," Vince said, holding his palms up. "Why so nervous?" The Walther was snake-black against the skin of his palm.

"Nervous? Damn straight. This whole Venegas thing sets me on edge."

Dane could hear Evohl snickering to himself like a kid in church.

"So, what did Vito want?" Dane asked. "Am I a problem?" From the corner of Dane's eye, he could see Evohl intrigued by the question.

Vince him-hawed around it for a second, running his fingertip down the length of the Walther, then admitted, "Vito has a thing for you Dane." He slipped the gun under his leather jacket into its holster. "He says it's intuition."

"What did I do wrong? Forget to kiss his ring?"

Evohl liked that one and ushered a laugh.

Suddenly, a voice yelled from the doorway. It was Blade Face. "Where's Mister Geraci?" There was urgency in his tone, his eyes panicked with a Peter Lorre fixation.

Vince turned to face him. "He's in the Library. What's up?"

"A helicopter is coming in low over the trees. I thought these assholes were coming by seaplane?"

"They are," Vince said as Evohl flew out of his chair.

***

Bobby dropped anchor in sixty feet of water, a good distance from the west shore of Open Bay, then dumped the propulsion sleds over the side.

"Are you ready?"

"Ready as I'll ever be," Tyra said.

Tyra fit the regulator mouthpiece between her teeth, then took a breath while she adjusted the mask over her face. Bobby went over first, backward, splashing into the water with the metal clang of tanks. Not to be surprised by the lack of air, he'd brought two extra cylinders, just in case. He made quick work of securing them to his sled, while the other sled floated aimlessly below the surface. Tyra set up on the gunwale, made one last tug on a zipper or two, then with a prayer in her eyes she too flipped back over into the water.

As they dropped below the surface in a shower of wet light, their arms stretched to full length, pulled taut by the power of the sleds. Down through the progressive darkness, from yellow to green to the murkiest of blue, Tyra felt herself sliding through successive layers of temperature, each colder than the last. The water was thick with sediment churned from the depths as if caught in a storm, and as the pressure on her eardrums increased in intensity, a faint ringing propagated in her skull as though a bandsaw was wearing on cold steel.

Bobby checked his dive watch computer and leveled off. The computer provided depth and navigation information, available oxygen, and a myriad more functions. He'd told Tyra that they'd descend to a level devoid of heavy currents, sensing his way to the path of least resistance. Tyra could feel her sled moving faster now than above, tugging more fervently on her shoulders.

Out of the murk, a school of sea bass crossed their path, clattering against her body, startling her with their giant eyes peering into her mask, causing her to lurch. Bobby glanced her way, a sump of water in his mask flirting with his eyes. There was a question in his gaze, one of concern, which Tyra rectified with a vibrant nod of her head. She had to appear fearless, for she knew if Bobby sensed her trepidation, his over-compensating for her welfare would put everyone at risk.

Several minutes passed, the soft whir of the sled's prop rhythmic, her wetsuit rendering a uniform layer of warmth under the artificial skin. However, several hundred feet of ocean lie beneath them. The sense of insignificance was pervasive. Tyra checked her watch, as if knowing the precise time would quell her anxiety.

Growing now in intensity came the sound of engines, and Bobby slowed to a stop. They floated motionless in the currents, while above them the waterline boiled with the props from a gaggle of whale watching boats.

Bobby checked his compass, gave Tyra a thumbs-up, then made a directional change. Tyra followed closely behind him, the bubble strings coming off Bobby's regulator like breadcrumbs through the water.

Three-quarters-of-a-mile from Open Bay, they emerged from a ganglion of seaweed at the base of Kellett Bluff. Bobby pointed to the flagpole, its image wavering through the water. The entrance to the tunnel was straight ahead.

***

Dane stood frozen in the courtyard, his hands jammed in his pockets, staring dubiously toward some yet unseen threat.

Evohl was beside him, his Beretta drawn, the muzzle pointing down at his side. The mechanical dragonfly had touched down. The thump-thump-thump of the helicopter blades were slowing to a whoosh, the whine of the engine's turbo entering the audible region of human capability on its way toward extinction.

***

Vince charged into the Library.

"Who is it?" Vito asked curtly.

"I don't know. It could be DEA."

"What makes you say that?"

Visions of Nick's confession were pounding rocks inside Vince's head. He shrugged his shoulders.

"Well, don't panic," Vito said. "We have nothing to hide. With any luck, it'll be some misguided pilot unaware of his location, and we'll be able to get him on his way quickly."

***

In a matter of minutes, the visitors became known. They weren't DEA. No flak jackets or helmets. No Quantico stares behind black glass, or blue windbreakers with bright yellow letters. And they weren't an unfortunate tour group whose pilot had plunked them down on the wrong clod of dirt in the San Juan Islands.

Dane came in first, his heart racing as though a gerbil ran loose in his chest. Behind him, Venegas' entourage came into the foyer, scouting out the corridors like a platoon of infantrymen stealing into a shelled-out village.

Leading the onslaught was a gorilla. It was impossible to determine where his eyebrows ended and his hairline began. The next was taller, leaner, his shoulders and waist moving fluidly with his legs in a choreographed slink. He had a face like a llama, and Dane expected him to spit on the floor at any second. The third was a mangy cur, wry in his tread, smelling of onion and charcoaled beef, with the white scarred mustache of a harelip.

They were dressed in leather boots, camo pants and T-shirts. Each had an ammo belt and an eight-inch blade strapped to their waist. Their torsos and arms were gnarled with muscle — sinew in a riot about to split the skin. Dane could feel their eyes strafe across his body. They were packing variations of enormous firepower from handgun to full-auto, and what they'd hidden in their foot-soldier ensembles was most likely as plentiful as effective.

The fourth man was different, slender, intelligent, a Latino with straw-colored hair. He wore a small ponytail at the nape of his neck, Gargoyle sunglasses, black jeans, black T, black sport coat, the points of his lizard-skinned cowboy boots curled into snouts. He was a hot wire of menace, packing a holstered Tokarev automatic and a superior attitude. Obviously in charge, his hands rested comfortably in his coat pockets, his face looking impassively around the room as though he were standing in a Taco Bell waiting for his nachos.

Blade-face came in next, looking jittery and stiff, endeavoring to mimic cool, then Evohl leading Venegas who had a female companion sporting his arm. Another one of Geraci's men with a silver mane remained outside with Venegas' pilot.

Venegas was a wiry, coiled snake of anger who walked with a cane. He had the eyes of a jaguar, his hair the black and shiny wetness of a raven's wing. He wore a gray silk shirt that rippled with a metallic sheen, a white silk suit, and an ornate gold cross from a leather thong about his neck. Forget the religious implications. He could blow out your lights as easy as turning the page in a comic book.

"Vito Geraci," Vince said, holding out a flat palm of introduction like some ironic butler. "This is Augustine Olade Venegas."

"It's my pleasure to meet you, Mister Venegas."

"Please, let's dispense with the formality," Venegas said with a perfect American accent. "You may call me Augustine. May I call you Vito?"

Vito stood speechless, curiosity raising his eyebrows.

"Does my diction surprise you?"

"Not to sound like some prejudiced fool, but yes," Vito said.

"Don't be. Many Colombians receive schooling in America. I for one have a master's degree in economics from Harvard. Rodrico, my eyes and ears," he said, casting a sidelong glance at the straw-haired Latino, "he has a degree in biology from NYU."

Venegas smiled the faintest of smiles. "I'm sure his study of anatomy has proved helpful in his present career."

Vito let his eyes roam to Venegas' companion. She was beautiful, yet plain. Wearing no make-up, but strikingly featured. Muscular, but not masculine. She smelled of sex and candy.

"You must forgive me," Venegas said. "This is Celida. My companion, my odalisque, my past and my future. She goes wherever I venture. We are inexplicably connected, at the hip as they say."

Vito reached out and took her hand. He kissed her lightly on the fingers. "It is my bounty that you are here. You are a flower amongst the thorns."

Celida pulled out a red-cherry sucker and put it in her mouth. She had on a black leather romper, cut high on her thighs. Period. *Finito.* The front was split to her navel, the leather narrow over her breasts, like two arms of a lover, hands joined about the soft curve of her neck. The back was non-existent, swooping to the crest of her pelvis like the eyes of every man in the room.

Dane was intrigued and wary in the same iota of thought. He believed Venegas would be a thug with the intellect of a wet noodle. But he wasn't. He was sophisticated, keen, even charming, to a fault. As soon as Venegas came in, his eyes swept the room, looking for adversaries. But he didn't see Dane. He simply didn't see him. And in that one act of non-recognition, he'd dismissed any semblance of prowess that Dane may have had.

It was clear. Dane posed no risk. No matter the pretensions, he wasn't a threat. But what was remarkable was that Venegas knew that without even making eye contact. When most people scan a room, they search for eyes. And if gazes meet, one of two things happens: either they hold the union for even so much as a brainwave, or they blink and shift away. The blink is the equivalent to a flip of the hand. You are dismissed. If it's between a man and a woman, sex is totally out of the question.

But Dane had been waiting for Venegas' look, staring at him as though he were some oddity of science, wanting to peer into the cunning soul of this well-oiled machine. But to Venegas, Dane was less than a blink. A blink. How in the hell did I get here? Dane mused. I should've been a priest, for in the world of intimidation, I rank lower than a footprint.

"We should move into the Great Room," Vito said. "The *Nez Pierce* will arrive soon. We can see her approach from there."

Venegas' eyes became slitted with private thoughts. He tugged at his earring. It was gold and the shape of a crescent moon.

Vince caught the gesture. "Vito, shouldn't we show Augustine the loot? He's come a long way." He looked around the room at the menagerie of goons. "I wouldn't want him becoming antsy with speculation."

"You must forgive me, Augustine. My anticipation is like pure adrenaline. Why don't you take Miss Celida to the Great Room, Vince, and I will show Augustine the fruits of his labor in the Library."

Venegas looked warily at Celida. She gathered the length of her licorice black hair and pulled it over one shoulder, the cascade reaching below her breast.

"It won't take but a minute." Vito held his hands out in front of himself, palms up, his face lit in saintly beatitude as though he were about to deliver a parable. "Then we'll join them." Charming was but a word until Vito embodied the term.

Celida nodded and Venegas turned, and like a pack of ferrets, his men spread out quickly, moving along the walls.

***

"Would you like a smoke?" Dane asked.

Celida's eyes were the color of cinnamon. Mercurial. Hungry. Clear as hate, fluid as water. She nodded with deliberate approval, a slight tip to her head.

He tapped out a cigarette from his pack, held it out for her grasp. Barefoot, she had a silver toe ring on her left foot middle. Coming closer, she stumbled accidentally on purpose against him, and the cigarette dropped to the floor. They looked at each other for a second, a gaze not a blink. Then she bent over in front of him, a little carelessly. The weight of her breasts was full against the leather.

Dane worked his lighter out of the front pocket of his jeans. Her left eye appeared gold and shimmered as he held the flame to the cigarette. Her face was a smooth palette of brown lust. When she exhaled, she blew her smoke around in the air like she was creating some form of artwork.

Vince offered a drink to Celida, but she turned him down, just as Michael walked in from the kitchen, staggering slightly.

"I thought Vito told you to go easy on the booze," Vince remarked.

Michael immediately flipped him off, wiggling his head in mock coolness, then, like skipping a track, scratched his neck. "Who was in the chopper?" He stared at Celida. "Boris and Natasha?"

Vince turned his back, looking out over the Sound through the tempered glass windows.

Celida moved to a chair, crossing her legs, the same motion as when a female panther stalks a wild goat. Dane imagined that if she wouldn't't've turned Vince down on a drink, it would've been exotic, made with dark rum and cherries in a highball glass.

"Has the *Nez* appeared yet?" Michael asked.

"Not yet," Vince said over his shoulder.

"I wasn't asking you. Dane, have you seen the *Nez Pierce?*"

Dane tore his eyes off Celida. "Uh no."

He walked to the window by Vince just as Vito and Augustine came into the room. They each were carrying a scotch, and deep in conversation.

Regarding the woman, Vince looked past Dane to Celida. "So, what do you think of Celida?" he said under his breath. "For a second, I thought you were going to melt under those eyes of hers ... just fall on the floor and let her ride you like a dime store pony."

"Vince," Vito said to draw Vince's attention. "Augustine is satisfied. He assures me we will be as well."

"That's what I like to hear."

Michael traipsed over and squatted by Celida's chair, cupping his hand on her forearm. "Hey, darling. Have you seen the kitchen in this place?" he said in an exaggerated whisper, loud enough to be overheard. "I bet Betty Crocker would give it up wet as a peach just to step foot in that motherfucker." He took a swig off his glass. "You cook?"

If looks could kill, Vito was packing a cannon.

Just then, Dane called out, "There she is," and all eyes turned to the ocean, where, like a mirage, the *Nez Pierce* had taken shape on the vaporous horizon.

***

Tyra and Bobby had been waiting for forty-five minutes under the dock, but Venegas' seaplane never came. They had their masks up on their foreheads, air hoses draped over their shoulders. They were hanging by their armpits from a steel cable that was part of the dock skeleton and talking in whispers.

Bobby's brow furrowed with worry. "Too much time has passed."

Tyra, too, wondered about Dane and the plan. Some part of her mind clued into the idle pacing of the two men on the planks above, the remaining portion on what was the next step. She shivered, her head and shoulders shaking.

"Are you okay?"

"Just getting cold," Tyra said. But she could not hide the pieces of fright in her eyes and sensed that Bobby wanted to calm her.

"Do you know either of these two?" he asked with a tilt to his head.

"I think the taller one is Lance. Dane told me about him. The other guy, I don't know."

Lance stuck two fingers in his mouth and whistled. Some seagulls took to the air, and the whistle sent Tyra's heart on a scurry around her chest. She splashed a little in the water. Bobby grabbed her arm in comfort, put a finger to his lips with his eyes.

Now there was another voice wearing camo clothes standing on the dock. He looked like a gorilla. From his front pocket, he produced a small wood case with a swivel top, and a ready-rolled joint emerged. The jay ignited; the air grew skunky with the smell of marijuana.

***

Dane stepped out to the top of the bluff stairs and fired up a cigarette. A nonchalant signal to the troops. Out of nowhere, Celida appeared beside him. She was working over a blue-raspberry lollipop, twirling it against her puckered lips. She took the cigarette from between his fingers and put it in her mouth.

The way she inhaled made his throat tingle. The first person he'd ever met that could turn smoke into fire. Words exploded from her eyes, and he went mute with their implications. Then, like a breeze off a block of ice, Rodrico appeared.

He surveyed the horizon for a moment, the *Nez Pierce* inch-by-inch growing larger to the eye. Then, as if directed by a tiny voice, he peered down the bluff toward the water, gazing as if he'd seen something in the shimmering surface.

He lifted his sunglasses, peering under the frames. Up close and exposed, Dane could see he had a glass eye shrouded with white film. The unnatural starkness of it made him hard to look at.

"Something is by the dock," Rodrico said.

Dane feigned surprise, then retrieved his cigarette from Celida and administered a calming inhale.

Rodrico pointed to a quiver in the water. "There." His hands were chaffed, his knuckles white as if left to soak in dishwater overnight.

Celida took the cigarette from Dane's lip and stole another drag.

Dane's eyes flashed on her face, then Rodrico's. "Oh, it's probably a sea lion." Dane knew it was Bobby or Tyra sure as shoes travel in pairs. "They're very common in these waters."

Celida flicked the smoldering cigarette butt toward the ocean, turned and walked off toward the house, once again her lips massaging the flavor out of the blue-raspberry candy.

Rodrico belched, his breath a slap akin to rendering plant slurry. He was staring serenely at Dane's forehead, and Dane had this strange feeling Rodrico was contemplating turning his skull into a fruit bowl.

"Sea lion, huh?" Rodrico turned and followed Celida.

***

"Tyra," Bobby said. "I don't know how, but Venegas must already be here. Dane gave us the signal to move to the tunnel. But I'm not ready here. You'll have to go yourself."

"I can't, Bobby." Tyra's eyes darted, looking for an escape. "I-I-I ..."

"Sh-sh-sh," he said, lifting his eyes to above. He paused, waiting for footsteps. When none came, he calmly said, "You can do it, Tyra."

Tyra stared at him, the gentle lapping of the water hypnotic like the tick of a clock. "But I'll get lost."

"Stay close to the surface. Remember, look for the flag-pole."

Tyra was in a death spiral. She envisioned running out of air, each passing second her lungs burning with an acid born of oxygen depletion, and then before she could reach the surface, the closure in her throat would break open, and she'd suck in a torrent of water that would fill her chest like cement. She'd sink to the bottom, eyes-glazed over like blue marbles, skin wrinkled and blanched white, and then the fish would come one at a time like beggars in a soup line to feast upon her poached ...

"Tyra?" Bobby shook her shoulder. "The tunnel?"

***

All the major players were in the Great Room except Dane, and that irritated Vince. He couldn't understand why Dane wasn't at his side at this crucial moment. Dane had left min-utes before in a full-bladder-meltdown, absent on his way to the bathroom.

They saw the *Nez Pierce* slow to a stop several hundred yards out, due west of the compound. The excitement was numbing. "Should we go to the lab to inspect the shipment?" Vince asked without thinking.

Vito glared at Vince. "No-no-no," he said, waving his hands in front of Vince like a marshaler ordering a plane not to land. "No one goes in that lab except Evohl. He will do the test."

Vince clucked his tongue, his mouth dry as an oven. Sean walked in and stood at the foot of the stairs that led to the second floor.

Venegas was fingering a wad of bills secured in a gold money clip. "I would like to see the test," he said casually, slipping the clip of money back into in his pants pocket.

Geraci threw his hand up, cutting him off like a good traffic cop. "You'll see the test if there is a need." Then his face contorted into a cynical twitch, and said, "Besides, if the quality is as good as you say, there should be no question."

Like finding out your fourteen-year-old daughter is pregnant by the pimple-faced geek sitting cross-legged on your couch. The cordial conversation had ended. Fifty kilos lie offshore and four million dollars in cash set in the next room. This was now business, do or die.

Eyes began shifting around the room, bodies cocked and loaded, those sitting were shifting their weight from one buttock to another in anxious anticipation. The shipment was like an approaching storm, the future uncertain what ravage it would take.

CHAPTER 45

San Juan Islands, Washington
January 13, 1996

Dane moved quickly to the bookcase. There was no time to lose. Like a chain caught in a gear, what he was about to do, there would be no turning back. He tipped the four books that controlled the combination out to a forty-five-degree angle, and as if there was a stirring giant behind the wall, the bookcase moved outward, the muffled whir of an electric motor driving the mahogany wall on a pivot.

Dane grabbed two of the four cases. The handles strained with the weight of millions. The bookcase slowed to a stop, and hastily he proceeded down the stairs, the stark white light of the lab igniting as he stepped on the first tread.

He could hear his feet clamoring on the metal steps, and defying the laws of physics, he tried to float like a balloon across the path. The lab felt cool on his face. The air seemed stale, compressed, forced through the kidneys of some air conditioner.

He set the cases down next to the shaft and spun the hand wheel counterclockwise. The hatch was heavy and bunched the fat of his hand as he lifted it on its hinges. He peered into the cistern, the smell of brine acrid and thick, charging up from the bottom. The hole was several feet in diameter and bored straight down into solid rock. Light died in its hold, the darkness amorphous and inky black.

Suddenly, a body emerged from below the waterline and clambered up the steel rungs of the ladder, rising out of the depth cloaked in a rubbery suit. It was a short distance, but it wasn't until Tyra emerged into the light and removed her regulator that Dane realized it was her and not Bobby.

"Where is Bobby?"

"He's rigging the dock. We were waiting for Venegas to come, but he never came, then Bobby saw your signal, and–and he wasn't ready, and he had to send me alone, and I didn't want to come at first, but ..." Her words were overlapping each other, each thought racing to get out first.

"I know. I know," Dane said, trying to calm her. "Venegas threw us a curve and came by helicopter."

"What do we do?"

"Just carry on as planned. Take the money and meet Bobby."

"But what about you?"

"I'll take care of this end. Where are the bags?"

Throwing one arm over the lip of the shaft, Tyra pulled on a thin nylon rope that was tied to her weight belt. She handed it to Dane, and he started hauling hand-over-hand a catch from the bottom. At the end of the rope were four waterproof bags.

Dane popped open the first case and started loading money, hand-sized stacks one-after-another into a bag. Tyra rose one more rung, then bent over the lip of the shaft and helped Dane maneuver the load. Once the case was emptied, Tyra zipped the bag closed and then the hermetic seal. While Dane unloaded the second case, she tossed the money-weighted parcel to the bottom of the shaft, the splash of a million dollars relatively slight compared to the weight of reprisal the action carried.

Seconds later, Dane raced to the stairs with the empty cases and returned with the other two. The process resumed. They worked in silence, each doing their part, a production line of such efficiency, Henry Ford would have marveled at the sight. Soon, all four bags were at the bottom of the shaft.

"Get yourself away from the tunnel as fast as you can," Dane said. "The divers will be here soon."

Dane grabbed the hatch handle, but as Tyra readjusted her mask, he saw the uncertainty in her eyes. He gave her a wink, as if to say things were in hand even though what lie ahead was the most treacherous of all, and in his heart, he felt a cry of hopelessness, closing the light on what may be the last time he'd ever see her.

***

"The divers should be in the water by now," Vito said.

Out over the Sound, boats peppered the water, some in search of whales, some in search of food, some in search of leisure. The *Nez Pierce* sat among them as innocuous as a virus on a doorknob.

Two of Venegas' men, Mangy Cur and Llama, had joined the ensemble of hoodlums. Not to be outdone, two of Geraci's men, Blade-face and Elvis, shadowed their moves, adding a snarling lip or piercing eye at every turn.

Michael started talking, swiveling his head from side-to-side as if speaking to all the hoodlums at once, "The testosterone is as thick as smoke in here and the way you boys are posturing I'm amazed at the idiocy of it all." He administered a drink of collusion, then joked out loud. "Could be one hell of a party, though." He raised his glass in a toast. "Enough coke to kill us all."

Vito looked at Michael sternly, as if he was trying to assemble a head to replace the one Michael was packing in his rectum.

"If the coke doesn't kill you," Venegas said. "You know you've paid too much." He looked very Scarfacian in his white suit and Latin mien, his jaded, heavy-lidded smirk nothing less than a towering masterpiece of intimidation.

Vito's eyes narrowed at Michael like someone aiming down a rifle barrel. They were liquid and rheumy, the whites tawny, the irises flecked yellow with rage.

Michael had gnawed on Vito's temper to where now Vince could see his eyes glaring hot as match heads, the tension existing between them spilling over the brim into business.

Venegas' nostrils flared like he was inhaling a crush of smelling salts, his eyes black and cavernous in his block-of-ice face. Celida unwrapped a fresh, violent-grape sucker and stuck it in her mouth.

Characters began moving in disparate directions. Michael plopped down in a chair, too drunk to care about who had the biggest *cojones*. Evohl edged closer to Rodrico, removing a margin of flexibility in case a fight ensued. Mangy Cur and Llama moved to positions at the odd ends of the room while Blade-face and Elvis spread out along the wall. Unaffected, Rodrico slowly scanned the situation with a slight twist to his neck while Sean slid in behind a couch of brown leather and touched the holstered gun which hung heavy against his ribs.

Vince could feel the tension building in his shoulders as if someone were filling his head with sand. He raised his hands in a placating way and took a step toward the sizzling space between Vito and Venegas. "Hey look. We're all a little tight. We're so close, let's not blow it on petty machismo."

Vito's eyes looked hard into Vince's. "You think you know what goes on in the mind of men such as Augustine or me?" He looked at his fingernails, then back. "I should shoot you for being a fool."

Vito's words were like a slap in the face, the action courting introspection instead of retaliation. It was brutally clear: Vince had committed *protracted* suicide, bringing Vito into his life. Unlike the jumper he'd seen from his office window, sprawled lifeless under a yellow tarp, he'd climbed the ladder of cruel ambition, blinded by the lure of wealth and power, to the rooftop of crime; but his expiration Vito controlled. His Adam's apple worked up-and-down with a dry click in his throat, trying to form words of rebuttal.

"What's wrong Vince ... cat got your tongue?" Geraci delivered the punchline with a maniacal gleam, paused a beat for effect, then threw back his head in a booming contagious laugh, slapping Venegas on the shoulder with delight.

"Evohl, go to the lab," Vito commanded him.

***

The empty cases back in position, Dane tipped the final book back in place and the bookcase retreated toward the wall.

"I'm sorry to find you here. I had hopes of you," Evohl said from the armchair where he was sitting, watching the deceit play out.

Startled, Dane turned on a heel. He looked at his hands, then rubbed his palms together. He was sweating heavier than a tuna in a sushi bar.

Evohl shrugged his shoulders. "So how bad is it?"

Dane rubbed his neck. "Pretty bad. Venegas will be one pissed-off *comanchero*."

"The money. It is gone?"

"Afraid so," Dane said.

"I see. What we do then?"

Dane pulled his gun. "I'm walking out of here."

Evohl looked as nervous as a brick wall. "Shoot me. Otherwise, you will not leave."

"Then I'll shoot you," Dane said, lifting the pointed gun a little higher.

"Then what? The gun is loud, and they will kill you."

"You have a better idea."

Evohl stood, flashing his toothy grin, and sauntered toward him. He was flexing his fists and popping knuckles. "Maybe you think you kill me with your hands."

"I don't want to kill you at all. All I want to do is leave."

Evohl moved to within a breath in front of him, Dane holding the Ruger only inches from his ribs. "You are a weak person, Avilla. As weak as your friend, Spinetti. I have no use for weak people. You should know, I was to kill you today. A risk you are, he said. Vince. Your friend." He laughed. "A risk."

Dane swung the pistol upward, whipping the gun barrel across Evohl's temple, a blow sufficient to take the big man down.

Or so he thought.

Blood trickled from the side of Evohl's head, staining his waxen skin, but he stood unwavering. A moment later, he knocked the gun from Dane's hand, then swallowed Dane in a bear hug. His arms were unyielding like links of a chain, and with a force of a machinist vise bearing down on a walnut, the albino squeezed.

Dane felt two ribs give way, the pain shooting down his side like a bolt of electricity, and with each passing second, precious breath was being forced from his lungs. He felt like a rag doll in Evohl's arms, his feet off the ground, his head jerking around, arms flailing against the albino's shoulders like waves crashing against a rocky shore, only he didn't have two millennia to wear him down.

The pain was excruciating, his brain pounding as if his heart had popped into his skull. Then, with as much force as he could muster, Dane boxed the albino's ears.

Evohl's eyes bulged for an instant, his grip easing as he staggered into the bar. Blood was draining from his ears, but the albino wasn't giving up.

Dane delivered another blow, but he was out of breath. Patches of his vision were turning dusky black. Colors streaked through his mind while his arms tingled with numbness from the giant tourniquet around his mid-section.

Dane fumbled for a next move, approaching death like an unwilling participant. He reared back, then butted his head forward, the force breaking the bridge of Evohl's nose and splitting Dane's forehead into the hairline. The albino reeled back against a barstool, the chair tipping and falling to the floor. But he never let go.

Evohl emitted a deranged laugh, a gleam in his eyes like Dane was the best joke he'd ever killed. It was over. Dane saw visions of white tunnels in his immediate future. Then by accident, his arms flopping, numb and deprived of oxygen, his right hand whacked the edge of the bar, drawing his eyes in that direction.

In his fading sight was an ice bucket, a bar towel, a tumbler half full of melted ice, and an ice pick. He stretched for the ice pick, his fingers working like a concert pianist trying to grapple the instrument. It was out of reach.

Evohl's breath turned sour, his teeth shimmering white with saliva, his gums crimson with homicide. Acting like a bear trap, Dane bit down on the albino's broken nose, tearing at the cartilage and flesh like a rabid dog.

Evohl merely grunted like a good ox, eyes crossed, but lumbered backward. The desperate measure had proved the distance. Dane's hand found the towel, then the tumbler, which he sent reeling to the floor in a crash, and then the ice pick.

A touch and it rolled into his grasp, and holding it like a microphone, the point directed up to the ceiling, Dane jabbed it into Evohl's back, puncturing his flesh between shoulder blades. But to no avail. The action perturbed the albino, but instead of relinquishing his hold, he tightened his grip.

Then instinct took over, a primal clarity that nullified all the pain, the numbness and the lack of oxygen, and Dane jabbed the pick upward, piercing the soft spot behind the albino's ear just under the base of his skull.

Curiously, the albino looked surprised by the move, his face almost comic with a how-dare-you stare, and then Dane did to the albino what he'd done to that frog in freshman biology. He started working the handle of the ice pick like he was going through the gears on his ZX, the action severing Evohl's brain from his spinal column like one would unplug a computer from a wall socket.

The albino's mouth opened and closed as though he was trying to clear his ears, exuding a smell akin to sardines and muenster cheese, then his face jerked to the side as if slapped. That was it.

Frozen in time, Dane could see his face reflected in the Evohl's sunglasses, then in the next instant, like somebody had pulled the pins out of the big man's joints, he folded up like a map of Leningrad, and the pair of strange lovers fell to the floor.

Dane gasped for air as if he was trying to inhale water. He tasted metal on his tongue. His mouth was bleeding, and he had blood on his palms. He got to his feet.

He wiped his hands in a crisscross on the dead man's chest, then bent over and grabbed the albino by the heels, endorphins taking the pain of his broken ribs on vacation.

Dane left him behind the couch, then backed away. He was bent over hands-to-knees, still laboring to catch his breath, when the door to the Library opened. He threw a sidelong glance at the man in the doorway. Michael Geraci. What next?

"Hey what's up?" Michael asked.

What's up? Oh nothing, Dane thought to himself, opening and closing his eyes to blink the sweat out of them. I just stole four million dollars, had my ribs broke, and just went about scrambling the albino's brains like I was making eggs for breakfast.

Michael waltzed into the room, headed for the bar and another drink. A few feet later, he realized there was blood on Dane's face. "Are you okay? You look like crap." Then he saw the albino's feet sticking out from behind the couch. "Oh whoa. Is that who I think it is? Those size-sixteen loafers are hard to mistake."

Still bent over, holding his knees, Dane was too winded to speak. All he could see was the ice pick sticking like a gearshift knob out of the back of Evohl's head.

Michael poured himself a scotch, then after a sip, he laughed.

Dane saw the butt of his Ruger laying half under a chair where it had fallen from his grip during the struggle. He wasn't about to fight anyone else. He'd just shoot Michael if he had to and take his chances. Dane fished the gun out, and with one hand on his hip supporting his aching ribs, he pointed the gun.

"She–it," Michael said, and he said it with proper emphasis in two syllables. "Hey, don't get excited there, Festus. I don't have any quarrel with you. I'm not even remotely sentimental about the big lug." He took a drink of his scotch. "Curious, though. What do you plan to do next?"

"Just like I told him," Dane said, waving the gun at the dead albino. "I'm leaving."

"Where to? Can I go? I'm bored with this group."

"Look Michael. I like you. But I don't have time for this." Dane made another round of inhales and exhales. "You see, I've stolen Venegas' money, and well, things are going to get ugly. I hated to see you in the middle of it, but you were a part of this I couldn't control."

"Is the money already gone?"

"Yes."

"Hmmmm. And of course, there's Evohl. So just how ..."

"I have a plan."

"A plan? I see," he said with an impish glint. "So far, it looks as though things are working pretty well."

"Michael, I don't have time to chit-chat, so this can go one of two ways. You either sit quietly as I walk out of here, or I kill you and take my chances."

"Hmmmm. Interesting. What did you figure would be the outcome of your little heist?"

"People will die."

Michael ran his finger around the rim of his glass. "So, let me ask one thing: were you hoping that my father would be a causality? I mean, if he isn't, pulling this stunt puts a bullseye on your back about the size of a bus."

"Vito dead? After all this? Yeah, that would be nice."

"And Vince?"

"I've heard there's a thin line between love and hate. I crossed it with Vince a while ago."

There was a moment of silence between them. Dane holding the gun, Michael swirling the ice in his drink.

Then Michael shrugged his shoulders and arched his eyebrows as though an impossible situation had been imposed upon him. "My father is a stubborn man. I remember as a kid, he killed a man named Willy Two-shoes, solely because he heard Willy had called him a cheater over some card game."

"Your father is not a boy scout."

"You know, when Carmen's gone, I die for conversation," Michael said. "That's why I drink. Jim Beam and Johnny Walker aren't big talkers themselves, but they get the voices in my head to carry on some weird conversations."

"Well, we all go through these chaotic periods."

Michael gazed at his mother's portrait over the fireplace and began speaking in a conciliatory tone, "She died for his love, you know." He chewed on his lower lip, put a hand on his hip. "My father. Seems there's an ugly possibility that he may die today." He paused in contemplation. "Then there is Carmen. Shouldn't there be some loyalty?"

"It's a two-way street," Dane said.

It took but a second more for Michael to decide. "Speaking of choices," he said. "You're right. There are only two options."

"So, which one do you want?"

"Now let me finish. My view is slightly different. If you don't trust me, which you probably don't, you shoot me and take your chances. However, if you trust me...and by the way, I've never given you any reason not to...you put the gun away, get cleaned up, and we walk out of here together."

Dane thought about it for a moment. He wasn't fond of the idea of killing Michael. He didn't even relish the thought of Evohl sprawled out behind the couch. Besides, he truly liked Michael and the chances of getting out of there alive after the multitudes heard the shot would be, well, zero. The hesitation was quick, the answer decisive. "If you so much as blink an eye in the wrong direction ... I will kill you. You understand that?"

"Definitely."

"You're not forgetting anything? The money? Your father?"

"Money. Nah, I have enough money, and as for my father; he's all that stands between me and Carmen. You're dealing the cards, and with that hand, he loses. In some respects, the old soldier will probably be proud of my decision."

"One last thing," Dane said. "I don't know how this is going to end. It was supposed to be simple, like a pack of rats fighting over a single piece of cheese in a bucket of water, but first Venegas comes by helicopter, now Evohl ... I mean worse case I always figured I could go back to Europe and just disappear. But you I can't predict."

"No one is asking you to. Hell, I may have to join you on the run, but even the prospect of living in flea bag hotels stringing from Budapest to Ankara is a better than what I'm going through now."

Dane stuck the Ruger back in his holster.

Michael smiled and tossed Dane the bar towel, then downed his drink. "So, what now, Sundance?"

***

When Tyra emerged from the tunnel, Bobby was waiting. He had both sleds untied, floating at an angle to the bottom. They quickly secured the bags to the sleds, then discarded their first set of air tanks, harnessed on the second set, and sped off due south, away from the compound and the possibility of encountering any of the *Nez Pierce* divers.

They approached the black shifting outline of the *Ecstasea* from the port side. Rising from the murk, Tyra could see the sunlight brighter on the surface, like a yellow flame dancing on the chop, the layers of current becoming increasingly tepid as they neared the surface.

The boat was slowly swinging in the current against the anchor, the cable singing under the tension like a steel guitar. Strings of bubbles rose from along its length. They slid along the hull in cool shadow. Tyra saw a school of perch flutter into the depths, their undulating bodies shimmering like a sequin gown.

At the stern, they secured the sleds to a cleat, then climbed onto the dive deck. They unloaded their dive equipment — flippers, air tanks — Tyra lost her weight belt in the process and watched it sink into the depths below.

The breeze felt cool on her face, the sky a welcome blue tent patched with white clouds. Overhead, a gaggle of seagulls filled the air with a cacophony. They did not know for sure who was aboard, but Dane's best guess was that Jimmy would be alone. Tyra pushed the hood of her wet suit back off her head.

Bobby was carrying a speargun, a moderately sized weapon with a quiver of five aluminum arrows, the tips barbed with razor blades. A good SEAL, besides the speargun and a knife, he also carried a blackjack.

They hurried across the aft, balancing themselves against the roll of the deck, then past the Game Room, which was empty, and into the hall. As they approached the Main Salon, they could hear music and, like fingerprints, they melted into the wall.

Jimmy was sitting on the couch, feet propped up on the coffee table, a Hot Rod magazine flipped open on his lap. Using Tyra as a distraction, Bobby rendered Jimmy unconscious, his blackjack striking against his temple.

Bobby took Jimmy's gun from his holster, then rolled him off the couch onto the floor. He pushed the furniture around to give himself room, then ripped a cord loose from a lamp and tied Jimmy up.

A minute later, Bobby shouldered the door to the monitor room and began shoveling video cassettes into the waterproof bag that Tyra was holding open like the mouth of an alligator. There were over thirty videotapes. It took less than twenty seconds to gather them all.

***

Vito was pacing. "Where the hell is Evohl?" he asked out loud, of no one in particular. Then he saw Dane and Michael enter the room. "Have either of you seen Evohl?"

Michael and Dane looked at each other with shrugged shoulders. Rodrico was absently tying a hangman's noose out of a piece of string.

"Dammit. What is taking him so long? Vince, go see what's keeping him."

Immediately, Vince headed for the Library. Dane and Michael followed. When they got outside the Great Room, Dane stopped Vince. He slapped a folded envelope in his hand.

"What's this?"

"Consequences," Dane said, walking off.

"What? Hey, where are you going? This deal is going down. I need you here."

"Just going down to the dock for a second," Dane said over his shoulder.

Vince stared at the envelope, his face perplexed, then slipped it in his pocket as Dane and Michael walked out the door into the spangled light.

Dane and Michael moved with calculated steps toward the bluff, not too fast, not too slow. The *Ecstasea* sat levitated in the distance on a flashing mirror of water, the sun close to the horizon in the short afternoon of winter.

"So, where's the money?" Michael asked. They were floating down the stairs, the smooth pipe railing gliding through their hands.

"You'll know soon enough."

"I don't get it. You can't be thinking of making an escape in that skiff."

A pause ensued, waiting for an answer.

"Let's take the X ..."

"Sorry, Michael," Dane said, shutting him down. "You're going to lose that boat."

Dane and Michael walked right by Lance and onto the skiff. The farm boy was, after all, naïve. The Gorilla stood scratching his face, while Darning Sock adjusted his belt.

Dane turned over the engine as Michael unwound the bow rope from its cleat, and the two pulled away from the dock. Then, with the flick of a switch on a box no bigger than a butane lighter, the dock went up like the Fourth of July behind them.

Bobby had set the charges to go off in succession, first the dock, the blast launching Lance backward into the water stunned from the concussion, leaving Darning Sock choking on a splintered plank, the obstruction sticking out of the side of his neck like an alien tongue.

The next explosion destroyed Vito's plane. A pontoon shattered into dust, the plane toppling sideways, its wing slicing into the water. Then Michael's Excalibur was gutted by a massive charge along its belly, the quarter-million-dollar speed boat sinking into the water with the same quickness that it had once traveled above the waves. Last but not least was Vito's yacht. The aft of the *Insatiable* shuddered with a blast that moved the engine room into the galley and made the great lady list to the starboard side in a slow death.

Dane looked back over his shoulder at the destruction in his wake and there through the dust and billowing smoke, he saw Gorilla impaled on a piece of pipe railing with a gun in one hand, his other clamped around the steel that exited his midsection in a torrent of blood, and as he slumped, recognizing his peril, Gorilla fired four shots obliquely into the water at his feet.

***

The sound of an outboard motor wound tight, racing across the Sound, the explosions detonating along the dock, the unmistakable percussion of pistol shots. Like a mother knows when their baby is in trouble, Venegas knew the deal was over.

He operated like a surgeon in an emergency room, casually lifting his cane — a modified rifle — and put a 25-caliber round behind Elvis' right ear, eliminating a tumor. The bullet went in as cleanly as a machinist punch through sheet metal, came out like a fist through his left eye socket, doing a Jackson Pollock in blood and tissue on the wall.

It was as if Dane had pranced out the door and tossed a flaming matchbook back inside, back into a house full of natural gas. The place exploded. Bullets bit chunks out of the walls, the curtains, the windows, the furniture. Muzzle talk and angry voices. Precision made autos — lawn sprinklers of death.

Vito dove behind a chair. A hollow point round splintered apart on the cement planter next to his head. Celida sat in an armchair primping her eyelashes, sucking on an outrageous-orange sucker, unaffected by the gunfight as if she lived in the heart of a force-field. Venegas slipped behind a heavy black walnut armoire for protection as Rodrico laid down a curtain of lead to shield his retreat.

It's one thing to own a gun, or even pack it, as Sean would soon find out. Quite another if you take the time to practice, arriving at the point where you can hit targets consistently, but in a real gun battle with real bullets and targets that fire back, that's where experience draws the line.

Sean had dropped to one knee behind the couch, wildly blasting shadows and vapors it would seem until he took one in the neck. Like a chicken bone had lodged in his throat, he struggled to stand, gagging, a hand to his neck, firing, moving for an exit, searching for more cover. The next one came in like a whisper, piercing his temple like a hot pencil shoved into his brain. He fell back over a small table, toppled like a mechanical robot on uneven ground.

With Rodrico, Llama and Mangy Cur still in the room uninjured, it was a total mismatch for Blade-face. Hearing the ensuing battle, Dimple Chin ran from the kitchen, entering through a swinging door only to get dished out a serving of death.

Dimple Chin never saw Rodrico until it was too late, the knife slicing through his throat with ease, the burning sensation of a blade through skin recognizable in his eyes. He opened his mouth to scream, a warm gurgling of air exiting from beneath his chin. He went down like a Chippendale dancer on his knees enticing the crowd, then fell on his face when the tips didn't come.

Seeing his impending doom, Blade-face stood to surrender, throwing his MAK 90 to the floor. Rodrico, Mangy Cur and Llama each moved out into the open, then looked at one another and laughed. Blade-face took the first one in the shoulder, jerking it backward, spinning him around. The next two came in stereo, their reverberation tearing through his back and turning his legs to water. He went face down on the carpet.

As the sulfur smoke cleared, Rodrico grabbed Vito by the hair and lifted him to his feet. He wore a large silver ring of a serpent, one with a raised knurled design. He blasted Vito in the face below the right eye. The gash that remained was a vortex, bursting with the color of torn plums. Vito fell to his knees, then his hands. He let out a wet sigh, laden with defeat, his head dropping like a dog whipped into submission.

Venegas started barking orders. Llama headed for the helicopter. Mangy Cur ran out to survey the destruction at the dock. Celida got up and went to the Library to check the money.

***

Looking back, Dane could see the dock area roiling with black curds of smoke and dark vermilion flames like those from an oil fire. The clatter of automatic gunfire emanated from the compound, the sound almost surreal, like a trilling of birds. Yet there was no time to waste on speculation about who was winning or losing the war. No doubt someone in a boat nearby would call the Coast Guard soon.

Seconds later, the skiff was alongside the stern of the *Ecstasea*, just in time to see Bobby and Tyra cut loose the zip cord from Jimmy's wrists and roll him off the deck into a waiting raft. Jimmy was unconscious and flopped over like a plucked chicken, the rubber tubes bending under the sudden weight taking in a small amount of water, then rebounding as the raft moved off in a slow twirl, one oar dipping into the water.

When Bobby turned to Dane, he stopped cold. "Who's this?" Bobby questioned, staring at the stranger.

"Michael Geraci."

"Geraci!" Bobby pulled his knife.

Tyra backed away.

"Put it away Bobby, he's coming with us," Dane replied. "I'll explain later."

Bobby hesitated — the tension so hungry it swallowed all sound.

"There's no time for a debate," Dane said at last.

Bobby relinquished, but his eyes still seared with reluctance as he sheathed his weapon. "I hope you know what you're doing." Then, without hesitation, he spun the cap off the jug of diesel he'd siphoned in the engine room and kicked it over on the deck. Dane and Michael were already helping Tyra down into the skiff. Bobby threw the four bags of money and the single bag of videotapes in after them.

As Bobby backed down the ladder onto the dive deck, he struck a flare, then tossed the flaming torch onto the flood of diesel. Within seconds, the air seemed to tear open with a yellow-blue flash like sheet lightning arcing in the clouds. The flames climbed quickly up the superstructure and a white nylon deck chair began to melt and burn with an acrid smell, producing black strings of smoke floating off into the air.

Dane stood almost hypnotized, watching in awe as the gluttonous flames danced across the flesh of the *Ecstasea*.

Bobby jumped aboard the skiff and pushed off. "Let's go," he said. "I radioed the all clear to McTarnihan two minutes ago from the bridge."

His words broke the spell, and Dane pulled his eyes from the flames. Michael revved up the engine, and the skiff nosed high in the water. Dane fell back in his seat. About twenty feet out, he could see Jimmy sitting up in the raft's bottom, rubbing the bump on his head.

Seconds later, they were lunging across the water, gaining distance from the *Ecstasea*, when Tyra stretched out and picked up a vial of coke that was laying at Dane's feet. It had fallen from his pocket. She handed it to Dane.

Dane stared at it for the longest moment, a lust in his eyes like that of a starving animal. Anticipation swelled in his chest, and he swallowed as a familiar taste was coating the back of his throat. Only the prospect of sex carries as much power over the human condition as cocaine. He closed his hand around it.

The skiff was headed for Open Bay and freedom. A new beginning. Bobby grabbed Dane's wrist. They exchanged stares. Coke, the ultimate conman, was already at work, but Bobby would not let go.

It was then that the tide changed forever. Tyra laid her hand on Dane's fist, the fist that clutched the vial desperately, and in her eyes, the answer was clear: she pitied him for his addiction, and in that instant, he resented what he'd become.

He motioned to Bobby to release, and with a mighty cock of his arm, he chucked the vial as far as he could out to sea, following its flight until it hit the water and disappeared with a flicker beneath the waves. Was it over? Already a part of him wanted to dive in after it.

Behind them the *Ecstasea* was building into a giant mountain range of flame, the compound a place of death and destruction fading from view, and there across the great expanse of water toward Port Angeles, Dane saw the clouds above the Olympics were stained red, lurid in the sun's afterglow.

***

When Vince saw Evohl stretched out behind the couch, he ran a finger under the flap of the envelope, tearing a ragged edge. Inside the envelope was a gold tooth and a note that read: *Sin always has a price.*

It took a second for it to register. It was Tony's tooth, and Dane was out of his freaking mind. Then the explosions began, and the gunfire ensued, and Vince knew that time had stretched thin.

He poured himself a bourbon, then walked to the window and stared out as if in shock, his body shrinking and losing resilience. Leaves on a Katsura tree flickered in a silver light outside.

Hearing the slide of the library door, Vince turned slowly with a swallow of bourbon, expecting to see Venegas' smirking face, for he knew the outcome. Evohl was a grim premonition of events lying on the floor. But seeing Celida surprised him. "I've been had," he said.

Celida said nothing, just started walking toward him, looking sidelong at the silver cases by the desk. One was partially open, standing askew.

Vince saw her interest. "They're all empty."

A single shot rang out from outside the Library. Vince focused, trying to pinpoint the direction.

Rolling an orange sucker on her tongue, Celida was on a slow and steady pace forward.

Vince pulled his gun. "Look, baby," he said, "I don't want to hurt you." He waved the gun at a chair. "Why don't you sit down?"

She kept moving.

"I'm not kidding. You're stellar, but not to die for."

Celida had moved to within a few feet of him, and as if Vince had blinked, she kicked precisely upward with her left foot so incredibly fast he had no time to react. The snap of her foot sent the gun sailing through the air.

He marveled at her dexterity.

Her next kick was a roundhouse blow that sent him reeling into the bar. Blood whipping from his nose, he turned fists cocked only to have another knife-edge-foot strike at his jaw, tearing his lip, bruising more than his ego.

The result was humiliating. He toppled over a barstool, the walls of the room taking off like a carnival ride. He ended up on all fours. His knees were barked; blood poured from his chin; his eyes were strobing like a cheap disco. He struggled to his feet, using the crippled barstool for balance. His teeth were slick with red, his taste buds wallowing in a warm, salty gag.

"Didn't your mother ever tell you not to jump around with a sucker in your mouth?" He was incensed, but not stupid. He was trying to be cute, draw her off-guard.

Vince threw a punch at her face, only to have it deflected. Celida countered with a masterful thrust to his solar plexus, a stiff spaded hand. It felt like she'd shoved her fingers clear inside him, the pain so intense he felt his heart stop and lightning bolts shoot out his knees.

He stumbled backward.

She came at him. For good measure, she followed the hand-knifing with a whirling kick to his ribs, the thrust of her heel akin to a Randy Johnson fastball. The blow was debilitating, the pain sharp, his ribs like knives in his chest. Time was a mystery. Space a clown. He couldn't focus, his ears were plugged. He was spinning, or the room was spinning one of the two, and he'd just realized that he'd wet his pants when she launched an ankle straight into his groin, the force of the blow lifting him a good ten inches off the Persian rug.

Vince doubled over in agony, falling forward onto the floor. How à propos, he thought, me getting pummeled by a woman. His sight was streaked with neon tubes of color, his brain pounding as if an angry cyclist had a bicycle pump shoved in his ear. The pain in his loins was voraciously acute. It sucked the air from his lungs, it drank the blood from his face. His kidneys felt as though they'd been thrown in a lemon press of stainless-steel design, and as he dry-heaved in pain, saliva ran from the corners of his mouth, every nerve from navel to knee ravaged and screaming, muscles stiff as welding rod.

Celida moved the sucker to the other side of her mouth. Vince gulped for air. He could feel his left nut swelling through walnut on its way to cantaloupe. He loped along the floor, one hand cupping his genitals. One shoe was gone, his sock pulled down over his ankle. He could see Celida watching him with disgust, like her cat had just sprayed the sofa.

Finally, Vince pulled himself erect. He was before her on his knees. He thought of groveling. Dismissed it. He could feel the weight on his barked kneecaps stinging hot on his skin. Desperate, he had only one card left. Charm. He could always charm the ladies.

It took a second to gather the strength, but then as he'd done to countless women, he looked up into Celida's dark eyes with a manufactured reverence, and said in a bourbon-drenched voice, "You're a beautiful woman, Celida." He took an agonizing breath. His tongue felt like calf liver. "And resourceful. God knows you can fight." Then he paused, shifting the weight on his knees, marshaling his shoulders, appearing to grow strong. "But I would venture to say your passion is as lethal as your kick." He took another breath, let the cool ice reach into his spastic lungs. "We could do such beautiful things together, Celida." He touched his raw and swollen lip with a dab of fingertips.

She seemed unaffected, but it was hard to tell. Even after all the exertion of beating the crap out of him she hadn't even broke a sweat. He swallowed a clot of blood but sensed his power returning. He could do this.

Inching closer, Celida pushed him back gently until he was sitting on his ankles. She was standing over him, straddling his thighs. She inched her black leather crotch toward his face, grabbed the back of his head and thrust his face there.

Immediately, he cupped the back of her thighs with his hands, awe-struck by how firm they were. He could smell horses in his nostrils. His arrogance was telling him he'd done it, then he stopped and looked up at her. Up the vee of flesh that ran from her navel to her neck, up between her breasts into the dark eyes that regarded him from above, her expression smooth as polished stone, her hair draped loosely about her face.

"Now that's more like it, Celida," he said cockily.

Still holding his hair in her grasp, as though the mane of a horse she was about to gallop bareback, in one smooth motion, Celida lurched forward, pushing Vince back over his ankles, his head slipping into the vise of her thighs as she rode him to the floor. His ankle snapped in transition and when they came to rest, Celida was sitting squarely on Vince's broken collarbones, his throat crushed, his chin wedged into her crotch, her legs extended long, and lean past his ears.

She had wrenched so hard on his head that clumps of hair had pulled loose in her hands. There was a trickle of blood from an eye, a beading of blood on the bare patches of his scalp. Yet with his head grossly askew, he didn't scream with anguish over broken collarbones, or ankles, or emancipated hair. He didn't move to swab the blood from his mouth, his nose, his eye. He didn't struggle to breathe through a throat incapable of passing air. It wasn't even a command of his will that made his bent and twisted legs suddenly spring out from under the small of his back like a pair of rubber pegs.

It was clear as a shout screaming through his mind. She'd broken his neck, and even though the snap had rendered him unable to control his limbs, or his voice, or his breathing, the lack of those abilities didn't mean the anguish he felt wasn't real. His brain was intact, and the thoughts connected to such torment were there in the acid, rioting in the streets of his intellect, and as if he'd sniffed a sock-load of spray paint the nightmare was swirling, a portrait of horror cast on the canvas of his mind.

Yet there was nothing to be done, like trying to move a mountain with your eyes, or attempting to hear the sun rise. His muscles lay dormant, unresponsive to the frantic commands, unable to scream, unable to move, unable to breathe one last breath, or taste the orange candy in her mouth, physically disconnected and mentally defeated, oh to smell the ocean again and feel the warmth of a woman's breast.

Celida brushed the tufts of black hair from her hands and pulled a small nub of orange candy on a stick from her mouth. She stared at it briefly, then discarded it, immediately un-wrapping a luscious-lemon sucker as Vince stared up blankly at her smooth brown face. She rolled the lemon on her lips, glistening her skin with flavor.

His neck had been snapped like a chilled carrot, and now memories were scattering from his mind like leaves on the wind; sensations of cold, pain, lust and anger vanishing like rodents scurrying away from the light, and in his collapsing vision he saw Celida, the sucker now bulging her cheek, watch with indifference as his milky greens drained to gray.

CHAPTER 46

Pawleys Island, South Carolina
May 21, 1996

It was in the Arts section of the *New York Times* the next time Dane got a glimpse of Michael Geraci. The headline read: "Geraci To Produce Love-Struck Comedy". Below it was a picture of Michael and Carmen holding hands, standing on a dock next to a teakwood yacht in Cannes.

Sitting comfortably in a beach chair, Dane could feel the sand between his toes. A gentle breeze was blowing from the south along the shore, the fronds of the palmettos bowing in cordial worship to the laid-back wind.

Tyra was out in the surf playing with Theo, a yellow Labrador pup. She looked happy, he thought, her skin brown as a chestnut, her hair long again, golden-blonde shimmering in the sun. She'd been a steadfast friend considering all the ground they'd covered, especially now during the slow transition out of the strange sense of boredom and melancholy that characterized his days.

Earlier in the day, he'd spoken to Bobby. He'd expanded the bait shop, and Natalie had opened a coffeehouse in Winslow. Next month, they were headed to Hawaii on a second honeymoon.

Dane let the paper rest in his lap. He adjusted his sunglasses and studied the waves. When they first reached the Black Thunder that day, Bobby sent Michael on alone with the money to fend for himself. Dane remembered seeing his hair whipped back in the wind as he circled the skiff out of Open Bay.

By the next day, the events on Henry Island had hit the papers. From McTarnihan's phone tip to Virchow, the Feds raided the compound with full tactical force, but came up empty-handed: Geraci and Venegas had escaped.

Three days later, Vito's body washed ashore at Neah Bay, and soon thereafter, Michael and Venegas forged an agreement. Michael returned the four-million dollars in lost revenue and gave Venegas an additional four-million dollars as security against reprisal.

A week later, Jenny OD'd. Suicide or mishap, Dane would never know, but the amount of smack in her body would've floated an elephant to Mars.

The beach can be therapeutic, the rhythm of the surf, the warm sun on a tortured face. Dane lifted a handful of sand, the granules slipping through his fingers like an hourglass of time, and he wondered if he'd ever be able to put Vince behind him.

Vince was the whetstone where they sharpened their wit, the sickle they used to reap their wild oats, but now he was dead, Blake and Tony too. Yet forever, they were bonded by one fraternal experience, one he knew existed for a reason.

He may never know all the answers, he mused, but their journey of friendship had taught him well. He realized now that truth is eternal, while trust must be earned and guarded to avoid extinction, and only forgiveness destroys bitterness, a choice he needed to make.

The phone chirped, and Dane grabbed the cell from Tyra's satchel. It was McTarnihan. The end was near. Chief Donovan and D.A. Green had been indicted thanks to the *Ecstasea's* videotapes. Dane knew the ointment of truth had eased the pain, but McTarnihan would carry the scar forever. Before the end of their conversation, McTarnihan said he'd visited the cemetery and put flowers in Erin's vase, and now a river of swirling currents, the memory of all the blissful moments they shared, came crowding over him.

Dane held the phone in his lap. He felt scared to love again, remembering the old-wives' tale of bad things coming in threes. But watching Tyra and Theo roiling in the surf, the gleeful cries of a woman, the playful barks of her dog, the sun coming like cylinders through the bolls-of-cotton clouds, white-white against a ceramic blue sky, he wondered if life was giving him another chance.

Then, as he put the cell away, he saw the small velvet case in her satchel, and it transported him back to weeks earlier when they'd returned to the Georgetown Inn, Tyra seeking her job back as a waitress at the Indigo Room.

***

The yard was mottled with shadows like so much of life. Camellia, wisteria and azalea were in full bloom, ancient oaks draped with Spanish moss; Jesse was hoeing weeds in a bed of hyacinths as they parked their car on the circular drive. Tyra saw him immediately and ran for his affection.

Jesse had wondered where she'd disappeared to, had missed the sweet call of her voice, the gentle warmth of her embrace. He'd spent many nights on his porch alone, pondering the fate of his friends. Jesse left the hoe leaning against a tree, sweat tickling his brow, and walked toward his modest abode, inviting them along for sweet tea and biscuits.

Jesse rocked in his creaky chair in the cool shade, smoking a pipe of tobacco, sipping his iced tea, and reached back to that night when his friend, Blake Hanson, paid him a visit, while Tyra and Dane listened in awe to the sometimes-rambling recollections of a forever lost piece of their human puzzle.

There was a well of emotion still untapped that Jesse was now dipping into. It wasn't hard to pull a bucket to the surface. Dane felt a stone in his chest where his heart used to be. Tyra fidgeted with the cool sweat of her palms.

From the bib of his overalls, Jesse produced the small velvet case that set this film in motion, rolling it around in his hand as if the action had a way of arranging his thoughts, telling how Blake had given him this case and that if anything should happen to him to make sure Tyra received it; and how he'd become anxious when Blake died and Tyra disappeared. Then he handed it to Tyra, a glow of relief in his eyes for finally fulfilling his commitment.

Feeling its size and weight, Tyra wept, but Jesse was quick to dry her tears, his words like the touch of a silken hand. There should be joy in this gift, he acclaimed, for as sure as the delicate Clematis needs afternoon shade, Blake intended to shade you from regret.

The case held a folded note:

Tyra,

My love for you is deathless, a love even omnipotence cannot break. This case once held a ring, one which I purchased but you'll never have, because I never want you to look back and wonder what could've been, but always look forward and remember what was. Promise me you'll take whatever memories you cherish of me and go on.

Out of my part of S.H.E., the legitimate part, I socked away some cash. Not much compared to what I've seen. But I want you to have it. For reasons that need not concern you, the account is held offshore, Geneva Swiss Bank, #154268, in your name. Dane will help you overseas with the money. His parents are Tiago and Brita Avilla in Kirkland, Washington. They'll know how to reach him. Tell him it was an honor being his best friend. Tell him to throw in a CD, Segar or Morrison, and sit back and have a cool one on me.

Now dry those tears, my dear. Do not mourn me dead. Think I am gone awaiting to see you again.

Love, Blake.

***

Dane gazed out over the Atlantic, his sunglasses cutting the glare, the sun like a rippling yellow balloon caught under the flatness of the ocean, remembering Hemingway's *The Sun Also Rises*, the future uncertain.

Tyra ran up and sat down next to him on the blanket, her legs pulled up at the knees. He handed her a towel, and she began drying off. Theo stood at the edge of the surf, shaking the water from his coat, then jumped in the air and ran off after a sand piper.

"You okay?" she asked. "You look worried."

"I'm fine," Dane said. "Just talked to McTarnihan."

"So, how'd that go?" She was ruffling her hair, her eyes flashing in the sun.

"Memories are like tattoos. Hard to get rid of."

"Oh, I see." She draped the towel over her knees.

"Tyra, I don't want to mess this up. I've been clean now for months, ever since I threw that vial into the ocean, but ..." Dane sighed as the thought dangled.

He could still feel her in the back of his throat like a dry hand reaching into his soul — the numb taste of sterility that was cocaine. She twists like fire around her victims in a forest of possibilities, and once destroyed, moves on to the next, and then the next, until the land lays in desolation. Cocaine, like any other drug, and the witchcraft it serves, is a living and dangerous entity, he surmised. To think of her any differently was to underestimate her power.

Tyra said nothing, simply laid her hand on top of his forearm. They were both staring out over the ocean.

"I can't get out of my head what Clayton told me about Circe and Pharmakeia. What if she comes back? What if being physically clean is not enough? And what if there is more to it, like Bobby said, 'Spiritual warfare that is more powerful than any conventional weapons'?"

"Listen. When I was with Bobby and Natalie, every night they'd pray for you. Honest...every night. I'd never seen that.

I don't know if that's the cure ... but they never gave up on you. And neither will I."

"This feels so good, you and me, and I'm worried that somehow, I don't know how that I'll screw this up, and ... I don't want to lose you."

"Well, I don't want to lose you either," she said.

Dane's head fell forward in contemplation. He let a handful of sand run between his fingers, then reestablished his gaze over the ocean. "But wanting and achieving are two different things," he said. "I'm just not sure how to do it...how to go forward."

Tyra put her finger on his chin and swiveled his head toward hers. "We've both been traumatized, so we keep it simple. Platonic love. Sex right now will only mess with our heads. If we're to be together, then we'll figure it out together. Even the hard stuff."

"I wish I could speak to Blake. A long time ago, he gave me his three laws of engineering," Dane revealed. "But besides memories, that is all I have left for advice."

"What are they?"

"One: there's always an open door. Two: there are no co-incidences. Three: confirmation follows every excellent decision."

"They sound like laws to live by," Tyra said. "Life's a maze. I don't know, maybe when you get to a dead end, the only door open is straight up."

Just then, Theo ran up, and between his jaws was a rect-angular object. He wanted to play tug-of-war. Dane grabbed the object with both hands, but Theo wasn't letting go. That's when Dane realized the object was a leather-bound book the color of brown sugar.

Theo was playfully growling and shaking his head, tugging and jerking until Dane wrestled him under his arm, squeezing the young pup against his ribs, and pried the book from his mouth. He did a quick search up and down the beach, expecting to see some frantic beachgoer running in their direction — but there was no one.

Dane and Tyra's eyes became transfixed by the book. The leather was worn and faded by the sun. The letters that formed a title were broken and discolored. Yet as Dane brushed away the accumulated sand from its cover, to their amazement, they could make out the words "New Testament", and stitched into the corner the initials BDH.

EPILOGUE

Seattle, Washington
May 21, 1996

Clayton lifted the snuff bullet to his face and violently sniffed, sending the cocaine deep into his left sinus, then flipping the bullet over and back, he reloaded the chamber and gave his right side an equal blow.

Face flush with blood, a curtain of warmth descended Clayton's body, his hands white-knuckled now, strangling the steering wheel of the Panel Delivery. The chemical darkness drained down from his sinuses, anesthetizing the muscles, prowling along the back of his throat like a jackal. His nose was wet with rush, plastic and cool. In seconds, his mouth watered as if biting tin, saliva pooling under his tongue while his swallow constricted with the numb taste of sterility.

The road to Avondale led out of the city of Kirkland across the summer countryside, traversing the fields of wildflowers, parting the stands of evergreens. Clayton stuck his hand out the driver's window, funneling the air into his face, his long dishwater-blond hair flapping in the wind.

The cool night air forced tears to emerge, the glistening moisture streaking back from the corners of his eyes like the mask of a raccoon. Clayton drummed the padded wheel with the palms of his hands, the music crisp in his ears; his mind shimmering like a crystalline ball, filled with all the colors of light.

I feel cracks drying on my temples, opening a chasm into my skull; he thought. I smell every honeysuckle in the meadows that rush by my window. I see every needle of every tree in the light that fans out before me. The world is mine. Mine for the taking. He pushed his shoulders back, his arms out straight to the wheel, the long and lanky body of his youth withered and gaunt.

He loaded the bullet again, and again, and again, and again, until his senses were a halo engulfing his flesh, his mind prime for an invasion.

***

Moments later, a spectral light filled the cab of the Delivery and Circe was sitting in the passenger seat, regal in all her seductive splendor.

"I can't wait to get to the party," Clayton said. "Will you come with me this time?"

"I'm with you all the time, Clate. They just don't see me... they don't believe I'm real."

"I try to tell them, but everyone thinks I'm psycho. I wish they could see how beautiful you are."

"That's because you and I have a special relationship."

Clayton rotated the bullet again. "But you *are* real, right?"

Circe knew that over the past few months, a crack in their spiritual relationship had formed, a sign that his usefulness had ended. She'd used Clayton as a demonic thread, weaving her presence through him into souls, souls that she destroyed, except for one, the one who had fled.

"Very real, Clate," she said.

"I mean, I see you, and I hear you, and I make love to you in my mind, but we haven't actually hooked up ... in the flesh, I mean."

"I understand, Clate. Remember the night we met face-to-face? The night Saber fell asleep."

"He's asleep?"

Circe's impatience with this buffoon was drawing thin. "He fell asleep, but now he's alive."

"That's cool. I thought he was dead."

"I promised that I'd never grow old, and I'd be with you forever. But I don't need your help anymore, Clate."

"I thought you were my girl?"

Circe smiled, exposing a dark fire behind her lips. "I'll always be your girl, Clate, but things are changing. Do you want to see Saber?"

"No, shit. That'd be awesome."

"Then let me take the wheel."

***

As the Delivery slipped through the night unsuspecting as a child, to cool his throat, Clayton took a guzzle off his beer, then returned it snugly to the console. His characteristic wide grin grew wider. The coke was exhilarating.

Circe accelerated Clayton's heart to a blur, and suddenly, like an adulterous lover cleaves the soul, Circe was in control.

Clayton laughed his gutty roll, then howled like a coyote as he twisted the throttle in his hand. The yellow lines blurred into a solid band while a rush of wind slid over the Delivery and vanished behind them. Circe watched him close his eyes as a blissful paralysis spread through his body like the warm rush of blow, his neck stiff against the headrest.

Circe's mouth was wet. Her nostrils flared with sex, her heart pounding through Clayton's ears. Let the strobe lights dance, she mused.

The stereo quelled at the end of a song, then shifted to a Saber favorite — "The Road to Hell". The soft-blue digital numbers tallied the display. Then, with the force of two atom bombs, the sound mushroomed from the stereo, the lyrics convicting those who seek currents of pleasure in a river of death.

At the end of the long straight-away, the road turned gently to the left and a small white gravel road peeled off from the corner. Clayton buried the nose of the Delivery into the embankment, the force driving the steering wheel through his chest, and while the night drew deathly still, Circe plotted her next move, wandering the dry places along the road to Avondale, looking for someone else to seduce.

www.ingramcontent.com/pod-product-compliance
Lightning Source LLC
Chambersburg PA
CBHW021524250626
47154CB00006BA/1962